WORLD IN CHAOS

BOOK 3 OF THE *GEMINI GATE* SERIES

STEVEN E. WILDE

World in Chaos (The Gemini Gate series, Book 3)
Steven E. Wilde
Hardcover edition 978-1-77342-096-7
Paperback edition 978-1-77342-095-0

Produced by IndieBookLauncher.com
www.IndieBookLauncher.com
Cover Design: Saul Bottcher
Interior Design and Typesetting: Saul Bottcher

The body text of this book is set in Adobe Caslon.

Also Available
Ebook edition, ISBN 978-1-77342-094-3

Other Books in the Gemini Gate series
Omega Crisis
Worlds in Collision
Battle for Aspen Valley
Door Between Twin Worlds

Dedicated to my fifteen grandchildren.
Thank you for keeping me young. I love you.

When the Sky is cleft asunder;

When the Stars are scattered;

When the Oceans are suffered to burst forth;

And when the Graves are turned upside down . . .

And the Wicked - they will be in the Fire,

Which they will enter on the Day of Judgment,

And they will not be able to keep away therefrom.

And what will explain to thee what the Day of Judgment is? . . .

(It will be) the Day when no soul shall have power (to do) aught for another:

For the command, that Day, will be (wholly) with Allah.

—Qur'an Transliteration,
SURAH AL-INFITAAR (82) (The Cleaving)
Abdullah Yusuf Ali Translation (Muslim prophecy)

12.2.10: The citizens will suffer greatly from cold, wind, heat, rain and snow. They will be further tormented by quarrels, hunger, thirst, disease and severe anxiety.

12.3.41: . . . men will develop hatred for each other even over a few coins. Giving up all friendly relations, they will be ready to lose their own lives and kill even their own relatives.

12.3.32: Cities will be dominated by thieves, the Vedas will be contaminated by speculative interpretations of atheists, political leaders will virtually consume the citizens, and the so-called priests and intellectuals will be devotees of their bellies and genitals.

—Srimad Bhagavatam (Hindu prophecy)

8: And I looked, and behold a pale horse: and his name that sat on him was Death, and Hell followed with him. And power was given unto them over the fourth part of the earth, to kill with sword, and with hunger, and with death, and with the beasts of the earth.

—Revelation 6:8, King James Version (KJV)

Prologue

Siem Reap, Cambodia, 9 July

Jaime strolled along the corridor of the ancient Angkor Wat temple holding the squirming hand of a rambunctious six-year-old—Jaime Jr.—with one hand. He and his wife, Jasmine, swung a giggling three-year-old, Angelo—Jasmine called him Angel—between them. It was the height of tourist season in Siem Reap, and, despite the dark skies and growing crowds, Jaime tried to focus on the battle scene painted on the wall. The mural made him think of the war taking place in other parts of the world. Other tourists passed, going the opposite direction, or stood looking at the wall. Many wore masks, due to poor air quality caused by nuclear fallout and earthquakes around the world, and several watched the young family, pointing, smiling and whispering in hushed tones, despite their concerns.

Without warning, the ground began to shake. The floor, ceiling and walls of the ancient temple groaned, and dust fell from joints between the old stones. With Angel in mid-swing, Jasmine lost her balance and fell, pulling Angel, Jaime, and Jaime Jr. down on top of her. As the ceiling started to collapse, Jaime looked to his right, toward the edge of the walkway. He quickly realized, as fear coursed through his body, that they were probably seven meters above the ground. But, despite the height, he thought that if they could get to the edge, maybe they could avoid the collapsing ceiling.

"Hold on to the boys!" Jaime yelled, trying to be heard over the rumble of grinding stone. Then he threw his arms around all of them and rolled to the right. They rolled over the edge and landed on a rock shelf two meters below and about two meters wide.

The fall knocked the wind out of him. Thinking they were safe he closed his eyes momentarily to catch his breath. But the grinding sound increased, causing him to look up from where he lay on his back, his arms still held tightly around his family. The outer wall leaned toward them, then the entire length of ceiling collapsed. He pushed his family toward the edge of the shelf, and the ground another five meters below, just as several tons of rock fell toward them and hundreds of other tourists.

Kuala Lumpur, Malaysia

Ben and Amelia stood in the glass-enclosed walkway that connected the forty-first floor of the twin Petronas towers in downtown Kuala Lumpur, the tallest twin towers in the world. It would have been a magnificent view from over five hundred feet in the air, if not for the dark clouds of ash that blocked the sun. Ben pointed out the wading pool and playground below, where they had played two hours earlier. Six-year-old Ethan jumped up and down excitedly, but eight-year-old Olivia wanted none of it. They had just returned from a quick stop on the eighty-sixth floor, with its dizzying views of the city, where Olivia had nearly passed out looking down from the height. Now she clung to Amelia, hiding her face against her mother's stomach.

"I don't want to look," Olivia whined. "I don't want to be here. I want to go home."

Amelia watched her husband lovingly attempt to persuade their anxious daughter to peer out of the clear glass panes, but it wasn't to be.

"Amy, maybe you should take her off the bridge," Ben suggested. She nodded and struggled to move, with her terrified daughter hugging her legs. She had just reached the end of the bridge—where the guide had shown them the massive sliding joints that allowed the towers to sway in the wind without damaging the glass bridge—when the bridge shuddered.

Amelia stepped off the bridge, dragging Olivia with her, as a male employee called out from behind her.

"*Emergency! Clear the bridge!*" he shouted in English, then repeated the warning in other languages that Amelia didn't understand.

When they had heard the rumors that a nuclear bomb might be smuggled into the United States, they had debated whether or not to cancel their vacation; but they had invested a lot of money in this trip, and they had trusted the government to manage the terrorist threat as it had similar threats since the 2001 attack in New York.

Amelia and her family had already arrived in Southeast Asia when the war started and, so far, the destruction had stayed north of them. Now, it seemed, it had spilled over into Malaysia. Amelia hoped her fears were wrong and that this was just a small earthquake.

Amelia turned and looked for Ben amid the staggering, screaming crowd trying to work their way off the swaying bridge. He was there—Ethan in his arms—holding onto the railing, working his way slowly toward her.

Then she heard a new sound—a screeching of metal on metal. She swiveled her head back and forth looking for the source of the terrible noise. Within moments, it became painfully clear that the sound came from the sliding joints, which looked like they might be extended too far.

She made eye contact with Ben and yelled, "Run, Ben!" just as one of the window panes in the middle of the bridge cracked, then shattered, sending glass shards in all directions.

Whether he heard her, or whether the screeching metal and

breaking glass motivated him, Ben let go of the handrail and charged through the crowd of frantic people who were screaming and running alongside him. Amelia watched as her husband, holding tightly to their small son, jumped over one man who had fallen in front of him. He was almost to the end of the bridge, when a large man bumped into him and sent him sprawling; little Ethan flying from his arms.

The glass panels began to break, one after another, from the middle of the bridge toward both ends. Ben scrambled to his knees, fighting the people who were now tripping over him, and reached his son, immediately tossing him toward his mother. Amelia pushed both children behind her—toward the elevators and stairwell—and moved toward Ben, fighting the river of bodies moving in the opposite direction. She lost sight of him for a moment, then saw him again, climbing over another person at the edge of the bridge. Ben was reaching toward the handrail at the end of the bridge when the structure reached the limit of its expansion. Amelia watched helplessly as the bridge popped loose of its housing and started to fall. Their eyes met for one terrible moment as Ben jumped toward her, missed the handrail by inches, and fell out of sight.

When his end of the bridge broke loose, it pulled the other end of the bridge out of its housing, and the entire bridge fell, collapsing the hinged support beneath it and pushing it toward the ground 170 meters—558 feet—below. Ben was in freefall, his screams indistinguishable from all the others. Amelia's voice caught in her throat as she watched the only man she had ever loved plummet to his death.

Singapore

The old, rusted cargo ship, almost two football fields in length, appeared to lay at rest adjacent to the Pulau Seborok oil storage and refueling port, south of Sentosa island. Even though she was tied up to the port, Captain Rupp kept the engines idling so he could make minor adjustments to her position in the mild current running around the southern tip of continental Asia.

"Captain." His radio squawked at his waist as he stood on the forecastle looking out at Sentosa Island. He easily distinguished the voice of his first mate calling from the bridge. He absent-mindedly pulled the radio from his waist as he peered away from the ship, trying to see the Merlion on Sentosa Island, that he had heard so much about.

"What is it Ted?" Rupp asked.

"Another earthquake north of here."

"Besides the ones in Thailand and Cambodia?"

"Yeah. This one really clobbered Kuala Lumpur, Malaysia."

"They're getting closer. The next one could be right under us. How full are the tanks?"

Ted laughed self-consciously.

"About half," he said. "We figured we'd need two-thirds to get to our next port."

"We're already sittin' low in the water because of the cargo. Let's disconnect and move into open water. Call the port and let 'em know.

"Aye-aye."

Captain Rupp re-holstered his radio as crewmen appeared to untie ropes from the bollards. The increased vibration from the engines told the captain they were underway.

"Captain." There was urgency in Ted's voice this time.

"What is it Ted? I'm on my way to the bridge."

"Earthquake south of our position."

Both men knew that an earthquake in open water could mean

a large swell, maybe a tsunami. Rupp also knew that he needed to turn into the wave and have enough water under him to cut through it, or they might not make it."

"Check distance and magnitude, then set a watch, and tell the engine room full speed ahead.

"Aye-aye."

Rupp reached the bridge just as the report came in from the watch.

"Swell building fast at twenty klicks, one-sixty degrees."

They were pointed due east and building speed as quickly as the old ship was able.

"We'll never make it," Ted said quietly.

"Turn into the wave, now" Rupp said. "We'll hope for the best."

"Heading one-sixty degrees," Rupp heard Ted call to the engine room.

The ship began a slow turn to starboard, while the wave built quickly, and was still turning when the sea seemed to drop out from under it—the water sucked into the wave. The ship's propellers hit mud and dug in; then the ship listed to starboard, driven by the rotation of the blades. By the time the wave hit, it had crested thirty feet above the deck, crashing down and driving the ship into the mud. Masts, derricks, winches, cranes, lifting rigs, and everything else that stood above the deck was bent, broken, or swept away. The bridge windows crashed inward, impaling Rudd, Ted and the other officers on the bridge before the water crushed them. The ship didn't resurface.

The wave crashed into Sentosa Island with enough force to shear the Merlion off at its base, and slam it onto the monorail that circled the park. The monorail bucked, ejecting a car full of tourists into the fast-moving water where they were swept away. The wave continued across the island into Singapore, damaging buildings and toppling several of the spectacular Super Trees.

Sydney, Australia

The Australian Tsunami Warning System alerted the cities along the east coast that a magnitude 9.1—Richter scale—earthquake had occurred in the New Hebrides Trench, part of the eight thousand kilometers of active tectonic plate boundary to the east, northeast and northwest of the country. Authorities worried that its strength could trigger other quakes nearby—nearly one-third of all earthquakes worldwide occurred along this boundary—but a quake of this magnitude hadn't been seen in this part of the world since 2004.

Following procedure, Geoscience Australia provided information to the Australian Bureau of Meteorology, which then ran a tsunami model to verify the existence of a tsunami; then estimate its size, arrival time, and potential impact locations. With less than four hours before the tsunami's expected arrival at the coast, the Bureau began sending warnings to state and territory emergency management services, media, and the public.

By the time the tsunami reached land, the beaches and coastal highways had emptied, the people travelling inland to escape the expected floods. In the larger cities—Sydney, Brisbane, Newcastle—the evacuation was slower due to traffic congestion, but the majority of the population had managed to move inland or to higher ground.

The shallow coastal waters slowly receded as the waves built offshore, exposing the sandy sea bottom. Then, faster than the warm, salty water had left, it came crashing back with a vengeance, washing over islands, through bays and inlets, and pouring into the cities. The high cliffs south of the Hornby Lighthouse, at the mouth of Sydney Harbor, which had protected Watsons Bay and points south for generations, were buried by the powerful waves. The Lighthouse was smashed, sending debris inland.

The beachfront communities to the north, and those in the mouth of the harbor, caught the full fury of the tsunami. Homes and other structures were levelled for over a kilometer inland. Pleasure boats resting in the bay at Balmoral were ripped from their moorings and washed ashore, deposited among the debris of shattered buildings.

The waves lost momentum as they moved inland through Sydney Harbor, but were still strong enough to damage buildings at Garden Island, uproot trees at the Royal Botanic Gardens, and flood the Sydney Opera House, high on its rocky cliff.

1

What's this?

Vice President Art Klemp—Early morning, 15 July

Two lousy women, Art thought, as he raced through the black night. It was a good thing he still had Dayron.

Despite the pouring rain and the lack of streetlights, with only the headlights to reveal obstacles, Art pushed the military truck he'd stolen, as hard and fast as it would go, toward Romney, West Virginia. Even a lack of sleep didn't slow him down. He now believed that the mutated smallpox virus he'd contracted had given him super-human energy and stamina. He looked forward to facing and punishing that creep, President Gregory McCormick.

The GPS and printed directions he'd demanded during his nighttime raid on the VEEP bunker suggested that he could reach the president's Prime bunker in about ten hours. Most of the ride would be on freeways before they had to leave the interstate and travel west into West Virginia.

He was replaying his attack on the bunker in his mind, pleased with the way Dayron—an ultimate fighter—had bested two security guards to get them into the house, but he was still trying to figure out how that fat old Colonel Johnson had turned the tables on him. He'd had everything under control and was going to kill Johnson and the others, when suddenly, Johnson had a gun on him. He'd had to settle for a quick retreat, but he'd gotten the information he'd wanted. He was distracted by his musings as he raced up the freeway onramp, when, almost immediately, his headlights lit up a major traffic blockage on the dark, wet road.

"What's this?" he yelled as he slammed on the brakes, causing the truck to skid and turn sideways on the wet pavement. He barely avoided colliding with cars that seemed to appear out of nowhere and block every lane. He cursed, straightened the truck, and weaved between the first few cars, only to discover that the congestion was continuous, forcing him to drive more slowly. He complained, cursed and talked to himself the remainder of the night. Dayron and the others stayed quiet, and Art knew none of them would speak unless spoken to. That was good; he was in no mood for a conversation.

They were still in South Carolina when the sky began to lighten, the sun hiding low on the horizon behind the clouds and haze from the explosions and nuclear fallout. It was Dayron, sitting in the passenger seat, who noticed the gas gauge.

"Excuse me?" Dayron said, making it sound like a question.

"What?" Art barked in irritation.

"I think we're low on gas."

Art glanced at the gas gauge and swore again.

"Why not? Everything else is going to hell," he said, looking around for a freeway exit.

"There's an exit two miles ahead," one of the women said from the back seat.

"What?"

"We just passed a sign," the woman said hesitantly. "It said there's an exit two miles ahead,"

"Oh. Right. Dayron, keep an eye out for the exit and let me know when we're close. It's taking all my concentration to avoid a collision." He swerved to avoid another automobile pileup and ended up on the soft shoulder. He cursed and laid the gas pedal to the floorboard. The truck tires spit rocks as they skidded and bumped along the uneven gravel surface to the offramp, finding it as difficult to navigate as the freeway.

The gas station at the bottom of the ramp was blocked by stalled cars.

"How am I supposed to get gas with all of those cars in the way?" he asked as he slammed on the brakes, causing Dayron to put his hand out to brace himself against the dash.

"Sir?" one of the women said.

"What?"

"I don't think the pumps are working. There's no power."

"Then we'll have to find another station," Art replied, as he twisted the steering wheel and gunned the engine toward another station across the road, then hit the brakes again when he realized he couldn't reach those pumps either.

"Sir?"

"*What?*" he asked, more irritated, if possible, than before.

"We could syphon gas from the stalled cars."

He thought about that as he stared at the cars between him and the pumps. He had no idea how to syphon gas from a car.

"What's your name? he asked.

"They call me M.C."

"Who does?"

"Well, everyone does," the woman finally said after a short hesitation.

"That's dumb. Does it stand for something?"

"Mary Catherine."

Art thought about that. M.C. was certainly easier to say.

"Okay, I'll call you M.C." Then, ignoring her, he turned to Dayron. "I see a mechanic's bay on the side of the station. Go see if you can find a hose to syphon gas."

Dayron looked surprised, but dropped down from the truck obediently, and hurried to follow Art's instructions. After a few minutes, with Art complaining and cursing the entire time, he returned with an engine hose about two feet long, bent on both ends, and too large in diameter to fit into the gas tank opening.

"Will that work?" Art asked skeptically as Dayron held it up for his inspection. Art had refueled his own cars often enough to realize that the hose looked too fat.

"It's all I could find."

"It's too rigid," a voice said quietly from the back seat.

"What do you suggest?" Art asked mockingly, as he turned in his seat. Then added, "What's your name? Is it another set of initials?"

"No sir. My name's Jean," she said meekly.

"Gene? That's a man's name. You have a man's name?"

"It's short for Jeanette, sir."

"Oh," Art sighed. "What's your suggestion, Jean that's short for Jeanette?"

"There's a house with a lawn next door to the garage. They probably have a garden hose that would work better. I watched my brother syphon gas a few times."

"Dayron, go see if they have a garden hose."

He hurried away, returning shortly carrying a spool of hose in both arms.

"Will that work?" Art asked Dayron, who shrugged.

"Maybe if you cut about four feet off the outlet end," Jean said.

Art watched impatiently, but quietly, as Dayron searched around in the glove box, looking for something he could use for cutting. He found a multi-tool with a knife blade and cut the hose where Jean showed him. Art was about to tell Dayron which car to syphon gas from, when Jean spoke again.

"Let's try that car," she said, pointing to a car that looked like it had been in the process of leaving the station when it stalled.

"Why that car? Why not that one?" Art asked, pointing to a car currently at the pump.

"Well," Jean said slowly, pointing to the car that she had suggested, "that car looks like it was just filled, and is leaving the station. The car at the pump looks like it was in the process of being filled, when the power went out. It may be full, but more likely it's empty or only partially filled. The hose is hanging at the side of the pump, like the driver didn't finish filling the tank before leaving in frustration."

"You're smart for a woman," Art said, thinking he was paying her a compliment.

"It just seemed logical," she replied and looked away.

"Okay, Dayron, let's get this done and get on the road again."

Jean showed Dayron how to syphon gas into a gas can, then pour it into the truck's tank. After choking on a mouthful of gas, then spitting it out and rinsing his irritated mouth several times with their precious water, Dayron listened to Jean's explanation about how to tell when to take the hose out of his mouth.

"You can feel the vibration and extra weight on the end of the hose, when the gas is almost there," she said. "That's when you need to take it out of your mouth and put it in the can." Dayron spent the next hour syphoning gas from several cars and filling the truck's large tank. Then he filled a five-gallon gas can that he found in the gas station.

In the dim morning light, Art could see farther ahead, through the freeway obstacle course, and made better time. As they continued north, in addition to stalled cars and traffic accidents, they encountered what appeared to be earthquake damage. The military truck could handle the cracked and broken roadbed, but Art felt like they were crawling.

By the end of the day, they were exhausted and hungry, but they'd reached North Carolina. When they left the truck to scavenge for food and fill up on gas again, their senses were assaulted by the sights and odors of decaying bodies. They spent the night in the truck with the windows up.

President McCormick - Prime bunker, 15 July, early morning

"Greg, we have six injured soldiers and one dead terrorist," Secretary of Defense, General James Seymour told the president. He was referring to the military surveillance and takedown of the terrorist: the one who'd attempted to bomb the CDC near Atlanta.

"No fatalities on our side?" President Gregory McCormick asked. He sat alone in the situation room of the Prime bunker, staring across the conference room table at the SEC DEF monitor, where he could see Jim sitting alone in his own situation room.

"No. The soldiers' vests stopped the bullets or they'd probably be dead. The vests don't absorb all of the impact energy, so the soldiers will probably be sore for a few days. Actually, I'm surprised at the shooter's accuracy; six shots to center of mass, in the dark, on moving targets."

"So, were you able to ID him?"

"His British passport said his name was Samuel Smith. You'll remember that's the name the Brits gave us for the suspect in the terrorist bombing in London last New Year's Eve. Can't say if this was the same terrorist who brought the nuclear bomb into Washington, D.C. from Mexico"—the bomb that had started the global war—"but it's a good bet. We've found no record of him entering the country through normal channels in the last two years."

"Didn't it surprise you that the terrorist had ID on him?"

"He didn't, Greg. The FBI agent who discovered which motel

the terrorist had stayed, returned to the motel later, with help, to look for evidence. They found his passport and some cash in the safe."

"Okay, so what happened at the car? The video of the takedown was dark. It was difficult for me to tell."

"Our soldiers spotted the car northwest of the CDC, smashed into a power pole. We set up surveillance and approached the car after dark, as you know. The soldiers must have given themselves away during their approach. That's when the target turned out his light and rolled out of the back seat of the car, onto the sidewalk.

"We lost him in the shadows for a few moments, until he fired at the soldiers who approached from the rear of the car. He hit two of them, then hid in a doorway across the sidewalk. The sniper, in the building across the street, could see him through his scope, but the soldiers on the ground couldn't, and they got too close before we could warn them. He shot one more soldier on that side of the street, then started firing at the soldiers crossing the street from the other direction, and hit three of them."

"That's when I made the decision to have the sniper take him out," Greg said.

"Correct," Jim said. "The sniper couldn't see him well, or he would have tried to put him out of commission without killing him. As it was, the bullet hit the terrorist in the chest, killing him instantly."

"Then why did the two soldiers that entered the doorway after that, go in shooting?"

"You'd made the decision; they just carried out your orders. They wanted to make sure he wouldn't hurt anyone else."

"I keep second-guessing that decision," Greg finally said. "It would have been good to interrogate him."

"Well, it's done," Jim said, "and I don't think he would have allowed himself to be taken alive."

"You think he would have committed suicide?"

"I do," Jim confirmed. "And he would have tried to take out more of our people."

"Okay," Greg said, wondering what else they could do to confirm the terrorist's identity, when Jim continued.

"Besides the passport and money that we found at the motel," Jim said, "and the gun he used during the attack, his backpack contained food, clothing, ammunition, a copy of the Quran and a throw-away cell phone. We had one surprise, though."

Greg motioned for him to continue.

"When the soldiers shined a light on him, they noticed that he had smallpox. I guess we should have expected that. We're convinced his car crashed into that power pole as a result of the explosion at the CDC. The entire neighborhood was a disaster and we've found others with smallpox in the area. I ordered the soldiers to cremate him on the spot."

"What? Why?"

"They took photos and fingerprints—it was difficult to do while wearing their hazmat suits—but they were reluctant to bring in his body, and I couldn't think of anything else that would help us figure out who he was."

Greg wondered if Dr. Anne Lister, the director of the CDC—which he had authorized to be destroyed, and where the smallpox had originated—would have had a different opinion. She'd been pestering him to conduct research on victims of the mutated virus.

"I'm not sure we would have learned anything from him if we'd been able to question him," Jim continued when Greg didn't respond. "But we did the next best thing."

"What?"

"We turned his cell phone over to Tom's people at the FBI.

They tried to trace the calls he'd made on the phone."

"Tom?" Greg asked, turning to Director of National Intelligence Thomas Mitchell, who sat quietly in the DNI bunker, a serious look on his face as he listened to the conversation.

"Yes, sir," Tom said. "It was a disposable phone and the only calls made from it were to a number with a Syrian country code. His calls went unanswered—ours did too, when we tried— so we're guessing the destination was one of the sites we destroyed during our allied offensive."

"Yes," Greg said, pensively. "Of course. That makes sense."

2

Maybe they're not violent

North of Johns Creek shelter, 15 July

"We're outcasts, displaced by war, exposed to smallpox, and disenfranchised by our own country," a woman behind Beth said. "What do we do now? Who are we?"

"You were a teacher," Beth stated bluntly.

"Close enough. I was a corporate trainer," the woman replied in surprise. "How'd you guess?"

"That was an educated question. I don't think most people realize how important it is to us humans to have an identity." The woman didn't respond, but Beth didn't know what she expected the woman to say.

Now nine women and three men trudged along the highway in the pale morning light, having survived the gun battle between the military and the vice president's security team in the Johns Creek Shelter the night before. Dr. Beth Byron, the Johns Creek shelter doctor and Dr. Melissa Gibbons, a CDC researcher, walked together in the lead, with the others trailing behind in ones and twos. They had escaped minutes before a backup team of armed soldiers had arrived to finish what the first team had failed to accomplish—the elimination of everyone in the shelter.

Beth and her followers had stumbled along in the darkness, afraid to use the one flashlight they had, for fear the soldiers would discover them. An hour after leaving the shelter, she had insisted that they stop for the night, using the excuse that she and Melissa needed to check the status of the three who had been wounded during the gun battle. Stopping for the night had also given them all an opportunity to treat the minor cuts and scrapes they had received during their frantic flight. Then they'd locked themselves in stalled cars on the street for the night.

When Beth had roused everyone in the morning gloom, she'd discovered that no one had slept well, and everyone was hungry and cranky. It would be a long day if they didn't get adequate food and hydration.

"Where are we going?" another woman asked from behind as they weaved between stalled cars. "And who made you the leader, anyway?"

Beth found herself unusually irritated at being questioned. Maybe it was the lack of sleep or the woman's attitude, but Beth's mood became sour quickly. Was it possible that the virus had had this effect on her—intensifying emotions—as she had observed in the others at the shelter? If so, she needed to cut them some slack. She tried to keep her voice neutral as she responded.

"We know there's a mess south of here, around Atlanta, because of the explosion at the CDC," she said, looking over her shoulder to see if everyone could hear. Since Callie, the last in line, looked up when she spoke, she decided she must be speaking loudly enough.

"The northeast and west coast are in shambles from the war, or so they said on the news before we lost power. I thought we could head west, toward the Rocky Mountains. Maybe we can find someplace where we can start over. I want to live in peace, without the fear of the government, or someone else, trying to exterminate me because of this mutated virus." Then, speaking so only the woman behind her could hear, Beth added, "If you have a better idea, feel free to take the lead."

The woman didn't respond, but she *did* slow down, creating more space between her and the leaders.

"Isn't there someplace closer where we could go?" the corporate trainer asked.

Beth shivered, as she thought about the grisly scene at the shelter the previous night, where seventy-seven men, women and children had died violently.

"We need to put more distance between us and the shelter," she said irritably. "The farther we can go before we have to stop, the better. Besides, there could be lots of places to hide in the mountains."

"Have you ever been to the Rocky Mountains?"

"No," Beth said. "Have you?"

"No, but how do you know that's a better destination than, say, Texas?"

Beth thought about the president's suggestion that people relocate upwind, to avoid fallout from the bombs in the northeast. Texas was upwind and on the way to Mexico, where she'd heard a lot of people were going to get out of the path of the missiles, so she thought that Texas wasn't a good destination; but that wasn't the point.

"I don't," Beth said, "but you don't know that it's not, do you? I'm going to the Rocky Mountains. You can go wherever you want."

They had followed State Bridge Road out of Johns Creek, and were now on the Old Milton Parkway, Highway 120. In every direction it was so dark, even during daytime, that they couldn't tell where the sky and land met. Shadows of silent cars loomed before them and blocked their view, but there were still signs on the roads, so at least they knew where they were. The lack of noise—no engines whining, no children laughing, not even birds chirping—was eerie.

"We don't have much food," Melissa grumbled quietly as she brushed soot off her clothes, "and I'm getting tired of the stink of death and breathing this junk in the air.". The air was thick with particulates that settled on their arms, heads and shoulders.

"Same here," Beth said. The air was nearly unbreathable and the death smell carried on the wind was nauseating. "I haven't seen dead bodies since we left the shelter, but there must be a lot of them lying around, decomposing, for the air to smell this bad." She didn't know what she'd do if she couldn't get used to *that*.

"Maybe we should be grateful for the cloud cover," Melissa said. "Think how bad the smell would be if we had normal July heat."

Beth was sure it was cooler than normal, which would keep the bodies from decomposing as quickly, but she hadn't really thought about it. She didn't seem to be getting cold.

"We'll have to stop soon," Beth said. "There has to be food and water around here. If you see something, speak up."

"I've seen houses through the trees every once in a while," Melissa said. "Maybe we can find someplace that doesn't have dead bodies lying around. Let's get off the highway at the next crossroad"

"Good idea," Beth said as she walked up to a car and looked in a window.

"It's eerie to see so many cars on the road and none of them moving," Melissa said, following Beth. "It's like a giant bumper car ride." Cars had curved into adjacent lanes or into each other and there were numerous collisions, some of them serious.

"Some of them must have continued rolling after the EMPs killed their control systems," Beth replied.

"There doesn't appear to be anyone in the cars," a young woman said from behind, causing both Beth and Melissa to turn their heads.

"Maybe people just left their cars and walked away," Melissa said.

Beth knew that the president had advised everyone to leave some of the largest cities, those that might be targeted by the enemy, so Melissa's suggestion made sense. People may have abandoned their cars and started walking, to their homes or someplace farther away, that they thought was safer. Wasn't that what Beth was doing?

"Let's spread out and look for food and water as we go," Melissa suggested. Many of the cars were unlocked, but they found nothing helpful.

"If there was ever anything important in these cars, it's been lifted by someone before us," Beth said.

They stopped on a bridge over Big Creek. The water flowed slowly and looked relatively clean in the meager light of day.

"Anyone want to take a bath while we're here?" Beth asked, brushing soot out of her hair and off her arms, where the smallpox sores were drying out. "I don't remember the last time I had a real bath. If your sores aren't weeping," she added more loudly, so they could all hear, "you should be safe from infection."

"In our clothes?" one of the younger women asked.

"Whatever you want," Beth replied indifferently. "If you don't want to walk in wet clothes, I suggest you strip down to your underwear."

"I'm not wearing any," the young woman replied, appearing embarrassed at the admission. "They itch."

"It's up to you," Beth said gruffly. "But I politely request that you gentlemen head upstream, out of view, please," she added sarcastically. Why was she being so ornery? This wasn't like her. She led the way through the thick brush under the trees, stomping them down to make a path—sort of—down to the edge of the water. Before removing her clothes, she watched the men, who had been quiet for the most part since leaving the shelter, trudge upstream and out of view. She removed her backpack, shoes and socks and set them aside. Then she removed her sleeveless shirt and cut-off slacks, laying them across a bush. Taking a bar of soap from her pack, she waded into the water in her underwear, shivering and gasping at the cold.

"Brrr . . . this is . . . refreshing," she said with a mock laugh.

Eventually, all nine women entered the water.

Beth washed thoroughly, then passed her soap to Melissa, who passed it on when she finished with it. Deciding that she didn't want to put dirty clothes on her clean body, Beth gathered her shirt and slacks from the bush and washed them in the stream, then placed them back on the bush to dry. Then she sat on the bank, on a bed of fallen leaves, and toweled off with a cotton hoodie from her backpack.

She looked out across the water at the other outcasts—the word the trainer had used seemed to fit—most of whom were now spread out along the near side of the shallow river, following her example and washing their clothes. She noticed that the young woman who'd said she wasn't wearing underwear, was up to her bare shoulders in the water, wringing out her tank top. Her jeans floated in the water next to her and she kept grabbing them to keep them from drifting away downstream.

Curious, Beth looked around for shy, eighteen-year-old Callie, the youngest survivor of the gunfight, at first not seeing her. Then movement caught her attention from the corner of her eye. She turned her head to see that one of the men had come back into view and had his back to her. Callie was behind him, backpedaling. Beth watched as the man reached out and grabbed the hem of Callie's shirt in one hand. With a firm grasp, he yanked it up, clearly trying to pull it over her head. Callie resisted, fighting the man and shaking her head no; but then she slipped, her head going under the water. By the time she came up, gasping and flailing her arms, the man had managed to lift her top partway over her head. Then Callie was able to catch her footing and get a fist on the top again.

"Hey! Leave her alone!" Beth stood and yelled, feeling protective of Callie. The others looked at Beth, then in the direction she was looking. Just as Beth made a move toward the pair, Ben Schick, the shelter nurse, ran down the slope from upstream, jumped in, and swam toward them. Clearly, Ben's gunshot wound wouldn't deter this rescue attempt.

"I'm just trying to help her get her shirt off so she can wash," the man replied as Ben reached them and pulled the man away from Callie. The men struggled in the water for a moment as Callie freed herself and staggered away toward the bank.

Beth watched as the man took a swing at Ben. Ben ducked just in time, then grabbed the man by the neck and pushed him under the water, putting his whole, considerable weight behind the move. The man's arms came up, trying unsuccessfully to get a grip on Ben, but his hands slid off Ben's bare, wet shoulders. After a few seconds, seeing that Callie had reached the shore, Ben let him up.

Just then Callie screamed and backed away from the bank, her hands going to her face. Ben waded over as quickly as he could, dragging his injured arm at his side, and pushed her behind him, away from the bank.

Lying on the bank, feet and lower legs in the water, was a mutilated, human female body, face up. It looked like animals had attacked her. Her clothing and flesh were torn, exposing her internal organs and skeleton. Blood had congealed and flies swarmed around the wounds.

Ben took Callie by the arm and turned her away, driving her toward the bank a little distance away, in the direction of the bridge. Callie had started to cry and her body shook as she scrabbled up the bank, kicking dirt into the river.

"What is it?" Beth called.

"A dead woman," Ben replied, breathing heavily, "probably attacked by animals." He winced when he attempted to climb up the bank behind Callie, then flopped down onto his back, holding his injured left arm with his right and closing his eyes.

"That's what I smelled," Melissa said, wrinkling her nose and standing in the water closest to Ben and Callie.

As Beth approached Ben, to see what help he needed, she saw, and smelled, the body. Then the sounds of splashing caused her to turn around. The other women were hastily exiting the water. She wasn't surprised. She would have done the same thing if she didn't think Ben needed her. She watched as the women tried to force their wet clothes on over their equally wet limbs, then gave up and carried them, wrapping them around their nearly naked bodies as they climbed back to the bridge. Water dripped from their hair and dirt clung to their bodies and clothes.

"You gonna' be okay?" Beth asked, as she knelt next to Ben on the bank. He opened his eyes and she could see his pain. What a brave man, she thought, and had a sudden urge to cradle him in her arms until the pain went away.

"Give me . . . a minute," he said between breaths.

Beth watched the man who had been dunked by Ben—Callie's attacker—as he struggled, coughing up river water. He finally looked up, first at Ben and Beth, then at the others, who were climbing toward the bridge. He staggered to the bank, throwing a dirty look their way, muttering under his breath and striking the surface of the river angrily with his fists. He disappeared upriver, then reappeared carrying the clothes he'd left on the bank. He followed the others to the bridge, breaking branches and kicking dirt and rocks as he went.

"Okay," Ben finally said, "if you'll help me up, I'll try to stand."

"Lean on me," Beth said, when she realized how difficult it was for Ben to find purchase on the sloping bank using only one hand. Melissa appeared shortly, likely having noticed their struggle. She had gathered Ben's things. She helped them hike slowly up the bank to the roadway where the others waited.

Melissa found a shirt and pair of dry pants in Ben's pack. They helped him pull his pants on, but they didn't bother trying to get his bad arm into his shirt; they just tied it around his arm and neck like a sling, making him as comfortable as possible. Then Melissa gave him some pills to help with the pain, and a drink of water.

"Okay," Ben said, after resting a few more minutes, "if you'll help me up again, I think I'm ready to travel."

Beth helped Ben up, pulling on his good arm, while Melissa stood on the other side of him, in case she was needed. Several of the others closed rank around Callie as they began to walk.

"It feels like my wet clothes are tearing open the scabs," Melissa said.

"Mine, too," Beth said. "It's making them itch. And it's making it awkward to walk."

"It looks like everyone else is having the same problem," Melissa said, after looking back at the others.

"Yeah. We need to stop soon and get cleaned up."

Twenty minutes later, they came to an intersection, left the road, and passed through a commercial area with several abandoned fast food restaurants. They broke into the first one they came to, and several of them starting stripping off their wet clothes.

"I'll put some water in a sink so we can wash before we put on clean clothes," Melissa said, opening a tap in a sink; but no water came from the faucet—no water pressure.

"I'll find some water," Beth said. After getting Ben to sit down at one of the tables, she found a large pot, went to a back room, and found the water heater. When she opened the drain, only a trickle of water came out.

"Melissa," she called, "will you please open a hot water faucet somewhere, so the water will drain."

"Sure," Melissa called back from the serving area. Seconds later, the water came gushing out of the drain valve, silty at first, then clearing. Beth filled the pot with water, carried it out to the serving area, and poured it into a sink. She repeated the process several more times, until there was enough water for all of them to wash.

"You don't mind if we take some water into one of the restrooms to wash, do you?" one of the young women asked when Beth set the pot down on the counter.

"Not at all," Beth said.

"We'd rather not change clothes in front of everyone," the young woman added.

Beth realized that she must have had a surprised look on her face, prompting that last comment. She noticed that Callie and both of the other young women were still dressed in their wet clothes. After seeing them all nearly naked at the stream, their modesty now made her chuckle.

"My scabs are bleeding," one of the women complained. She

was standing naked in the serving area, oblivious to the looks from the men. Beth watched the woman dab at the sores on her stomach and upper legs with a paper towel before applying an antibiotic that Melissa had given her.

"I'm rubbed raw from walking in my wet clothes," another woman said, standing in her underwear in front of the sink, washing the sores on one arm.

By the time everyone had cleaned up and changed into dry clothes, two women had begun to argue. Beth listened from a distance. They hadn't found any food here, so they disagreed on whether to search other restaurants in the area or go back to the shelter. As the argument began to heat up, Beth wondered why she felt the need to babysit these people, but these two clearly needed a referee. So, she walked over to the women and stood there until they noticed her.

"What do you want?" one woman asked, turning to Beth.

"You know," Beth said sternly, "everyone is free to do whatever they want. I'm going to look around here for food. You're welcome to come with me, or go your own way. I really don't care what you do. But the fighting isn't helping." Beth couldn't believe those words came from her mouth. By nature, and as a doctor trained to care about people and their problems, she had always listened carefully, to assess people's needs and consider what she could do to help. Her sudden indifference toward these women was a surprise to her.

Sure, they'd all suffered since they went to the shelter, but she couldn't believe how irritating it was to watch grown women fighting and squabbling over what should be a common-sense approach to this crisis. They didn't dare go back to the shelter, because soldiers might be there, so they had to move on.

She realized that she actually *didn't* care what these people did.

With Melissa, Ben and the three young women by her side, she would be fine. The rest of them—she actually hoped they would walk away and not come back.

There was some grumbling, but when Beth started walking, everyone followed.

President McCormick—Private meeting with his SecDef, 15 July

"Okay, Jim, what is it?" Greg asked, staring at the SEC DEF monitor. At Jim's request, he'd excused his other advisors following their discussion of the terrorist takedown. What Jim needed to discuss didn't require the others to be present, he'd said, but Greg suspected it was more than that. Jim had seemed unsettled by Greg's outbursts of frustration. *Maybe he's worried that I'm falling apart,* Greg thought. Maybe he was.

"We lost three security personnel last night when Art and his gang entered the VEEP bunker with guns blazing, demanding directions to your bunker. Colonel Johnson wasn't worried about giving Art the directions, knowing that we could track him by satellite, now that we knew where he was, but Johnson was hoping that one of his security teams would arrive while Art was still there, and get him in a crossfire. His team arrived, but not before Johnson was forced to take action on his own. He managed to outsmart Art, kill two of his gang members, and get Ambassador Porter and Corporal Prettyman safely out of the room."

"How did Art get in?" Greg asked, nodding. He wasn't surprised that Johnson, with his battle experience, had outsmarted Art; but this didn't sound like the sniveling coward he knew, to be so bold and cold-bloodedly efficient.

"He broke in through an upstairs bathroom window. How he managed to knock out two armed guards without alerting bunker security is a mystery, and neither of the guards, who were found disarmed and unconscious on the floor in the upstairs hallway, has been able to explain it. Everyone who interacted with Art or his gang members has been vaccinated and placed in quarantine while we wait to see if they've contracted smallpox."

"Wasn't everyone in the Johns Creek shelter vaccinated against smallpox?" Greg asked.

"As far as we know."

Greg realized that he was nervously tapping his foot beneath the table and forced himself to stop.

"Then what?" Greg asked, feeling his pulse start to race. "He just waltzes into the bunker?"

"He had the security codes. We realize now that we could have avoided the whole thing if we'd changed the codes while he was at the shelter; but we had no idea he would try this, or that he would get so far before we stopped him."

"We still haven't stopped him!" the president shouted. He could feel his stomach churning. Was it possible that Art now had the courage and the resources to carry out his threat to go to Prime and kill him? "Why can't we get things under control?" he asked, not expecting an answer and not getting one. "Nothing's going right. First the war devastates the infrastructure, then the virus escapes containment, now Art spreads the virus unhindered. At this rate, we'll have total chaos within months . . . maybe weeks. None of this should be happening."

Jim stared at him without speaking.

Greg took a deep breath and let it out, wondering if Jim was right. Was he falling apart?

"Okay, anything new from Dr. Lister?" Greg asked once he had himself under control again. He'd ordered Lister to determine exactly how the virus had mutated. She'd already told him that she suspected her deputy director and an associate had removed the experimental samples from the CDC to protect them from being destroyed. The research notes in the CDC database were incomplete, but she believed it was because they hadn't had time to complete the evaluation of their modifications, not because it was part of some mysterious conspiracy.

"She still doesn't know the extent of the mutations," Jim said, "but she said the VEEP security team should be vaccinated and quarantined as a medical precaution."

"Great," Greg said sarcastically, again fighting for control. "Keep me informed. Were we able to account for all of the occupants of the shelter?" He didn't want another surprise like the missing researchers from the CDC.

"Unless Art left people outside when he attacked the VEEP bunker, there are still a dozen people unaccounted for."

"Why not?" Greg fumed, trying to ignore the pain in the pit of his stomach. "So, we could have another group of violent people show up somewhere else. Is that what you're telling me?"

"Maybe they're not violent," Jim said. "We're still looking for them."

"Fine. Anything else?" Greg asked, sending a dirty look in Jim's direction.

"Yes," Jim said. "One of the backup teams we sent to the Johns Creek shelter stayed out until it started to get light, to look for the people who had escaped. They didn't know Art was at the VEEP bunker at the same time. When they hadn't seen anyone around Johns Creek—I mean, anyone moving—I told them to return to the shelter, cremate the bodies, and gut the building with fire, as we'd discussed."

"You mean, they saw people, but they were dead," Greg said, acknowledging that he understood what Jim was telling him.

"I don't know why this hasn't come up before," Jim said, "maybe because we're in bunkers, with filtered air, instead of out on the streets. When the team reported in, they said the smell of death was so strong that even the rebreathers in their masks didn't filter out all of it. In the early morning light, if you could call it light, they could see rotting, bloated corpses lying in the streets. There must be a trail of them all the way back to the CDC."

"You mean they only saw them between Johns Creek and Atlanta?" Greg asked.

"That's the only place they were looking. I'm sure there are bodies everywhere. They're going to spread disease."

"Ok, Jim. Take care of it."

"Flamethrowers? We don't have the manpower to gather them up and move them."

"Whatever. Anything else? Wait. What did you mean about the light?"

"Greg, the teams are reporting that the sky is so dark, and the air so thick with ash and soot, that there's almost no light around Johns Creek. Between that and the death odors, it smells like hell—literally—at least what they think hell would smell like."

The president tried to imagine it, staring at the wall to his right. He didn't know if he could handle any more bad news.

3

Anyone hungry?

The Outcasts—North of Johns Creek, Georgia, 15 July

They searched shelves, cupboards, freezers and back rooms in one restaurant after another, each more thoroughly than the last. They were getting desperate; not because they were starving—yet—but because the lack of food and water in places where they should be found was making everyone act crazy, bickering over every little thing. If the restaurants didn't have supplies, where would they find them?

"This is ridiculous," one woman complained, sounding miserable. "There's no food here, just like the last five places we've looked."

"We're going to die," another said.

Beth didn't know what to do. Maybe she was right.

"I think I found something," one of the men said, sticking his head out of a freezer. "I'll need help and something to chop ice."

Suddenly hopeful, Beth found a couple of knives in a drawer, which Ben took from her, offering to help.

"Let me do that," Ben said, wincing.

"You don't have to, Ben," Beth said. "Why don't you go sit down?"

"I need to be helping," he said, taking the knives to the freezer

The two men walked out of the freezer a few minutes later, the first one carrying a chunk of ice. Ben followed, holding his bad arm, which was still in a sling, with his good one.

"I found some meat encased in ice in a corner of the freezer," the first man said triumphantly. "I could see it through the ice, probably because the ice has been melting."

He put the chunk of ice in one of the sinks, and continued stabbing at it with a knife, to break the meat free, while he continued to talk animatedly.

"The freezer was cool, but not cold, because of the power outage. It looks like hamburger patties. I'll cook 'em if we can get a fire going."

"The grills won't light," Melissa said. "No gas or electricity."

"We'll have to start a fire with wood then," Beth said. "I'll find some. I'm pretty sure we'll find a grill in the back. This restaurant advertised flame grilled burgers."

As the various members of the group scattered to find a grill, or to continue to look for food, Beth realized that she was smiling. She couldn't remember the last time she'd felt good. She wasn't exactly happy, but watching the group working together for the first time, she thought maybe they could get through this. Maybe they should call themselves Outcasts, with a capital "O".

"Melissa, can you help me?" Beth asked as she tried to tear a wooden door off of a cabinet.

"Have you tried removing the screws from the hinges?" Ben asked, watching Beth's futile effort. "I saw a screwdriver when I was searching a back room. I'll go get it if someone else can operate it." Melissa followed him to get the screwdriver.

Another woman entered dragging a portable grill, just as Beth had assumed.

The self-designated cook used cardboard to get the fire started and smashed the wooden doors with a booted foot to use for kindling. When he had a good fire going, he set the metal grill down over the fire and cooked the hamburger patties.

Beth and Melissa found a couple of empty plastic bottles that had contained pickles and went to find the water heater. Beth rinsed her pickle bottle with a little water, then put more water in the bottle and tasted it. "Awful," she said, making a face.

"Shake it," Ben said, coming up behind them. "It will improve the flavor." Beth looked at him skeptically, but started shaking the water in the bottle.

"Why is that?" Melissa asked.

"It's called aeration," Ben said. "Mixing air with water removes gases and minerals, along with its flat taste—something I learned in Boy Scouts," he added with a sheepish smile.

Beth shook her bottle again, then tasted the water. "It'll do," she said. They filled the bottles and took them to the front.

☢

When they finally sat down to eat, Beth's mouth was watering. The smell alone was overpowering. She took her first bite, and even without bread or condiments, she relished the flavor. The meat was overcooked on the outside and undercooked in the middle, but nobody complained. Eating warm food must have improved their attitudes, because they started talking.

"Our first warm meal since . . . when?" one of the young women asked.

"Since the power went out in the shelter," someone else said.

"Let's not talk about the shelter," another said, cringing.

"How did you end up in the shelter?" Melissa asked Beth.

Beth's first impulse was to tell Melissa to mind her own business, then she realized that with her medical background, Melissa probably knew that talking through a bad experience could be therapeutic—a way to improve a person's mental health. Maybe Melissa was fighting her own demons. It would be a good idea for everyone to share something about themselves. It might even make them feel closer to each other. She hadn't been ready to be the de facto leader of this ragtag group—these Outcasts—and didn't enjoy it. But medicine, and this group's emotional health, that was her thing.

"You all know me, I think," Beth said, speaking to the group. "I worked in a clinic in Johns Creek when the call went out for volunteers, and I was assigned to the Johns Creek shelter." She considered saying more, maybe tell them about her brother, Brian, but that was too personal and she couldn't think of anything that she thought would be interesting to them.

"Who wants to go next?" she asked when she noticed that of the eleven others—three men and eight women—only a couple were even looking in her direction. They must all be struggling with this. Now was her time to really lead. The people needed to open up. Sharing thoughts and feelings with each other could bring a closeness and forge a bond, and should improve their attitudes. People who liked each other, and really knew each other were more likely to help each other. Beth suddenly had a new goal. Survival was important, but trust was paramount.

"How about you Melissa?" Beth asked.

"I'm Melissa," Melissa said without hesitation. "I was a scientist at the CDC, with Evelyn—Dr. Shumann." She teared up suddenly, likely thinking about how she'd last seen Evelyn, lying on the floor in the shelter, but continued quietly. "Dr. Shumann was shot in the back by a soldier's weapon. We—Evelyn and I—were studying flu viruses, trying to understand why new ones appear each year. We chose to go to the shelter because we were convinced by Vice President Klemp's argument, that the VEEP bunker might be damaged by the explosion at the CDC because of its nearness."

"Ooo . . . don't mention that evil man's name," a woman said. "I hope the military found and tortured him for the terrible things he did in the shelter."

"They'll probably kill him, alright," one of the men said, "but not for what he did. They'll kill him for having smallpox, just like they'll kill us if they find us."

"Stop that kind of talk," Beth said. "Let's not talk about the vice president or smallpox. We were introducing ourselves. Who's next?"

"I'm Lisa and this is Kerri," one of the young women said after a slight pause. "We were interns together at the United Nations in New York, working for Ambassador Daniel Porter. The Ambassador invited us to follow him to the vice . . . I mean, the VEEP bunker to continue working for him." She chuckled self-consciously. "It flattered him to have young women around. Like the vice . . . I mean, like Melissa, we were afraid the bunker wasn't safe, so we opted to move to the shelter. What a mistake."

"Ditto," Kerri said, looking up long enough to make eye contact with Beth, then looking down again.

Beth noted that it was Lisa, more outspoken than Kerri, who had commented about being sans underwear at the river. She had also been the most helpful in the kitchen earlier. She seemed to be a people person, aware of her surroundings and willing to help where needed. That may be why the Ambassador liked having her around.

"I'm Karen," a gray-haired older woman said, whose face told of a hard life *before* the war interfered and made it worse. "My husband, John, and I lived on a farm just north of Johns Creek. We went to the shelter when we heard the warnings. I tried to call our three married children while John drove. We could only get one of them, our daughter, who was living in Kentucky with her husband and four children. They were headed to a shelter as well. I hope to be able to find them when this is over." Karen started to choke up. "John was killed in the gunfight at the shelter." Beth knew that Karen had also been shot in the gunfight, a superficial wound to her left side that was healing nicely. Beth had helped clean and bandage it.

"I'm Pepper," said a slim, middle-aged woman with bright red, frizzy hair and gray roots. "I was just starting a second marriage when we got the warning to go to the shelter. I left New York after the divorce and haven't a clue where my first husband and two kids are. Met Lyle in Atlanta. He was also killed in the shelter."

Beth remembered that Pepper wore lots of makeup in the shelter; and without it now, she was rather plain looking. She realized that it was Pepper who had questioned her authority to lead the group and who had argued in favor of returning to Johns Creek when they couldn't find food earlier. She had also been the one who stood in her underwear in the serving area to wash. The way Pepper talked now, Beth couldn't tell if she was sorry at the disruption in her life, or not. She's a survivor, Beth realized.

There was a pause and Beth noticed Ben looking around.

"I'm Ben," he said quietly. "You all know me as Nurse Schick." He struggled to smile but still looked sad. "Like Beth, I was working in a clinic in Johns Creek—not the same one—and volunteered to work in the shelter if they needed me."

Beth wanted to ask if he had someone special. Then she realized that her reason for wanting to know was that she had begun to like him. It had nothing to do with the trust she was hoping to garner and grow in the group. But Ben was more than just an associate to her, even more than a friend. It wasn't romantic, but while she was helping him dress at the bridge, wearing only his wet jockey shorts—blue with yellow smiley faces—she had definitely felt a physical attraction to him. Although she was sure Ben was a few years younger than her, Beth thought there was some chemistry between them that might, over time, develop into something. But she decided it wasn't fair to ask; she wasn't afraid to tell him how she felt, but if he had feelings for her, it would become apparent with time. She would wait.

"Where are you from, Ben?" Melissa asked.

"Pennsylvania. How I ended up in Johns Creek is a long story. Ask me about it sometime if you're interested."

"That would be nice," Melissa said, with an attempt at a smile.

"I'm Suzanne," said another middle-aged woman, this one with curly, dark brown hair. "I'm a corporate trainer from Florida. I was visiting my sister in Johns Creek when we were told to find shelter. She died in the gunfight." A pause, a sniffle, but no tears, like she was forcing herself to hold it in. "I tried to contact my husband, but got voicemail. I have no idea if he and our children found shelter." Suzanne started to cry and looked down at her feet.

Seeing Suzanne cry made Beth feel badly that she had been so quick to judge these people. Maybe Suzanne appeared mean and ornery because she'd developed an emotional shell to help her deal with a world that wasn't always nice to her. Right now, she seemed vulnerable. Suzanne, like others, would take more time to get close to. Beth determined she would make a greater effort with Suzanne.

"I'm Candy," a woman in her thirties, who had been movie-star gorgeous before smallpox put sores all over her body, said with a sigh. "Single, no significant other, no children. I've done modeling, commercials, was back-up singer in a small-time rock group. It was a dead-end. Then my agent called and said he had a big part for me if I could get to Nashville. I went and auditioned, and they liked me. It looked like I was going to get the job; it was going to be my big break. I was just on my way home to Jacksonville, Florida, when I ran into a roadblock north of Atlanta and they directed me to the Johns Creek shelter. Great timing, huh?"

Beth remembered that it was Candy who had stood naked behind the counter to change clothes. Maybe she did more than modeling, Beth thought, then scolded herself for thinking unkind thoughts. Candy sounded angry—at whom, Beth couldn't tell.

"Do you have family, Candy?" Karen asked.

"Hah!" she said, with tears in her eyes and spite in her voice. "I'm from Denver. Got kicked out years ago, because I didn't want to stay *down on the farm* after this New York agent saw my portfolio and told me I'd be crazy not to take the gig he had for me. Went to New York and never looked back."

"Candy doesn't sound like a farmgirl name," Karen said. "Is Candy a childhood nickname?"

"No. Candy's my stage name. I don't like the name my parents gave me, so when I left home, I quit using it."

"I'm Bryce," a man about thirty finally said to break the silence that followed Candy's explanation. He was medium height and weight—medium everything—except for his hair; he had a receding hairline and was going bald in the back. It was Bryce who had found and cooked the hamburgers. "I'm a tool salesman. Grew up in Johns Creek and met my wife in high school. We were trying to have children—we'd started in-vitro—when we heard the warning to go to the shelter. She . . . " He started to bawl, put his head in his hands, and didn't go on. The wrapping on his left hand was a reminder that Bryce had also been shot in the gunfight. The bullet had gone cleanly through the palm of his hand, possibly chipping a bone, but there didn't seem to be any infection and he didn't complain about pain.

"And you make good burgers," Lisa said, smiling and holding up the last half of her second piece of meat between her fingers. Kerri snickered and bumped Lisa with her shoulder.

That left Callie and her attacker to introduce themselves. Several people looked at her, expecting her to be next. She finally looked up, and with tears running down her cheeks, tried to speak.

"You all know, I think . . . I'm Callie. Mom . . . and Dad . . . both got murdered in the shelter. Mom . . . was the kindest person. So was Dad. They didn't deserve to die like that." She bawled unashamedly. "I wish I were dead, too."

Beth wanted to say, "you don't mean that," but Callie probably *did* mean it right at that moment.

"Where are you from, Callie?" Beth asked, instead.

"Johns Creek," she said, then paused. She had thanked Beth for her kindness, explaining that her mother had been her closest friend, and that she really didn't want to go on without her. She choked out the next few words with venom in her voice. "We believed the president . . . when he said the terrorists didn't have a bomb. It was a lie. He probably just . . . didn't want anyone to panic. Well, he waited so long to warn us, that we couldn't get away. Now look at us; we're a bunch of mutant outcasts. If anyone from the government finds us, they're going to murder *us,* too." Then she cried harder, great sobs pouring out, and tears dropping onto her t-shirt. Beth knew this would be a hard one. At her age, this type of trauma could lead to suicide. Another one to watch carefully, Beth thought.

Everyone sat silently while Callie cried. Beth thought about the stark reality that Callie had just described. The others, in their silence, may have been thinking about it, too.

Beth thought again about the name, Outcasts. They had just

begun to share bits of themselves with each other. Maybe having a name would speed up the healing process. So, she told them about her conversation with Suzanne and asked them what they thought about the name. A few of them nodded their approval; Lisa cheered and shared a high-five with an amused Kerri.

After a few minutes, Beth turned to the last man—Callie's attacker. He looked to be in his late forties, large build, with a fringe of hair around his head like a halo. Beth wanted to laugh at the image *that* brought to her mind—a molester with a halo. She realized she really didn't care if he introduced himself or not.

"Do you want to tell us your name?" she asked bluntly.

"Doesn't matter," the man said indifferently, after a few moments. "You all hate me. You think I'm bad. Well, I'm just a man with normal male needs."

"Oh, brother," Melissa said as Candy snorted derisively.

"His name is Jared." Pepper said, sounding a little defensive—protective.

"Well, Jared," Beth said seriously. "I hope you can get your *male needs* under control, for the sake of the women who don't want your attention."

Jared's comments, and the women's responses, put a damper on further polite conversation.

Beth motioned for Melissa to follow her. They went to the kitchen and found wrapping paper to wrap the remainder of the meat that they had cooked, which wasn't much. Lisa appeared shortly, trailed by Kerri, and asked what they could do to help. They refilled the plastic bottles with water, then placed them with the meat in a backpack.

While the others were preoccupied, Beth pulled several sharp knives from a drawer under the counter and gave half of them to Melissa.

"Just in case," Beth said, and they stuffed the knives in their separate packs.

Some of the Outcasts picked up their trash and placed it in the garbage bin.

"Like, who cares if you throw it out?" Pepper asked, laughing sarcastically. She swept her trash onto the floor with her arm, then stood, grabbed her pack in one hand, and walked out.

Once everyone was outside—it was early afternoon, but didn't seem to be any lighter than it had been when they'd started out that morning—Beth pointed to their right.

"This is the way we were going," she said, "if you're going with me." She started walking with Melissa and Ben, one on either side.

The others followed eventually, spread out over a considerable distance.

After they'd walked for a few minutes, Beth began to speak. It was in her nature to solve problems. "Melissa, what do you think about our medical prognosis?"

"Well, based on the accelerated progress of the disease," Melissa said, leaning toward Beth and speaking quietly, "I figure the pustules should drain and crust over within the next two days."

"I agree," Beth said. "And they should begin flaking off after that, leaving pigmented scars."

"My thoughts exactly. We shouldn't be contagious once that begins." Melissa snorted. "Wouldn't it be something if we were?"

"Were what?" Beth asked, stopping and turning quickly to face her, afraid that she already knew what Melissa was suggesting.

"Still contagious," Melissa replied innocently.

"That would be horrible!" Beth said angrily. She reigned herself in, was frustrated at herself for her inability to cope with the problems they were facing. "Anyway, we've been vaccinated. The one thing we have to hope for is that we're not contagious. That way, maybe the government will stop hunting us. Don't take that away from me—from us." Melissa stopped walking and turned to look at Beth. The innocence in Melissa's eyes made Beth feel guilty for having said anything. "Melissa, I'm sorry. I don't know what's come over me. It's like the virus is causing a personality change."

"I think that's exactly what's happening," Melissa said kindly. "Do you remember what you said back in the shelter about the changes that you were seeing?"

"You mean, that everyone's emotions were more intense?" Beth asked.

"It was more than that. We were all pretty strung out just before the gunfight, but what I remember you saying was that everyone's personality traits were enhanced. The aggressive people, like Vice President Klemp, became violent. The shy, like Callie, became despondent. At least, I think that's what you said."

"Yeah, I remember saying something like that," Beth said, "and now, besides that, all of us have more endurance and less sensitivity to temperature changes."

"It's not like we've become stronger," Melissa added, "or Callie could have defended herself better against Jared or Vice President Klemp."

"I see what you mean. Should we tell the others?" Beth finally asked.

"I'm sure there'll be a time when it's appropriate. You decide. Anyway, normally, we wouldn't be contagious after we've been vaccinated, but with this mutated virus I don't know what to expect."

Beth stared at Melissa, distressed at the possibility.

They walked for several hours after that, with very little talking. Beth thought about where they'd been, what they'd experienced and where they ought to go. They were the last twelve of close to a hundred people that had been in the shelter, unless Art Klemp was still out there somewhere, picking on people. She wondered if she should take off on her own, rather than being saddled with all these emotional people, then realized that she might be the most emotional of them all, which brought her to tears.

They encountered no one, and saw only glimpses of people behind closed curtains and doors. When the meager light of day appeared to be fading, Beth pointed to a neighborhood that looked as deserted as the others they had passed.

"That looks like a good place to stop for the night," she said, then turned to see if they had left anyone behind. "Look," she said, pointing back toward the group following them. Melissa looked over her shoulder.

"No surprise there," Melissa said. At the back of the string of Outcasts, Pepper walked and talked with Jared.

"Do we need to worry about them?"

"And do what, tell them they can't talk to each other?" Melissa asked, and barked a laugh. "They're probably doing us a favor. If they hook up with each other, maybe they'll leave everyone else alone."

The smell of death was stronger once they entered the neighborhood. They couldn't tell where it was coming from and didn't want to find out. Beth approached the first house they came to and knocked. She saw the curtains move, but no one answered the door, so she moved on. She tried several more houses, saw a few curtains move, but no one answered at any of them. She finally found a house that Melissa agreed must be unoccupied, tried the doorknob and found the door unlocked. She cautiously opened the door, with Melissa standing next to her. The smell of death that swept over them was so strong that Beth gagged and Melissa turned her head and vomited off the side of the porch. Beth quickly closed the door and they moved away.

They checked another five houses before finding one that was empty and didn't smell of death.

"Anyone hungry?" Beth asked as they filed into the house, but the experience had caused all of them to lose their appetites.

4

He's never gone against my instructions before

The Preserve, Aspen Valley, 16 July

Six women sat at one end of the dining room table—actually three folding tables placed end-to-end down the middle of the room, in their dinner configuration—as far away from the kitchen as they could get, to reduce the distraction of the laughter and clanging.

Lunch had been cleared away, and the current cleanup crew was busy washing and drying dishes in the kitchen, which was separated from the dining area by a doorway with double swinging doors. The long, narrow shape of the dining/kitchen area and the metal shell of the room, acted like an echo chamber, carrying the kitchen sounds toward the women.

Lillie had asked Amos one time why they didn't have a dishwasher in the Preserve, since it would cut down on the noise. He had explained that a dishwasher used a lot of water, and since all their water had to be treated and recycled, it was a poor use of resources—water *and* electricity. "Besides," he'd added with a mischievous smile, "requiring people to do the dishes will give them something to occupy their spare time."

As the designated house manager and Emily's mother, Lillie had called this meeting to plan Emily's wedding, and none of the women wanted to be left out. The men, on the other hand, had gratefully accepted their exclusion.

"Let's keep it simple," Lillie said as she watched her twenty-one-year-old daughter, who seemed distracted. She knew Emily had been thrilled when they'd invited her boyfriend, Matthew Green, to join them at the Preserve. Then Emily and Matthew had shed tears of joy when Amos had said he could legally marry them using his authority as the minister of the Church of Aspen Valley.

But Emily didn't seem happy now. She kept touching the cast on her arm, which had been in a sling since she fell and broke it during the earthquake. Maybe there was an infection. Lillie would have to ask Amos to look at it when they finished this meeting.

"I'll plan the luncheon and make a wedding cake," Becca Stephens said, interrupting Lillie's thoughts. Since Becca's primary responsibility in the Preserve was food preparation, it was a logical suggestion.

"Excellent," Lillie said, making a note on her tablet.

"I hope they're being careful," Becca added, looking toward the kitchen. She'd made it clear that she wouldn't tolerate horseplay that resulted in broken dishes, of which they had a limited supply.

"Do you want me to check on them?" Katie, Becca's daughter, now twenty-two, asked enthusiastically. She'd been bubbling over with anticipation and excitement since her mother had given her a beautiful dress for her birthday three days earlier. The wedding party would be her first opportunity to wear the dress and she would dance every dance with Mike Blund.

Before Becca could answer, a crash from the kitchen, amid exclamations of surprise, startled them all.

"Be careful in there," Becca called, as the kitchen became deathly quiet.

"Yes mother," Chris, Becca's nineteen-year-old, called back. His comment was followed by whispers; then the normal sounds of laughter and clanging returned.

"I'd be happy to make Emily a wedding dress," Brittany Carlsen said. Lillie knew Brittany made most of Sydney's clothes, as well as some of her own. "I just need time."

"That's great, Brittany," Lillie said. She would have less than two weeks.

The planning continued for another hour, and Emily still hadn't smiled.

Rachel Blund, eighteen years old and the only woman at the table—besides Emily—that had yet to contribute, had been thinking about the birthday party where Emily and Matt had announced their engagement. Like most of the others, she'd been startled when her dad had explained that he could perform the wedding. Trust Dad to think of everything.

Now Katie had captured Mike's attention with her new dress, and would spend an entire evening dancing with him.

She sighed, wishing she could think of a way to get Chris to do more than hold her hand; but Chris still needed to figure out what he wanted, and she didn't want to push him into anything. She decided that she would have to be a little more obvious with her flirting.

"I think that does it," Lillie said. "I'll review the list, if Emily and Rachel are still with us."

"What?" the two young women said at the same time, coming back from their thoughts.

Lillie smiled at her daughters, as the other women laughed,

then read from her tablet all the things that needed to be done in the next few days and who had accepted the assignment.

"Emily and Rachel," she added, "you can decide where you want to help. Remember everyone, keep it simple." They all agreed, but Lillie was certain they would all go out of their way to make the wedding preparations elaborate and special, because this wedding was a break from the daily routine of the Preserve, something that was badly needed.

"Emily." Lillie said as the others rose to leave.

"What Mom?" Emily asked, turning back to look at her mother.

"Is your arm bothering you?"

"It itches a little. Why?"

"You look troubled and keep touching it."

"It's nothing, Mom," Emily said, looking around. Everyone had left the room. "It's just that . . . I've wanted to marry Matt for so long, and now that it's going to happen, I suddenly have doubts. Is that normal?"

"Yes, it's normal, dear. Do you love him?" Lillie asked with a knowing smile.

"With all my heart and soul, Mom. I can't imagine living without him." Emily returned the smile.

"Well, sometimes we have to take a leap of faith." Lillie placed an arm around Emily's shoulders and they walked out together, talking about the wedding plans.

☢

"You know, I'm going to need a haircut before the wedding," Amos said distractedly as he ran his fingers through his unruly hair. At the age of fifty, his hair was still full, hanging below his collar and graying at the fringes. "I haven't had one since . . . I don't know when."

"Hmmph. Same here," Terry said. "Do you think Lillie will give us free haircuts now that we don't have a barber? Doesn't she cut your hair all the time?"

Amos chuckled despite the seriousness of the things they had been discussing. "Yeah. She gave good haircuts, until she got too busy with her career. Now she says she likes my hair hanging on my shoulders; says it reminds her of pictures of the Chippendales."

"You mean those male strippers?"

"Yeah. But don't tell her I told you. It would embarrass her." They both laughed. "What was your question, Terry?"

"After Mike told us he was mapping the area from Ogden to the north end of Bear Lake, I took a look at what he's done. He must be spending a lot of time in the lab when he should be taking care of the gardens." Since they had discovered that the Observer created a door or gate to a twin world, Mike had started jumping the gate from one place to another, virtually mapping locations in the parallel world as the Observer tracked the three-dimensional coordinates. It had become an obsession and appeared to be impacting his other duties.

"He's been to Logan, Brigham City, Ogden, Garden City and everything in between," Terry continued. "He's mapped out just about every square inch of the Smith's parking lot in Logan," he exaggerated.

"You think he's preparing for a trip through the gate?" Amos asked, remembering his earlier concern about Mike trying to get around his rules.

"He made it pretty clear that he thinks you should let him go."

"So he's researching the area to learn all he can from this side of the gate?"

"That's what it looks like to me."

"He's never gone against my instructions before."

"He's never seen anything like this before. Neither have we. It's got to be tempting."

"Maybe we should have him show us what he's been doing. Better to know now than be surprised later, don't you think?"

Terry nodded.

The Outcasts—Northwest of Johns Creek, Georgia, 16 July

When Beth and Melissa entered the kitchen from the bedroom they shared, Lisa was searching the cupboards.

"What are you looking for," Beth asked.

"Something to eat," Lisa said, "and I'm not finding anything."

"Where's the backpack with the food and water?" Beth asked.

"Gone," Lisa said, "along with Pepper and Jared. And good riddance."

Eight of the women had slept in beds, while Ben and Bryce slept in the family room in recliners. Pepper and Jared had stayed in the living room, by the kitchen and front door.

"Are you surprised?" Lisa asked.

"Not really," Beth said, "but I wish they hadn't taken our food. They didn't leave anything?"

"Not even a note."

Beth barked a laugh and shook her head.

"If they'd left a note, what do you think it would have said?" Beth asked.

"Got my male needs covered, thank you very much."

The others, hearing Lisa and Beth talking, straggled into the kitchen to see what was going on.

"Well, we better look for more food and water," Karen said.

"And let's hope it's not as difficult to find this time," Candy added.

"Let's divide up and search houses," Melissa said.

"I saw a gas station nearby," Beth said. "I'd like to see if they have some road maps that'll show us how to get to the Rocky Mountains."

"I'll go with you," Melissa said, "to see if there's any food. Maybe they'll have a vending machine with candy bars. Wouldn't that be a treat?"

"All the houses we checked last night were stinky," Suzanne griped, wrinkling her nose. "I don't want to go in them."

"Maybe the stinky ones will be where there's food," Beth said, challenging Suzanne. "If there's a dead person in there, it means the people didn't leave and take all of their stuff with 'em." After thinking about it for a moment, she added, "Wrap a wet towel around your face. Maybe it'll filter the air you're breathing and keep the smell down."

Suzanne gave Beth a dirty look and walked away.

"I suggest you divide up in pairs," Beth said before she and Melissa left, "so no one has to be alone." When they returned, an hour later, she set a map on the kitchen counter, then turned to the others, who sat at the table eating what they'd found.

"Was I right?" she asked Suzanne.

"Unfortunately," Suzanne said, as she forked a slice of peach into her mouth from a can. "I guess it makes some kind of sense, that if *we* don't want to go into a house because it stinks, it would be the last place *anyone else* would want to look as well."

"Only problem," Lisa said, "was that it was hard holding my breath long enough to find the food and get out of the house again."

"That bad?" Beth asked.

"The worst smell seemed to be coming from upstairs," Lisa said, "so we avoided that and looked on the main floor only."

"The pantry was full," Kerri said, not looking up from her breakfast. It was the first full sentence Beth had heard her speak.

"Here," Melissa said to Beth, as she set an open can of fruit cocktail, and a spoon, in front of her.

"Thanks," Beth said. "Are you disappointed that the vending machines were empty?"

"Yes, but let me get something in my stomach and I won't notice it so much."

"You really wanted a chocolate bar, didn't you?

"Chocolate bar?" Lisa said, jerking her head up to look at Beth. Several others looked up, too. "You found a chocolate bar?"

"I wish I had," Melissa replied. "The vending machines were empty. Well, actually, they were broken, smashed to pieces and lying on the floor."

Lisa went back to her canned peaches, disappointment clear on her face.

When they finished eating, Beth inventoried the rest of the food they'd collected, while Lisa and Kerri went to find containers for water.

"Could be two days' worth of food if we're careful, and if no one else disappears with it," Beth said, looking around at the others, trying to determine if she had to worry about any of them.

"We figured that's about as much weight as we can carry in our packs at one time," Suzanne said.

"Any more and we'd have to leave our clothes behind," Candy added.

"These should fit nicely into our backpacks," Lisa said when she and Kerri returned carrying several empty glass quart jars.

"Hmm . . . not such a good idea, ladies," Beth said. "If the glass breaks—"

"You lose the water," Lisa finished for her.

"You could also ruin whatever else is in the backpack."

"Oh! Yeah. We'll try again," Lisa said. They returned a few minutes later with plastic, two-liter Coke bottles. "We filled them from the water heater like you showed us."

"What was in them before?" Suzanne asked.

"Nothing," Lisa replied innocently. "They were sitting in a re-cycling bin by the back door."

"Did you—" Suzanne started to say.

"We rinsed them out," Lisa said, interrupting her.

Beth studied her map, giving the exchange only part of her attention, so the others gathered around to see what was so in-teresting.

"This map shows several southeastern states," Beth said and pointed to a spot northwest of Atlanta, Georgia. "Here's where we are. To get to the Rocky Mountains, we need to cross the Missis-sippi River." She ran her finger along the river from New Orleans to the upper edge of the map.

"Here's the nearest bridge that crosses the river, at Memphis, Tennessee. I suggest we work our way northwest across Alabama and Mississippi, to Memphis, and cross there."

"Then what?" Suzanne asked.

"We'll figure it out along the way," Beth said, controlling her sudden anger at being questioned. She didn't know all the an-swers. She was making this up as she went along.

As they left the house, Beth was again struck by the lack of noise—the normal sounds of life—and the sky was as dark as it had been the day before. Maybe the birds thought it was perpetual night.

They left the too-quiet neighborhood, and a few minutes later, left highway 120 to follow Rucker Road.

Without Pepper and Jared in tow, Beth thought she would feel safer; but as time passed, she began to worry that they were being followed. She had no idea where the pair of misfits had gone, or if the government was looking for them; but as they walked, she watched their back, and the nagging feeling that they were being watched stayed with her.

The Preserve, Wedding preparations, 17-18 July

"I wish you would call him Matt, Mom," Emily said for the hundredth time since she had started dating him. Brittany pinned up the wedding dress while Lillie fussed with the lacy outer layer, tilting her head to one side as she looked at the fit critically.

"Oh, it's okay Emily," Lillie said, "Matthew doesn't mind. And I think Matthew sounds so much more dignified."

"Ouch!" Emily said, as Brittany stuck her with a pin.

"Hold still," Brittany said, through lips that were closed over the pins set between her teeth.

"What's Matthew doing today?" Lillie asked.

Emily sighed. No way was Mom going to call him Matt. "Dad started Matt's medical training this week." Amos had committed to complete the training Matt had missed by leaving his residency and coming to the Preserve with them. "Matt's been spending most of his time in the library studying. Today, Dad has him in the hospital, practicing what he's been learning."

"Who's the patient today?"

"I think they're doing an appendectomy on Mike."

"Michael has already had his appendix removed."

"Mom," Emily said in exasperation, "Dad's not going to actually cut Mike open."

"I know. And I know that's why they picked an appendectomy. They can look at Michael's scar and compare his x-rays with the medical books. They could even use a plastic knife and pretend to make the incision."

Emily started to laugh.

"Hold still," Brittany said, through closed teeth, "or I'll stick you on purpose."

☢

"We can use my art set to make wedding invitations," Sydney Carlsen said.

"That would be fun," Rylee Parker agreed. Rylee was the only survivor of the car crash in Logan Canyon that took her parents and brother, as well as Aaron Carlsen and his friend. Lillie had informally adopted fifteen-year-old Rylee and taken her to the Preserve, rather than risk leaving her at the scene of the accident, or in Logan, where she could be found and questioned. That could have caused authorities to begin looking for the Preserve.

Sydney and Rylee sat at a table in the community center, drawing, while Brittany sat across the room making final adjustments to Emily's wedding dress.

"Would that be okay, Mom," Sydney called to her mom.

"I think that would be wonderful," Brittany said distractedly.

"Do you have any suggestions?" Sydney asked. "I've never made wedding invitations before."

Brittany chuckled, set down her sewing, and walked over to where the girls worked.

With Brittany's suggestions, the girls completed the invitations that afternoon. They awoke early the next morning and tried to sneak down each tunnel, to tape the invitations on bedroom doors before anyone else got up. As they tiptoed, their quiet laughter and whispers echoed through the bedroom tunnels, making so much noise, that by the time they got to the room shared by Mike and Chris, the two young men were waiting for them. At just the right moment, they whipped the door open and yelled, scaring the girls, who ran off screaming and laughing.

Katie had asked Mike to help her design and make live table decorations, since Mike was responsible for the greenhouses, and she knew he would do anything for her.

"What did you have in mind?" he asked, as she took his arm and they walked slowly through the garden common room, then into one of the greenhouses.

"What do you recommend?" she asked, watching him closely, her lips curled into a smile. She remembered how, ever since grade school, he had tried to get her attention by showing off—hanging by his knees on the monkey bars, jumping out of the swing at the end of its arc, trying to dunk on a 7-foot-high basketball hoop, and other pre-teen boy antics. Mike hadn't really known how to talk to her, but he had obviously wanted her to notice him.

That had changed when—as a teenager—Mike had started dating and had developed better social skills; but he had still seemed reticent about opening up to *her*. Katie had been pleased when that had changed, after they'd arrived at the Preserve and they'd spent more time together. Now, if she could just get him to kiss her.

Mike talked about the various plants that they could use, making suggestions about how to combine different plants to make bouquets. Katie watched and listened, pretending to be impressed, but Mike's suggestions were terrible. He might be able to grow plants, but it appeared he had no idea how to combine them to make aesthetic flower arrangements.

Eventually, Mike turned toward her—likely to see her reaction—and stopped talking about plants when he saw her face.

"You're beautiful," he said, spontaneously, and with emotion.

Katie smiled at this intelligent, handsome, but not too creative man that she loved. She leaned toward him, her face tilted up toward his, her lips parted slightly.

He leaned toward her, placed his hands on both sides of her face, and kissed her.

Finally, she thought, closing her eyes, *he noticed.*

They separated, and he backed up far enough to look into her eyes, then he grabbed her shoulders, pulled her close, and kissed her again. She returned the embrace, enjoying his touch, as he ran his hands up and down her back. She wished they could stay that way forever, but knew it had to end soon, before someone came along and noticed.

She broke the kiss and backed away, running her hands along his arms as she did. He held her arms and looked into her eyes.

"Can we do this again? Soon?"

She nodded, smiling, not trusting herself to speak. The sooner the better.

5

We let our guard down

The Outcasts—Georgia, 17 July

Seeing the broken-up roads and cracks in the ground, it looked to Beth like there had been a large earthquake. She knew Georgia had small quakes, but this was different; and she still wondered about the ash and soot that constantly fell from the dark sky. Was it nuclear fallout, fires burning out of control, something else, or a combination of all of those things? Whatever it was, she was uncomfortable being outdoors.

"I didn't feel an earthquake strong enough to do this kind of damage," Suzanne said.

"Maybe the explosion in Atlanta caused it," Lisa suggested.

"I don't know," Beth replied, "but I think we need to be careful. If it was a quake, there could be aftershocks, which would probably open up these cracks. A fall into something like that, in this darkness, could be disastrous."

"Okay, which way do we go now?" Melissa asked.

"According to the map," Beth said, "Interstate 75 gives us more options for crossing Lake Acworth, and it's shorter."

"We don't seem to tire from walking," Melissa said, "and staying on the interstate could leave us pretty exposed. So, maybe we should just stay on this road."

"You think we're more vulnerable to an attack on the interstate, is that it?" Beth asked.

"Well, what if we're being followed?" Melissa asked.

Beth jerked at the suggestion. It was exactly what she had thought earlier. "You mean, by Jared and Pepper, or the government?" Beth asked.

"I don't know if the government can track us, or if they're trying to," Melissa said, "but it feels like we're being watched."

"That's what I think, too," Beth said. "With the lack of light, plus the road damage, I think we should take the route that gives us more options. We'll just have to be careful."

Beth looked around at the others to gauge their feelings, but it was difficult to see their faces in the dim light, and most of them had become adept at hiding their emotions behind blank faces. Lisa was the exception; her body language gave her away every time, and this time she agreed with Beth, as she usually did.

Beth led them up the onramp onto the interstate, where they spread out and began weaving their way between stalled cars that were turned at all angles, some of them blocking multiple lanes—a graveyard of obsolete technology. Maybe they should have stayed on the other road, Beth thought, second-guessing her earlier decision; but the longer they stayed on the interstate, the easier it was for her to conclude that this was the best choice, because it offered "more options".

"Some of these collisions look like they occurred at a pretty high speed," Lisa said.

"Well duh. We *are* on a freeway." Suzanne replied caustically.

"They've turned this into a real obstacle course," Lisa continued, as she and Kerri walked up to a car resting upside down on the asphalt. Kerri bent down to peer into a broken window as Lisa approached.

Kerri squealed and moved away so fast that she fell on her backside.

"There are bloody bodies in here," Lisa said, also backing away.

"This one too," Suzanne said. "I think I'm going to be sick."

"Everyone," Beth called, "it's easier travelling over here by the center median." She and Melissa had worked their way over to the depression between the westbound and eastbound lanes. Eventually, everyone else weaved their way toward them.

After a while, they were strung out over several car lengths—in ones and twos—and fell into a routine, talking quietly to one another, or just looking around. They hadn't seen a living soul all day.

Without warning, a screaming man ran out of the dark, between two cars, with a tire iron raised over his head. His route took him directly toward Karen, who was near the back of their procession, with only Callie and Ben behind her. Ben, who'd been bringing up the rear to keep an eye on Callie, had been distracted by a crumpled Maserati that had rear-ended a pickup on the other side of the median. He heard the scream and turned just as the man swung the tire iron down toward Karen.

"Look out," he yelled—too late.

The metal bar landed with such force on the top of Karen's head that it caved in her skull with a sickening "squishy" sound, and she crumpled to the pavement with an *"umph"*. The attacker paused only momentarily, then turned toward Callie, screaming incoherent threats.

"Noooo," Callie said quietly, closing her eyes and placing her hands over her face, frozen in place.

Ben raced past her and intercepted the attacker in mid-swing, knocking the tire iron to the side with his left forearm. His right fist connected with the attacker's head, spinning it around with a loud crunch of bone. The attacker fell backward in a heap.

Attracted by the noise, the others ran back toward the incident.

"Melissa, check Karen," Beth said; but as she passed, she could tell there was nothing they could do for her.

"Lisa," she continued, knowing Lisa would be right behind her, "check on Callie. Bryce, help me with Ben." She ran up to Ben, who was now kneeling on the ground, clutching his left arm with his right, obviously in serious pain.

"I'm pretty sure it's broken," Ben said, as Beth knelt beside him. She took his left forearm in both hands and carefully felt around. Ben bravely held still, closing his eyes and gritting his teeth.

"It hurts, Beth. I need to sit down before I fall over."

"Over here," Bryce said, opening the rear door of a nearby car. With Bryce's help, Beth removed Ben's backpack, then they lowered him into the car, just as he fainted. He fell sideways onto the seat, leaving Beth holding his broken arm. She produced a knife from beneath her loose-fitting shirt, and cut his sleeve open to the elbow.

"What can I do to help?" Lisa asked from behind her.

"It feels like both bones are broken," Beth said, without looking around. "The radius must have taken the worst of the blow. It has almost broken through the skin. It needs to be set, then we need to immobilize the arm. See what Melissa has in her pack that we can use."

"Okay."

Beth heard Lisa hurry away.

"Wait!" she called, turning to look at Lisa, who had stopped and turned her head. "We'll need pain killers as well."

"This is going to hurt, Ben," she told him when he woke a few minutes later. "Take these," she added, as she held some pills in her open palm and a bottle of water in her other hand.

He nodded once, without speaking. Bryce supported his head from the other side of the car while he swallowed the pills dry and chased them down with water, emptying her bottle.

Beth watched his heavy breathing as he closed his eyes against the pain. "We can wait a few minutes, until the medicine takes effect," she said, but he shook his head, without opening his eyes.

"Hold him tight," she told Bryce, who pressed Ben's shoulders against the back of the car seat with Ben's left arm on top where she had access to it. When she set his arm, he screamed and fainted again.

Beth splinted his arm, then asked Lisa and Kerri to stay with him while she went to see what the others were doing. She needed a break from the stress; her shoulders and neck were sore and her head ached. As she walked away, she again considered her feelings. She realized she was reluctant to leave Ben. She wanted to be there when he woke so her face was the first thing he saw. More than that though, she was tired of being in charge. She was angry that the others assumed she would take care of everything—that she would tell them what they needed to do. She couldn't explain her anger. She was trained in medicine, and except for Melissa and Ben, the others weren't. She knew that, but still felt as though she was surrounded by morons.

As Beth's thoughts raced, and her heartbeat continued to rise, she saw Bryce and Melissa leaning against the side of an SUV, talking quietly. The others were sitting on the slope of the median, seeming to have little interest in what was going on. There was no sign of Karen or her attacker.

Beth slowed her breathing, and soon calmed down.

"What'd you do with 'em?" she asked Melissa.

"We laid Karen in the back seat of this SUV, but no one wanted to touch the guy."

When Beth looked at her questioningly, she nodded toward the median, where the attacker's body lay crumpled. "We rolled him over there with our shoes."

"Did you look at him first, to see if you could tell what made him act that way?"

"Yeah. Not much light to see by, but what I thought at first were scrapes from an accident, are actually scratches over radiation burns, probably made by the man himself. He was probably in serious pain and going crazy from it."

"That's what I thought, too," Bryce said. "Is that normal?"

"I don't know," Melissa said. "Maybe he had a serious case of radiation poisoning. Or, maybe he had some other problems that complicated his reaction to the radiation. We haven't seen anyone else acting that way."

"Poor Karen," Beth said. Things were getting worse. What was going to happen to them? Would they all become victims? Would they run into more crazed attackers? And why was she so angry. That was the question that lingered as she returned to Ben.

☢

Beth found a spare shirt in Ben's pack. When he woke, she smiled at him with genuine pleasure, which he returned drowsily. She and Lisa helped him into a sitting position and tied the shirt into a sling. They leaned him back against the seat and he fell asleep again within a few minutes.

"How do you plan to move him?" Melissa asked, when she wandered over and handed Beth more pills from her medical pack and a bottle of water.

"Let's just hope he can move on his own power," Beth replied, taking the pills and water. "After all, it's not his legs." She shook Ben gently until he stirred, then stuffed the pills in his mouth.

"Ben, swallow the pills," she said. He swallowed without opening his eyes. "Drink this," she said, as she tipped a water bottle to his mouth. Most of the water ran down the front of his shirt and what he tried to swallow, he choked on.

"How long can we stay here?" Beth asked Melissa, without looking at her.

"Assuming our guy doesn't have friends lurking, I'd say a couple of hours max. We need to get into some kind of shelter before we lose what little daylight we have."

"We let our guard down," Beth said, looking around at the jungle of broken cars and trucks. She noticed the others sitting down, not bothering to check their surroundings—a bad sign. She handed the water bottle back to Melissa, who dumped half the remaining water on Ben's face. He sputtered and came awake, moaning and reaching for his arm. Beth threw an angry look in her direction and blocked Ben's hand.

"Just thought I'd speed things along a little," Melissa said casually, with a backward glance, as she walked away toward the others. "It worked."

"Should we try to get him to stand?" Lisa asked from behind.

Beth jumped in surprise and let out a little squeal, then relaxed when she realized who had spoken to her.

"Get on his right side and push him this way. Let's see if we can get him out of the car and standing upright." With effort, they managed to get Ben's feet on the ground, pushing and pulling him into a standing position. Ben tried to help, pushing off and standing up. A suppressed moan escaped his lips. He took a tentative step, then another. He leaned on Lisa for support, but she was collapsing under his weight.

"Here," Beth said, quickly taking Lisa's place under Ben's good arm. "Let me take him. I'm a little more substantial than you." Lisa got behind Ben, took hold of one of his belt loops, and lifted. Ben winced and moaned with pain as they walked him along the side of the car. They had only reached the front of the car before they were exhausted from the effort and Ben was ready to collapse again.

"Lisa," Beth said, "let's get him back in the car, so we can sit him down. This isn't working." They got Ben turned around and back into the car, but when he tried to lay down, Beth pulled him back upright. "Don't lay down, Ben," she said. "We need to decide what to do." He was asleep almost immediately, his head falling back against the seat back.

"What do you want to do?" Melissa asked from behind. Beth turned to find Melissa ushering the others toward the car.

"What do *you* want to do?" Beth threw the question back at her in frustration.

"Well, we have three in favor of moving on and three who don't care whether we go or rest a while."

"Make that four who don't care," Lisa said.

Beth studied Melissa, impressed that she had taken the initiative of polling the others, while she was focused solely on Ben.

"Then I suggest we take time to eat," Beth said, "and check out some of these cars. Let's see if there's anything useful in any of them." Melissa shrugged, then opened a pack and started laying food out on the hood of the car.

☢

Beth sat next to Ben, watching him sleep, and absently rubbing her finger across the blade of a straight-bladed kitchen knife.

"Where'd you get the knife?" Lisa asked quietly, coming closer.

"The restaurant we ate at yesterday," Beth said without hesitation; but she remained focused on Ben.

"Are you worried about our—your safety?"

Beth nodded without speaking or turning to look at Lisa.

As Lisa watched Beth, the thought struck her that maybe Beth's concern for Ben was more than just a doctor-patient relationship. They had been together in the shelter and inseparable since then. She thought Beth must want to be alone with him—worried about his condition—so she started to turn away. She stopped and turned back when Beth spoke.

"After the episodes with Art at the shelter and Jared at the river, we decided we should have some protection," Beth said with a sigh, finally looking up at Lisa.

"You said 'we'."

"Melissa and I each have several knives."

Lisa thought having a knife for protection was a good idea and wanted to ask for one, but hesitated—she couldn't say why. Beth had always been kind and generous, except when she was frustrated with Suzanne. Maybe the stress of herding the Outcasts was wearing her patience thin. She hoped that Beth had noticed how she always tried to be a calming influence on the group and help out whenever she saw a need.

Beth was still looking at Lisa, possibly waiting for her to ask the obvious next question. When Lisa didn't ask, Beth opened her backpack and handed two knives to her.

"One for Kerri." Beth said and smiled briefly—a sad smile—which Lisa returned. Then Lisa tucked the knives into her pants and went to find Kerri.

☢

Beth watched Lisa walk away quickly and head straight for Kerri. She sighed and thought how much easier this journey would be if all of the Outcasts were as caring and helpful as Lisa.

She woke Ben and got him to his feet again. He was still in considerable pain, but she walked him to the next freeway exit, two hundred yards farther along the freeway, and to a service station at the bottom of the ramp. The windows on the station were shattered, so they let themselves in and Beth let Ben rest again. Then, while she stayed with Ben, the others went out looking for food, water and other supplies. Later, over a meal of canned fruit and cold vegetables, that they'd found in the cellar of one house, they discussed their next steps.

"We need to get out of Georgia, away from all this death and violence." Candy said with a shiver.

"It's got to be better in less populated states, west of the Mississippi River." Melissa said.

Beth wondered if that were true, or if the entire country had now been affected; but she was counting on finding a hideaway in the Rocky Mountains.

"I'm in no condition to travel, at least not for a while." Ben said groggily. "You should just leave me. I'll fend for myself and find a way to follow you."

"No Ben," Beth said. "I won't leave you." Ben opened his mouth to protest, but Beth held up a hand to stop him. "I've decided. If you have to stay, to continue your recovery, I'll stay too." She had almost added that she couldn't leave him because she thought she loved him, but had changed her mind at the last second.

There were groans and protests from some of the others.

"I say, if he wants us to go, we should go," Suzanne complained.

Beth became defensive immediately. "You go right ahead, Suzanne." She looked around at the others. "Any of you who want to go are welcome to. I'm not your boss, and you're not mine. Do whatever you want." There was venom in her voice, and she quickly reigned herself in. "Sorry," she added, then looked down at her feet.

"Come on, Beth. We need to put some distance between us and Johns Creek," Candy added after a few moments. "Maybe some of us should go ahead and the rest catch up."

"I'm not going without Beth," Lisa said, standing between Kerri and Callie, with an arm around each of them. "And neither are you two. Am I right?" They nodded.

Torn between wanting to keep everyone together and feeling like she couldn't leave Ben, Beth was relieved to see that most of them supported staying. She looked at Bryce, who winked at her and smiled. That settled it.

"How about we sleep on it and decide in the morning?" Lisa said diplomatically.

"Good idea, Lisa," Beth said. "Ben will probably be good to walk tomorrow. The medicine will dull the pain and he'll be good to go—slowly. Will someone please help me get him to the house where we found the food." She would stay with Ben as long as it took, until he could travel farther; but she really believed Ben would be fine by morning. It was only his arm after all. They would bandage it tightly to stabilize the break, and then he'd be able to move. But if not, if anyone wanted to continue, she would show them on the map where she thought they should go, and she would try to catch up.

"The house where we found the food is stinky," Lisa said, with a smile at Suzanne, who liked to use that word, "but there's one close by that's not. We could go there."

Bryce lifted Ben by his good arm and draped it over his shoulder, then followed Lisa outside and down the street. Most of the others followed immediately. Suzanne and Candy moaned and looked at each other, then followed.

Vice President Art Klemp, 18 July

As daylight was disappearing, Art thought he could see torches ahead on the roadway.

"What's that?" he asked, as he slowed the truck.

"Looks like a roadblock," Dayron replied.

"It looks like they're armed," M.C. added.

"What?" Art asked, surprised at her comment.

"Looks like those torches are reflecting off metal weapons, like maybe they have guns."

"I think you're right," he said, seeing what she meant. He squinted, but it didn't help. "We need to be ready for a fight." He picked up his automatic weapon, the dead soldier's handgun he had acquired at the shelter, and weighed it in his hand. "Do you all still have your guns?" Before anyone could respond, he added. "I'm going to ram the roadblock. Be prepared to use your weapons."

Art began accelerating a hundred yards from what appeared to be cars placed bumper to bumper across the roadway, aiming for the gap between two cars. As they approached the make-shift barricade, the torch-bearers began waving their torches back and forth, as if they were flagging him down. Closer, he could see that the weapons were rifles, and that they were being leveled at the truck.

He wondered if they were warning him of a danger beyond the barricade, then dismissed the thought. Their weapons told him that this was an attempt to get his truck, or anything else of value that he might have.

At fifty yards, the people at the barricade started firing. Art and Dayron ducked reflexively until Art realized that the bullets were hitting the truck body and windshield, cracking the glass, but not penetrating. "Bullet-proof glass and hardened chassis," he said, triumphantly.

The defenders jumped out of the way, just before the truck hit the barricade at sixty-five miles per hour, spinning two cars out of the way. Metal screamed in protest and glass shattered, as the truck pushed its way through the barricade and hit a second barricade twenty yards beyond, this one made from concrete lane dividers. The truck rose up over the barrier and came to a halt—high-centered—when the front wheels couldn't get traction. Art, and the others, were thrown forward against their seatbelts and the airbags deployed, hitting them in the face. Art's chest hurt and it took a few moments to reorient himself and deflate the airbag.

"We're surrounded," Jean said from the back seat. "Do we surrender?"

"No way!" Art said defiantly, looking around to confirm that they were, indeed, surrounded. But their enemies, as Art now thought of them, were being cautious, showing little of themselves.

"Soldiers, surrender your weapons and we'll be lenient," came a voice from a blowhorn.

"They think we're soldiers," Dayron said, unnecessarily.

"I guess we'll have to shoot our way out of here," Art said as he took one last swipe at the airbag, his feelings of invincibility strong.

"Maybe we should wait until they come out from cover before we start shooting," Jean said. "Right now, we'd have a difficult time hitting them."

"What do you know about it?" Art barked, hyped-up and ready for a fight.

"I used to hunt deer with my husband," Jean replied. "We had better success when we let the game come to us."

"Hmm . . . let them come to us. Okay," Art said, unbuckling his seatbelt and sitting back in his seat, but not relaxing. "Let's wait a minute and see if they come to us."

Although they were difficult to see in the dark, within a few moments, the defenders from the barricade started creeping out from their hiding places and approached the truck. Art didn't know if it was because they thought the truck's occupants were unconscious, or they were just impatient, but he was impressed with Jean's suggestion.

"Now would be a good time to start shooting," Jean finally said.

Art looked around and noticed that about two dozen men and women—some armed with rifles, some with handguns, but most with clubs or garden implements—were coming from the direction of the barricade. The closest ones, the ones with guns, were only a few yards away.

"Open the doors just far enough to shoot, but stay inside the truck," Jean said.

"Okay, shoot those with firearms first," Art instructed, frowning at Jean. "What she said. *Now!*"

The attack started so suddenly that the approaching defenders were caught off-guard. Although Art and his followers were not experienced shooters, except for Jean, the defenders closest to the truck were hit and went down immediately. Those farther away fled, a couple of them limping. The few shots fired at the truck ricocheted away harmlessly, or missed completely.

"Okay, let's gather weapons and move on," Art said with bravado.

"Sir," Jean said, stopping him with his hand on the door handle, "I suggest we wait a few minutes, to make certain the survivors aren't waiting to attack again when we're in the open."

Without responding, he removed his hand from the door handle and continued looking around, until his patience was spent.

"Enough waiting. Everyone out!" he finally said, waiting until the other three were in the open and no shots were fired before opening his own door and cautiously stepping down from the truck, his handgun at the ready. They walked quickly to the bodies lying on the pavement, took their guns, and searched the bodies for anything of value.

"What now?" Dayron asked.

"Now we walk," he said and headed north into the darkness.

6

You want us to ask for volunteers?

"Well, Mike, how's the research coming?" Amos asked as they followed Terry toward the lab after lunch.

"Wha—?"

"Looks like you've been doing some research on our twin world. What have you discovered?"

Mike should have realized that he couldn't hide what he'd been doing, but he didn't think they would notice so soon. He hoped they didn't suspect his real intentions.

"Well," Mike's thoughts ran in several directions, trying to decide what to say to deflect their suspicions, "when we took the gate down the canyon, we saw that the people drive on the right side of the road, just like *we* do. And from the newspaper, we saw that they speak English. So, I wondered what else we could learn, just by looking."

"And?"

"What? That's it."

"Terry?" Amos asked, looking at his partner.

"From the tracks you've created in the Observer's memory," Terry said, "it's apparent that you've spent a lot of time in the lab."

"Not really."

"Michael," Amos said, "with your duties in the gardens, when are you finding time for this?"

"It really hasn't taken that much time," Mike said defensively, hoping his dad would drop it. He didn't know how long he could continue telling half-truths.

Amos studied Mike for a few moments before going on.

"So, what have you learned?"

"Well, besides the things we already saw, I've learned that they have similar coinage."

"How did you find that out?" Amos asked, his curiosity apparently overcoming his suspicions for the moment. Mike was so relieved, that he almost forgot to look embarrassed by his next confession.

"Well, I found a quarter on the ground outside the Smith's store, so I reached through and picked it up." He fished the coin out of his pocket and showed it to his dad, who turned it over in his hand, then passed it to Terry.

"It certainly looks and feels the same as ours," Terry said, while Amos studied his son again, making him squirm.

"That's all I did, Dad, honest," Mike said. He could tell that his dad suspected there was more, but he didn't want his dad to know he was considering going through the gate into the twin world.

"Mike," Amos finally said, as if reading Mike's mind, "I want you to promise me, again, that you won't go through the gate without one of us being here."

Mike's heart sank. He didn't want to lie, but he *definitely* intended to go through the gate. As his dad continued, his mind searched for a way out.

"We don't know how our presence in the other world will contaminate their environment," Amos said, "or what it might do to us. And you need to have someone with you who knows how to operate the Observer, in case of an emergency."

That was it, Mike realized. He would teach Katie how to operate the Observer.

"I promise, Dad," he said, contritely. "No unattended travel." He hoped his dad couldn't hear the elation in his voice or the condition he'd placed on his promise.

Amos studied him for a few more moments, then nodded.

"Okay, Mike. Terry said you've been from Ogden to Bear Lake. Show us what you've found."

"Great Dad," Mike said as he entered coordinates, then opened the gate. They were looking at a hillside, with construction equipment moving dirt. "Remember the new medical facility that was under construction above the Weber State University campus, the one we couldn't find a few weeks ago? They've finally started working on it in the twin world."

Amos looked at the construction site through the gate, then stared at Terry, who stared back.

Prime bunker, 19 July

"Thank you for joining us, Director Lister," the president said. "How are your patients coming along?"

"You know that four nights ago," Lister said, "Ambassador Porter, Colonel Johnson, Corporal Prettyman and a couple of house guards were in close contact with Vice President Klemp during an attack on the VEEP bunker."

"Yes, yes," the president said impatiently. "How are they doing?"

"All of them were immediately vaccinated and quarantined. Rashes have appeared on everyone's face, neck and hands, except for the Ambassador, who we've separated from the others. They look very similar to radiation burns—"

"Director," the president said, cutting her off, "we're not blaming you for this. Just tell us if they have smallpox."

"Yes," she said with a sigh, not meeting his eyes. "I think they do." She'd tried to find some other explanation for what they were seeing, but couldn't. "Based on what we encountered in the Johns Creek shelter. I think they have a mutated version of smallpox."

"Thank you. That means we can now say for sure that this *mutation* of the virus accelerated its progress and made it more virulent, correct? So, when Vice President Klemp carried it to the VEEP bunker it contaminated seven people."

"Seven?" Lister asked, looking up sharply. "I only treated four."

"There were three dead security personnel," SecDef Jim Seymour interjected.

"Oh. I didn't know. Yes. That's how it appears," Lister said.

"And you're sure that Art—the vice president—and the others were vaccinated at the shelter?" the president asked.

"I thought so, but now I don't know. They shouldn't have been contagious after they were vaccinated." Lister looked away. Worry lines spread across her forehead.

The president shook his head, his expression grim.

"What did we find out about Ft. Detrick, Director?" the president asked, trying to keep the dialogue going. The Director looked back at him, her face now defiant and angry. Greg knew she took this matter personally—a breach in the protocols and security measures in place for facilities such as her own. Her own colleagues had caused this.

"Well, as you know, the director of the Ft. Detrick facility is now in the bunker of the secretary of defense. He told me that two scientists disappeared from his facility as well. One was the deputy director, who was also the primary contact with the CDC, through my deputy director."

"So, your deputy director stole samples from the CDC and his counterpart stole samples from Ft. Detrick. This just gets better and better. No idea where they went, I suppose?"

"We haven't found them," Jim replied, "but we're not checking all the bodies before we incinerate them. Reports are that at least some of the people appear to have contracted smallpox before they died."

"Meaning that we have an outbreak of smallpox near the Ft. Detrick facility, I suppose?" the president asked.

"Unfortunately," Jim said

"Wonderful. Any response from our contacts at the Level 4 facility in Russia?"

"No official contact with anyone in Russia," Secretary of State Cy Hutchison said. "We're calling, but they're not answering."

"Director Lister?" the president asked.

"I've been unable to get in touch with any of my contacts there, sir."

"Director, is there any possibility that the doctors who took the virus samples conspired to release them intentionally, for whatever reason?"

"Oh, no, Mr. President. I can't imagine a conspiracy of that nature," she said. She hadn't known her deputy, Dr. Thomas Strang, for very long, but he had come to her attention, two years earlier, highly recommended for the position, and with exceptional credentials and experience. He had performed his duties well, right from the start, but had some unusual habits—like biting his fingernails—and she had had to stop herself from calling him Dr. Strange on two separate occasions. Even so, she couldn't believe anyone as professional and polite as Thomas, could harbor such feelings as would permit him to release a deadly disease on the world.

The president stared at her for a few moments, making her squirm uncomfortably. She wondered if he had read her mind and waited for her to confess her doubts about Dr. Strang.

"You didn't think they would remove them in the first place though, did you?" he asked.

Anne was shaken by the president's comment. She *had* denied the possibility that the virus could escape, originally.

"I've had a lot of time to consider that, Mr. President," she replied confidently. "From all the evidence—from their research notes and what they reported—I don't believe there was a conspiracy to intentionally release the virus." She hesitated for a few moments, her initial doubts returning, then continued apologetically. "I don't know any way to confirm it either way, unless we can find one of the doctors alive, and ask. But based upon notes and records, it appears the doctors may have just wanted to protect their research. Nothing more. Stupid, I know, but innocent enough, I believe."

Greg studied Director Lister. She spoke with confidence, but her body language told him she was nervous. About what? The virus? The possibility of a conspiracy? He was caught in a dilemma. As a humanitarian, he should protect everyone—the infected and the uninfected—but if he couldn't control the virus, or if there was a conspiracy to spread the virus, he had an obligation to protect the uninfected, even if it meant the infected had to go. Could he make a life or death decision for millions, possibly hundreds of millions of people? Did he have a right to make that decision?

His head ached. His stomach churned. He swore under his breath. Did he have the right? He was the president of the United States of America, the greatest republic in the world. Half the country was dead or dying. What would happen to the rest of the country—the rest of the world—if he failed to make the tough decision, or made the wrong decision? He needed all the information he could gather before making this decision.

"Director Lister," he said, and felt like he was pleading with her, "I'm about to make the toughest decision of my life, and it could affect the lives of millions of people. Is there anything you're not telling me, anything at all?"

Lister looked shocked by Greg's question, but she slowly shook her head.

"Anyone?" he asked his advisors. Nothing.

"Ok," the president began, prepared for a rebuttal from one or more of them. "Jim, keep up your search for smallpox victims. You know the symptoms. Neutralize threats—especially if you run into Art and his band of thugs."

"Colonel Johnson said Art only had three people with him when he left—a black man and two white women," Jim said.

"Who knows how many followers he'll have next time we see him?" the president asked. "And I'm sure we haven't seen the last of him. He's probably moving as fast as he can toward the Prime bunker. Didn't you say Colonel Johnson gave him a map?"

"Yes sir. Art has GPS and a printed map. We've tracked his truck into North Carolina."

Anne Lister had opened her mouth but nothing came out.

"Director," the president said when he noticed, "I told you this was a difficult decision, but you have to understand that these people are a threat to our survival. What we need you to do is to find a cure for the mutated virus. How long do you think it will take you?"

"I . . . I have no equipment," Anne sputtered, "no facility, no specimens. I have no idea what it will take."

"Ok. Jim," Greg said, adapting to the new input, "let's modify the plan. We need you to find some volunteers for the director."

"You want us to ask for volunteers?" Jim asked, a questioning look on his face.

"Of course not. Just don't eliminate all the candidates before the director finds us a cure." Greg smiled at Lister, but it was not a friendly expression. Jim raised his eyebrows in surprise.

"Tom, get with the director. Find out what kind of equipment she needs and get it for her." Tom nodded.

"Director, you have scientists in both the VEEP and SEC DEF bunkers. I'm placing you in charge of both groups. The Ft. Detrick director will report to you. I don't think we have room in the bunkers for you to set up shop, do we gentlemen?" His advisers shook their heads.

"Mr. President—" Lister tried again to interrupt the president, but he continued to talk over her.

"Right, so here's what we'll do. Tom will secure space in public shelters near the VEEP and SEC DEF bunkers so your scientists can get back and forth when they need to. Jim, doesn't the military have special hazmat suits, that can be worn 24/7?"

"Yes, sir," Jim said with a smile.

"Good, let's issue them to the scientists, to wear until a cure is found. Tell her about them, Jim."

"Mr. President, I must object—" Anne began, but the president cut her off again.

"No, you mustn't, Director. Listen to what Jim has to say."

"Mr. President!" Anne screamed unprofessionally.

"What?" Greg asked with forced calm, finger-tapping on the tabletop the only indication that he was annoyed.

"The rashes from radiation burns look a lot like smallpox rashes. You could mistakenly kill people whose only problem is that they were caught outside when the bombs started falling."

"Good point," the president said, thinking about everything

that had been said and done.

Anne smiled, probably thinking she had won a small victory.

"Director," Greg finally said, "the public was warned to find shelter. Granted, they weren't given a lot of time. In the parts of the country where there wasn't a CDC or Ft. Detrick, I can agree with you that we should leave those people alone—give them a chance to recover. However, here, where we know the virus has been released, and that it's contagious, we can't take any chances. If the people are outside, and show signs of having smallpox, we will treat them as if they do. Do I make myself clear?"

Anne slowly nodded her head, defeat evident in her posture and movements.

"Besides," President McCormick said, "I said we won't kill them. We'll detain them for your research."

"Research on living people," she said, shaking her head. "How many will the research kill?"

He felt her sorrow, and shared it. But he had made a decision. The guilt, and lasting ramifications, would be his. He hoped Director Lister would come to understand with time.

"Tom," Greg said to his DNI after Lister had left, "my gut tells me the director has more information than she's shared with us." Tom nodded. "I want you to have her phone records searched. In fact, let's find out the names of the missing people from the CDC and Ft. Detrick facilities and search their phone records, too."

"I'll set that up immediately," Tom said. "Is there anything specific you want us to look for? Director Lister said the assistant directors were the interface between the two facilities. There are bound to be many phone calls between them."

"Let your people know that we're concerned about any indication of a conspiracy to release a mutated smallpox virus on the public."

Vice President Art Klemp, 20 July

"This is President McCormick's doing," Art said. "That's why we're going to his bunker, to make him pay."

Walking had given him time to think. He knew what he wanted to do, but he needed transportation and more people. The four of them would not be able to take over Greg's bunker.

"I thought the terrorists did this." Dayron said, his self-confidence evident after his role at the VEEP bunker.

Art turned on Dayron suddenly, cursing. "It's that idiot McCormick's fault. If he'd let me help," Art snarled, convinced in his own mind that he was right, "none of this would have happened."

He sped up, a subconscious reaction to being questioned. His followers kept pace, which surprised him when he thought about it. No matter how long or how fast he walked, they didn't seem to tire. He was surprised at his stamina, and theirs.

Art could see and smell the bloated and decaying bodies that were lying everywhere. When he noticed Jean wrapping a damp rag around her head, to cover her nose and mouth, he realized it was to keep out some of the smell, so he did it, too.

Georgia and Maryland, 20 July

As sightings of the mutated virus spread outward from Georgia and Maryland, and reports piled up on the SecDef's desk, the military organized what came to be known as *elimination squads*. Their orders were straightforward, but grim: cremate the dead using flamethrowers; and detain anyone living who was not in a shelter, who showed any of the symptoms of smallpox or radiation sickness, and deliver them to Director Lister to help with the search for a cure.

Shortly after the orders were given, a truckload of soldiers in camouflage hazmat suits stopped on a street corner where the

Atlanta explosion, six miles to the south, had severely damaged the homes.

"You three," the sergeant said through his helmet mic, "take that street. We'll take this one."

The first three soldiers—a corporal and two privates—climbed out of the truck into a street overshadowed by thick, dark clouds. The truck headlights provided the only real light, even though it was the middle of the day. Wind and rain pummeled the soldiers, adding to the visibility problem.

The rain-soaked streets reflected the dim light from the truck's headlights, causing warped shadows to dance across the corporal's vision. Turning on his flashlight, he walked carefully down the center of the dark street, flanked by the two privates, a step behind. They walked all the way to the end of the street without seeing anyone, dead or alive.

As they returned, the corporal noticed movement in the ruins of one of the houses.

"Hey, you there," he called. "We're here to help. Come out where we can see you."

A woman and three children, likely under the age of ten, had to be coaxed, but eventually crept slowly from their hiding place. They were difficult to see until they were fully out in the open. The youngest was probably two or three, holding the woman's hand, with a thumb in his mouth. Their clothes were dirty and shredded. The woman had thrown a blanket around her shoulders, probably attempting to cover her torn dress. The rain and wind lashed at the blanket, sending it whipping in all directions.

"The woman has some rashes," one of the privates whispered into his helmet mike. "Looks like the older kid does too."

"It's okay," the corporal called to the woman. "Come on out," he beckoned with his hand, carefully keeping the light from his flashlight out of their faces. "We have water and chocolate bars."

That was all that was needed. The woman ushered her children ahead of her and approached the corporal, who was holding a water bottle in one hand and candy bars in the other.

The oldest boy, about ten and farthest from the woman, yelled, "It's a lie!" Then he turned and ran. One of the privates gave chase and caught him only twenty-five yards or so from the group, where he was handcuffed and returned to the others. Then all four were loaded into the back of the truck and given the water and chocolate, with instructions to "stay put".

The corporal sighed as he closed the truck door. This was just the beginning. If a ten-year-old kid thought it was a trap, so could anybody else. Their assignment was not going to be easy.

He was roused from his musings by the sound of flamethrowers. The privates had lit up the family's hiding place and the houses adjacent to it. Then they walked away, leaving the homes burning.

"With any luck," the corporal said, "the whole neighborhood will burn to the ground." But his words didn't reflect his mood. He acted tough, but his emotions were close to the surface.

☢

The sergeant led the other three soldiers down the adjacent street. In one of the collapsed houses, an inner wall leaned against an outer wall forming a type of lean-to shelter. In the light from his flashlight, the sergeant could see a gaunt dog, obviously starving, frantically chewing on something. He strained his eyes through the rain and the darkness, but couldn't tell what it was.

He tried to shoo the dog away, yelling loudly at it, but it wouldn't leave its treasure. When he approached closer and stomped his foot at it, the dog growled and tried to drag its meal away. One of the soldiers drew the sergeant's attention to an adult body that lay partway out of the rubble, with an arm extended.

"You think the dog did that?" the soldier asked his sergeant.

"Whoa," the sergeant replied, shining his light on the body and seeing the chew marks and shredded skin on the outstretched arm. "Never seen a dog attack an adult like that, starving or not. Must have given up. So, what's he got now?"

He moved his light back to the dog and looked closer, realizing that the dog had hold of a child's arm, still attached to the rest of the body. In anger, the sergeant charged the dog, stomping and yelling. The dog growled louder and tried desperately to drag the child's body away; but a fragment of the small pair of jeans, still wrapped around the child's waist, caught onto something. The dog jerked on the arm, separating it from the body, and dragged it away quickly.

One soldier raised a rifle and shot the dog, hitting it in the back. The dog collapsed and began to yelp in pain. The soldier fired again and the dog lay still.

"Private," the sergeant asked sternly, "why'd you shoot the dog?"

"Sergeant, sir," the private replied crisply, "the arm is probably contaminated. That means the dog probably is too." The private choked on his next words. "I have a wife and child that I haven't seen or heard from since the fourth. I would hope someone would do the same for them."

"I understand private," the sergeant replied sympathetically, thinking about his own family in a shelter somewhere. "Sorry for the rebuke." He turned to the soldiers with flamethrowers. "Burn everything."

7

Are you losing your soul?

The Preserve, 20 July

"Well, Emily," Amos said with a smile, as he checked her arm after removing the cast, "the break is healing nicely. I think we can replace the cast with a semi-rigid bandage. But you should probably continue to wear a sling for a few more days."

"But the wedding is only a week away," Emily complained. "I've got to get out of this thing."

"Maybe Brittany can make a *white* sling," Lillie said, as she gathered the material for the bandage. "It'll match your wedding dress, and that should help you relax a little."

"Should I cover the bandage with lace?" Amos asked, with a smug look on his face.

"That won't be necessary, thank you," Lillie replied, then spoke conspiratorially to Emily. "Men never understand what a woman goes through."

Her comments had the desired effect. Emily smiled at her mother's humor and visibly relaxed.

☢

"Next on the list," Lillie said, setting her tablet aside, "is to change the furniture in Matthew's bedroom." She was pleased when she realized that Michael had anticipated Emily's marriage, before they'd even arrived at the Preserve, and had placed Matt in a room by himself. All she had to do now was move Emily out of the room she shared with Katie Stephens and into Matt's room.

"Michael," she said, "I'm a little surprised you anticipated this marriage."

"Surprised? I've got a sense for these things."

"I'm sure you do," Lillie said with a knowing smile.

"It was pretty obvious, you know, when you invited Matt to join us, that this would be the first change we'd have to make." He chuckled.

"Well, thank you anyway," Lillie said. "Now, will you get some help and meet me in Matthew's room? We need to convert it into a newlywed apartment."

"Sure Mom." He arrived a few minutes later, with Chris, Rachel and Katie, and started dismantling Matt's double bed.

"Good. Let's move the bed to the storage room," she said, then looked in the bathroom. "Spots on the mirror and hair in the sink," she thought aloud. "What else?" she wondered, looking around.

Mike peeked over her shoulder. "Doesn't look too bad to me," he said.

"I could never live with myself if I let Emily move into a room looking like this. I'd have nightmares." She shivered, then frowned at her only son. "Do I need to inspect your room, too, Michael?"

"Hey Mom, I clean my room every week, as ordered." He stood up straight and saluted her.

"Good," she said, "because I'm going to inspect it next week, after we get through this wedding."

"Chris," Lillie pleaded, "will you please go find Rylee and Sydney and bring back cleaning supplies. I want to clean this room from top to bottom before bringing in the queen bed."

"Sure thing." Chris said, laughing at Mike's exchange with his mother. He took Rachel's hand and they walked out together.

"Katie, we can't move Emily's personal belongings until Friday, but why don't we go look in her room and see what else we can do today."

✵

"You know what else is this week, besides the wedding?" Lillie asked Amos.

"It's not my birthday," he said, as they sat on the couch after everyone else had gone to their rooms, "so it can't be too important."

"Pioneer Day is on the twenty-fourth," she said. "Should we celebrate?"

"You had ancestors that crossed the plains with the Mormon pioneers, didn't you?"

"They were in the Martin Handcart company, and three members of the family died at Martin's Cove in the freak, early snowstorm that hit Wyoming that year."

"How would we celebrate? We don't have fireworks."

"And we can't have a barbecue, since we don't have any more meat. I guess we could cook veggie-burgers, and we have corn-on-the-cob in the freezer."

"I guess it's up to you," he said, giving her a squeeze and a kiss.

"I'll talk to Becca and Brittany. Maybe we already have enough to do with this wedding."

President McCormick—Prime bunker, West Virginia, 20 July

"Director, these suits allow for eating and eliminating waste while being worn," Jim told Director Lister, who was frowning at a camouflaged hazmat suit that Ambassador Daniel Porter held up to show her. "They're not fun, but they're functional. Soldiers . . . the scientists can wear them for several days without taking them off.

"We're converting shelters near the VEEP and SEC DEF bunkers into labs for your research teams," Jim continued, "and we're already gathering contaminated people for you to use as guinea pigs. You can sort out which ones have only radiation burns and we'll relocate them to shelters where they can be treated with the rest of the population."

Anne's nose wrinkled in disgust as she studied the hazmat suit, but Jim continued, straight-faced, as if he hadn't noticed.

"And your people can go to the bunkers every week for showers, and to recycle the suits. The military has transportation that wasn't affected by the EMPs, so we'll have no trouble getting you back and forth."

"You have two months to produce a cure," the president said, seriously.

Anne stared with her mouth open.

"What's the status on Art and his gang?" the president asked after Director Lister and Ambassador Porter had turned off their video link.

"The truck stopped in North Carolina, at a makeshift barricade controlled by a local militia," SecDef Seymour said. "Maybe they're all dead."

"Don't let your guard down, Jim. We can't be that lucky. He'll pop up again, somewhere."

"What do you want me to do?"

"Let's change the instructions to the elimination squads. Between here and there, until we know Art is dead, they need to actually *eliminate* anyone they see with smallpox symptoms, instead of just bringing them in for Dr. Lister's medical research."

"Consider it done, Greg," Jim said seriously.

"Greg," Liz McCormick said to her husband as he entered the private quarters that they shared with their two sons and their families, "I heard that the military is killing anyone who has this mutated smallpox virus, even if they only *look* like they have it. Was that your doing or is Jim acting on his own?"

Greg had been trying to shelter Liz and the rest of his family from the details of the battle against the virus, but it appeared others were not as judicious.

"Who told you that?" Greg asked defensively. He had known that she would think his decision to stop the virus at any cost, was harsh. He scrambled to think of the best way to answer her.

"Greg, are you having innocent people killed?"

"No, dear," he said through clenched teeth. "We're gathering them up to help with research to cure the disease."

"That's not what I heard," she said. "I heard that you're having these—what do you call them? Elimination squads—go out and find anyone who's different from us and kill them, then incinerate them with flamethrowers? Are you losing your soul?"

He thought about his latest instructions to Jim. He couldn't lie to Liz. "Liz, a few may have to be eliminated to protect the rest. These are not innocent people. They are a threat to any chance we might have to rebuild our society." She had no idea what he'd been through in an attempt to save the world. In the last three weeks, he had watched their enemies destroy the nation's capital; had made the decision to retaliate with nuclear weapons as he had threatened at the United Nations General Assembly; had failed to stop the release of a deadly mutated virus; and had watched helplessly as his own vice-president had turned traitor and spread the disease, hoping to kill them all, no doubt.

He noticed Liz take a step back from him, as if afraid, and realized his face was flushed and hot, his hands balled into fists, and he could feel his rapid pulse beating in his neck. He looked at her face and saw fear. He knew he had to say something to reassure her, so he tried to calm himself before speaking. He took a deep breath and let it out.

"Liz," he finally said, stepping up to her and taking her hands, which were shaking, in his. "We're at war. We haven't had a war on U.S. soil since the Civil War, and it's ugly. We've had to make some tough decisions, and I'm trying to protect the lives of those still able to be saved, under extreme conditions."

He thought about Amos Blund, hiding in his Preserve, with enough food, water and power to survive for thirty years or more. What if he could get Amos's technology and scale it up to save millions of people? Was there any way Amos would share what he knew? As he thought about how many times Amos had turned down opportunities to join his team, he started to tense up again. Liz must have felt it, because she pulled away from him, and backed up another step.

"I'm not sure I know you very well anymore," she said, her voice shaky.

"Liz," he said, and took another step toward her, reaching for her. She held her hands out to stop him.

"Don't . . . touch me right now," she said hesitantly, and turned her head as though she feared he would strike her.

It shook him to the core. He dropped his hands, turned, and left the room without another word. He went to his office, sat at his desk and rested his face in his hands. Had he changed so much that Liz didn't recognize him? Was he an evil person? Once before he'd wondered if he would go to hell for his role in this war.

Now he wondered if his marriage would be a casualty of the war as well.

A lot of people had died, or were dying, but that wasn't his fault, he told himself. He couldn't stop fighting for those who were still out there trying to survive. He had to do everything he could to bring sanity back to the world.

President McCormick—Prime bunker, private meeting with his SecDef, 22 July

"Is Director Lister getting everything she needs?" Greg asked distractedly.

Jim studied his Commander-in-Chief—his good friend—thinking that Greg looked more beaten down with each passing day. The stress must be eating him up inside. Jim knew he couldn't get Greg to take a vacation—nowhere to go anyway, and the death and destruction outside the bunkers were depressing; but maybe he could convince Greg to see a doctor. They couldn't afford to have him fall apart.

"We've given her and her scientists several shelters to work in," Jim said, but Greg didn't seem to hear. Jim waited quietly while the president returned from whatever dark place he'd gone.

"What is it, Jim?" Greg asked, finally noticing the look on Jim's face.

"What's wrong, Greg?" Jim asked. "You look strung out. I think you should see a doctor."

Greg's face collapsed, his shoulders sagged, and he looked down at the table in front of him. Jim was about to speak again, when Greg looked up.

"Liz kicked me out, Jim," Greg said tiredly. "I've been sleeping on a cot in the office. I told my security detail I needed to be close to communications. I'm not sleeping well."

Jim had heard the rumor that Greg was sleeping in the office, but didn't know why. He didn't want to pry, but he was more concerned now than before this revelation. He was still trying to decide what to say when Greg spoke again.

"Someone told her about the elimination squads. She'd already questioned me about retaliating against Russia, North Korea, and Al-Qaeda, using nuclear weapons, and why I felt the need to drop a nuclear bomb on Atlanta. Now we're killing more *innocent* citizens. Is she right, Jim? Have I lost my soul?"

Jim didn't know how to answer. He had encouraged the president to stand up to Al-Qaeda and their co-conspirators rather than let them win.

"Greg," Jim said quietly, "we knew Al-Qaeda would use the nuclear technology Russia supplied. The only way to stop them was to threaten retaliation. Russia should have known better than to be involved with madmen."

"Is that right, Jim?" Greg pleaded. "Was there no other way? Couldn't we have made our point with conventional weapons?"

Jim scrambled to come up with a satisfactory response.

"I . . . I don't know how, Greg," Jim said. "I'm sure Russia backed the terrorists because they thought we were weak-willed and would back down from a nuclear confrontation. They pinned us into a corner, with no other options than to retaliate, or prove them right. If we hadn't held them accountable for destroying Washington, D.C., it would have proved to the world that we were no longer the global protector of freedom and right."

Greg snorted a laugh. "How did we protect freedom and right by blowing up the world?"

Jim tried to understand Greg's pain, but couldn't think of anything to say that would help.

"What about my decision to drop a nuclear weapon on the

CDC?" Greg finally asked. "Wouldn't a tactical air strike have destroyed the viruses without all the collateral damage?"

"We don't know," Jim said. "We had to take action, and that was our best choice, the only one we knew would work. We used the available time to evacuate everyone from the shelters, out of the blast zone."

"What about people who chose to stay at home instead of going to the shelters?" Greg asked. "Do we know how many people died because we didn't take time to find and relocate them farther away?"

"Greg, you know we didn't have time to go door to door, looking for people who'd already made the decision to take their chances at home. We deployed all of our resources to relocate the people in the shelters before the CDC's backup generators ran out of fuel and allowed the viruses to escape their containment."

Jim wondered if he had been too quick to recommend the most aggressive course of action. He had wanted, his entire military career, to take the battle to the bad guys—terrorists, communists, dictators, anyone who fought against freedom. This war had given him that chance and he had pushed Greg to take on their enemies. Had *he* lost his soul?

"Okay," Greg said, conceding to Jim's logic. "What about the elimination squads?"

Greg didn't look as desperate as he had a few minutes earlier, so maybe Jim's arguments were helping the president calm down,

"Greg, we've already stopped killing people just because they have smallpox, except in the area where we think Art is currently located. We're collecting the contaminated and sending them to Dr. Lister, as you requested. She's testing them for smallpox and letting anyone that tests negative go home or to a shelter. Now, she's got more guinea pigs than she knows what to do with."

Greg nodded his understanding.

"Why doesn't Liz understand?" Greg asked.

Jim just shook his head. Even though he'd been married for fifteen years, before his wife made him choose between her and his military career, he'd never figured out the way she reasoned. He wasn't about to make suggestions to the president about women.

The Preserve, 23 July

"This is how you turn it on and off," Mike told Katie. He'd been waiting days for an opportunity to bring her to the lab and show her the Observer. When he'd tried to explain the discovery of a gate to a parallel world to her earlier, she couldn't comprehend it. Now, standing next to him at the controls, she still didn't seem convinced—of the existence of the gate or of its possibilities—but now was the moment, whether she understood or not.

Mike's dad and Terry were in the hospital, working with Matt on his medical training, and no one else had a reason, or permission, to be in the lab.

"Are you sure it's okay for me to be here, Mike?"

"You're with me, so it's perfectly alright," he said, brushing away her concern with a wave of his hand, and bouncing excitedly on the balls of his feet. He checked once again that the correct control panel was in the Observer. "Besides, I need you to learn how to operate the gate, so you can help me with an experiment."

"Can't this wait until your dad, or mine, are finished up in the hospital?" she asked, fidgeting nervously. "This just doesn't feel right." Mike was shaking his head before she finished speaking.

"They have other things they need to do when they're finished there. Now, I'll talk you through the startup and shutdown steps. They're simple. Then we'll look at some of the other controls."

"Why are we doing this?"

"Don't worry about it." At her questioning look, he added, "We'll talk about it later. I need to get back to the gardens before I'm missed, so we don't have much time."

The Preserve, Aspen Valley, 26 July

"They're pouring foundations for the new medical center in Ogden," Mike said, as Amos and Terry entered the lab. Mike was sitting in front of the Observer, watching the gate. He wanted to make them think he was just curious, so they wouldn't question him about his real motive. He wanted to avoid another awkward conversation about going through the gate.

"Typical engineer," Terry said with a laugh. "He'll miss a beautiful sunset because he's so focused on a construction project."

"You've got him pegged," Amos agreed, chuckling.

Mike was briefly offended at being stereotyped, then realized that he probably had missed a few conversations over the years by being too focused on a project. But, if that kept his dad from questioning him about the gate, he'd tolerate it.

"How do you know they're building a medical center?" Amos asked.

"I, uh, well, I looked at their blueprints," Mike admitted reluctantly. When his dad just stared, he continued. "I moved the gate—carefully, when no one was close—into the construction trailer and looked at the drawings." Amos studied him for a few moments before speaking.

"So, they're what, two months behind the construction in our world?" Amos asked.

"Well, I'm sure the construction in our world has stopped because of all the chaos out there. Otherwise they would be exactly seventy-two days behind," Mike said.

"Is that significant?" Terry asked.

"I don't know," Amos said. "At a minimum, it means the two worlds are running parallel courses, but that they aren't identical."

"We know they aren't identical, because we don't live in Logan in the twin world," Terry said.

Mike thought about seeing his dad's name in the newspaper. His dad, at least, was in that world, just not in the same place. Were the rest of them there? The twin world had evolved differently and he wanted to know why. When he looked up, his dad was studying him.

"What are you thinking, Mike? Do you know something we don't?" Amos asked.

"What? No," he said. "I was just thinking about what you said. I agree—parallel, but not identical, like you said."

Amos studied him for a few more moments.

"What other differences have you noticed?" Amos asked.

"That's it, really," Mike said, "but I'm wondering how far we can take the gate from here. Can we go to Salt Lake City? Denver? Washington, D.C.? Is there a limit?"

"Let's test it," Amos said. "But Mike, we agreed there would always be two of us here whenever we work with the Observer. Will you please respect that?"

Mike nodded, not trusting himself to speak, not wanting to tell a lie.

8

We're starting a new tradition

Vice President Art Klemp, 26 July

"Where is everybody?" Art asked as the four of them walked down the main street of a small town, trying to ignore the smell of death that was everywhere. Art led, with Dayron a step or two behind and the two women farther back. He'd left the freeway to look for anyone willing to join his little army and help him take on the president. He'd already passed through several communities and was surprised at how few people showed themselves. Jean and M.C. had mentioned seeing curtains move or people ducking around corners, but no one was out where he could easily talk to them. Did he look that scary, or was the whole area deserted?

The road they followed bent to the left, back toward the freeway they'd left thirty minutes earlier. As they turned the corner, a group of five people stood on a corner, talking. Art approached them boldly and called out.

"Hello there," he said, "can we talk to you?"

They looked nervous, but stood their ground until he was close.

"What do you want? We don't have anything to share."

"Nah. I'm not looking for a handout. I want to know if you're happy with the way the president is handling things, or if you'd like to help me bring him down."

Art had kept walking and was finally close enough that the people should have been able to see the spots on his face.

"Who are you and what's wrong with you?"

"I'm Vice President Art Klemp and I caught a disease that President Greg McCormick caused. I know where he is and I'm going there now."

"Is it contagious?" one person asked.

"How are you going to do that?" another asked at the same time.

Their spokesman put a hand up to stop the questions, then he spoke. "Right. If you're the vice president why aren't you in a bunker with him?" the spokesman asked.

Art couldn't believe that they didn't recognize him, then realized that his disfigurement had fooled them. As he struggled with how to address the man's question, the man added, "and are you contagious?"

Art's anger at the president boiled over.

"He tried to kill me," Art said and swore, his body shaking. "I wanted to help, but the incompetent fool kicked me out where I would get sick, maybe die. But I'm going to show him. I'm on my way to his bunker now to give him some of his own medicine."

"You're going to break into a bunker protected by the military, possibly the secret service, and threaten the president of the United States? Are you a fool, or just crazy?"

Art started swearing at the man and took a step toward him. The man looked nervous and backed away a step.

His associates started backing into a side street and one of them touched the man's arm. He turned and they all hurried away, leaving Art and his gang standing in the street.

"Idiots!" Art called after them, then turned toward the freeway and started walking.

"May I make an observation?" Jean asked.

"What?" Art barked, then stopped and turned toward his followers.

"Sorry, sir, but maybe their lives have to be threatened, like ours were back at the shelter, before they'll feel the same anger toward the president that we feel."

Art thought about that. Maybe Jean was right. Maybe he would threaten the next group of idiots and see if that made a difference.

The Preserve, Wedding Day, 27 July

Lillie ensured that all the wedding arrangements—food, decorations, the wedding dress—had been completed. The invitations had been distributed, and the girls received sincere compliments on their artwork, to their obvious delight.

The anticipation had been building for two weeks and Em was a nervous wreck.

"Emily," Lillie said at breakfast, when she noticed that Em hadn't eaten anything, "you need to eat, and you look like you didn't sleep well."

"I'm fine, mom," Em replied as she pushed her food around her plate with her fork and yawned.

"We're going to move your things into your new room after breakfast. If you have any special instructions for us, you should be there."

"Okay, mom. Thanks for all your help." She yawned again.

By lunchtime, Em could barely keep her eyes open and ate so little that Lillie worried she had made herself sick. Matt, sitting on the other side of Em, appeared concerned, but said nothing.

"You should lie down after lunch," her mother said.

"I'm not tired," she replied tiredly, her eyes half-closed.

"A little nap will do you good. It will settle your stomach."

"I don't think I could sleep."

When Em put down her fork, Lillie escorted her out of the dining room and down to her new bedroom. Matt started to get up to go with them.

"Sit down," Lillie told Matt. "Go find something to do for an hour." Matt sat, and Lillie noticed Mike hiding a smile.

☢

Em lay on her side on the bed, fully dressed except for her shoes, with a throw over her. It felt strange knowing this was Matt's room but would soon be hers as well—her personal belongings were already in the room—and that she would be sleeping in his arms tonight. The thought made her feel warm inside, but she wondered, not for the first time, if they would be compatible, in bed and in life. It was one of many questions she would soon be able to answer.

She studied the picture of a family vacation to Yellowstone National Park, that sat on her night stand—one of her favorite memories—and was asleep, resting peacefully, when Lillie and Brittany came to help her into her wedding dress.

☢

While Em slept, the family scrambled, following Lillie's directions, to get the community center ready for the wedding, and the dining room set up for the dinner that would be served afterward.

Lillie helped Em into her wedding dress with Brittany on hand for any last-minute adjustments or alterations. So, when Lillie and Brittany hurried into the community center and sat with their families, everyone knew it was time to start.

Rylee sat next to Lillie, regularly looking toward the back of the room. Lillie thought it was her excitement about Emily and the wedding, but noticed that when Nathan made a brief appearance, she sat up straighter. Then when he left, after looking at Chris and Rachel sitting together, her face fell and she slumped in her chair.

"How long do you think it will take Michael to ask Katie to marry him?" Becca whispered, breaking into Lillie's thoughts.

"It shouldn't take long after this," Lillie responded distractedly.

"I hope not. Katie mopes around whenever Michael's not with her."

"Maybe we have Michael too busy. I'll talk to Amos about it."

Em appeared in the doorway holding Terry Stephens's arm, since her father, Amos, would be performing the wedding, and Terry was just like a member of the family. Sydney, who had been playing appropriate music on the synthesizer, only occasionally making Lillie cringe by missing a note, started playing a version of Christina Perri's *A Thousand Years*, made popular as a wedding processional by the Piano Guys, after being used in the Twilight series. She didn't have a copy of Mendelssohn's *Wedding March*.

All eyes turned to the back of the room.

"She looks like an angel," Becca said, smiling. From the *oohs* and *aahs* and other appreciative noises, Lillie knew that the others agreed. Emily's face glowed, and she looked lovingly at Matt as she walked with Terry down the aisle.

Terry handed Em off to Matt and sat next to his wife. Then Em and Matt stared into each other's eyes until Amos cleared his throat to get their attention.

Lillie had worried that with Amos's witty, and sometimes sarcastic, sense of humor, he would say something to ruin the solemnity of the ceremony; but she needn't have worried. Amos had told her that he knew how important this day was to Emily, and proved it by conducting a serious wedding ceremony, howbeit with a mischievous twinkle in his eye. Seeing the loving look that passed between Em and Matt, as they faced each other, made Lillie very happy for them.

When Amos finally said, "You may now kiss the bride," family members would argue for years whether Matt grabbed Em first, or Em, Matt. They both seemed to be in a hurry. Em's arm, still in a bandage, didn't seem to keep her from giving Matt a crushing embrace, and everyone clapped and cheered.

In the rush of trying to leave Logan for the Preserve, weeks earlier, no one had thought to buy wedding rings, so Amos and Lillie had donated theirs. After the ceremony Matt and Em tried to return them.

"They're yours," Amos said.

"Dad, we can't take your wedding rings," Em said adamantly.

"We're starting a new tradition, dear," Lillie said, encouragingly. "They're yours."

Em gave her mom a tearful hug. "Thank you, Mom," she said. "This means so much to us."

Matt, also moist-eyed, shook Amos's hand exuberantly. "Yes, thank you."

"Dinner's on," Becca said a few minutes later, then ushered those still in the community center into the dining room, where she and her current dinner team had turned out a lavish banquet, bigger than the one they'd had the day they'd first arrived at the Preserve. They'd called that one their welcome home dinner. This one would be Emily's wedding supper; and this time no one was surprised at the variety of fresh fruits and vegetables, casseroles and juices. They'd all seen the gardens and pantries, and knew that the only thing in limited supply was meat, because it wasn't renewable.

Following dinner, they returned to the community center to

dance. The chairs were cleared away and Mike started a music CD that he'd prepared in advance.

Amos danced the first dance with Emily. Matt cut in partway through the dance and Amos handed off his daughter to the new man in her life. After that, everyone joined in. Katie, wearing her new dress—the one her mother had given her for her birthday—danced the entire evening with Mike. Lillie could tell that they especially enjoyed the slow dances, where they wrapped their arms around each other and held each other close.

Chris danced with Rachel, when they weren't at the punchbowl or snack table. Sydney and Rylee danced with each other for a couple of dances, then asked Chris and Rachel to follow them. Lillie, amused by the girls' swinging arms and wiggling bodies, asked them later if their dances had names. Giggling, they told her the names of several dance styles, which she didn't understand, and promptly forgot. Then Sydney told her that Chris and Rachel had helped them decorate Matt and Em's bedroom. They'd placed flower petals on the bed, a fruit bowl on the dresser, and—she confessed with an embarrassed laugh—suggestive comments, written with soap, on the bathroom mirror.

☢

Nathan watched Rylee dance with his sister, picturing the exercise outfit she'd worn the last time she was in the weight room. He decided he wouldn't mind getting together with her, after all. Next time she came to the weight room, if she came again, he would talk to her, maybe help her lift some weights, and see where it led from there. Then he left the dance and went to exercise.

☢

Jason had left the celebration right after dinner. Now he sat in a comfortable chair in the library, trying to read a novel he'd picked at random off a shelf; but his mind was elsewhere. Amos had all the angles figured out. The Preserve was self-contained, so no one needed to go outside. He controlled all communications—he'd even blocked the cell phones—so no one could contradict what he said about the *supposed* war. And now, he'd made himself a minister so he could perform marriages.

It rankled him that he didn't have access to news outlets, so he could catch Amos in his lies. When he asked questions, he couldn't even get a straight answer. So, if he didn't show up for a work assignment once in a while, he didn't feel guilty. There were plenty of good books here to read—although this one was stupid, he thought, as he flipped to the last page to see how it ended. There was always the weight room and exercise room; but Nathan used the weight room, and everyone else used the exercise room, and he didn't like being with any of them. Nathan, especially, made it painfully clear that he didn't want anyone else in the room when he was working out, even his dad. *Ha!* Won't those two be surprised when they find out they're not really married.

Jason set the book down on a side table and got up to look for one that was more interesting.

☢

When Rylee and Sydney returned to the dance, Mike was left alone in the bedroom with Katie.

"Would you like to see how big my room is now that Em has moved out?" Katie asked.

Mike didn't need to go to her room to see how big it was. He'd helped build the Preserve, had placed the furniture in all the rooms and had helped move Em out of Katie's room. But he had a pretty good idea what Katie had in mind. He'd been a little slow on the uptake, but now understood, since that day in the garden.

"I'd love to," he said.

Katie took Mike's hand and led him down the tunnel and into her bedroom. Mike turned and closed the door. When he turned back around, Katie threw her arms around his neck, pulled his head down to hers and kissed him. He placed his arms around her back and returned the kiss.

Between kisses, Katie whispered, "See how big my room is?"

"I think it could be two feet square and be big enough," Mike replied.

"Well, as long as this is all I do when I'm here."

"As long as it's with me, we're fine," Mike said, in a husky voice.

"Then you better come often so I don't get bored standing here by myself," she replied mischievously.

She began humming, swaying back and forth to her own music. He pulled her close and followed her rhythm.

She backed away from him, concern in her eyes. He didn't know what he'd done wrong, but he'd offended her somehow, and didn't know what to do. He just stared at her, trying to understand.

Suddenly, she smiled and took his hand.

"We better get back to the dance," she said, leading him, reluctantly, out of her room.

☢

Em wore out first, dancing awkwardly because of her bandaged arm; so she and Matt escaped to their room, amid cheers, catcalls, and laughter.

The others followed gradually, until Lillie and Amos were

alone, sitting together quietly on a couch. Lillie remembered how amused, then a little concerned, she'd been earlier in the day, when Sydney and Rylee had discussed how the members of the four families should think of themselves as one big family now—the Aspen family—and had gone through the family, renaming each of them. It had gone well until Rylee had said "Nathan Aspen" and Sydney had objected. She didn't want her brother to be part of the family.

☢

At the same time, Amos was thinking about how he and Terry, good friends and partners, had been preparing for a crisis for years. There had always been natural disasters in the world, but the worst Logan had seen was heavier than normal snowfall. Wars had always been in far off places, mostly caused by greed, hatred and religious intolerance. Amos had wanted to be ready when the crisis became personal and was not surprised when Al-Qaeda and North Korea had started this one—they'd been threatening for years.

Amos's retreat—the Preserve—had been ready, complete with all the resources the families would need to survive below ground for at least thirty years, including a patented power supply system of their own design. The graphite composite technology they'd used in their patented medical prosthesis designs, along with Mike's engineering skills, had made construction of the Preserve possible. What they hadn't envisioned was the neighbors figuring out what they were doing and insisting that they be included. Now, after less than a month, they'd been cut off from the outside world by nuclear war.

"Why so serious, Amos?" Lillie asked, interrupting his thoughts.

"Just thinking about everything we've been through in the last few weeks."

"We have a good life here. You saw how happy Emily and Matthew were today."

"Everybody's happy, is that what you're trying to say?"

"Well, most of us are happy."

"I wonder what lies ahead for us and what we'll find when we're able to go outside again."

"Do you think there are other survivors out there in hidden retreats, the way we are? Do you have a way to find out?"

"I do, but I'm not sure we want to let anyone know we're here. I'll have to think about it."

"Well, in the meantime, we have everything we need. We have each other."

"Well said," Amos replied, giving Lillie a squeeze.

9

You wanna work out with me?

The Preserve, 28-29 July

"Katie?" Becca asked as they carried their dishes to the kitchen after breakfast.

"Yes Mom?"

"What happened between you and Michael last night after the wedding?"

"Nothing Mom. Why?"

"When you two came back to the dance, Michael looked like he'd eaten a lemon."

Katie considered lying to her mom, or just downplaying the previous night's events. realized that if Mike's moods were that transparent to her mom, maybe her mom could tell her what to do about him.

"Mom, I'm in love with him, and I think he loves me," she said with a sigh.

Becca nodded knowingly.

"Ever since Amos explained why he could perform marriages; I've been trying to figure out how to get Mike to propose to me. He's *so* busy every day, and the only time I can see him is at night, after his chores are complete. He has to check the gardens each night and has been helping his dad and Terry with their research on the Observer." She paused, trying to decide how to go on.

Her mom made an encouraging motion and Katie rushed on.

"After the wedding last night, I was making myself sick with frustration. I usually wait for him in the community center. Sometimes I read—or pretend to—until he shows up. I ask how his day has gone, but he usually just brushes it off with comments like, 'Oh, you know,' or, 'Just more of the same.' When he talks about the gardens, or says something interesting about his research, I ask questions—I really want to be part of his life—but he clams up or changes the subject. It's like, what he's doing is some kind of secret. He's always so tired by the time we meet, that it must be too much effort for him to carry on a conversation." Katie had been looking down as she spoke. When she looked up, she could see determination in her mom's expression.

"What should I do?" Katie asked.

"Lillie and I have discussed Michael's workload. We want you to have more time together, and Lillie was going to ask Amos to do something about it. I'll check with Lillie to see what she's done. So, what changed last night?"

Katie sighed. "During the wedding," she said, "I decided to try to move our relationship along, so I invited Mike to my room on the pretense of showing him how big it appears, now that Emily has moved out."

"Mike already knows how big the rooms are."

"I know. It was just an excuse."

Becca's face showed concern, even though Katie was sure her mom was trying to keep a neutral expression.

"I know Mike helped design the Preserve. He also helped us move Em's furniture into Matt's room, but he followed me when I took his hand." Katie paused before continuing, trying to decide how much to say. "I hadn't planned for anything to happen. I just wanted to see where the relationship would go. When Mike became too personal—"

Becca's eyebrows shot up, so Katie went on quickly.

"It was awkward Mom. I backed away and it broke the mood. That's when we went back to the wedding."

Becca looked relieved. "I'll talk to Lillie this morning."

Rylee went to the weight room, just as she had each day, at a time when she knew Nathan would be there alone. She knew that everyone avoided him because, as quiet as he was, he was also intimidating. She knew that when he wasn't in the weight room, he was usually in his bedroom, sleeping. He slept a lot during the day, missing work assignments, ignoring people when they tried to correct or challenge him, and walking away when they wouldn't leave him in peace. Mike had even moved some of the exercise equipment out of the weight room and into the exercise room, so others could use them without having to deal with him. It was just easier for everyone.

Now, Rylee felt certain that Nathan had noticed her at the dance the previous evening. Maybe he had begun to see her as a kindred spirit, since they'd both lost close family members recently.

As she entered the room, dressed in her exercise outfit, Nathan stopped and looked at her. A shiver ran up her spine. She walked over and sat on a bench at the side of the room where she always sat, kept her eyes on him, and waited.

"Hi," he said, meeting her gaze. "You wanna work out with me?"

Suddenly, she was tongue-tied and her heart beat faster. Was he serious or teasing her? She nodded.

He set down the weights he was holding. "Come and try this," he said.

She hesitated, still unsure of the situation.

"Come on," he said, and waved her over.

She rose slowly and walked unsteadily over to him, her eyes not leaving his. Her heart pounded in her chest; her palms were sweaty. Up close, she noticed that his eyes were dark and mysterious. She felt so inferior to him, yet here he was talking to her as if she were important.

"Let's start you with something light," he said, looking her up and down once. He picked up a couple of weights—she had no idea how heavy they were—and set them on the floormat in front of her.

"These are free weights. Bend at the knees, not the waist, like this," he said, lifting his own, heavier weights to show her how.

As she bent to pick up her weights, he placed one hand on the small of her back and the other on her shoulder, making her body tingle where he touched her. He used his hands to control her posture, as she lifted the weights and flexed her arms the way he'd shown her, and left them there. After a few repetitions, he removed his hands.

"Very good," he said.

She grinned stupidly at his praise. She could hear her blood pounding in her ears.

"Let's try something else," he said and moved over to one of the exercise machines. She followed. He sat down and leaned back on the reclining seat back, brought his feet up and rested them on a vertical plate, then pushed on the plate with his feet, straightening his legs. The motion pushed the plate away from him and lifted some weights at the side of the machine. When he bent his knees, the plate and weights returned to their original positions. He repeated the movement a couple of times.

"This is called a leg press," he said as he stood up, adjusted the seat for her shorter legs, and reduced the weight. "Your turn."

She was nervous and responded slowly.

Nathan put his hands on her waist and guided her over to the bench, pushing her gently onto the seat.

"Place your feet high on this pad, about here." He said as he placed a hand on the vertical plate. When she didn't move, he smiled and moved his hands to her feet. He gripped her bare calves and positioned her feet on the pad. She stared at his face, unable to move a muscle. The butterflies in her stomach went crazy.

"Put your hands on these handles," he said, taking her hands out of her lap and placing them on the hand grips. She stared at one hand, trying to understand her reaction to him. He was so close that she could smell his sweat. It was surprisingly intoxicating, messing up her mind.

"Now push with your legs," he said.

She could barely breath, but she managed to push on the plate.

"Very good," he said. "Now let's increase the weight." He adjusted the machine twice, until she was straining to push. "Do ten repetitions, then we'll try something else," he said. She was breathing heavily, a light perspiration on her forehead before she'd finished.

"Very good," he said, then showed her a couple more exercises.

She wondered at her physical reaction each time he touched her. The feel of his hands on her skin, and his musky smell whenever he came close, played havoc with her senses.

"That's all we'll do for today," he finally said. "I'll show you more another time."

Rylee turned her head slightly to look up at Nathan's face, inches away from her and smiling! She was so surprised she froze, forgetting to breathe.

"Are you okay?" He asked, his face turning serious.

Did he care how she felt? First a smile, then a show of concern. Had everyone misjudged him completely?

"I . . . I'm fine," she croaked when she finally found her voice, "thanks," she added hesitantly after a moment.

"You can practice these exercises on your own or come back and we'll continue," he said as he took her hand and helped her up from the bench.

Nathan watched Rylee walk away and smiled mischievously, convinced she would be back the next day. He had wondered if it would be a good idea to let her work out with him, but after seeing her responses, he decided it had been a good call. Maybe they could have a little fun together. He wondered if his face had betrayed his thoughts.

Katie had waited all day for something to change; but here she was again, waiting for Mike to finish in the garden before he could go to bed. She knew how serious he took his work; he was just like his father. She knew their parents had good intentions about trying to help them arrange more time together, but nothing had changed so far. She would have to continue stealing his time at night.

She considered going to her room to get ready for bed, but didn't want to miss him; so she waited, as usual, in the community center. Mike entered a few minutes later and dragged himself—she thought he looked like he could fall asleep standing—across the room. She stood and went to him, glad that she hadn't left.

"Hi, handsome," she said after a quick kiss. "How was your day?"

"Hi, Katie. More of the same," he said tiredly.

She led him by the hand to a couch, sat him down, and cuddled next to him. Within moments, he'd fallen asleep.

Chris had been frustrated when he'd discovered that his mobile phone wouldn't work in the Preserve. He'd been studying political science when they'd left Logan and he'd been active on social media with friends and associates around the world. He had even made contact with several people in the State Department and had high hopes of landing a job through them after graduation. Now he'd lost contact with the world, overnight, so to speak.

He knew that the adults had communications with the outside, since his parents had mentioned watching videos of the explosion in Washington, D.C., and the subsequent panic and violence. Amos had told them he would keep them informed, and Chris really wanted to know what was going on; but he'd been treated like one of the children, left out of all the important discussions.

"Your dad knows President McCormick?" Chris asked as he and Rachel sat on the couch in her bedroom cluster common room. "And he's talked to him since we arrived?" Chris was shocked by Rachel's revelation. "Why hasn't he said anything about that to the rest of us? Is Jason right? Is your dad holding back information or outright lying to us? Is it because we're just children and can't handle the truth?" He told himself that he wasn't upset, but Rachel's response told him that she thought he was.

"Don't be angry, Chris," Rachel said, taking his hands in hers, "I just found out myself. Mike told me last night that Dad and President McCormick have been friends since they were kids, and that the president has called Dad several times."

"I'm sorry, baby. I'm not mad at you. This is just such a surprise. Do you think Mike knows what's going on outside now? Do you think if I ask him, he'll tell me?"

"I don't know, but maybe you should try."

"Yeah, maybe I will," Chris said, and went to his room. As he'd expected, Mike wasn't there. He knew that Mike and Katie sometimes stayed up late in the community center, but he was sure Mike wouldn't be long. He went to bed, but decided to sit up and read until Mike arrived, so he could ask him tonight.

☢

Katie dozed, off and on. She thought that Mike's light snoring was what kept waking her, but trying to sleep sitting on this couch wasn't comfortable. She knew it was late, but she didn't have the heart to wake him. She ran her fingers through his hair affectionately, smiling at this wonderful, hard-working man, then leaned back and closed her eyes again.

☢

Chris woke with the desk lamp shining in his eyes.

Mike should have turned that off when he went to bed, he thought drowsily.

"Mike," he said softly. No answer. "Mike, you there?" he asked, a little louder. When he still didn't get a response, he raised up on one elbow and looked over at Mike's bed. Mike wasn't there, and the bathroom door was open with the light out. Was it possible that Mike hadn't come to bed?

Chris looked at the clock. It was after two in the morning. His first reaction was to find Mike and get him back to the room before their parents found out.

Katie woke when she heard a whispered, "Mike?" She opened her eyes and saw Chris standing a few feet away, barefoot, in pajamas, and with his hair sticking out in all directions.

"Hi Chris," she said groggily, "Are you looking for Mike?"

"Sorry to trouble you, Katie. When I noticed that Mike hadn't come to bed, I thought I should find him."

"Sorry Chris," she said, trying not to laugh at Chris's appearance. "He was so tired, he fell asleep as soon as he got here, and I didn't have the heart to wake him. I'll wake him now. Sorry if you were concerned about him."

"It's alright Katie. I don't know what I was concerned about. Now that I think about it, where could he go?" Chris chuckled self-consciously. "I'll go now. Sorry I woke you."

On his way back to his room, Chris remembered why he'd wanted to find Mike, to ask about Amos's relationship with the president. He decided it could wait until morning.

The Preserve, 29 July

"Ready for something else," Nathan asked after they'd repeated the exercises from the previous day.

Rylee nodded, her face flushed from exertion, then followed him over to another machine. He grabbed an overhead bar, sat and locked his knees under another bar in front of him, adjusted his hands on the overhead bar and pulled down a couple of times with his arms.

"This is a lat pull," he said, standing up and releasing the bar. He reached down and adjusted the weight for her. "Your turn."

She sat on the bench and reached for the overhead bar. It was just out of her reach, so he pulled it down for her to take with her hands. He adjusted the bar over her knees, resting his hand on her leg just below the hem of her gym shorts. She stared at her leg where his hand rested, so he left it there a little longer than necessary, smiling inwardly. Then he reached up and moved her hands to a more comfortable position on the overhead bar.

"Now pull down on the bar," he said.

☢

Struggling to look away from him, she took a deep, shuddering breath, her leg tingling where his hand had rested on it, and pulled down. He had her stand and made an adjustment to the weight, resting his hand on her waist in the process. Her heart skipped a beat. Her stomach fluttered. He helped her pull the bar down again so she could sit and lock her knees, then she remembered to breathe.

"Now give me ten reps," he said.

☢

"How's the construction coming," Amos asked as he and Terry entered the lab to find Mike looking through the gate.

"Fine, Dad," Mike said, self-consciously, as his dad walked over to look at what he was doing.

"That's not the Smith's store in Logan," Amos said, seeing that Mike was looking at a newspaper; but the counter it rested on wasn't the one they'd seen before.

"I found another newspaper in Ogden," Mike said.

"Why do you need another paper?"

"I'm looking for information about the twin world. I can only see the top half of the front page. I thought that I could learn more if I found another paper that featured different stories."

"That makes sense. Are there different stories?"

"Some are different, some are the same."

"Are you looking for something specific, that you're not seeing in the Logan paper?"

Mike felt trapped. He couldn't think of any way to avoid telling them that he was looking for more information about his dad being a presidential advisor in the twin world. Then Terry rescued him.

"You know, Amos, I've been thinking about Mike's coordinate mapping in the twin world. Eventually, we want to see what's happened in *our* world as a result of the war. If we can copy the mapping information that he worked out for the original control panel, panel A, onto the panel for our world, panel B, we can jump from place to place in our world, knowing in advance where we're going, and minimize our exposure to radiation and other hazards."

"I'd like to see what's going on in Logan," Amos said. "I've thought a lot about all the people we knew there. How much notice did they have before the fire reached Cache Valley? How many were able to find shelter? Knowing now how bad it got, I wish we could have found a way to help more of the neighbors."

"I know what you mean, Amos," Terry replied seriously. "I keep thinking about Patrick and Kathy McKensie. Patrick was quite a character," he chuckled, "and Kitty was so sweet and grandmotherly. They didn't want to live underground, but I hope they found someplace to go to be safe."

All three men were quiet for a few moments, lost in their thoughts. Mike felt like they were sharing a moment of silence for the dead. Then Amos brought them back to the subject of the control panels.

"We know that Panel B is a gate like Panel A," Amos said, "but are there other differences? We might need to do some testing with Panel B to make sure it would function the same way as Panel A, but it could be months or years before the radiation contamination in the valley allows for us to make jumps outside the Preserve. Mike, what do you think?"

Mike was so relieved at the distraction that he almost missed what his dad had said.

"Huh? Um, a way to test Panel B? Uh, maybe we could test it here in the lab, without leaving the room." Mike knew he wasn't getting enough rest and it slowed down his thinking

"You mean, jump from one part of the room to another?" his dad asked.

"Great idea, Mike," Terry said. "Let's start by downloading the coordinates, then see if we can copy them to Panel B. If it works in the lab, we can expand to different parts of the Preserve. Then we can test it out in the valley, wearing hazmat suits until we know it's safe to go out without them."

"Okay," Amos said. "Let's think about it and we can continue this discussion later. Mike, I came in here to tell you we really want you to be part of our research, but I made a promise to your mother. She asked me to reduce our dependence on you so you can spend more time with Katie. Don't tell your mother I told you, but she wants Katie to help you in the gardens whenever she can."

"But Katie's responsible for exercise and education. How does it solve the problem if you take away some of my responsibilities and give Katie more?"

"Well, your mother's going to change the schedule, so Rachel takes over schooling for Rylee and Sydney, and Katie has more assignments in the gardens with you.

Mike smiled and his eyes lit up as he thought about it; then, realizing that this might be his dad's way of getting him away from the gate, he frowned again. "What about the research. I won't know what's going on."

"You can spend some time with us each day, catching up and redirecting our experiments if we need it." Amos got that silly grin on his face that said he was making a joke.

"Very funny," Mike said, but he couldn't help but smile when his dad draped an arm over his shoulders amiably.

"Now, do me a favor and act surprised when your mother tells you about it," Amos said. "Alright?"

"How can I say no? You're the boss," Mike replied.

10

We'll take whatever you have

Vice President Art Klemp, 30 July

"What do you mean, 'we're out of food'?" Art asked Dayron. They sat on wet grass in a city park, in the rain. "What happened to the food we took from that couple yesterday?"

"Sorry sir, but that was two days ago and we've eaten it all," Dayron said.

Art swore. He was doing that a lot lately. Nothing seemed to be going his way. Every truck or car he checked was dead, no one had agreed to join his army, and he had to keep stealing food from the poor creeps they ran into that wouldn't join his army. M.C. had suggested they search homes for a larger food supply and carry more on their backs, but Art hadn't wanted to take the time, although it seemed like it was taking a lot of time to find people to steal food from. Maybe she was right.

He heard voices and followed the sound to a group of adults who seemed to be arguing in front of an apartment building. A few of them wore backpacks, as though they were travelling as well.

"Hello," Art said, drawing their attention.

"What do you want?" one man said angrily.

"Whoa," Art said, trying to sound friendly. "We're just wondering where to get some food and water around here."

"There ain't none. Now go away."

"You must have some or you'd be dead by now." Still friendly, but challenging.

"Not for you. Now get lost."

Art thought about what Jean had said earlier, about people needing to be threatened before they would cooperate.

"I think we'll take whatever you have in the backpacks," he said as he drew his gun and pointed it at the man.

"You wouldn't," the man said cautiously.

"I would. I tried to ask nicely, but you chose to be a moron. Now, hand over your backpacks and we'll be on our way."

"Look, I'm sorry. We really only have a little. We're trying to figure out where to get more ourselves." Some of the others in the group had started to look around, likely looking for an escape route without being the first to draw attention to themselves.

"I'll give you a choice. You can give us your food, or you can join my little army."

"Your army?" he asked, his eyes darting between Art and his three followers.

"Yes. President McCormick—" he said sarcastically "—did this to us. Now we're going to his bunker to pay him back. Which do you want to do?"

The man looked around at the others in his group, but got no signal from them.

"I don't see how you can take on the president and win," the man said, "and we really don't have any food to share."

Art shot him in the chest from fifteen feet away. Everyone jerked in surprise, then watched in shock as he fell—dead. One anxious woman cried, her hand over her mouth, shifting her weight from one foot to the other, as though she wanted to go to the downed man, but was afraid.

"Now, who else has an opinion?" Art asked with a fake smile.

Those with backpacks laid them on the ground and backed

away, never taking their eyes off Art's gun.

"Check 'em," Art said to his followers, motioning toward the packs. Dayron, M.C. and Jean rifled through the packs, finding a little food and water, just as the dead man had said.

"That's it?" Art asked and swore when Dayron nodded. "Okay, put it in one of the packs and you carry it. Let's go." Dayron dumped the contents of one of the packs, with an apologetic look to the owner, stuffed the food and water into it, and put it on his back.

As Art turned away, the anxious woman rushed to the downed man, wailing.

"That didn't work out quite the way you thought it would, did it?" Art asked Jean, who wisely kept her opinion, if she had one, to herself.

The Preserve, 30 July

Jason tried the doorknob, finding it locked. It was the third one he'd tried and all he'd discovered was that Amos kept all the doors locked except those in the family areas. He turned back toward the community center just as Mike turned a corner and stopped abruptly.

"Oh. Excuse me," Mike said. "Can I help you?"

"What's behind this door," Jason demanded, trying the doorknob again. He'd already decided that if anyone caught him snooping, he'd try to keep them off balance by taking the offensive.

"It's a storage room," Mike said.

"Why is it locked?"

"Because . . . there's no reason for you to go in there," Mike said apologetically.

"What's your dad trying to hide?"

"I'm sorry Jason, but Dad keeps all the doors locked unless

there's—"

"I want to know what Amos is hiding."

"He's not hiding anything in there . . . really. What are you trying to find? Maybe I can help."

"You're a bad liar!" Jason fumed. "If you worked for me, I'd fire you on the spot." Jason brushed past Mike, pushing him out of the way, and continued on toward the community center, leaving Mike standing in the corridor with his mouth open.

☢

"Do you want to go to the lab and see what we're doing with the gate?" Amos asked Lillie as he studied the back of her hand. They sat on the couch in the community center after everyone else had gone to their bedrooms.

"Don't look at my hand," she said, trying to pull it away, "it looks old."

"You know I love everything about you."

"I know you do. *I'm everything I am because you love me,*" she said, quoting a line from one of Amos' favorite love songs, and making him smile, since it was usually him quoting them to her, "but I'm embarrassed about how my hands have aged."

He brought her hand to his lips and kissed it.

"You call it a gate now?" she asked.

"The machine is the Observer. As you know, we first thought we were looking at an image, but it turned out to be an opening." She nodded: she'd heard this before. "We called it a portal. Now we call it the Gemini Gate—the door between twin worlds."

"The door between twin worlds?" Lillie asked, looking startled, then skeptical.

"What we're seeing on the other side of the gate is so similar to our world that we believe it's some kind of parallel world."

"Amos! Is that even possible? It sounds like fiction. Are you teasing me?"

"Honest, honey, it was hard for us to believe at first, too—I can't explain it—but that's what we believe."

Lillie stared at him, trying to understand what he was telling her. He had never intentionally lied to her—that she knew of—although he'd withheld information before, until he was ready to share it. But this was different: he was sharing information that was unbelievable, and yet, she could tell he totally believed what he was saying.

"Why Gemini gate?" she asked.

"That was inspired by Mike. He called it a twin world because Katie had been asking him about his astrological sign, Gemini—the twins. It just stuck."

"Okay," she said tentatively. "When do you want to show me this twin world?" Lillie had her hands full as the house manager for the fifteen people in the Preserve, and she'd taken personal responsibility to mother Rylee since her parents had died in the automobile accident. She also had her eye on Emily and Matthew's marriage, Michael and Katie's courtship, Chris and Rachel's budding relationship, Nathan's obsession with Chris and Rachel, and Rylee's infatuation with Nathan. She drew the line at watching Jason—that was Amos's job.

"We could put it off until tomorrow if you're too busy," Amos offered.

"Actually, right now might be the best time. My days are always so hectic."

"Do you want to see if Becca would like to join us?"

"I'll go see if she and Terry are still awake."

When the four of them arrived at the lab, Amos was surprised to find Mike and Katie sitting at the table, next to the Observer, looking through the gate, which Mike had set at about one-foot diameter. Startled, Mike reached over to the controls, as if to change the setting or shut it down.

"Stop right there!" Amos said and Mike backed away from the controls. "What's going on? You two should be in your rooms."

Looking embarrassed and uncomfortable, Katie opened her mouth to explain, but Mike stopped her with a hand on her arm.

"It's okay Katie," he said, "Dad's been suspicious for some time. I better explain." He turned to his dad.

"Dad, you wanted to know why I've been spending so much time looking at newspapers." Amos nodded, so Mike continued. "While I was looking at the Logan paper a few days ago, I saw your name mentioned as an advisor to President McCormick."

Amos opened his mouth to speak, but couldn't formulate a question or comment. Mike had caught him totally off guard. His mind flew a hundred miles an hour, in several directions at once.

"What does he mean, Amos?" Lillie asked. "You've turned down all of Greg's requests to work for the government, haven't you?"

"Just a minute, honey," Amos said, deferring her question while he tried to understand. He turned to look at the gate. "What are you seeing now?" he asked anxiously.

"We're looking at the Logan newspaper, but there's nothing about you in it."

"Amos?" Lillie repeated.

"Just a sec, honey." He thought about what Mike had just said, took a deep breath, glanced at Terry's serious expression, and turned to Lillie and Becca.

"Okay," he started, "what I wanted to show you was Aspen Valley. Mike, will you jump to the valley so they can see?" They all took a couple of steps and turned so they could see the gate. It was dark, because of the late hour, so Mike enlarged the gate to about six feet in diameter, to allow the light from the lab to illuminate the trees and brush, which were obviously green and healthy.

"There's no fire damage!" Becca exclaimed.

"This is what you were trying to tell me, isn't it?" Lillie said. "This looks like our valley, but it's not."

Amos nodded.

"Becca, what I was trying to explain to Lillie earlier, and the reason we invited you here, was to show you that we've discovered a parallel world," Amos said. Becca looked confused, and Lillie, pensive. "We call this the Gemini Gate—the door between twin worlds. Mike, move out twenty feet and show them the cliff."

It was difficult to see the cliff, but the heavily wooded valley was obvious.

"This is directly above the Preserve," Amos said.

"There are no trees above the Preserve," Lillie said.

"Correct. In this world, we never built the Preserve. Mike, jump to Ogden, to the construction site."

"Is this what made you so frustrated before we left Logan for the Preserve?" Lillie asked. "The hillside you said should show a medical building under construction, but there wasn't one."

"Correct again. You can see that it's now under construction. Mike has confirmed that it is a medical building by looking at the blueprints, but it was started two and a half months later than the one in our world."

"Terry," Becca said, "what's going on?"

Terry looked at Amos, who nodded for him to go ahead.

"You know that we built the Observer for medical research," Terry said. "We wanted a way to diagnose internal medical conditions, non-intrusively. We've partially accomplished that. Watch."

Mike jumped back to the valley and moved the gate toward a large aspen tree, stopping when the gate had dissected it, vertically. What they were looking at appeared to be cut dimension lumber with bark on the edges. They could see the growth rings as near-vertical lines in the tree.

"And there's no damage to the tree?" Lillie asked. Mike backed the gate out of the tree, and the tree looked fine.

"We've done the same thing with animals," Terry continued, "but they can either sense the gate—or actually feel it—and move away, so we don't get a chance to study them, to know if there's permanent damage.

"What do you mean, 'feel it?'" Becca asked.

"Mike and I have both reached an arm through the gate," Amos said. "It tingles, but we can't see any damage." At Lillie's distressed look, he explained. "I've run some medical tests and don't see anything wrong."

"Then, we can go through the gate and walk around in the valley?" Lillie asked.

Amos looked at Mike when he answered, to reinforce his previous instructions.

"We don't know if it's safe for *us,* or what impact we would have on our twin world, so *we've agreed* that *no one* goes through the gate until we know more—more about the twin world and more about the gate." Both women turned back to the gate, looking longingly at the valley.

"It even smells wonderful," Becca said to Lillie

"This all sounds so impossible," Lillie finally said, turning and noticing Mike and Katie again. "So, Mike, what are you doing *here* when you should be in bed?"

"It's my fault, Lillie," Katie said. "Mike was telling me about his research and I asked him to show me."

"I'm sure you had to twist his arm, didn't you?" Lillie asked.

Mike and Katie looked at each other, a message passing between them.

"And this was the only time of day you both had available?" Amos asked.

"Actually, Dad," Mike said, yawning "that's pretty close to the truth. With our other responsibilities, it's pretty hard to find time for this."

"I told you we have them too busy," Becca whispered loudly to Lillie, making Terry laugh.

"This sounds like they're trying to find a way to get out of their chores," Terry said.

"Okay," Amos said, "that's enough for tonight. Mike, I want to know more about this report you saw in the newspaper, but that can wait until tomorrow. You two need to go now."

"Wait," Lillie said. "Michael. What you said earlier—you think your Dad is an advisor to the president in this parallel world?"

Mike looked at his dad, likely asking for permission to explain, so Amos nodded. He wanted to know more, as well.

"Mom, if this really is a parallel world—and I think it is—then we should all be there." He stopped talking and watched his mom, probably expecting a response or another question.

"You're thinking that somewhere in his life," Lillie said, "your Dad had to make a choice between becoming a doctor or accepting Greg's requests to work for the government, and that he chose differently in this twin world. Is that it?"

"I don't think it's that simple—I mean, it could involve lots of choices—but essentially, that's what I'm wondering. Are you and

Dad married in the twin world? Are we a family there, like we are here? If not, what decisions led to the differences? *I want to know where we are!*"

Amos finally understood Mike's motivation. Either he'd need to watch Mike more closely, or expend more effort making sure it was safe for him to go through the gate.

"Mike, what are these?" Terry asked as he held up a stack of five- by seven-inch images from the table. The others joined them.

"After I saw Dad's name in the paper, I remembered that he wanted me to find a way to record what we were seeing through the gate. I didn't want to miss the next opportunity, so I've been practicing, taking pictures with my phone and printing them."

"So, what are these?" Amos asked.

"Nothing important. I'm just practicing. I haven't figured out how to get the Observer to record anything."

"Terry, let's talk about this tomorrow, see what we need to do to get the Observer to take pictures."

"Right," Terry said.

"Now, off you go," Lillie said as she ushered Mike and Katie out of the lab.

11

Where's the surface

The Outcasts—Georgia to Tennessee, 31 July

"About time," Suzanne griped. She closed the romance novel she'd been reading and dropped it on the end table. "If I have to read another romance, I'm going to puke."

"Let's go" Candy said, jumping up from the couch and heading for the bedroom.

"You're that anxious?" Lisa laughed. "Beth said 'today', not 'this second'."

"I'm going stir crazy," Candy replied. "If we're going to the Rocky Mountains, let's get going."

"Actually," Beth said, entering the room, "we should be ready in about an hour. I just need to check Ben's arm. The break seems to be healing well. Bryce and Melissa, will you check with everyone to see that we have enough food and water to last a few days?"

Within the hour, the Outcasts were on the move. They crossed Alabama north of Birmingham and south of the Tennessee River, leaving the road at times and travelling through fields to avoid car pileups and sick, wandering people. Their scabs had dried and fallen off. Now they were covered with pigmented spots. Even if no one recognized the signs of smallpox, Beth was worried that strangers would be cruel because of the difference in their appearance.

When they reached Interstate 22, they followed it all the way to Memphis, walking for hours at a time. They stopped only when

Beth noticed that Ben—who was obviously in pain, but didn't complain—looked like he needed a rest. No one else seemed to tire of the walking.

The air, which should have been hot and humid this time of year across the South, was cool; and it was thick with smoke from explosions and fires. Soot fell on them constantly.

As they walked, Beth and Melissa discussed changes they'd observed in themselves and their travelling companions, which they attributed to the virus: intensified emotions, increased strength and stamina, and less sensitivity to temperature changes. Beth knew she should be worried about the changes, but instead, against all instincts, she felt invigorated. Her prior fear of these unknown conditions had been replaced with surprise, then anticipation. Her thoughts were interrupted when Melissa spoke from beside her.

"How long do you think it should take us to get to the Rocky Mountains?" Melissa asked.

"If we can keep moving at our current pace, and assuming we don't run into more problems, we could be there in a few weeks."

Beth and Melissa were talking about what they might find in Memphis, when Candy cried out. They looked up to see her stopped in the middle of the roadway, where the road turned slightly to the north. Beth ran forward, the others on her heals. Still twenty miles from Memphis, trees were blown down, there was evidence of forest fires, and the road was broken up. Beth stood and stared in shock, as did the others.

After a short, animated discussion, the only explanation they could come up with for the damage was an explosion, possibly nuclear. Beth knew she should be worried about fallout, but she wasn't. She had faced violence, death and disease in the last few days, and survived. She felt no fear as they continued to move into the wreckage.

As the road continued to turn, they got their first glimpse of Memphis; or rather, where Memphis should have been, but wasn't. The terrain was so flat that, with the trees blown over, they should have been able to see downtown buildings; but all they could see was flat, level ground, broken up by mounds of debris and a monster crater where Memphis used to be. The bridges, on the two interstates that crossed the Mississippi River, should have been visible if they were still standing.

"It's gone," Candy said, her anguish turning to anger. "I was here just a few weeks ago. I can't believe it's totally gone."

"I don't suppose there's any hope of finding an intact bridge to cross the river, is there?" Beth asked.

Candy shook her head. "I can tell from here. Both bridges are gone. What do we do?" she asked, wringing her hands, then tucking them under her armpits and hugging herself.

"Beth," Melissa said, wrapping her arm around Candy's shoulders, and winking at Beth, "why don't we cross over to the river below Memphis? Maybe there's a boat we can use to cross the river."

"Great idea," Beth readily agreed, thinking that if this damage were caused by a nuclear explosion, they would encounter burned and mutilated bodies closer to Memphis. And, of course, even though she felt no real fear of radiation, she was also smart enough not to test the limits. She suspected that Melissa's thinking ran along the same lines.

They headed west about ten miles south of the city, following a country road. They soon discovered that there was so much damage to the roadway, they may as well have been travelling cross country. The stink of human decay was stronger here, and the few bodies they saw looked bloated from death, possibly from disease, and certainly from severe radiation poisoning.

Stopping on a knoll, where they should have been able to see the Mississippi river, they were shocked at the sight of a mile-wide mud flat, divided by a river of water that was, maybe, a few hundred yards across.

"Wow," Melissa said. "What does that mean?"

"And how do we cross that?" Lisa asked.

Beth sat on a blackened, fallen tree and stared at the shrunken river. The others found places to sit and waited quietly for Beth to tell them what to do.

"I think my eyes are playing tricks on me," Lisa said. "It looks like the river is shrinking. That's not possible, is it?"

"Well duh," Suzanne said. "It's obviously shrunk. Just look at it."

"I mean, it looks like it's gotten smaller since we stopped here."

"That's enough, Suzanne," Beth said angrily. She thought Lisa might be right, but what could be affecting the river so dramatically?

She heard crying and turned to see some of the women in tears. Now seemed like a good time to tell them what she and Melissa had discussed about the personality changes being caused by the virus. Perhaps, if they believed that the virus made all their emotions more intense, they would be more self-aware and in control. It was time for the crying and anger, at unexpected and inconvenient times, to stop. Her anger at Suzanne's comments and suggestions needed to stop. They would all need their new strength to get through their current trial, so she told them what she and Melissa believed.

☢

They skirted Memphis to the east, hoping to find another river-crossing farther north. She cautioned everyone about what they might encounter, including people with radiation burns, diseases, and mental illness. They might see people in worse shape than they'd seen before.

"We'll avoid all of it if we can," she'd said, knowing that that was unlikely, and not really caring. Thankfully, after her explanation of the side effects of their exposure to smallpox, the mood had lightened, and there had been fewer negative comments from the group. Beth was relieved. She felt as though a new chapter had started, and she felt more in control of herself and her Outcasts, than she'd felt before.

The wind out of the southwest had been blowing most of the odors away from them—burning chemicals and charred flesh among them—but as they passed to the east of the city, all of those smells assailed them. So strong was the assault to their eyes, noses and throats, that they soaked cloths in their precious water and tied the wet cloths around their faces, to try to reduce the intensity of the attack.

A few people wandered aimlessly and bodies lay everywhere—on the ground or leaning against partially collapsed walls—but few were close enough to tell if they were alive or dead. What surprised Beth most, and what they couldn't avoid, was the constant wailing, which beset them from every direction.

"Help us, please," a woman cried from fifty feet away as they passed. She sat on the ground facing them, her clothes dirty and torn, with sores on her exposed skin, large enough to be visible at that distance. Two filthy children sat on the ground next to her, crying, their hands out in front of them in a pleading manner.

Beth heard weeping behind her and turned to see Callie and Kerri crying. After the strength her friends had begun to show, Beth realized that this scene was more traumatic than any of them had ever experienced, but she didn't share her thoughts.

"We should help them," Callie said, tears streaming down her face. Beth opened her mouth to respond, but Callie hurried on. "I know. I know. It just hurts to leave them like that."

"Move faster," Melissa said, and Beth turned to see two men approaching on an intercepting course.

"Bryce, take the rear," Beth said, as they began to run.

The men sped up, but tired quickly, and slowed to a staggering walk, then bent over and coughed—tremendous, wracking coughs. With their increased stamina, the Outcasts easily passed out of reach before slowing again. Beth thought she heard one of them, between coughing fits, beg for help, but she didn't listen.

They reached Highway 51 and followed it north, leaving the dying city behind. They saw people in the communities on either side of the highway, but they hurried past, and the people showed only cursory interest in them.

"We'll be too far away from the river to see it until we get to Dyersburg, Tennessee, about fifty miles ahead," Beth said. "That's where the next bridge is shown on the map. We'll cross there."

"What if that bridge is gone, too," Suzanne asked.

Beth wondered briefly if she should give Suzanne a straight answer, tell her to shut up, or punch her. Then she remembered that she was going to cut Suzanne some slack.

"If we can't cross at Dyersburg," she said, forcing a calm into her voice, "it looks like the next bridge is at the confluence with the Ohio River, another seventy miles, or so, to the northeast. We'll find a bridge. We've got nothing better to do anyway."

"Get serious!" Suzanne said. "There have to be other bridges between here and there."

"I don't see any on my map," Beth replied angrily.

"Then you need a better map."

Beth thought Suzanne was probably right, but didn't want to admit it. She was still considering how to respond when Lisa distracted her, probably on purpose to prevent an argument.

"Do you think the fires and road damage were caused by the explosion in Memphis," Lisa asked, as she jumped over a large crack in the roadway. The farther north they traveled the more damage they encountered to the roadway, including gaps on the side of the road where large chunks of asphalt had sloughed off, leaving holes that had to be avoided.

Beth wasn't surprised by Lisa's intervention; she was becoming accustomed to Lisa stepping in to defuse a difficult situation or to help with a task, without being asked, as if she could sense a need and the appropriate response.

"Looks more like earthquake damage," Melissa said.

"What do you know about earthquakes?" Suzanne asked.

Beth wanted to respond, but Melissa beat her to it.

"That's a stupid question, Suzanne. For your information, I've been through two earthquakes. I was on vacation in Los Angeles in 1991 during the Northridge earthquake; then I—"

"Alright," Suzanne said, holding up both hands in front of her, defensively. "I get it. You know earthquakes. Sheesh."

Beth had to smile at Melissa's spunk. She'd never been quick-witted enough to have comebacks like that.

Small groups of people passed them periodically going the opposite direction, on the other side of the highway, fifty or sixty feet away. They pulled wagons or pushed wheelbarrows filled with what appeared to be mostly junk. Finally, Beth's curiosity peaked and she called to one of them, a group of four that looked like a family—parents and two teen-aged children.

"Hello!" Beth said, stopping and turning toward them.

"Hello yourself," the man said politely, lowering his wheelbarrow to the pavement and turning toward the Outcasts.

"May I ask why you're headed south? Is the road impassable to the north?"

"Floodwater's rising. Had to leave. Didn't know where else to go."

Beth remembered the president telling the people in the northeast to move upwind—southwest—to avoid fallout from the Washington, D.C. explosion, but everything had changed since then. She was just thinking what to ask, when Lisa spoke quietly from behind her.

"Is it a mistake to go north?" Lisa asked.

"So, you don't know if it's safe to go north?" Beth asked the man.

"Nope. No power, so no reports on the radio to tell us what to expect, north or south. I suppose there are problems in all directions. You're coming from the south. What's going on there."

"Memphis is destroyed. There are communities on both sides of the road between here and there. We didn't stop at any of them."

"Well, be careful if you're going to continue north."

"Will do. You take care, too."

The man tipped his hat to Beth, picked up the wheelbarrow handles and continued south.

Beth wondered if she should change her plan; but she couldn't think of any other place, besides the Rocky Mountains, where they could have a chance to start over. Nor could she think of any other way to get there.

"We haven't seen evidence of more explosions," Melissa said. "The damage must be from earthquakes."

"The smells have decreased," Lisa said, "and the smoke and

haze seem to have drifted off toward the east."

The air was clearer, though the sky was still overcast and dark. Beth could see the flood water the man had mentioned, to the east. It filled the streets in the community on the east side of the highway. She couldn't tell how deep it was; it could easily be too deep to wade through, and swimming through murky water, with whatever might be down there, not knowing when they'd be able to stand, wasn't an option. Beth decided that they would stay on the highway, which was high and dry so far.

"At Memphis, the river was so low," Candy began. "Here, there's too much water. Did the Mississippi River change direction, or something?"

"What would that take?" Lisa asked.

"I used to have family in this area," Suzanne said. "They told me once that the river changes its course whenever there's a major flood. Maybe the river just moved again."

"Is your family still around?" Beth asked, thinking maybe they could get some friendly information about what's going on and where they should go.

"No, they moved to California years ago," she replied, "but they told me a story about a massive earthquake, actually a series of them, that occurred in 1811 and 1812 in this area."

"Folk tales?" Lisa asked.

"I didn't believe them at the time," Suzanne said, "then someone else mentioned the New Madrid earthquake of 1811, so I looked it up. You may find this boring, but I was fascinated by it. There were three earthquakes over seven magnitude between December 1811 and February 1812, with hundreds of aftershocks. Besides structural damage to the few buildings in the area at the time— the United States was still expanding west that long ago, and the few people that lived this far west lived in log cabins—there were river bank failures, landslides, sunken land, and something they called sand blows."

"What's a sand blow?" Candy asked.

"The way I understand it," Suzanne chuckled, "giant plumes of sand shot out of the ground, into the air. Scientists have since decided that, because of the earthquakes, huge pockets of coal found seams to the surface, and blew clouds of black dust into the air that were nearly unbreathable, making the sky so dark that people couldn't see, and the air so thick that they couldn't light a flame."

"Sounds like a folk tale, alright," Lisa said.

"The damaged area was over two hundred thousand square miles," Suzanne continued, "all over Missouri and Arkansas to the west, and Tennessee, Kentucky, Illinois, and Indiana, to the east. Some of the sunken lands were big enough and deep enough to become lakes and the uplifted areas became permanent hills."

Beth believed that Suzanne was telling the truth about what she'd read, but wondered about the accuracy of the reporting of an incident that happened two hundred years earlier. No one seemed to know what to say, so the conversation died.

The floodwater became deeper the closer they got to Dyersburg, eventually covering the highway. Spread out, and with Beth in the lead, they walked in oily water more than a foot deep, filled with floating debris, making it difficult to see where they were going. Beth thought about the sink holes that Suzanne had mentioned, big enough to become lakes, and was just turning to warn the others to watch their step, when Candy cried out and fell, disappearing under the surface. Beth expected her to pop back up at any second, but she didn't.

Bryce, a few feet behind her, looked startled and hesitated, possibly expecting Candy to reappear; but when she didn't, he fell to his knees and reached into the water, moving his hands around.

A shocked expression registered on his face as he frantically thrust one arm, then both, around in the water, up to his shoulders, in an effort to locate her.

Beth, Melissa and Lisa arrived just as Bryce took a deep breath and fell forward, also disappearing under the water. They all went to their knees, feeling around in the water with both hands. There was no bottom.

☢

Candy dropped straight down. At first surprised, she told herself not to panic. She'd swallowed a little water before closing her mouth and worried that she might catch something from it, but she expected to pop right back up out of the water.

When she reached out, she could feel a wall of dirt behind her, but it crumbled in her hands when she tried to pull herself up.

She knew how to swim, so she moved her arms, and kicked her legs, but couldn't tell if it made any difference. She thought that maybe her backpack and clothes were weighing her down, and considered trying to take them off. Then she got a cramp in her left thigh and nearly cried out with the pain. She couldn't move that leg.

Her lungs started to burn, and her brain told her to breathe, but her instincts told her that that wasn't right. She wanted to scream, but that also seemed like a bad idea.

She became confused, not sure which way was up. She thought her kicking should move her toward the surface but it hadn't worked yet. Maybe she was pushing herself down. Then her right leg, which had been treading water, began to cramp.

Where's the surface? she wondered. Her panic increased and she began frantically scrabbling with both hands on the wall of dirt.

Gradually, her movements became more sluggish, until her arms hung limply in the water and her brain told her to relieve the pain in her lungs by taking a breath.

She imagined herself under the surface of a cold ocean, looking out at Bryce, who lay on a warm beach in the sun, smiling and waving for her to join him. She moved sluggishly toward him, and opened her mouth to call out, when a hand caught in her floating hair and pulled.

Beth knelt in a foot of water, with Melissa and Lisa kneeling next to her and the others standing nearby. Suddenly, Bryce and Candy popped up out of the water a few feet to the side, startling them. Bryce gasped for breath. Candy looked dead.

"Wha—?" Beth blurted.

Bryce had one hand in Candy's hair and used it to drag her up onto his lap as he sat on the edge of the hole. He held her mostly out of the water—face down—slipped her backpack off her shoulders, and set it in the water to the side. He held her in place over his knees with one arm and pounded on her back with a fist, trying to get her to breathe. He breathed heavily from his exertion. Moments later, he turned her over, plugged her nose, and moved toward her face, with his mouth open. Suddenly, she bucked and took a gasping breath. Bryce moved his face away as Candy started coughing up water and everything else in her stomach.

Beth felt helpless; she could only sit and watch Bryce's attempt to save Candy's life. No one spoke. Finally, Lisa came forward cautiously and rested a hand on Bryce's shoulder. The others approached cautiously, testing the ground ahead of them before taking a step, and waited impatiently.

Bryce forced Candy to sit on his lap so she was mostly out of the water. Leaning forward, she shook violently and continued to cough up water, wracking coughs making her body jerk spasmodically. He pulled her against his chest and hugged her tightly. It took several minutes, but she finally stopped choking and tried to sit up on her own.

Bryce, still breathing raggedly, finally looked at Beth.

"There's . . . a hole there," he said, pointing to where they'd come out of the water.

"Yeah, I guess so," Beth said.

"You mean, like a sink-hole?" Lisa asked.

"I don't know . . . about a sink-hole. But . . . something made a hole . . . big enough to get lost in," Bryce said. "I had to swim . . . around to find her."

"Candy, are you okay?" Suzanne asked with concern.

Candy didn't respond. Her skin was pasty white, and she'd tucked her arms between her chest and Bryce, leaning her bowed head against his chest.

"Give her a minute, okay?" Beth said, holding a hand up to Suzanne.

Candy's long hair hung, limp and dirty, littered with twigs and other debris. Bryce gently wiped the spittle that ran down her chin and dripped onto her lap, with the palm of his hand. She opened her eyes and smiled weakly at him, plucked a piece of a leaf from the stubble on his chin, then placed her arms around his neck and squeezed weakly. Hanging on his shoulders, she returned her head to his chest. He looked around at the others, then closed his eyes and rested his head on hers.

Beth watched them, surprised at the tears that fell from her eyes. She was grateful for Bryce's bravery, time and again along their journey; and of course, for Candy's safety. She thought about everything they'd been through—the evacuation to the shelter, the vice president, the soldiers, the virus, Karen's death and now Candy's near-drowning—and wondered if any of them would live to see the Rocky Mountains.

Now, as had occurred frequently, it was her own feelings that gave her pause. Hours earlier she had lectured the group about the need to control their new emotions, certain that the changes were not improvements, but amplification of negative impulses; but she had been wrong. The intense relief and joy she felt for these two should not be tamped down, but enjoyed.

12

Who'll be the first guinea pig?

The Preserve, 1 August

"Someone has been raiding the pantry at night," Becca said, as she looked around the office at the other members of the board. "I think it's Nathan, since he doesn't show up for regular meals anymore, but it would be nice to know for sure." Now that the wedding was over and things had settled down, Amos wanted to know if anyone had questions or concerns. Becca had been the first to speak up.

"Is anything damaged?" Lillie asked.

"No. I'm just concerned because this has been going on for a couple of weeks now."

"What does Nathan *do* with his day?" Mike asked. "He doesn't show up when he has work assignments and he doesn't show up for meals. He can't be exercising all day long, every day."

"Do you want me to monitor all the rooms?" Terry asked Amos.

"They're all set up, we're just not recording," Amos replied.

"Do you have one in my bedroom?" Emily asked, her face flushing with embarrassment. Being a newlywed, she was likely concerned about someone watching her and Matt.

"No dear," Lillie said with a smile. "There are none in the bedrooms."

"Let's start recording, Terry," Amos said. "I'd like to know what Jason is doing with his time, too. Anything else?"

"Can I tell everyone what we're doing with the gate?" Mike asked excitedly.

"Go ahead," Amos replied, having already allowed most of it to be revealed earlier.

Emily was the only member of the board who hadn't heard about the discovery of the twin world, so Mike brought her up to speed, then promised to show her the valley, the construction site, and their neighborhood. Then he shared with everyone what he and Terry had been working on.

"This morning," he said, "we took the gate all the way to Salt Lake City using the control panel for the twin world—the one we call panel A. There appears to be a stability problem at that distance, but we're looking into that."

"Our next objective was to map the lab and other parts of the Preserve—to compare panels A and B—before we try to go outside in our world using panel B. Since the Preserve doesn't exist in the twin world, we can't map anything in the Preserve with panel A.

"What we did, instead, was copy the data we developed with Panel A—from Bear Lake to Ogden—into the database for panel B; then used panel B to jump around inside the Preserve, mapping the common areas. You may have seen something out of the corner of your eye that wasn't there when you turned your head, since we've seen most of you."

"I did!" Becca exclaimed. "In the kitchen."

"So did I," Lillie added. "In the community center."

"Great," Mike said. "So, now we need to combine all the map points from the two panels and see if they form a continuous map."

"What does that do for you?" Emily asked.

"If it works," Mike explained, "it means we can make short-duration visits to the outside, to see what's going on in our world, without too much radiation exposure."

"Wow," Emily said. "That would be interesting."

"It's great that we've discovered that the Observer has these phenomenal capabilities," Amos said seriously, "but I want to remind us all, that our ultimate goal hasn't changed. We built the Observer to look inside the human body, as an aide in medical diagnosis. I've been thinking about the extensive testing and protocols that would normally be required before we could test it on a human body."

"That may not be in our lifetime," Mike said.

"With the world in chaos, as it is," Terry said, "we might never get all the testing done."

"You're right—both of you—but are either of you even thinking about it? Or, are we too distracted by what we're seeing in this twin world? Can we spend a few minutes talking about how to direct our research?"

"Are you suggesting that we can do something now?" Terry asked.

"Maybe—" Amos paused, considering how to proceed.

"What?" Mike asked anxiously.

"Well, if we assume that we're not restricted by normal medical protocols—"

"Who's going to turn you in?" Mike asked.

"Right," Amos said. "Well, maybe we could do some limited testing on a person. Our only limitation would be our concern for personal safety." Would he really skip steps to begin testing on live, human patients? And who would volunteer to be his first patient?

"Dad?" Mike asked.

"I know, Mike. It's a radical thought. But I may be more anxious to see the results in my lifetime than I thought previously."

"Really?" Emily asked.

"Are you ready for that?" Lillie asked at the same time. "Maybe you should conduct more research."

"Lillie, we don't have any way to do more research. We've passed the gate through a deer with no visible signs of distress, but there's no way we'll get a deer to stand still long enough to look at its insides. We could capture a rabbit or mouse to study, but their bodily construction and metabolism are so different from humans, that it would tell us little more than what we already know."

"Who'll be the first guinea pig?" Lillie asked with a smile, looking around at the others.

"I thought we could start by looking at the ankle you sprained during the earthquake," Amos said, smiling mischievously,

"But—" Lillie said as her smile fled and Emily chuckled. Amos turned his smile on Emily.

"Then, if Lillie lives," he said, "we'll check Emily's arm." Emily choked on her laugh. "I don't know if we're ready to tell the others, but when we do, we can also check the back of Sidney's head. After that, we'll start looking at other parts of the body, like colons, for indications of pre-cancer polyps."

Apparently, nobody thought that was funny.

"Dad?" Mike asked again.

Amos had thought Mike's concern was about beginning the testing now, without more research, but maybe it wasn't. "What is it Mike?" he asked.

"Dad, even if we succeed," Mike said, "with the world in its present condition, who's going to know about the Observer's capability and use it?"

Amos didn't have an answer, but maybe that explained why Mike was more interested in the twin world than in medical research.

The Outcasts—Tennessee to Missouri, 5 August

"I hope the bridge is still intact," Suzanne said. "With all this water, I don't think we can go much farther north."

Beth's temper flared again. Why did she let Suzanne's comments set her off like that?

As they continued west toward the river and bridge, the interstate rose out of the water. They traveled just far enough to be able to sit on dry ground, then stopped to let Candy and Bryce rest. Candy continued to have coughing fits—Bryce was staying close to her—and Beth was concerned that she might have caught something; but it couldn't be worse than smallpox and radiation poisoning, could it?

Their backpacks had gone under the water with them, so all their clothes were soaked. Candy was taller than the other women, but they offered her dry clothes that mostly fit. No one's clothes were large enough to fit Bryce, but he claimed the cold didn't bother him and he seemed no worse off after his underwater swim. Beth decided to worry about both of them anyway.

As they walked toward the bridge, they speculated on the conditions around them—broken roads, flooding, underwater hazards—it was all too surreal.

"The bridge is still standing," Melissa said as they got closer, "but look at its condition." Some of the steel girders and supports were deformed—twisted—as if they'd gone soft.

"I didn't know steel could bend like that." Lisa gasped.

"Is it safe to cross?" Suzanne asked quietly.

The concrete on the approach to the bridge was cracked and tilted, and the west-bound lanes looked blocked with stalled cars and trucks; no surprise, since the president had told people to go west and south.

"If we stay to the left," Beth said, "where there are fewer obstacles, maybe we can work our way across."

"What's that in the roadway?" Melissa asked. "Looks like people."

"I count seven," Lisa said. "They're holding things in their hands."

"Weapons?" Bryce asked, hurrying Candy forward so they could catch up.

Beth had been preoccupied with the bridge and hadn't noticed the people. This could only mean more trouble.

As they approached slowly, Beth could see that seven men blocked the roadway. They each held some sort of weapon, mostly shovels and hoes. They were obviously trying to look menacing.

"Can we get past them without a confrontation," Melissa asked quietly.

"Doesn't look like it," Beth said. "Only four of us have knives."

"Where did you get knives?" Suzanne asked.

"Later, Suzanne," Beth said. "We need to see if we can talk our way through this. A knife is for close-in fighting. A shovel beats a knife, unless you have a throwing knife and know how to throw it. Let's ask, nicely, what it will take to let us pass. There's no doubt they want something. Melissa and Bryce, come with me," Beth turned to the others. "The rest of you, wait here, please. We'll see if we can get safe passage."

Beth approached the group, followed closely by Melissa and Bryce.

"Hello," Beth said when she was within shouting distance. "Nice day for a walk. Mind if we pass over the bridge?" *That was lame,* she thought, of course they minded or they wouldn't be in the way.

Two of the men stepped forward a couple of steps. The older one, on the left, spoke.

"The bridge belongs to us now. Ya can't pass unless ya pay a toll."

"And what will it take for you to let us pass?" Beth asked.

"Give us all yer food, water, medical supplies—anything of value." The younger man leaned over and spoke quietly to the spokesman, who then leaned to the side, to look beyond Beth at the others standing farther back. "We'll also have the younger women—those three," he added.

"That's unacceptable," Beth called back, thinking furiously for a solution. Suddenly, a plan coalesced in her head. She turned to Melissa and Bryce, explaining quickly.

"Get the others to move up here, casually," she said to Bryce. "I'm going to try a bluff. Follow my lead." *This better work,* she thought.

She turned back to the men and spoke in a casual voice, loud enough to be heard, as she sauntered toward them.

"That's not a good idea," she said. "We all have smallpox. We're contagious. If you don't stand down and move out of the way, you'll all become contaminated."

"Hah," the leader said, "you don't have the red spots."

"You must have some medical training," Beth said. "I'm impressed. Melissa, here—" she motioned at Melissa, "—worked at the CDC in Atlanta before it was bombed by the government. The virus escaped—mutated—because of the radiation, I guess, and we caught it. When I get close enough, you'll be able to see the dark splotches on my skin where the pustules used to be." She intentionally used the word *pustules* because it frightened most people.

While the two men discussed what Beth had said, the other men moved up to see better, and Beth could hear the other Outcasts catching up to her.

"Yeah, we can see the splotches, that means the virus is past it's contagious stage. You're not dead, so you must have survived it.

But you're not contagious." He must not have been scared by the word *pustules.*

"We were vaccinated. But it mutated, accelerating the incubation process and leaving us contagious."

The spokesman laughed. "Good try. We'll take our chances." Another young man leaned over quickly and said something to the spokesman. They argued for a minute, until the spokesman backhanded him on the shoulder and pushed him away.

"Now get on with it," he said, turning back to Beth. "All your valuables and the three young women."

"Ok," Beth said, removing her backpack, "but you'll pay the price, possibly with your lives, if you get the hemorrhagic version." The others had been listening and started removing their backpacks.

"Yeah? What we have is no kind of life, anyway," the spokesman said bitterly.

Lisa leaned into Beth and asked, "What if they don't take the bluff?"

"Just make sure Callie goes along. I think the young man on his right is the weak link."

Beth motioned for the others to follow her and began walking toward the group of men, her backpack in her outstretched hands. The men began moving around nervously, talking to the spokesman.

"Ok, we accept your terms," Beth called, "all of our supplies and the three young women, in exchange for the rest of us being allowed to cross the bridge, right?"

The closer they got to the men, the more agitated the men acted. Then Candy coughed. None of the men knew she had fallen into a sink hole. The cough clearly rattled some of them, and Beth had to control a smile that tugged at the edge of her lips, imagining what the men were thinking. Here was a group of nine people, possibly contagious with smallpox, readily approaching as though they were unafraid, ready to hand themselves over, with nothing to lose. Had Beth been in their shoes, she would have been wondering if this was a bluff, but certainly would have thought something was wrong with the situation.

"Wait right there," the spokesman said, holding out his hand, as several of his associates approached him, appearing agitated and whispering loudly.

The Outcasts stopped.

The men put their heads together and had an animated discussion, then the spokesman faced the Outcasts. "Leave your valuables where they are and you'll be allowed to pass," he said.

As the Outcasts were setting their packs on the pavement, Melissa called out. "I guess you realize that anything we've touched is probably carrying the smallpox virus."

The men huddled again. Some started moving off the roadway, shaking their heads and obviously just wanting to get away. The arguing continued until, one after another, the seven men left the roadway. The last two to leave moved reluctantly and threw up their hands in frustration.

The Outcasts put their packs back on. Lisa said something to Kerri that made her smile.

Beth noticed and glared at Kerri. "Get rid of that smile until we get across the bridge. We're still being watched."

As they passed the men, who were now about twenty feet off the road, Beth took a chance and called out. "What happened to the river?"

She didn't think they were going to answer. Then one of the older men said, "There was a huge earthquake. It shook the bridge—rippled like a wet noodle." That explained the twisted metal and maybe the sink-hole. "The river's been slowly drying up, like the water is going someplace else."

"Maybe that's the water we saw to the east and north?" Beth asked.

"Don't rightly know. Somebody said the Missouri and Ohio Rivers backed up, spread out, found new paths. I don't know."

The other Outcasts followed the conversation, moving slowly toward the bridge. Callie lagged behind the others as usual. Ben, walking a few feet in front of her, held his injured left arm with his right.

One of the younger men, apparently not satisfied with the smallpox story or the outcome of the confrontation, suddenly dropped his shovel and rushed toward Callie.

"Colin, stop!" someone called.

Callie and Ben turned just in time to see the young man reach the pavement. Callie, as usual, froze. Ben, despite his injury, hurtled toward Callie and Colin. Colin reached Callie first and swept her off her feet, threw her over his shoulder, and began carrying her away, before the others could react and come to her rescue.

"Fight him, Callie," Ben called.

Beth feared that if Colin managed to get Callie off the highway before Ben reached them, it would be difficult to win her back. She didn't know what Ben could do with his injured arm and she noticed a couple of Colin's associates running toward them.

Callie must have finally realized that she needed to do something to save herself—probably remembering her near-rape by Art and the attack by Jared in the river. She began to kick and struggle as hard as she could, scratching Colin on his face and arms, forcing him to slow down to keep her under his control.

Ben finally reached them and grabbed Colin by the neck, pulling and twisting until Colin lost his balance and fell, Callie landing on top of him. The two men running toward them stopped and watched the confrontation. Ben winced as he pulled Callie to her feet and pushed her toward the bridge. Beth passed her and went to Ben, whose arm hung at his side and whose expression said he was about to faint from pain. Kerri and Lisa reached Callie, placed her between them, and frog-marched her away.

Colin scrambled to his hands and knees and scurried off the highway toward his fellows. They backed off, warning him not to touch them.

"Better quarantine Colin," Melissa called out to the men. "It takes two days for the rashes to appear, three days for lesions in the mouth. If he develops smallpox, he'll be contagious forever, a leper in your midst."

Colin approached the rest of the group, pleading as they continued to back away. All six of the other men raised their shovels and rakes menacingly, repeatedly telling Colin to stay back. The group continued to back away from Colin, down a slope, and out of sight around a small hill.

Bryce approached as Beth helped Ben sit on the pavement and unwrapped his injured arm. Without supplies to cast it, Beth had wrapped it tightly and put it in a sling. Ben passed out while she ministered to him.

"We need to get him across the bridge and out of here," Bryce said, glancing over at the hill where the men had disappeared.

"He's reinjured his arm," Beth replied. "I don't think he rebroke it, but it's already starting to swell. Help me carry him." Beth took Ben's legs while Bryce struggled with his head and shoulders. As they worked their way toward the bridge, Lisa and Kerri came over and tried to help, but they were just in the way.

"It's ok, ladies," Beth said. "We've got him. Encourage the others to get across the bridge before those men change their mind and come after us."

"I'd try a fireman carry," Bryce said, "if it wasn't Ben's arm that was injured."

"I'm okay if you are," Beth replied, keeping Ben's legs raised off the pavement. Bryce shifted Ben's weight to get a better grip, and they stumbled along.

They worked their way slowly across the tilted bridge. Cars had slid down to the median, forcing them to go up and over. Several times, Bryce had to stop to get a new grip, because of Ben's weight and the poor footing on the sloping surface. Others offered to help, but Beth declined.

During one rest stop, near the middle of the bridge, Beth could see the river's low water level. It seemed even lower here than downstream.

By the time they reached the other side of the bridge, Beth was exhausted, and Bryce looked the way Beth felt. Ben had stirred a couple of times, moaning and fainting again—or maybe falling asleep.

"We can't stay here," Beth said, when Melissa showed her on a map that the nearest town, Caruthers, was several miles away. "We're too close to Colin and his friends."

"Maybe they'll leave us alone now."

"Colin has nothing to lose. Once he realizes that, he may come after us. Maybe there's a farmhouse nearby."

"Can you keep going?"

"Not yet," Bryce answered for both of them, breathing heavily. "We need to rest a bit. Let's try to get Ben into a car and take a break. With our increased stamina, I don't think it will take long to recover."

"This disease does have a few benefits, I guess," Beth replied. "Melissa, why don't you take someone with you, and see if you can find a place for us to spend the night? The rest of us will stay here unless we're forced to move to stay safe. In that case, we'll keep going, but we'll stay near the highway, and watch for you."

"I don't want us to get separated," Melissa said, but Beth insisted. By the time Melissa agreed to leave, Bryce wanted to go with her, 'to walk the kinks out' he said. So, Melissa took Bryce, Candy and Suzanne. Lisa, Kerri and Callie stayed with Beth and Ben.

"We'll come back for you when we find something," Melissa said.

13

Who's Sheryl?

"It looks like a farmhouse about a half-mile away on the left," Melissa said, pointing. This was farm country, so they expected to see homes spread out between the farms. "Looks like another one ahead, about the same distance, just off the highway, on the right."

They decided to try the one on the left first. Being farther from the highway, Melissa figured it had the better chance of being unmolested by travelers like themselves. They were in the yard before an old man came out the front door, a shotgun in his hands, and warned them away.

"Stop right there," the man said, aiming the shotgun in their direction.

Melissa raised both hands, palms toward the man and said, "Don't shoot. We're harmless."

"Go away. You're not welcome here."

"We have an injured man," Melissa said. "We're looking for someplace for him to rest for a while."

"Liar. I don't see an injured man."

"He's back at the bridge. He has a broken arm. He's too—"

"We don't have anything to share," the man said, interrupting her. "The last people . . . just go away." The man started waving his shotgun, scaring Melissa.

"Fine. We don't want trouble," Melissa said, backing away.

"Couldn't you just let us rest in the barn overnight?"

"*No!*" the man screamed. "Now go away before I make trouble for *you.*"

They backed hurriedly out of the yard, turned, and ran toward the highway.

Bryce could see smoke rising from the second farmhouse while they were still a half-mile away. It must have started while they were at the first farmhouse, and still burned in several places.

"Is anyone there?" Bryce called as they approached, spreading out across the yard. He wondered if anyone might still be inside the ruined house, but didn't see any way to enter safely. He approached the front porch, while the others split up and moved to either side of the burning structure. He noticed what looked like a body on the charred remains of the porch and went over to investigate, but the roof collapsed before he could get there, forcing him to pull back. He pulled his shirttail over his nose and braved the smoke, to lift a blackened beam off the man, then squinted to see him better.

"What is it?" Melissa called.

"A middle-aged man, badly burned. Looks like he died from a knife wound." It was an understatement; his throat had been cut so deeply that he had been nearly decapitated. "Watch out for someone with a knife."

The others stopped and looked around.

"Melissa," Suzanne said and drew Melissa's attention to something on the ground leading away from the house. "There's a trail here." In the gloom of the overcast sky, it looked like someone had been dragged from the house to the barn.

Alerted to the possible threat, they moved more cautiously toward the barn, which appeared to be intact. Melissa pulled knives from her pack, handed one to Suzanne and another to Bryce as he walked up to her. Candy didn't want one.

"Where'd you get these?" Suzanne asked

"The restaurant, a few days ago. Have you ever used one?"

"Not on another person!" Suzanne said defensively.

"Be prepared to use it," Bryce said, as he approached the large double doors on the front of the barn. Melissa followed him cautiously to a smaller door—a man door—cut into one of them, while the others stood back and to one side. He held his knife in front of him and motioned for Melissa to have hers ready, then pushed the door open quickly. He released a grateful sigh when nothing jumped out at him.

"Anyone in there?" he called loudly. No answer. He carefully approached the dark opening and could see hay motes in the air immediately in front of him, from what little light spilled in from the doorway and from a window high in the side wall. He shook his head and mouthed, "nothing moving", without looking at Melissa.

He motioned for her to follow him in, then move to her left. They entered, crouching, with their knives out in front of them, one going to each side of the door. As their eyes adjusted, Bryce could neither see nor hear movement; but there had been someone in there, evidenced by the disturbance on the floor. The trail that led them to the barn continued into the darkness.

Bryce pointed to himself then toward the trail, offering to check it out. Melissa, her fear evident in her expression, nodded shakily and stayed by the door. Bryce disappeared into the interior of the barn, reappearing after a few moments, and motioned for Melissa to follow him. What he'd found was a plump, middle-aged woman, lying on the hay in the middle of the barn. Her throat had been slit and her clothes were in disarray.

He heard movement above him and turned, just in time to hear a grunt, and see a body fall toward him from the loft. A knife blade flashed momentarily in the dim light. He instinctively raised his arms to protect his face and moved slightly to the side, away from Melissa and the assailant's knife.

The assailant landed on top of him, knocking him to the ground, but didn't follow up the attack. Bryce rolled over, throwing the twitching assailant off him.

Melissa approached cautiously, looking around. She reached Bryce as he was rising to his knees. The assailant—a man—lay still, Bryce's knife buried to the hilt in his chest. Bryce couldn't immediately see the assailant's knife.

"Bryce! Melissa!" Suzanne called from the door.

"We're ok," Melissa said. "Be careful. Let your eyes adjust before you come over."

A flashlight beam flared near the door and reached out to them. Candy led Suzanne over.

"Where'd you find the flashlight?" Bryce asked.

"On a shelf by the door," Candy said.

"That's convenient," Bryce said, as he looked at Melissa and shook his head. Why hadn't he bothered to look? He took the light and quickly found the assailant's knife, a few feet away, the handle protruding from the hay. He weighed the knife in his hand and decided he liked it better than the kitchen knife Melissa had given him—more balanced. He pocketed the knife and carried the flashlight to the loft to verify that it was empty. "How'd you know to look for the flashlight?" he asked Candy.

"My uncle had a barn," she said. "I liked riding his horses when I was a little girl. I expected to find a lantern. The flashlight was a bonus."

"Her body's still warm," Melissa said, feeling the dead woman's throat for a pulse.

"Do you think she died before or after he molested her?" Suzanne asked, shining the flashlight on the woman's face.

"He may not have molested her," Melissa replied, looking away. She didn't want to think about it. "He wouldn't have had a lot of time, since the house was still burning." She looked around, assessing the barn as a place to stay for a while. "I think this barn will do. We need to go back to the bridge to get the others. Who wants to go?"

"Whoever's going, needs to go soon," Suzanne said. "I felt raindrops while we were waiting for you outside."

"Ooo, I don't think I can stay here knowing two dead people are in here," Candy said.

"Candy, will you go with Bryce to get the others?" Melissa asked. "Suzanne and I can get rid of the bodies while you're gone."

"That works," Bryce said, kicking the bottom rail of a horse stall gate and breaking the small log free. "Help me knock down this gate so we have a couple of poles to make a litter."

"Here are some horse blankets we can take," Candy said as Bryce kicked another rail and broke it free.

"Ugh, they smell like horses," Suzanne said, turning her head away.

"That's because they're *horse* blankets," Candy said, heading for the door.

Bryce picked up the logs and followed.

"Melissa," Candy said, "the barn doors can be locked from the inside."

"Really?" Melissa asked, looking where Candy and Bryce were standing by the open door.

"Yes, my uncle's barn was set up the same way. You place this board in the brackets mounted on the doors to make a horizontal barricade. This one is for the large doors and this one is for the small door. As good as having locks on the doors."

"Why would you need to barricade the barn from the inside?" Suzanne asked.

"I don't know whose idea it was," Candy replied. "Normally, barns are barred on the outside, and this one has the brackets for it; but it should make you feel safer while we're gone."

A sudden, brilliant light flashed through the cracks in the barn walls, followed immediately by thunder that shook the structure. Bryce jumped and Candy squealed. Then the rain started, thundering as it pelted the roof and west wall of the barn.

After waiting for the heaviest rain to pass, Bryce and Candy departed in near total darkness, since Melissa had asked to keep the flashlight. They would have to be careful in the dark; and they wouldn't try to return tonight unless Beth insisted.

☢

Suzanne helped Melissa drag the bodies out and around to the back of the barn, where they dropped them into a ditch. They covered them with a horse blanket and a few rocks, to make it difficult for animals to get to them. Unless the others got curious and went looking, they would never know. Then they barricaded the doors from the inside, against the weather and any unwanted visitors.

"They could just burn the barn down if they couldn't get in," Suzanne said.

"Be quiet, Suzanne," Melissa replied, hoping they didn't have to worry about roaming pyromaniacs. "I didn't need that to worry about." Nevertheless, Melissa looked for and found another door in the back wall, and barricaded that one, too.

"Do you have your knife handy?" Melissa asked Suzanne as they tried to find a place to dry out and sleep.

"I don't think I could use a knife on a person," Suzanne said.

"Me neither," Melissa said, "but why don't we have them available just in case."

Suzanne removed her wet clothes and laid them over the top rail of a horse stall. She must have seen Melissa's surprised expression. "I think I'll dry out faster this way," she added, then sat on a pile of hay.

At first surprised by Suzanne undressing in front of her, Melissa decided that Suzanne's idea was a good one, and removed her clothes as well. They laid their knives next to them in the hay, then sat, leaning against a log wall, staring at the flashlight beam and talking quietly. They couldn't sleep with the rain beating on the roof and the wind howling through the walls. They jerked at every sound the old barn made. They checked their clothes periodically, finding them still wet, then found dry clothes in their packs and put them on instead.

Hours passed. Finally, they decided to try to sleep, so they wouldn't be totally exhausted when the others arrived.

"Melissa! Suzanne!" Lisa called from outside the barn door.

"Eek!" Suzanne squeaked as they both jerked nervously.

"It's Lisa. We're here. Let us in."

"I think I just wet my pants," Suzanne said, sounding embarrassed.

Melissa carried the flashlight to the man door and lifted the bar. As the door opened, the light spilled out on Lisa's face.

"Better open the large door," Lisa said, "so we can get Ben inside. The litter's too wide to fit through this one." Soaked from the rain, her hair hanging limply around her head, she looked strung out.

As Lisa, Kerri and Callie staggered into the barn, wet and tired, Melissa and Suzanne lifted the bar on the large doors and swung one side open.

The rain had stopped but the sky was black, with no stars or moon visible. Ben lay, covered, on the horse blankets they'd wrapped around the poles, spaced about three feet apart to form a litter. Bryce held the poles at the near end, dragging the other end on the ground. Beth and Candy stood behind and to either side, each holding onto one of the poles, trying to ease Bryce's load. Melissa thought they all looked like they'd been beat up.

Bryce leaned the poles on a rail about two feet off the ground—part of a horse stall—and stepped away. All three collapsed onto the hay, huffing from the exertion, to join the others, who'd already settled onto the hay and closed their eyes.

"Why didn't you wait until morning?" Melissa asked Beth as they passed.

"It wasn't safe to stay there," Beth said. "People were roaming around. We didn't know if Colin and his friends were among them. As it was, we had to be sneaky to get here, even in the dark and the rain."

"I'll get Suzanne to help me bar the doors again, then we'll get you something to eat, and you can crash until morning."

"No, I want to look around a little before settling down for the night. Who'll go with me?"

No one wanted to get up again. They had all taken turns dragging the litter, and even with their increased stamina they were exhausted.

"Lisa, Kerri, come on. I need your eyes and ears," Beth pleaded.

"Okay, sure," Lisa said, grudgingly, as she and Kerri struggled to their feet.

Melissa and Suzanne barred the large door, and guarded the man door, until the three women returned.

⊛

Beth's flashlight had died, but it was just as well. She didn't want anyone to know where they were. She left Melissa's flashlight in the barn so her eyes would adjust to the dim, outside light. Then the three of them walked around the outside of the barn, identifying landmarks. They found the place Melissa had said to use as a latrine.

Satisfied that they were alone and not in immediate danger, they returned to the barn, where Melissa and Suzanne had laid out food and water. Bryce and Candy were sitting in their underwear, Callie had changed into dry clothes from her pack, and they were all sitting on the hay, eating.

"What's this?" Beth asked.

"I suggested that everyone dry out before going to bed," Melissa said.

⊛

Beth checked on Ben, finding him asleep, likely from the pain killers she'd given him earlier: but he was soaked to the skin.

"What are you doing?" Melissa asked. Beth had spread out some hay next to Ben's litter and bunched a sweatshirt at one end.

"I'm going to sleep next to Ben," she said, stifling a yawn. "I want to know when he wakes, so I can check on him. You're welcome to sleep here, too."

"Thanks, but Suzanne and I decided to take the first watch. She's making us a bed near the door."

"You got friendly with Suzanne while you were waiting for us, did you?"

"She was telling me about her job as a corporate trainer. I'd like to hear the rest of it, if I can get her talking again."

"She hasn't been bashful about complaining," Beth said quietly. "I don't know why you'd have trouble getting her to talk."

"You'd be surprised, Beth. She's had a tough life, being a black business woman in the South. Maybe you should cut her some slack."

"Maybe. We'll see. Here, do you need the light to see what you're doing over there?"

"I think Suzanne's got it. Good night, Beth." Melissa turned to leave.

"Melissa," Beth said tiredly, "will you help me undress Ben?" Between them, they were able to get Ben undressed and into some dry clothes that Beth found in his pack. Then Melissa walked away into the dark.

"We'll take the light if you're done with it," Lisa said, coming up behind Beth. As Beth handed her the flashlight, she wondered how long Lisa had been standing there and how much of their conversation she'd heard. Whatever she'd heard, she chose not to say anything about it.

"Bryce," Lisa said, "if you'll follow us, you can have the light next."

❂

Candy watched Bryce as he followed Lisa and Kerri to a corner of the barn, away from the doors, then returned a few minutes later with the flashlight. He was so masculine . . . and so brave. She smiled as she waited quietly for him to approach.

"Callie," Lisa said, coming back into the light. Callie had been looking around, as though lost. "If you're looking for a place to lie down, I found a good spot in a horse stall back here. We've laid a lot of fresh hay on the ground and there's plenty of room for all three of us."

"Okay," Callie said quietly as she walked over, head down. As she reached Lisa, Lisa placed an arm around her waist and spoke quietly to her as they walked away. Candy smiled as she watched them go. She had become fond of these people.

"Are you ready?" Bryce asked and Candy nodded. "Best place in the barn is in the loft. You go first and I'll carry the light." He held the flashlight where it gave him a good view. He liked the way her jeans hugged her backside as she climbed the ladder ahead of him.

They all slept the troubled sleep of those who've been through daytime nightmares.

The Outcasts—Missouri, 6 August

Life didn't look so dismal to Beth after a few hours of rest. Over a light breakfast, they discussed their plans.

"Obviously we need food," Beth said, "but someone needs to stay with Ben while he convalesces for a few days." She wondered if the others would allow her to stay with him while they took turns looking for food.

"How about we take turns staying with him," Melissa said, answering the question for Beth, "while the others scavenge for food."

"Sheryl and I can stay with him first," Bryce said, looking at Candy. "I think the knife I recovered from the assailant feels like a throwing knife, so I'd like to set up a target on the outside wall of the barn, and practice throwing it."

Beth stared at Bryce and Candy, trying to understand his comment.

"Sheryl?" Suzanne asked. "Who's Sheryl?"

Beth smiled. She'd guessed that Sheryl was Candy's real name and that Candy had shared her real name with Bryce while they were being chummy in the hayloft.

"That's Candy's real name," Bryce said proudly as he hugged Candy to him.

"You want us to call you Sheryl?" Suzanne asked.

"Just call me Candy," she said, with a frustrated look at Bryce.

There was a town a few miles to the northwest—Caruthers, Missouri—with lots of farmland in between. A few—mostly men—worked in the fields and gathered water from the nearby stream. Anyone else was likely staying indoors to shelter from the radiation.

Beth, Lisa and Kerri approached a farmer harvesting his corn by hand, placing the cobs of corn into a basket at his feet. A four-wheeled hand truck stood on a dirt path a few yards from him, with a basket full of corn already resting on it.

"I don't think we should get near him," Lisa whispered to Beth.

"I would prefer to avoid contact, but we should ask for food before taking it, since we know who owns it," Beth replied quietly.

It was a mistake. The farmer pulled a handgun from a holster on his belt as soon as he saw them.

"Go away," he said, pointing his gun from one to another of them.

"Please sir," said Beth, "we just need a little food."

"I said go away," the farmer repeated, becoming agitated.

Beth held up both hands in front of her as they backed away. "We're leaving. We're sorry we disturbed you."

Bryce, standing about twenty feet from the barn, threw his knife at a target he'd drawn on the wall with mud, then walked up to the target to retrieve the knife. Beth walked up to the target and studied it.

"Is it working?" she asked.

"Nine of the last ten within six inches of center," Bryce replied proudly. "Even better if I'm closer."

"I couldn't get my knife to stick in the wood at any distance," Melissa snorted. She was sitting on a tree stump eating from a can. "Not with any of the other knives, and Bryce won't let me try his."

"Nope." Bryce said. "The way you throw, I'm afraid you'll break my knife."

"I guess we'll have to use our knives for cutting meat, if we ever have meat again," Beth said with a short bark of laughter.

"I see you didn't bring home any food," Melissa said.

"He has that whole field of corn," Lisa complained angrily, as Melissa handed her a can of something, and a spoon, "and it's spoiling on the stalk because he can't harvest it fast enough."

"Why didn't you just take some?" Melissa asked Beth.

"Pork and beans," Lisa said.

"What?" Beth asked distractedly, looking at Lisa, who held up her can so Beth could read the label. Beth turned back to Melissa.

"Stealing is wrong," Beth said, taking a half empty can of beans from Melissa. "I thought I'd give him a chance to share."

"How did that work out for you?" Melissa snorted.

"We're almost out of food," Beth said, thrusting her spoon in the can of beans, feeling it hit the bottom of the can. "We'll have to go back and steal some soon; but not when the farmers are out in their fields."

The Outcasts—Missouri, 8-11 August

Out of food, Beth, Melissa, Candy and Bryce went to a different field, late at night, hoping to avoid another encounter, especially with the same farmer. They worked separately, a little distance from each other, tearing cobs of corn off stalks and stuffing them into backpacks. Suddenly, the same farmer appeared out of the maze of corn stalks and confronted Melissa, shining a flashlight in her eyes.

"You have three seconds to be out of my sight before I start shooting. Three, two—" the farmer said, his handgun pointed at Melissa, ten feet away. Melissa didn't have time to react—she stood frozen in place—so he couldn't miss. "One," he said and fired, hitting Melissa in the chest and knocking her down.

He turned his gun on Candy, but his second shot went wild. His eyes got big, and he turned; and as he did, Beth could see the knife sticking out of his neck, with Bryce hurrying toward him from about fifteen feet away.

The farmer tried to reach the knife. He tried to speak. He could do neither. He collapsed in a heap as Bryce reached him and pulled the knife from his neck, wiping it quickly on the farmer's shirt and tucking it into his belt. Then he picked up the flashlight that lay on the ground, shined its light briefly into Melissa's dead eyes, then flashed it around the farmer's body on the ground.

"I can't see the gun," he whispered.

"Forget it," Beth said as she knelt next to Melissa and felt for a heartbeat. Then she looked at Bryce, shaking her head.

Bryce walked quickly away, picking up Melissa's backpack, as he headed for the path leading out of the field. Beth stood and turned to follow him, then noticed that Candy hadn't moved, but stared at Melissa's body, tears running down her cheeks.

Beth looked back at Melissa's body, then grabbed Candy's arm.

"Snap out of it. We have to leave before someone responds to the gunshot," she said.

Bryce returned and grabbed Candy around the waist, then the three of them fled, taking the corn with them. They ran all the way back to the barn.

"Where's Melissa?" Lisa asked.

"He shot her," Candy cried while trying to catch her breath from running. "He was going to shoot me, too." She buried her face in her hands. Bryce pulled her to him and wrapped his arms around her. She buried her face against his chest and continued to sob.

The others looked to Beth for an explanation, shock on their faces, but Beth was struggling with her own emotions and couldn't speak; she just shook her head and dropped onto a pile of hay to rest.

"We should leave, right now," Lisa said.

"And go where?" Beth asked, choking on her words and wiping tears from her eyes. She would miss Melissa's companionship and advice.

"What do you mean?"

"Which way do you want to go, back toward the men on the

bridge, or through the farm we just left, that might be full of armed men by now."

"Oh."

"Here's what I think," Bryce said. "We don't know what happened to Colin. If we go back across the bridge, we risk running into a group of possibly angry, possibly contaminated men who think they now have nothing to lose by attacking us."

Callie moaned and shivered. Lisa, sitting next to her in the hay, put an arm around her and pulled her close.

"If we wait a few days," Bryce continued, "there's a chance that things will calm down in Caruthers and we can sneak past. Of course, they could also come looking for us, in which case we better be prepared to defend ourselves or run."

"There are trees about fifty feet from the barn," Lisa said, "over by the highway. We could stay there tonight and watch the barn to see if anyone comes."

"We'll get more rest if we stay in the barn," Bryce replied.

"Then we better set a watch tonight," Lisa said. "We'll take the first watch. From the trees we'll be able to see any lights approaching from the highway or coming across the fields from the direction of Caruthers. We'll warn you if we see or hear anything."

Beth sat in the hay and cried silently. She could handle Karen's death, but not Melissa's. Were they all going to die? Would any of them find peace?

✵

"What happened to Caruthers?" Suzanne asked, "No one has come looking for the farmer's attackers."

"His murderers, you mean?" Candy asked.

"Candy," Beth scolded kindly, "we're not murderers. We tried to reason with him earlier, but he wouldn't listen. Bryce was just protecting us. He prevented you from being shot. But I'm surprised, too. That farmer had to have had family or friends. At the same time, I'm grateful they didn't come looking for us." Are we murderers? The question left her unsettled.

"I'm sorry, Beth," Candy said sadly. "You're right, of course. I think I was just upset about the violence. We've seen too much of it." Beth agreed.

After waiting three more days, just to be sure, Beth pushed them north, past Caruthers, toward St. Louis. They followed Interstate 55 to New Madrid, where Suzanne had said the 1811 earthquakes had started. They could see the Mississippi River again, where it made a huge double horseshoe bend. The river was no wider than it was at Memphis.

"The guy at the bridge said he thought the Ohio and Missouri Rivers had changed course," Beth said, looking at a map. "If we get off the Interstate and follow county roads, we can stay closer to the river and end up at the confluence of the Mississippi with the Ohio."

"That'll take us northeast instead of west," Bryce said, pointing at the map. "If we stay on Interstate 55, we get to St. Louis faster and may still be able to see what's happened to the Mississippi River."

"But we *could* miss it," Beth said, giving Bryce a dirty look. "It won't take us out of our way much."

"It's okay with me," he said, throwing his hands in the air.

No one else had an opinion, so Beth turned them northeast.

14

Nothing's going to go wrong

The Outcasts—Missouri, 14 August

"We're going way out of our way," Suzanne complained. They didn't tire easily, but this time they'd been chased for close to a mile. They'd finally stopped—bent over, holding their stomachs, and breathing heavily—in the front yard of an earthquake-damaged home on the outskirts of the town, without having replenished their food and water supplies.

"Do you have a better idea?" Beth asked when she could finally speak.

"Sorry," Suzanne said sarcastically, as she moved over to the front porch and sat on a wooden step. "You're the one who suggested that we go east, when what we really need is to go west to get to the Rocky Mountains."

Beth plopped down on the dead lawn next to Ben and gritted her teeth to keep from exploding. She already felt the stress of having made the—possibly bad—decision to go east instead of west. She didn't need to be reminded.

They'd traveled for days in a northeasterly direction, encountering earthquake damage and sometimes friendly, sometimes angry people. Beth, feeling personally responsible for Melissa's death, had been compelled to stop and help anyone she found sick or injured, who were friendly enough to allow it. Because of the shortage of clean water and antibiotics, she did what she could and moved on. How she missed Melissa.

"So, we're travelling through populated areas, competing for food and water with the locals, and trying to stay ahead of people who think we're diseased, or have something they need worse than we do, right?" Suzanne asked. Getting no response, she continued. "I'm too old to run all the way across the country. I think I'll just sit here and rest for a year or two."

"It's alright, Suzanne," Lisa said jokingly. "Let us know if we need to carry you. We need to keep up with the others."

Beth ignored Suzanne, and watched Bryce and Candy walk away from the group, wondering what they had in mind.

"You all need to see what's ahead of us," Bryce said, walking briskly back to them with Candy following, equally animated. He walked over to where Beth was trying to help Ben stand, put Ben's good arm—the one that wasn't in a sling—across his shoulders and helped him up, lifting him right off the ground because of their height difference.

"Ahhh!" Ben complained as his feet left the ground and he had to run on tiptoes to stay with Bryce.

Callie laughed, apparently amused by Ben's distress.

"Callie! That's delightful," Candy said, obviously embarrassing Callie, who looked down self-consciously. Candy touched Callie on the arm, affectionately.

"Was that Callie?" Beth asked, turning to look. She had also been watching Ben running on his tiptoes, but with concern, rather than amusement.

"Callie, you have a beautiful laugh," Candy continued. "I wish we had more to be happy about."

Callie looked up timidly and smiled tentatively.

"You've all been . . . so good to me. I haven't felt like I . . . really belonged since—" She couldn't finish, but Beth knew she meant since her parents had been killed in the gunfight at the shelter.

Callie looked down again. The others had heard the conversation, stopped, and watched without speaking.

"I could use a drink right now," Lisa said. Beth suspected that Lisa was intentionally drawing attention away from Callie, to allow her to recover from her embarrassment.

Beth looked in the direction Bryce had taken Ben, as she handed Lisa a bottle of water—their last.

"What's Bryce showing Ben," she asked Candy.

"I think it's the confluence with the Ohio River," Candy said. "I suggest we take a break before going on."

"Bryce," Beth replied when he and Ben returned, "you were about to tell us what you saw up ahead." She went to Ben and touched his bad arm carefully. "Are you okay?" she asked.

"No, I was going to show you," Bryce said. "I'll show you when you're through sitting around wasting daylight—well, half-daylight," he continued, looking around at the monotonously gray sky.

☢

From a hilltop, they could see the confluence of the Mississippi and Ohio Rivers. Most of the water that flowed beyond that point was from the Ohio, but even that had to be less than normal.

"Both rivers must be diverted, upstream," Candy said, noticing that Bryce seemed particularly upset. "Are you okay, Bryce?" she asked.

"I've always been fascinated by the Mississippi," Bryce said, suddenly looking away. "Mark Twain was my childhood hero." He turned back and made eye contact with Candy. "I dreamed of riding the river on a raft like Tom Sawyer. For my thirteenth birthday, my dad took me for a paddle boat ride."

Candy stared into his eyes, oblivious of the others watching them, and smiled.

☢

"There's another bridge at the confluence," Beth said, looking at a map, "and the roads on the east side of the Mississippi are closer to the river than on the west side, so we might be able to see what happened to the river if we cross here."

"If we cross here, won't we have to cross back, farther north, before we can go west?" Suzanne asked. "Maybe we should stay on this side."

Her question rattled Beth, as they usually did. She didn't understand it. Melissa had been right to challenge her attitude toward Suzanne, but what could she do about it? She couldn't stand her. Thinking of Melissa, Beth choked up and didn't trust herself to speak. While Beth struggled, Lisa spoke up in support of continuing and Bryce and Candy started walking toward the bridge, so Beth followed without a word—decision made—as it began to rain. The others followed, and by the time they reached the bridge they were in a drenching downpour.

They crossed the bridge without incident and continued toward St. Louis.

The Preserve, Aspen Valley, 15 August

"I still don't know, Mike," Katie said, concern etched on her face.

"You've got it down, babe," Mike said, giving her a quick kiss.

He'd been teaching her how to operate the Observer for several days now and they'd just completed her twentieth run-through on the controls; everything he could think of, including contingencies.

"Tell me again why you have to do this."

He'd been ready—and anxious—to step through the gate, but paused to reassure her.

187

"I need to know what happened to us in this other world," he said, forcing himself to appear calm. He worried that their parents might pull another surprise, middle-of-the-night visit to the lab and stop him before he could get started. "We didn't build the Preserve and Dad became an advisor to the president. Why? And what happened to your family?

"In today's newspaper that there's another article about the president, so I've got to get a copy and study it, to see if it tells me anything about my dad."

"Then why aren't you going *into* the store, instead of *in front* of it?"

"There's a copy on the ground in front of the store. I figured that if I took that one, it would be less like stealing." Mike said.

"Then why don't you just reach through and pick it up?"

"Don't you see? I've got to do this. Maybe I'll look around a little before coming back." At Katie's look of frustration, Mike stepped over to her and planted another kiss on her lips. "It will only take me ten seconds."

"Ooh, Mike," she said, "what if something goes wrong?"

"Nothing's going to go wrong," he said with a reassuring smile, "and if it does, you'll handle it just fine. Now, wish me luck." He leaned over and kissed her again.

"Be careful. I love you."

"I love you, too."

☢

Mike stepped through the gate into the deserted parking lot, in front of the Smiths grocery store. He turned to remind Katie to keep an eye on him, when a deep voice spoke from his right.

"Well, what do we have here?"

Mike spun around to face three men about his age, sitting cross-legged on the ground and leaning against the building, about fifteen feet away. They wore sleeveless t-shirts, and had long, dirty hair, tattoos, and multiple piercings. Smoke from whatever they were smoking—an unfamiliar smell—wafted past him.

There shouldn't have been anyone here. He'd checked out this location thoroughly, just fifteen minutes earlier.

He glanced around to see if he could spot the gate, but it had closed behind him—no sign of it.

"Katie," he called quietly in case she could see him, even though he couldn't see her.

"They call me Duke," the deep-voiced man said, chuckling, "not Katie. You have a friend with you, do you? Bring her out here so we can get to know her." His voice suggested what he had in mind. He stood slowly and moved casually toward Mike, the other two following and moving to either side of him.

Mike looked around again, this time for a way out. The few cars in the dimly lit lot were spread out, with no one around them. He considered running, but didn't want to turn his back on these three.

His mind raced. What had happened to the gate? Had Katie accidentally closed it? When it didn't reappear immediately, he wondered if she'd forgotten her instructions. Would she remember how to reopen it? Did she know he was in trouble? How had he missed seeing these guys, and how dangerous were they? *Come on Katie, get me out of here,* he thought.

He looked back at the three men. They had cut the distance to him in half, and had spread out, trying to cut off any escape.

Back in the lab, the last thing Katie heard as the gate shut down, was a deep male voice say, "What do we have here?" She realized immediately that Mike was in trouble.

"Mike," she called, but he didn't respond. "Mike, *Michael!*" she called again, frantically looking at the controls, and around the room, trying to figure out what had happened to the gate. Mike had shown her exactly what to do to minimize the portal without closing it completely, so she could monitor what he was doing and then open it again if he had to return quickly.

She tried to remember exactly what he'd said and shown her, but now she couldn't think clearly. She realized she was panicking.

"That won't help Mike," she thought aloud. "Get control of yourself."

She took several slow, deep breaths, to steady her nerves, shook both hands in the air, and tried to think.

Turn this knob to the left, but not all the way to the zero. She'd done that, and it still wasn't on the zero. To get it back, she had to turn it to the right. The larger the number, the larger the opening. She turned the knob but nothing happened.

Had she accidentally turned it all the way to zero without noticing?" She turned the knob back and forth several times with no result.

She made a frustrated sound and stomped her foot. She didn't know what to do. Mike had told his dad he wouldn't try this on his own. And he hadn't—she was here—but instead of helping, she was messing it up, and didn't know how to fix it. She started to cry.

"Mike, I'm so sorry," she whined.

Maybe she had accidentally kicked a plug or something. She looked around for a power cord and soon found one that came from the Observer. She followed it to the outlet on the floor, under the worktable. It looked okay. She got down on her hands and knees and crawled under the table, then wiggled it to see if it was plugged in all the way, which it was.

What else? She'd watched Mike input coordinates, but she didn't know enough about changing them to try it. Besides, he'd told her to leave them where they were.

She couldn't think of anything else to try.

Mike had told her they were doing this at night because he didn't want their parents to accidentally walk in and stop them, the way they had the last time. She realized she really wanted her dad or Amos to walk in right now, but they were probably sound asleep.

Why did Michael insist on doing this on his own and after midnight? She realized, with tears streaming down her cheeks, that if she didn't get help, she might lose Mike forever—and she was wasting time.

"I'm sorry Mike," she cried, as she ran from the room.

☢

Katie was screaming her dad's name by the time she reached his bedroom, which was much closer than Amos's. Terry whipped the bedroom door open before she reached it, grabbed her by both arms, and tried to calm his hysterical daughter.

"Mike went through the gate and I can't get him back!" she screamed through her tears.

"Becca," Terry called back into the bedroom, "get Amos to the lab and Lillie to control the family, so we don't have a panic." Then he ran, dragging Katie behind him.

☢

Amos arrived while Terry was still looking at the coordinates to see where Mike had gone. Katie was sitting on the edge of a chair, rocking back and forth, as she watched her dad and sobbed into her hands.

"You're here," Terry said. "Good. Katie, tell Amos what you told me."

Katie repeated everything Mike had told her about why he was going through the gate.

"He said it would only take him ten seconds to get the newspaper and step back through the gate," she bawled.

"What's your plan?" Amos asked Terry.

"I've reset the coordinates, in case they got messed up somehow. I'm ready to open the gate, above and on the far side of the parking lot. Ready?"

"Do it."

Terry opened the gate; a medium sized opening facing the front of the store, but thirty yards away and above it. He didn't immediately see them, but Katie let out a startled squeal.

"There," she said, pointing to the left side of the gate.

"Katie," Terry said sharply, "leave the room." He didn't want Katie to see what he saw—what was happening to Mike.

"Why?" Katie asked.

"Leave! Now!"

Amos stood between Katie and the gate and ushered her out of the room. She tried to look around him, but he moved with her to block her view. After he'd locked her out, he returned to stand by Terry.

"What did you see?" he asked, then he could see for himself. Terry had moved the gate closer to where Mike lay, balled up in a fetal position on the ground. Two of the three men kicked him, while the third leaned against a car, smoking, and all three laughed.

"Get around behind the blond one, where I can reach his ankle," Amos said.

Terry moved the gate immediately, without question. Maybe he'd guessed what Amos had in mind. He reduced the gate to fist size and moved around behind one of attackers, while Amos dimmed the lights in the lab.

When the gate was in position, Amos reached through and yanked on the foot that was supporting the attacker's weight, dropping him on his face on the pavement. The attacker rolled on the ground, holding the wrist that he'd used to break his fall, and screamed in pain.

The second attacker started to laugh and raised his foot to kick Mike again, then his foot came out from under him and he fell, turning sideways and landing on his shoulder. With both men on the ground, cursing and crying, the third man pushed off from the car, flicked his cigarette away, and took two steps forward.

"Stupid incompetents," he said as he approached Mike, who had stopped moaning, likely unconscious. He raised his foot over Mike's head, as if to stomp on it, when his other foot came out from under him and he fell forward, over Mike.

He rolled off Mike, onto his back, then a disembodied hand grabbed his neck and pressed a thumb into the soft tissue of his throat, cutting off his air. He tried to grab an arm, but nothing was attached to the hand. He flailed his arms through the air and began to panic. Then a voice spoke to him from out of nowhere.

"You worthless piece of garbage!" it said, menacingly. "I should choke you to death, right now."

Fueled by his fear, he rolled to the side—breaking the choke-hold—then stood and ran, coughing, not looking back to see what would happen to his associates.

Amos repeated his threat with the other two attackers, with similar results. The one with the injured hand rolled away, stood, and ran. The one with the injured shoulder tried to roll, but was in too much pain. When he started to cry, Amos felt like he'd scared him enough, and let go. The man was finally able to roll onto his good side, stand, and hobble away holding his shoulder with his opposite hand.

As soon as the last man had moved away, Terry maneuvered the gate to Mike's side and opened it far enough for Amos to perform a cursory check on Mike's vital signs and injuries. Then he ran to the hospital, using an emergency service tunnel not known to most of the family and returned with a gurney.

They lifted Mike—awkwardly, since they passed only their arms through the opening—onto the gurney. It frustrated Amos that they couldn't just move the gate past Mike and drop him onto the gurney; but they'd already discovered that a *moving gate* passed *through* stationary objects, and Mike could not move on his own power.

As they worked, they discussed their options, and the risks associated with moving Mike without thoroughly diagnosing his injuries. They agreed that the urgency of getting him to the hospital outweighed the need for more triage; besides, they could work on him while they transported him from the lab.

15

Is that a mirage?

Vice President Art Klemp, 20 August

"We'll have to search houses for food," Art said, with a warning look at Jean, who'd suggested it days earlier. Art hadn't wanted to take the time to find their own food, but he couldn't shoot everyone who refused to share what little they had.

"I see houses through the trees on this side of the road," Dayron said helpfully. "It looks like there's a street just ahead."

Art led them into the neighborhood and approached the first house on the street. He knocked on the door but no one answered. Was it empty? Was everyone dead? Would he find stinking, decomposing bodies inside?

"The curtains moved," M.C. said.

"What?" Art asked, distracted by the sound of her voice and looking at her.

M.C. pointed at the curtained window to the left of the front door, but the curtains were no longer moving. Art knocked again, then tried the doorknob. Finding the door locked, he pulled out his gun and shot the lock—the door squeaked open an inch, then Art waved Dayron through the opening. Dayron pulled out his own gun, pushed the door open slowly with his other hand and looked around the door.

Suddenly, someone slammed into the door from the other side. Dayron's head banged into the door frame and he fell outside, his nose bloodied, as the door closed. Art pushed on the door, feeling resistance, then fired several rounds through the door. A quiet 'umph' from the other side let him know that he'd hit whoever was behind it. He gave it a hard shove and it opened a foot, stopping against a body that lay across the opening.

Art stooped to check on Dayron, finding him unconscious, laying on his side, blood running from his nose.

"One of you stop the bleeding and the other come with me," he said, and waved the women forward. M.C. knelt down next to Dayron, but Art didn't wait to see how she handled the situation. He waved Jean through the door, then followed.

"I think they left," Jean said, as a door slammed somewhere in the back of the house. "There should be a pantry near the kitchen."

Art followed Jean into the kitchen and watched, as she went through the cupboards and pantry, removing things she thought they could use and setting them on the kitchen table. Art looked around, through doorways and out the back window, holding his gun in front of him, *just in case*. When he looked back, Jean was filling a backpack with the things she'd found.

He let her finish, then moved back toward the front door, only then stopping to examine the man he'd shot. He'd hit him three times in the chest and abdomen. Nudging him with the toe of his shoe—the man didn't move—he stepped over him and out the door. Dayron sat in a porch chair, his head tilted back, holding his damp, bloody shirttail against his face. Jean was gone.

"Where is she?" he asked. Dayron looked puzzled, then must have realized Art meant Jean.

"She went to check the garage," Dayron said, his voice sounding funny. "She wondered if they had a car that worked."

Art rounded the corner of the house as Jean was returning.

"Well?" he asked.

"There's a car and the key's in the ignition, but it won't start."

"Then let's go," he said and started walking away, assuming that Jean, Dayron and M.C. would follow.

The Preserve, 20 August

"You've all heard that Mike had an accident the other night," Amos told those who had gathered in the community center.

"We figured that out from all the shouting in the middle of the night," Jason said. "Why'd you take so long to tell us?"

"I'm not prepared to go into details about the accident just yet, but we need to make some adjustments to work assignments, until things get back to normal."

"Why can't you give us the details?"

"Because we don't *know* all the details and what we *do* know is personal." Amos knew he was stretching the truth again, but there was no way he was going to tell Jason about their discoveries. "We need to be sensitive to the feelings of those involved, so I would appreciate you not speculating about it. Mike will tell us what he wants us to know, when he's prepared to talk about it." He also didn't want to tell them that he'd placed Mike in an induced coma, to allow his body to recover from a concussion, six broken or cracked ribs, a herniated disk, multiple cuts and abrasions, and bruised kidneys; that would only invite questions that he didn't want to answer. Mike might not be in any condition to talk for weeks or months, and this might be the best way to keep people from trying to get more information about the accident, the Observer, and their research. He hoped the whole thing would blow over without the details coming out.

"Mike's in the hospital, so we'll need extra help in the gardens until he's better. Terry, Lillie and I will take turns monitoring his condition. Needless to say, Katie will also be spending time in the hospital with him. What we need is for Emily to give Lillie more help managing the Preserve. We also need Matt to take over the gardens. Matt, you'll have the work teams to help you on a daily basis, and we'll put a hold on your medical training, so it isn't a distraction." What Amos wanted was to remove any reason Matt might have to interact with Mike in the hospital before Amos was ready. "Rachel, you'll need to take over Rylee's and Sydney's education until Katie can help again."

Jason opened his mouth to say something. Amos suspected, from the look on his face, that he was going to raise the issue of his management experience again, and insist that he be allowed to take Lillie's duties, so Amos went on quickly while looking directly at him.

"I'll also be more visible in the day-to-day operations of the Preserve, to help Emily, Matt and Rachel. Each of you can manage your own exercise programs while Katie's preoccupied, but I'll spend more time in each area to answer questions and offer suggestions.

"Now, any questions?"

"Did Katie get hurt, too?" Rachel asked.

"No, she didn't, Rachel."

"And you're not going to tell us how he got injured, or how serious the injury is?" Jason asked.

"No. Any other questions?"

"Well," Jason said, "that doesn't leave much room for questions."

"Fine," Amos said bluntly. "We'll give you regular updates when we have them."

☢

"Mom." Rachel hurried after Lillie as they left the meeting. "What happened to Mike?"

"You heard your father, Rachel. We're not in a position to say anything, yet. Give it some time."

"I thought that was intended for the others. He's my brother. You can tell me."

"You better wait for your father." Lillie hurried off, leaving Rachel standing, with a surprised look on her face.

The Outcasts—Missouri, 21 August

"Is that a mirage?" Candy asked. Beth had stopped to study the horizon to the north and east, where it appeared that the dim morning sunlight reflected off large bodies of water.

"If it's not, that may explain where the Mississippi River diverted to," Bryce replied, sharing a smile with her.

"What city is that?" Lisa asked Beth, as she had each time they approached a town of any size.

"Waterloo is just ahead of us," Beth said, looking at her map. "We're about 20 miles south of St. Louis."

"There must be more people here," Lisa said, pointing. "That window has been boarded up and those fallen trees have been cut up and moved aside."

"I see what you mean," Bryce said. "Someone has propped up that wall with plywood and dimension lumber."

"It stinks of death," Suzanne said, "just like everywhere else."

"But it's not as bad as it's been," Bryce said.

"Look!" Lisa said, "There are some people."

"I don't see anybody," Suzanne said.

"They were there, but they moved behind that house."

"Let's not go looking for them," Beth said, "and let's hope they don't come looking for us." She thought about all the people she'd tried to help—had helped. There was a never-ending supply of them and she was running out of medical supplies. Then there were those angry people who chased them. No, they were better off to avoid other people.

"This wind and fire damage are similar to what we saw in Memphis," Candy said as they got closer to Waterloo.

"Wow!" Bryce said, looking farther ahead. "There's water covering everything as far as you can see."

"That's where St. Louis should be," Beth said, consulting her map again. "No city. No Gateway Arch. There must have been an explosion here too, to cause this much damage. I wonder if anyone escaped before the rivers backed up."

"That's the Interstate 255 bridge ahead of us," Beth said as she waded through knee-deep, oily, opaque water full of charred wood, tree limbs and other debris from the fires and explosions, pushed by the gentle waves of this new Lake St. Louis. In the half-light, Beth noticed that Candy walked next to Bryce, holding on to his arm and taking mincing steps—testing the ground ahead with each foot—before committing herself to take a step. She had slowed down so much that everyone caught up.

Bryce had a concerned expression on his face. The last time they'd walked in knee-deep water, they'd almost lost Candy.

"It's okay, Sheryl," Bryce said, using Candy's given name, which he preferred over her stage name. "I'm right here and I'm holding onto you."

"Stop," Beth said, holding up a hand and looking around. "We need a plan to avoid an accident."

"What are you doing?" Lisa asked.

"Looking for a pole to test the water ahead of us," Beth said.

"I saw a thick tree branch floating in the water back a little way," Lisa said. "I'll go get it."

"Be careful. Take Kerri with you and hold on to each other," Beth said. Lisa and Kerri looked at each other, then locked arms and walked back to where Lisa had seen the tree branch.

"Candy, I'm sorry," Beth said. "Would you like someone to go ahead of you?"

"We'll be fine with a pole to test the water for holes," Bryce said. "Won't we, baby?" Candy nodded cautiously, still holding tightly to Bryce's arm with both hands. She closed her eyes for a moment and swallowed hard, likely reliving the horrible experience of almost drowning.

Lisa ripped smaller branches and twigs from the main branch before handing it to Bryce. With his free hand, Bryce used the branch to test the water ahead and to both sides for depth and underwater hazards. They stayed on the crown of the highway, where the water would be the shallowest, with the others following directly behind.

The water didn't get any deeper than Bryce's knees; but twice Bryce warned them of fallen trees lying across the roadway that they had to step over. They steered clear of anything that looked suspicious, like body parts.

As they approached the interstate, it looked to Beth like a giant snake emerging from the lake on the right, rising up to swallow the bridge on the left. The Mississippi riverbed was dammed up a few hundred yards north of the bridge; a huge berm of earth that extended as far as they could see in both directions, backing up water. The top of the berm looked to be a few feet above the bridge deck and the water level was obviously near the top of the berm, since water leaked over the top and seeped through in places. The charred bridge leaned dangerously to the south, away from the berm, as though an angry giant had kicked it with a very large foot. The steel girders were twisted worse than the Caruthers bridge.

"That dam looks like it won't hold back water much longer," Bryce said.

"Why do you say that?" Candy asked.

"It's not compacted like a normal dam. When the water goes over the top, it will erode the dirt, washing it away."

"Then nothing will stop all that water from flowing downstream, right underneath us."

"Hopefully we'll be across the bridge before the berm fails; but yeah, when it fails, the water will escape downstream, probably in a gushing torrent. It could cause crazy flooding all the way to Louisiana."

"What would it do to the bridge?"

"It could be washed away, too," Bryce said, looking from one end of the bridge to the other. "This bridge has been seriously compromised. I don't know what it would take to bring it down."

Beth had the same thought. She studied the bridge, trying to decide if it could be crossed and how long it would take them. She didn't want to be on it if—when—it collapsed.

Stalled cars and trucks jammed the west-bound lanes—obviously people trying to get away from the city before the explosions. They had all slid sideways toward the median. There were fewer vehicles in the east-bound lanes and they, too, had slid across the tilted lanes and come to rest at the damaged walkway and railing. From the gaps in the barrier between the west- and east-bound lanes, and the one gap they could see in the railing on the low side of the bridge, Beth figured that at least one car—maybe a heavy truck—had crashed through the barriers and fallen off the bridge.

"If we stay on the left side walkway," Beth finally said, "where there are fewer obstacles, I'm sure we can work our way across." Her words sounded more confident than she felt.

"I'm scared," Callie said quietly.

"Me, too," Candy agreed. "I don't think I can do it."

"I'll help you," Bryce said, smiling at Candy.

"I knew we should have stayed on the other side of the river," Suzanne said, "instead of crossing at the confluence with the Ohio."

A nasty retort came to Beth's mind, but she constrained herself. It would be stressful enough getting over this bridge, without her contributing to it.

"Bryce," Beth said, "if you'll lead, I'll bring up the rear."

They started across, holding onto the railing. Candy, holding Bryce's hand and shuffling carefully along next to him on the tilted surface, stopped at the gap in the handrail halfway across the bridge and refused to continue because there was nothing to grip for safety.

"I knew this would come in handy," Bryce said. Pulling a coiled rope out of his backpack, he walked back through the group, tying everyone together to form a human chain.

"Look!" Lisa said, concern in her voice as she pointed at the earthen dam to their right.

Beth saw what troubled Lisa. Water had started to flow over the top of the dam and was quickly deteriorating the berm in several places. Near the eastern end, where they had passed minutes before, a waterfall of muddy water cut into the wall, cascading down the face of the dam, carrying dirt and rocks with it, the noise making her nervous.

"Don't worry," Beth said, trying to reassure everyone, including herself. "Let's just keep moving."

As each person passed the narrow gap in the railing, mincing along to prevent slipping, one eye on the deteriorating wall of earth, the others held on to anything they could find that gave them purchase.

Suddenly the bridge shook and women screamed. Beth looked back and saw that the eastern end of the bridge had been undercut by the now raging waterfall. She realized that the rising background noise she heard was from the increasing torrent of water which cascaded over the dam and had begun to fill the riverbed. If the bridge supports failed, she feared that they would all fall to their deaths.

Without warning, Suzanne lost her footing and slid toward the gap.

"Help," she called desperately, as her feet slid off the side of the bridge. She dangled from the waist, over the edge; held in place by Callie, a few feet in front of her, and Ben behind.

Then Callie lost her grip and was dragged backward.

"Nooo," she cried, the sound lost in the noise from the waterfall, as she scrambled frantically for a foot- or hand-hold. She snagged a door handle as she slid past a car, jerking her arm, and causing her to cry out painfully. Kerri, ahead of her, wrapped her arms and legs around a tilted bridge column, and held on tightly.

Ben moaned at the pain in his shoulder, as he held on to a car wheel well, straining to hold Suzanne's weight.

Suzanne slipped again and caught the edge of the bridge with her fingers; a thin lip of metal.

"Help me," she whimpered, as she hung suspended in the air, looking down at the raging river below.

Beth worked her way forward, to take hold of the rope ahead of Ben, while Bryce, in the lead, worked his way back past the others, toward Callie.

"Give me your hand," Bryce told Callie, calmly. With panic in her eyes, Callie reached toward his hand, nearly losing her grip on the door handle. Bryce stretched farther, grabbed Callie's wrist, and slowly pulled her toward him, while she tried to get her feet under her. She was so close to Suzanne, whose wailing had diminished to quiet sobbing, that Beth feared she would accidentally kick one of Suzanne's hands, knock her loose, and drag them all off the bridge.

Bryce held on to a car frame with one hand while pulling Callie slowly toward him with the other.

"Beth," Bryce called, "let me pull them to this side of the gap."

Beth, who'd been pulling on her end of the rope, saw the wisdom in his comment immediately. If she pulled Suzanne to her, Suzanne would have to cross the gap again. Instead, Beth held the tension on the rope, concentrating on keeping the stress off Ben's shoulder, and let it out slowly as Bryce pulled it toward him. Lisa held Bryce's belt and pulled each time Bryce adjusted his stance.

Bryce focused on pulling Callie to him until Lisa cried out from behind him.

"Suzanne!" Lisa yelled.

His eyes flew to Suzanne, who was slipping out of the rope tied around her waist. It had already slipped up to her chest and she couldn't move her hands from the edge of the bridge to take hold of it. In his surprise, he almost let go of Callie; but she held onto his arm with both of hers.

Finally, Bryce pulled Callie against him.

"Thank you," Callie said. They looked into each other's eyes and Bryce smiled to cover his concern.

"Take Lisa's hand," he said with forced calm, his arm still around her. "I'll help Suzanne."

As Callie moved to pass Bryce, the ground shook again, and Callie squeezed Bryce tightly with both arms. Suzanne lost her grip, slipped out of the rope, and fell away from the bridge.

"No!" Beth yelled as the rope went slack and Suzanne screamed in terror. Beth would forever wonder if she heard the splash of Suzanne hitting the water, felt it in the vibration of the bridge or just imagined it. She shivered at the thought. The world stopped for a moment as she prayed for Suzanne and asked forgiveness for all her unkind thoughts.

When her world started moving again, Beth looked at the others and saw her own fear reflected in their faces. Callie hugged her savior, Bryce, who then passed her off to Lisa. He took a quick look over the edge of the bridge then made eye contact with Beth. She thought his expression said Suzanne was dead.

"Let's keep moving," he called. "Keep the slack out of the rope." Beth watched the rope between Callie and Ben go tight, the loop between them now empty where Suzanne should have been. Tears came to her eyes and spilled over, running down her cheeks. She had to blink several times to see well enough to continue.

"Maybe I should come over there and tie myself between you two," Bryce yelled, looking over at Beth and Ben, who were the last in line.

"No," Ben said. "Just give me a couple more minutes to catch my breath."

"You don't have to be a hero," Bryce said. "Let me help you."

"It's okay," Ben said, still breathing heavily. He opened his eyes and looked at Bryce with a nervous smile. "I got good shoes. It's all in the shoes."

"You jerk," Bryce snorted. "If you make us all fall and we don't die, I'll kill you."

"You got it," Ben said as he pushed himself ahead of Beth, preparing to cross the gap. "I'll even help you."

Bryce shook his head and tightened his grip on the rope. Just then, the bridge shook again, violently, and Ben stopped moving. He looked into Beth's eyes and she saw the insecurity he must be feeling and hiding with false bravado; then he looked back at Bryce.

"Whenever you're ready," Ben said. The others kept the slack out of the rope so Bryce could release and get a new grip every few moments.

Ben's face registered his torture from the pain in his arm. He was breathing raggedly, his eyes closed. But he must have been right about the shoes; he crossed the gap without incident. Then he helped Bryce pull Beth across, where she threw her arms around Ben and hugged him, laying her head against his chest. He returned the hug awkwardly.

"Thank you, Ben," she said, listening to his pounding heart—or was it hers?

"We gotta' go," Bryce said anxiously, just as the bridge shook again, this time feeling like it had begun to settle at the eastern end. They followed the others quickly to the far end of the bridge, where the bridge deck leveled out, but didn't stop to rest until they had cleared the bridge and were standing on solid ground. Beth sat between Ben and Bryce, breathing heavily from relief rather than from exertion.

"Should we go check Suzanne," she asked so only Bryce could hear, already suspecting that if she had survived the fall, she would have been washed downstream.

"Suzanne's dead," he responded so everyone could hear. "There's no doubt," he added. He didn't explain how he knew and no one asked for details.

The ground beneath them shook violently as the bridge structure started to fall toward the right—the downstream side. Metal screeched as girders bent and anchors broke out of the concrete bridge abutment. Where there had been several v-shaped gaps in the rim of the dam, where water cascaded over the edge, now a huge section, from the far end to the middle, busted out, allowing a deluge of water to shoot out into the air, smash against the metal and concrete structure, and splash in all directions. They were showered by the spray.

They scrambled farther from the end of the bridge, then stopped to watch as it collapsed into the roiling mass of muddy water before being dragged, bucking and screaming down the chasm. Beth sat, open-mouthed, her heart pounding in her chest, as the dam failed and millions of gallons of muddy, rock-filled water rushed past. The mist-filled wind caused by the movement of earth and water, blew their hair and tore at their clothes, a solemn reminder of the power of nature.

"That was too close," Beth thought out loud, then heard crying and turned to see Candy leaning against Bryce, crying into his chest as he rubbed her back. Kerri and Lisa cried on each other's shoulder. Callie sat stoically, staring straight ahead, appearing almost catatonic, with tears streaming down her face. Ben scooted closer to Beth and placed his good arm around her shoulders. When she turned to look at him, he wiped a tear from her cheek and, still breathing heavily, smiled.

16

A world in chaos

The Outcasts—St. Louis, Missouri, 22 August

"We need to make a decision," Beth said. "There's less damage on the West side of the freeway. Should we stay on the interstate or look for shelter in a neighborhood."

When they'd left the bridge, they'd discovered that the entire downtown area to the north and most of the surrounding suburbs were under water, their populations—almost three million people—gone or dead.

The concrete on the bridge apron had been shattered from the heat. The asphalt had bubbled and burned. Beth could still taste the grit in the hazy air and feel it on her skin, even weeks after the explosion.

To the west and southwest, she could see the damaged homes and buildings and smell the fires. She had no way to tell how many people had stayed in the area; she saw nothing moving except a few trees—those that hadn't blown over—swaying in the breeze. She had pushed them as hard as Ben's injury would allow, walking alongside to help him, to see if conditions would improve farther west.

Now, as the freeway curved toward the north, it appeared to sink into the floodwater. Convinced that her last decision had killed Suzanne, Beth wanted someone else make the decision on where to go from here.

"I vote we sleep in cars on the freeway," Candy said.

"We need food and water," Bryce said, hugging Candy and smiling possessively at her, "and we don't have much daylight left. Let's take the next off ramp and look for shelter."

Relieved that Bryce had made the decision for her, Beth led them along a residential street not far from the freeway entrance. Every home looked damaged, with roofs blown off and walls caved in. Trees were uprooted or broken off like matchsticks, some lying across cars and houses. At first, no one was in sight, but before long they began to see signs of life.

"Look," Lisa said, pointing to a bicycle standing upright, as though recently ridden.

"Over there," Kerri said quietly.

"What?" Beth asked.

"Somebody stacked boards next to that door," Lisa answered for Kerri. "Looks like they're trying to clean up."

"And there's a tent set up in that backyard, next to a cold campfire," Bryce said.

"Hmm . . . " Beth said. "Maybe all the homes are occupied here. Maybe we'll have to look somewhere else."

They reached an intersection and stopped abruptly. A tent city filled a vacant lot that looked like it had once been a neighborhood park. Broken trees had been piled around the perimeter of the lot, forming a partial visual barrier. A break in the barrier faced them across the street, 12 feet wide and about 50 feet away. Two people, a man and a woman, stood on either side of the entrance; whether guards or greeters, Beth couldn't tell.

"Should we go over?" Bryce asked.

"I say we turn around or go another direction," Lisa said.

The man at the barrier noticed them immediately and picked up a baseball bat that leaned against a nearby tree trunk. The woman turned and called out to someone inside the barrier. Within seconds, three men appeared in the opening, walking quickly. They stopped just outside the opening, facing the Outcasts.

"Identify yourselves, please," the one in the middle called politely.

"I don't like it," Lisa whispered to Beth. "I think we should leave, quickly.

"I'm Beth," Beth called, waving her arms to either side. "These are my friends. We're travelling"—she was going to say to the Rocky Mountains, then changed her mind— "west. We need to find a place to spend the night."

"Do you have something to trade?"

"Like what?"

"Food, water, medical supplies."

"Tell him no," Lisa said quietly. "Maybe they just want to rob us."

Beth turned to look Lisa in the eyes, and saw her disquiet. When she looked back, one of the men turned away from the spokesman as though he had just said something to him. Maybe Lisa's right, she thought. Maybe they have a one-sided trade in mind.

"No," Beth called, looking back at Lisa. "We were hoping for a meal as well."

The spokesman nodded to the men next to him, who then turned and disappeared into the maze of the tent city.

"We can probably manage that," the man said slowly, in contrast to his earlier abruptness. Why did it sound like he was trying to delay them? "We usually require something in exchange," the man continued slowly, "but I'm feeling generous. You look like you could really use some empathy today. Come on over and we'll find something for you."

Beth and Lisa made eye contact again. Lisa mouthed, "let's go".

"Maybe we'll just move along," Beth said, remembering her decision to let the others help with the decisions. Besides, her gut told her something was wrong with the man's offer. She turned and motioned for the others to follow.

"Wait!" the man called anxiously. "I just sent my counselors to find a place for you."

"Beth," Lisa said, nodding down the street to their left. Beth turned in time to see a man cross the street, a block away, and disappear behind a house. "There were four of them."

Beth looked down the street in the other direction to see if they were being flanked.

"Don't mind them," the man called out anxiously, and continued talking; but Beth had quit listening. It was obvious that the man knew what they were seeing and Beth was now convinced he had unfriendly intentions.

"Knives out," Beth said, making eye contact with Lisa again and nodding. She turned back toward the freeway, with the others following. Ben was holding his arm, which slowed him down, so Beth placed an arm around his waist and tried to help him. They'd just reached the first cross street, when they saw the four men approaching from the right at a run.

"Bryce, take the rear," Beth said, starting to jog and nearly dragging Ben.

☢

Bryce nodded and slowed long enough to let the others pass, then picked up his pace. He could tell when the first man caught up, from his heavy breathing. He turned quickly, braced himself for an impact, and held his knife in front of him at chest level. The man had raised a large club over his head and was swinging it down at Bryce, as Bryce raised his other arm to protect his head and shoulders.

They were eye-to-eye and Bryce could tell the man was startled by the sudden confrontation. It appeared the man didn't know he'd run into Bryce's knife, burying it all the way to the hilt in his chest, until Bryce retracted it, covered with the man's blood, and stepped back.

The man looked down at the knife, then at his chest, which pumped blood from a punctured artery. The fight went out of him and he collapsed, the club bouncing away. The other three men stopped suddenly, alternately looking at Bryce and their fallen associate. Bryce turned and ran to catch up to the other Outcasts, looking over his shoulder once, to verify that the three men had given up the chase.

They locked themselves into cars on the freeway for the night, as Lisa had suggested earlier.

"I won't be able to sleep," Beth said as she helped Ben into the front seat of a crew cab pickup truck, then began climbing in next to him. She had selected a truck that sat where she could see the off-ramp, so she could alert the others if anyone came up the ramp.

"Me neither," Lisa said from beside her as she, Kerri and Callie piled into a nearby SUV. "I'll be awake all night. We'll take the first watch."

Beth relayed Lisa's message to Bryce and Candy, who waved in acknowledgement without turning to look at her.

The Outcasts—Missouri, 23 August

Bryce banged on the hood of the truck, waking Beth and Ben. Beth had raised the center console to convert the front seats to a bench and reclined the seats as far back as they would go. She was sitting close to Ben, leaning her head against his good shoulder, with his arm around her. Dim sunlight shown through the windows from a weak sun on the horizon.

"I thought you were going to wake one of us," Bryce said as Beth opened her door.

"I'm sorry," Beth said, trying to apologize. "I fell asleep. Ben—"

"Forget about it," Bryce said. "No harm, no foul. None of us slept well. I'm sure I would have heard if anyone had come by."

They gathered to share what food was left. Beth sat close to Ben, thinking about each person they'd lost. She wasn't too upset about Pepper and Jordan leaving them. Losing Karen was difficult, but losing Melissa was excruciating. And she felt so guilty about how she'd treated Suzanne that she didn't think she would ever get over it.

"You thinking about Suzanne?" Lisa asked.

"And Melissa and Karen," Beth said.

"Yeah. Tough, isn't it? Everyone's depressed this morning. I guess the run-in with the men from the tent city last night affected all of us. Do you want to give up?"

Beth wondered what she meant by "give up". It must have shown on her face, since Lisa corrected herself. "I mean, are you going to be okay?"

Beth realized that if she wasn't strong, they might all decide to "give up". She straightened up and gave Lisa a nod. Lisa smiled.

Ben grimaced as Beth tied his arm back into a sling to reduce motion and gave him a couple of pain pills with a drink of water—their last.

"How are you doing Ben?" she asked with genuine concern.

"Great," Ben said through gritted teeth.

"Let me know if you need anything," she said, laying her hand against his chest. "Anything."

They made eye contact and Beth thought she saw in his eyes, for the first time, realization that she must like him more than as a friend.

"Okay, folks," Beth said, turning toward the group, "let's put as much distance as possible between us and St. Louis."

When the interstate turned north, they exited and headed west, toward Kansas City. They learned how to get food by raiding fields at night, after setting a lookout to watch for farmers, so they seldom went hungry. They filtered river water through a piece of cloth. Beth didn't worry about bacteria. How could they be worse off than they were already?

As the days passed, they settled into a routine. They had some tense moments, avoiding farmers, but no confrontations. When they stopped at night, Beth would study the maps they'd picked up along the way, looking for a destination that looked suitable for outcasts. It was a big country and they were on foot; inspiration didn't come easily.

Beth started noticing references on the maps to the Old Oregon Trail, which headed west from Kansas City. She'd heard of the Oregon Trail but didn't know much about it. Being this close, she looked for and found a trail map at a convenience store. It showed cities and historic sites along the trail that had become tourist attractions.

"What are you looking at," Lisa asked during one meal break.

"The Oregon Trail passes by here a little to our north. The more I read about it, the more interested I am in following it."

"It goes to Oregon, obviously; but other than that, why the interest?"

"The people who settled the northwest, including the Rocky Mountains, used the Oregon Trail to get there. They didn't have cars or roads back then. They either walked, like we are, or rode in wagons." Kerri and Callie looked over when they heard Beth's response.

"Wasn't that a long time ago?" Lisa asked. "Is the trail still there?"

"A large portion of the trail has been obscured by time. But in places you can still see it. And there are tourist stops in a few places that look interesting."

"You want to go to tourist attractions?" Kerri asked, then laughed. "Do you think you're on a vacation or something?"

Beth chuckled self-consciously. "No. I just think it's interesting that we have to travel just like people did back in the nineteenth century. It would be interesting to see how they did it. Some of the tourist stops have artifacts of their travels."

"So," Lisa said with amusement, warming to the subject, "you want to follow the Oregon Trail, to see how people over a hundred years ago traveled thousands of miles on foot."

"Well, they didn't have to deal with nuclear fallout. And actually, it was over a hundred and fifty years ago," Beth said. "But yes, I want to see how they traveled. Think about it. The world progressed for over 150 years to what we all knew and loved. Then, in less than two weeks, we left that world and we're back in this other world; a world of yesterday."

"Which one's real?" Lisa asked sarcastically.

"The one we're in now," Beth said. "a world in chaos."

"Separated by two weeks and lots of bad government decisions," Lisa said.

"You're romanticizing," Bryce said, coming up and standing by the group that had formed around Beth. He had his arm around Candy's waist.

"Maybe so," Beth replied. "But aren't we pioneers of a sort?"

"That we are," he replied with a snort.

"Look, that's the direction we want to go, so it's not really out of our way. And, it'll get us off the highways."

"Yeah," Bryce replied as others nodded in agreement, "most of our problems so far have been near the interstate."

"Well, you can't say our travels have been boring," Lisa said, "but it would be nice to travel without running into hostile people or damaged bridges. There aren't big bridges on the Oregon Trail, are there?"

"Not that I can see," Beth said. "We'll just have the Rocky Mountains to cross."

"Oh, just the largest mountain range in North America." Candy said sarcastically.

"I wish we could just go back to the way things were," Callie said quietly.

"There's nothin' to go back to," Candy said wistfully, possibly thinking about her lost performing career.

"Unless you want a bullet in the head," Bryce added, obviously thinking about the gunfight in the Johns Creek shelter.

"Well, what do you think about following the Oregon Trail?" Beth asked, trying to recapture their attention.

"Why not?" Lisa asked. "Anyone have anything better to do?"

There were mumbles and grumbles, but no one else had a strong opinion.

"It'll get us off the highways," Beth said. "It'll be better. You'll see. I'll let you know each time we're approaching a historic site, and I'll tell you what happened there, ok?" Beth was trying to build some enthusiasm for the trip.

"I've never had this much endurance," Lisa said, seemingly ignoring Beth's effort. "I'm feeling healthier, with more strength than I can ever remember."

"I knew you were going to say that," Kerri said. She and Lisa had been joking about being able to read each other's minds—telepathy—for several days.

The Preserve, 23 August

"Have you figured out why the gate shut down on Mike?" Amos asked Terry, who was looking over a printout from the Observer.

"I think so."

"Well?"

"Just a minute, Amos. This programming language isn't as easy for me to follow as it is for Mike. I'm confirming my hypothesis, then I'll explain."

Amos paced the office for a minute, then sat at his desk and drummed his fingers on the desktop, ran his hand through his hair, and coughed.

"I didn't get a real good look, but one of the attackers looked enough like Nathan Carlsen that it could have been his brother," Amos said, standing and pacing again.

"Aaron?" Terry asked, without looking up from his papers. "The one that was in the collision with the Parkers' SUV?"

"I'm not positive, but that's my guess. The ringleader looked tougher—hardened—the criminal type." Finally losing patience, Amos added, "What are you doing, Terry?"

"Hold your horses, pardner," Terry said. "Almost done." Finally, Terry looked up and smiled.

"Well?"

"I've been comparing readouts from the Observer during Mike's little foray into the unknown, with the readouts from the two times you two put your arms through the gate. I also looked at the program, line by line, to try to understand what I was seeing in the readouts."

"Get to the point," Amos said, making Terry smile.

"Okay. I think what affected the gate when Mike went through, was a small electrical charge that changed the settings. I can see a small change in the readings at the time he went through."

"Caused by his body's natural electrical impulses," Amos guessed. "What about when we put our arms through?" he asked excitedly.

"The same type of charge, but a lower magnitude."

"Because the SA node is near the heart."

"That's my conclusion, but I wanted to checked all the readouts before telling you."

"Can we compensate or control it?"

"That could take some time to figure out, but I'll design some experiments, and run the plans past you, before we test them."

"Anything else?" Amos asked excitedly.

"Yes. While I was checking the readouts for low magnitude charges, I found more than just those two excursions."

"Meaning?"

"I think Mike reached through the gate more than once. The other *seven times* were at night."

Amos gritted his teeth, realizing that Mike had planned his trip through the gate some time ago.

"Thanks, Terry. I'll have to think about this."

Prime Bunker, 28 August

"What's the emergency, Jim?" the president asked sourly, looking at the monitors on the wall across the table. He was beginning to hate this room because it reminded him of the military's failure—his failure—to stop the nuclear bombs that destroyed three bunkers and killed hundreds of government leaders as he watched, many of whom were personal friends.

"I received an update from the Army Corps of Engineers regarding the blockage on the Mississippi River," SecDef James Seymour said. In Jim's last report, he'd said that the Corps had yet to figure out a way to drain the water from behind the berm wall blocking the river above the Interstate 255 bridge south of St. Louis.

"Do they have a plan for draining it?"

"It's a moot point now, Greg. The river—or should I say ocean—of water that was backed up, overflowed the dam three days ago. It disintegrated the dam—what we feared—and washed everything downstream, along with the bridge. I ordered helicopter overflights as soon as I heard about the breach . . . "

"When was that?" the president interrupted.

"Yesterday morning. According to the army spokesperson, the floodwater has scoured the river bottom and carved a new path. Farther downstream, the water has spread out and slowed. The flooding is the worst ever recorded, and the volume of debris carried on the flood and left in its wake as the water receded, is staggering."

"Casualties?" Greg asked, feeling helpless.

"No idea," Jim said. "We don't know how many people were in the way. I'm waiting for a report on the flood's impact downstream.

Greg closed his eyes and thought about the conversation he'd had with Jim about losing his soul. Was there a threshold on how many deaths he could cause before God sent him to hell? He folded his hands under the table to stop them from shaking.

"Greg," DNI Tom Mitchell said, to get the president's attention, "I have an update on the smallpox epidemic. Would you like to hear it?"

Greg nodded his head, not trusting himself to speak.

"We're seeing cases of smallpox in Mississippi, Tennessee and Missouri," Tom said, "generally along the Mississippi River, and as far north as St. Louis. That's besides the reports in the northeast and along the east coast."

"Is that the old Mississippi River or the new one?" Greg asked sarcastically, his voice shaky. No one laughed or responded.

"I think we can blame the missing occupants of the Johns Creek shelter," HomeSec Chuck Dickson finally said, breaking the silence. When Greg stared at him, he added, "for the wide and rapid spread of the virus."

"I'm sure we can blame Art Klemp and the scientists from the Ft. Detrick facility for the spread of the virus along the east coast," Jim said. "I have a hard time believing those others could get all the way to St. Louis this fast, especially if they're on foot. Think how quickly they'd have to travel to get that far. They'd have to have a specific destination in mind."

"Maybe they're headed to Canada," Tom suggested

"Send teams to find out and cut them off!" Greg ordered Jim, agreeing with Tom that Canada was likely, if they were heading north.

"Yes, sir," Jim said.

Prime Bunker, 30 August

"What is it now?" Greg asked HomeSec Chuck Dickson after the president and his advisors had all settled into the situation rooms in their respective bunkers. "More distressing news?"

Chuck hesitated for a few moments, making eye contact with Greg before continuing.

"You'll remember," Chuck finally said, "that I mentioned we were running out of generator fuel and spare parts for the life support systems in the bunkers. Some of the equipment in the bunkers is in worse condition than we thought."

"What are you doing about it?"

"We're robbing Peter to pay Paul. We're taking equipment and fuel from shelters, that can't afford to share it with winter coming on. The long-term forecast is for the coldest, wettest winter on record, because of the nuclear fallout."

"Amos said he could survive for thirty years or more with his power supply!" Greg exclaimed, then swore. "Why can't we last a year?"

"*What is* Amos's power source?" SecDef Jim Seymour asked calmly. "What could last for 30 years?"

"I don't know," Greg complained. "Find out."

"Yes sir," Jim said.

"No, not you, Jim. Chuck, put some resources on it."

"Yes, sir," Chuck said. "It has to be nuclear. Maybe he has a patent for it."

"Knowing Amos," Greg said, "it may be difficult to find out. He's so secretive."

"I'll see what I can find."

"Good. What else?" Greg thought about the argument he'd had with Liz and her concern that Greg didn't seem to care about the people. "What about the people who are in the shelters you're stealing from?"

"They'll be okay," Jim said. "We're coordinating with Chuck to move the people to other shelters where they'll be safer, even though the shelters are already overcrowded. Chuck, you said Amos's power source had to be nuclear."

"That's what I believe," Chuck said.

"Our subs and some of our naval ships are nuclear," Jim said. "Is there some way to take advantage of that?"

"I'll see if I can find someone who can answer that."

As Chuck finished making a note on his tablet, he added, "Our scientists at the National Oceanic and Atmospheric Administration are reporting that the heavy cloud cover is changing weather patterns globally, warming the polar ice and cooling the warmer climates. As a result, the melting glaciers are raising ocean levels and flooding coastal areas."

Greg realized his mouth hung open and shut it. The whole world was in chaos. Looking at his advisors on the wall monitors, he could tell they were as shocked as he was—all except Chuck, who'd had time to absorb the information he was presenting, but his expression was grim.

They sat in silence for several minutes. Greg didn't know what to say and the others probably felt the same.

"Has the NOAA offered a forecast of the situation?" Jim finally asked.

"They have no way to predict what will happen," Chuck said. "The amount of polar ice melt depends on how long the cloud cover lasts. There are estimates on how much the oceans would rise if *all* the ice melted, but no one is predicting that. They say it's best if we get people to move away from the coasts." Chuck shrugged apologetically.

Secretary of State Cy Hutchison cleared his throat, drawing everyone's attention.

"Greg, when you mentioned Amos surviving for thirty years in his . . . did you call it a Preserve?" Cy asked.

Greg nodded.

"Well, it reminded me that there are groups of people in the country who prepare for emergencies by setting up shelters like Amos's. They're called preppers."

"I think Amos used the term 'preppers' in one of our conversations," Greg said with a nod, "but it didn't mean anything to me."

"There are preppers all over the country," Cy said, "but the movement seems to be strongest in the Mountain West states—Montana, Wyoming, Utah and Idaho specifically. It's possible Amos isn't the only one with a unique power supply. The preppers may also have hardened electronic equipment, which the country sorely needs. I don't know what else."

"Can you find out who they are and where they are?" Greg asked, a ray of hope suddenly shining on their dismal future.

"I'll get people on it immediately and see what we can find."

Prime Bunker, 2 September

"We've made a list of the prepper groups we've been able to identify so far, through an internet search," Secretary of State Cy Hutchison said. "Some of them advertised the location of their survival retreats, so we have a few locations to check out. We're coordinating with Jim to send a military team."

"From the information on their websites," SecDef Jim Seymour said, "most of these survivalist groups are peaceful, but some are racist or anti-government extremists. Some have organized militias and are well armed. If we find them, we may not receive a warm welcome."

"We know Amos is underground," the president replied, "so some of these others may be, too. Let me know what you find."

17

I just saved your lives

"It's been over two weeks, Amos," Jason said. "When are you going to tell us what happened to Mike?"

Amos had called a family meeting with the intent to give everyone an update on Mike's condition, but he was exhausted from worry and his extra workload. He knew that Lillie, Terry and others were also worn out. Jason's abrupt question, before he could even begin the meeting, set him off. He stood and pointed a finger at Jason.

"Jason, what happened to Mike is none of your business. Just keep your mouth shut and let me handle this meeting my own way."

Jason bristled and turned red in the face. He may have been trying to decide how to respond, but Amos didn't give him a chance.

"If you don't like it, you can leave the room."

Jason balled his fists and started to stand, then sat back down and crossed his arms with his fists in his armpits. Amos noticed that the others in the room had gone still, likely trying to avoid drawing attention to themselves.

Amos had decided to give them a little information, to satisfy their curiosity. Even if he couldn't tell them how the accident happened, he could tell them about some of Mike's injuries. He needed everyone to continue taking on extra chores.

"Mike's accident was more serious than we thought. He's still in critical condition, with broken ribs and internal injuries. I induced a coma to let his body heal itself, and it is; but it's going to be a slow process."

"Did something fall on him?" Chris asked.

"Yes, Chris," Amos said, visualizing the three men kicking Mike, and the one, about to stomp on his head. "We appreciate how each of you have taken on more of the work around the Preserve, and will appreciate your continued help. Right now, Terry and Katie are with Mike, and Lillie is taking a well-deserved break.

"Emily, filling in for Lillie as house manager," he continued, looking at Emily, "said she'll make the rounds again today to check on housekeeping assignments, school work and exercise." After a short pause, long enough to realize that his anger at Jason probably upset Emily and others with sensitive feelings, he decided to apologize; not to Jason, but to the others. "I'm sorry if I was a little short-tempered a few minutes ago. Caring for Mike has taken an emotional toll on his mother, me and the others."

Prime Bunker, 6 September

"What have you learned?" Greg asked, hopefully.

"We've approached over two dozen prepper groups," SecDef Jim Seymour said. "We've divided them into three classifications; Those that are friendly and don't have underground shelters; those that *have* underground shelters; and those that are unfriendly.

"The first class, the friendly groups, had food and water for a while, but have now run out and have to scavenge like everyone else. Part of their problem was that other people knew they had emergency supplies and they decided to share what they had. Now their emergency food and water are gone. Some have hardened power supplies, but mostly the hand-crank type.

"The second class, those that are underground, have locked themselves in and don't want to be bothered. The two groups that we convinced to open their doors to us—and we only convinced them by swearing that we didn't want anything from them except information and that we actually had supplies for them—are in a little better shape because they haven't shared their food and water. They have only conventional power supplies, but some are hardened.

"The third class, the unfriendly groups, could be more aptly described as hostile. We didn't even get close before we were warned off by signs and recorded messages threatening violence to trespassers. We didn't think our task was to start a war with them, so we left them alone."

"So, none of the groups you spoke with have their own, unique power supply. Is that what you're saying?"

"Actually, one group did. The leader of the group was a former submarine technician. He knew enough about the nuclear reactors on subs to build his own. He refused to say where he got the radioactive material, but swore it was legal."

"You didn't try to confiscate it?"

"We'd already told him we were only looking for information. He was pretty nervous about telling us about it, and if we show up again, he may not be as willing to let us in.

"Hmm . . . "

"And before you suggest it, I'll tell you I've already spoken with General Peatross, asking him to find out if we have submarine reactors on the shelf that can be copied and applied to the power grid."

"Great. Thanks. Do you have recommendations for our approach with the preppers?"

"I do and I'll send them to you today."

The Outcasts—Missouri, 9 September

Kansas City had been bombed, so they passed to the south of the worst damage, avoiding the tent cities scattered around, and found the Oregon Trail near Lawrence, Kansas.

Just before crossing into Nebraska, Beth looked for and found Alcove Spring, north of Blue Rapids, on the Big Blue River. It was on a dirt road—not much there besides the spring—originating in an unusual rock formation. Many of the emigrants' names—carved in the rocks surrounding the spring—were still visible, alongside more recent additions to the artwork, in spray paint. There were a few tents set up near the spring with people moving around; but they quickly disappeared into their tents or the surrounding trees and brush when the Outcasts showed up.

After a drink of the cool, fresh water, Beth encouraged everyone to fill their water containers, then they took a short, brisk bath in the spring, with the men serving as lookout while the women bathed and vice-versa. But they needn't have worried, the locals stayed hidden until the Outcasts left.

Beth led them north into Nebraska, the roads straight and the terrain mostly flat. There were fields of grain and other crops on both sides of the road as far as they could see. There were a few farmhouses scattered among the fields, and fewer people. It appeared that each farmer farmed a lot of ground. However, without power, most of the grain was still in the fields. They raided the grain fields at night and figured out a way to separate the grain from the chaff, boiling it to make a bland, course cereal.

Vice President Art Klemp, 17 September

"How can you be so stupid?" Art asked. "The president caused all these problems. If we get rid of him, we can put everything back to normal."

"You want to take on the president and the military, when we're all starving?" the man asked Art, speaking for what looked like two or three families, huddled around a meager campfire, trying to heat something in a big pot. "We just want to be left alone so we can try to survive."

"Idiots! All of you! Can't see the truth when it's in front of you. You deserve whatever you get."

"He shouldn't talk to us that way," the woman sitting next to the man said quietly. "We haven't done anything wrong." The man stood and reached behind him, bringing a gun around from his back and pointing it at Art. Before he could get a shot off, he was hit twice in the chest and fell backward into another man.

Art watched the man fall, then looked to his left, where the sound of the gunshots had originated. Jean had fired from the hip, her face serene, her smoking gun still pointed at the group.

The woman who had spoken collapsed onto the man, bawling, one hand going to his face, pleading for him to live, while the other hand tried to stem the flow of blood on his chest as he bled out. Most of the rest stared in shock at Jean, Art or the crying woman. Art nodded toward Jean, then turned and walked away, the others following.

Vice President Art Klemp, 18 September

Art and his followers had finally reached Harrisonburg, Virginia, and it was still just the four of them. Turning a corner, he recognized a group of smallpox survivors from their splotchy skin. Like Art and his followers, their scabs had fallen off, leaving pigmented spots in their place.

"Are we going to try to recruit them?" Dayron asked when Art stopped.

They'd encountered several people the day before who'd gone

through the change and had invited them to join his small army. They'd refused and he was frustrated, after all the others who'd turned him down. He was anxious to get to Prime—they were almost there—so maybe the four of them would have to do it by themselves.

On the other hand, he didn't know how he would get into Prime without more help. He'd just decided that he *would* talk to this group of men and women, and was considering his approach, when he heard an engine. He backed up and watched from the corner of a building as a military truck approached and stopped short of the group. Two soldiers in hazmat suits stepped down from the cab, the passenger moving around to stand by the driver, with their arms up in a friendly gesture. The people moved away at first, then paused, as if reassured by the soldiers' friendliness.

Art couldn't hear what was being said, but from the posture of the group, he figured the soldiers had asked a question. Two members of the group responded, and they had all begun to relax, spread out so Art could clearly see all of them from his position.

Suddenly, the canvas side of the truck rolled up and a barrage of automatic weapons fire spewed from the exposed truck bed, killing all of the civilians.

Art was shocked. M.C. cried out; her cry covered by the sound of the guns. Dayron moved away from the others and vomited against the side of the building.

"We could have been out there," Jean said quietly. "We could have been killed."

Art continued to watch as some of the soldiers dropped down from the truck bed with flamethrowers and cremated all of the bodies.

"No bodies, no virus," Art said quietly to himself, already wondering how he could use this information to his advantage.

For the remainder of that day, Art followed discretely, as the truckload of soldiers drove through the streets slowly, watching the scene repeat itself twice more. He studied the soldiers' M.O.—their Modus Operandi—wanting to know if they followed a pattern, and if their approach had a weakness that he could exploit. By the end of the day, he'd come up with a plan, which he explained to the others, knowing that he needed all of them for it to succeed.

Vice President Art Klemp, 19 September

They spread out—staying within sight of each other—watching for other smallpox survivors and listening for the sound of a military truck. It was Jean who first heard it and whistled to get Art's attention. A small group of people sat against a building across the street from her position. The truck stopped in the road between them.

As in the previous encounters, two soldiers stepped down from the cab and faced the group, who had all stood and looked prepared to run away. This time the soldiers were on the passenger's side of the truck. Art's team crept to the back of the truck from the far side and waited. When Art figured the soldiers were about to raise the canvas, he motioned for the others to begin. M.C. tossed a stun grenade into the back of the truck, and Jean began shooting the soldiers inside. Dayron rounded the back of the truck and shot the driver and passenger, who were still reaching for their guns. The stunned civilians dropped to the ground to avoid being hit.

The battle lasted less than a minute. The soldiers never fired a shot. The three in the truck that hadn't been shot, dropped their automatic weapons and raised their hands in the air. Dayron ordered them out of the truck, then ordered them to remove their hazmat suits. While the two women held them at gunpoint, Dayron went inside the truck and shot each downed soldier in the head, "for insurance," Art had said.

Art, who showed himself only after the shooting had stopped, spoke to the group of survivors, trying to recruit them to his cause.

"What just happened?" one man asked.

"I just saved your lives," Art gloated. "Those soldiers were going to shoot all of you."

"Why?" a woman asked.

"Because we're different, you and I," Art replied with a smirk. "President McCormick is afraid of us, so he's trying to eliminate us."

"You mean, because of the virus?" the first man asked.

"Yeah. This super mutated virus. Ain't that a bummer?"

"What do you mean, 'super mutated virus'?"

"Oh, didn't they tell you? This virus continues to be contagious. We can still contaminate people. That's why they're afraid of us. We go through all this pain and grief, while President Gregory McCormick sits in his secure bunker and orders our deaths. What do you think we should do about it?"

"I think we should tell him to stop it," a young woman said.

"You think that would convince him?" Art asked, laughing.

"We should go and give him some of his own medicine," the first man said, angrily.

"I'm with you." Art continued to laugh. Jean had been right when she'd said that people needed to be threatened before they would get involved. "That's where we're going now. Who wants to go with us?"

Five of them agreed to join Art—four angry men and an equally angry young woman. The others decided they should get off the streets as quickly as possible, so they wouldn't contaminate others, and they wouldn't become targets.

Art's expanded team of nine—including himself—stripped the dead soldiers of their hazmat suits and weapons, dumped them out of the truck, and incinerated them with their own flamethrowers, which Art thought was entertaining.

He considered killing the surviving soldiers, too, but decided to bring them along in case they were still useful. With their own weapons aimed at them, the soldiers didn't resist having their hands and feet tied with plastic ties.

"Try out your new power to contaminate others, on these soldiers," Art suggested, looking directly at the young woman. She stared at Art for a moment, then a sly smile erupted on her face. She approached the three men, who began to struggle.

"Hold them," Art said to his new recruits. With all three men pinned to the ground, the woman knelt down next to the youngest soldier, a private.

"Hi honey," she said. "You look good enough to eat." The soldier got a panicked look on his face. "I think I'll have a taste," she continued, then licked his face. She used one hand to squeeze his nose closed until he had to open his mouth to breathe; but he kept his teeth clenched as she licked his teeth and gums.

"That was fun," she laughed when she'd finished. The private turned his head and spit, probably trying to remove the contamination from his mouth. He had obviously been warned that the virus remained contagious. The other two soldiers had already started to struggle with their bonds when she turned her attention to them and repeated the process, careful not to let them bite her tongue.

"Two days and you'll know," Art laughed, as his followers laid the three soldiers in the bed of the truck. As Art turned to leave, one of the soldiers, a sergeant, spoke.

"Wait! We have to report in."

Art studied the sergeant for a few moments. He wouldn't be able to intimidate the sergeant like he had the female soldier in the VEEP bunker; but maybe he could use the young private as leverage.

"Good idea," he said. "First, you're going to give me the security keywords, so I know you won't give us away." The sergeant looked away from Art briefly, then looked back, the lie already forming in his eyes.

"I see in your eyes that you plan to lie to me," Art said, pointing his gun at the young private. "If you do, this young man dies . . . slowly. Think about it before you make your decision."

The private looked panicked and turned toward his sergeant, who returned the look briefly.

"You'll have to kill all of us. I'm not giving them to you and the others don't know what they are."

"Good try, sergeant, but I know better than that." Art shot the private in the elbow. He screamed in agony and fainted as blood and bone fragments flew into the air. The sergeant looked grim, having challenged the vice president of the United States and lost.

Art pointed his gun at the private's knee. "What's it going to be sergeant?"

"Okay, okay," the sergeant said quickly. "No reason for this."

"Oh? And what did you have in mind for my friends here?" he asked, waving his gun around the back of the truck, dangerously. "Here's what you're going to do, sergeant. You're going to tell me the keywords, right now. Then you're going to report that everything went as planned. Is that clear?"

The grim-faced sergeant nodded and gave Art the keywords.

"Now, will you get him some medical attention and untie me so I can operate the radio?"

Art laughed and motioned to Dayron to stop the bleeding.

"I'll operate the radio for you," Art motioned for the radio.

While the sergeant was reporting, one statement seemed unnecessary and incongruous to his report. It didn't contain either of the security keywords that the Sergeant had given him, but Art believed he had been tricked. He thought the sergeant wasn't very good at this game, but he couldn't kill all the soldiers or his plan wouldn't work. He needed information on the Prime bunker that the sergeant might have, so Art shot the sergeant in the knee, causing him to scream into the radio. It wouldn't take long for this report to get back to the president.

"Was that a gunshot?" came a voice from the radio, which Art had taken and placed against his own ear.

"This is Vice President Art Klemp. You can tell Greg—President McCormick—that we're coming for him. He won't know when or how, but you tell him it's pay-back time."

President Gregory McCormick—Prime bunker, West Virginia, 19 September

The president was notified within minutes that Art was near Harrisonburg, Virginia.

"What happened, Jim?" Greg asked.

"A Sergeant in one of the elimination squads called the SEC DEF bunker and was making a report to Security," Jim said. "In his report, he used one of the security keywords, to alert Security that he was in trouble. The operator heard a gunshot and scream, then a new voice spoke into the radio." Jim looked down and read Art's words from a paper in front of him.

"So, now Art has hostages, automatic weapons and another truck," Greg said. "I had hoped that when his truck stopped moving at that barricade, it meant he'd been taken out of the picture. How does that imbecile keep surprising us?"

"He has nothing to lose," Jim replied, "so he doesn't hold back."

"And he doesn't care how many people he harms," DNI Tom Mitchell added.

"All true," Greg replied. "Okay, what do we do? Should we send a regiment of soldiers after him."

"Let him come to us," Jim replied. "Art's so desperate to get back at you, and possibly me, that he'll make a mistake, sooner or later."

"How many people do we let him hurt in the meantime?" HomeSec Chuck Dickson asked.

"I like Jim's suggestion," Greg said. "Let's keep our people out of his way. Make him come to us. If he harms anyone else, it's no different than what we've been doing."

"What does that say for us?" Secretary of State Cy Hutchison asked.

Greg gave Cy a dirty look, but Cy had a point. Were they any better than Art? He thought about his conversation with Liz a few days earlier. She'd been so upset with him that she'd asked him to move out of their bedroom. He'd had his security team find a cot and set it up in his office where, he'd told them, he could be available at any time of the day or night.

Vice President Art Klemp—Harrisonburg, Virginia, 19 September

"Five new team members and three hostages," Art said with glee. "But I want more."

"What do we do with the soldiers," Dayron asked hesitantly, concerned that the vice president was beginning to sound a little crazy.

"What? Oh, put 'em on their stomachs in the back of the truck," he said. "Have the others point their guns at 'em." His cackle gave Dayron shivers. "That'll keep 'em in their place. You ride up front with me."

Dayron passed along the instructions and joined Art in the cab. The remainder of Art's team sat on the benches that ran along either side of the covered truck bed, watching the hostages. Each time the truck hit a bump, turned a corner, or swerved—which was constant due to Art's reckless driving—Dayron could hear the injured soldiers screaming in pain.

18

What have I done?

Prime Bunker, 22 September

"What is it Chuck?" The president asked his HomeSec, who had requested this meeting.

"Greg, it's not working. We've been meeting with industry and utility leaders for weeks and we're no closer to solving the problems with water treatment and distribution, communications, and electric and gas utilities, than we were back in July."

"Come on, Chuck, it's got to be better than that," the president said. "We released the government stores of hardened equipment and spare components to industry, didn't we? That should have helped some."

"Well, okay, it's slightly better. We have small pockets of working power, mostly in the mid-west, which was less impacted by the explosions and EMPs. But the rest of the country is still without clean water or power. The only reason we've made that much progress, is because we quit listening to the individual utility leaders, and made the decisions based on where the equipment would do the most good."

"Meaning?"

"Some of the largest utilities thought they should have priority because they had the most territory to worry about. But they were also in the most impacted regions, with damage from explosions, tsunamis, earthquakes and fires. When they realized they weren't going to get their way, some of them became difficult, refusing to provide skilled workers to help in other regions, using the excuse that their people feared the radioactive contamination, the diseases spread by the rotting dead, and the possibility of violence."

"Legitimate concerns."

"They are, but in this case, they were just excuses. We assured them the military would be present at every work site; but as yet, we still don't have a manufacturing plant on line that can provide the controls we need to build new transformers."

"What about the reactor design from the prepper group?" They'd agreed to approach the former submarine technician about duplicating his design in exchange for food and water for his group. He'd accepted, possibly because he didn't trust what the government would do if he refused.

"We've built a few small reactors, using their design and they work fine in isolation. But we can't seem to make them work with the power grid. Whether it's a problem of incompatible components, a lack of skilled labor, or something else, we're still trying to figure it out."

Vice President Art Klemp—Harrisonburg, Virginia, 27 September

They spent the next eight days driving around Harrisonburg, where Art thought their chances of finding more smallpox survivors would be high. During a rest stop on the first day, one of the men he had recruited—one with medical training—was able to treat the hostages from a medical kit he'd found in the truck; so, hopefully, they wouldn't get an infection from the gunshot wounds. But he couldn't do much about the fractured bones. They would probably be crippled for life.

On the second day the hostages had rashes, and on the third they had lesions in their mouths. No one in the truck had much sympathy. They had all been through the painful transition.

The vice president found plenty of candidates for his army, but few were interested in his plans.

"The president has the whole military behind him," one man said. "Are you going to take on the army?"

"Nah, he only has a few soldiers protecting him in his bunker," Art laughed, "but you go ahead and hide in your hole, like the other sissies. I'm going to take these brave soldiers"—he waved his arm to encompass those who had agreed to follow him— "and find that S.O.B.-of-a-president; and I'm going to pay him back, for me *and* for you."

He recruited enough people to fill the truck to capacity, then decided it was time to move ahead with his plan. He briefly considered why the president hadn't sent more soldiers to stop him, but didn't really care in the end.

Vice President Art Klemp—West Virginia, 28 September

As Art and his truckload of armed men and women, all smallpox survivors, traveled toward Prime, Art revealed his strategy to Dayron.

"I have GPS coordinates," he said, "but I need the layout, access locations and passcodes. I need enough people to storm Prime, then contaminate everyone inside and kill the president."

Dayron didn't answer, which was expected. Art knew that Dayron had figured out how this worked. Art talked, Dayron listened. Nearly every time Dayron had tried to speak over the past several days, Art had talked right over him. It had been intentional. Dayron was a good solider, but Art was in charge.

"What I need," Art continued, mostly to himself, "is to capture soldiers from Prime."

The sergeant noticed that whenever they stopped to take a break, Art gravitated to the hostages. This stop was no different.

"You know the president's responsible for what's happened to you," Art said, "just like he's responsible for what's happened around the world."

The sergeant had wondered why they hadn't encountered teams of soldiers out looking for them. They had to be close to Prime by now and the vice president had admitted over the radio that he was going to attack Prime.

The sergeant hoped that the military had a plan to capture the vice president and were just waiting for the right moment to spring it. What could he do or say that would help that plan along? After spending time with the vice president and listening to his twisted logic, the sergeant was convinced that he was crazy. Maybe he could encourage the vice president to do something that would be his undoing, like attacking armed soldiers. He decided to take a chance.

"I think you're right, Mr. Vice President," the sergeant said, "and I think your best chance to access the president's bunker is to capture soldiers from Prime. They'll know the approaches and access codes."

The sergeant's response must have surprised Art, because he didn't respond right away.

"How's the best way to capture some soldiers from Prime?" Art finally asked.

"Well," the sergeant said, "the president probably has soldiers out looking for you now. Being in a military truck, they'll probably think you're one of them. If you handle it right, you should be able to fool them." The sergeant didn't believe the vice president could fool anyone; but having watched his crazy rants for days now, he thought the vice president's ego would convince him it was true.

Art looked thoughtful, then nodded and walked away.

President Gregory McCormick—Prime bunker, West Virginia, 28 September

"Greg, Art has stopped wandering around Virginia and is headed your way," Jim said. The military had been tracking Art's progress using military satellites, so Jim was notified when Art stopped wandering and headed west, toward Prime, instead of north, toward the SecDef bunker. "We've initiated the operation to infiltrate his group," Jim said.

"Details?" Greg asked.

"You sure you want to know? I can handle this," Jim said.

"Absolutely. I'm sending more people into harm's way. I want to understand the risks."

"Fine. We're using only volunteers. They'll allow themselves to be captured and they understand there's a substantial risk of contamination. There's also the risk of violence. Art has demonstrated that he places no value on the lives of others."

"Why would anyone volunteer under those circumstances?" Greg asked.

"The volunteers know we're working on a cure, but don't have one yet. Most of them have already learned that their families are dead. Perhaps they don't think they have much left to live for and want to go out with a bang. Maybe it's out of love for their country. I don't really know. But we have them, and they're ready to move."

"How will they convince Art to go along with our plan?"

"Psychology. Art has demonstrated that he believes he's smarter than us. Most importantly, he's sexist. He believes all women are inferior. That works to our advantage. We're sending Captain Alyssa Marston and a team of five soldiers from Prime, who will show their inferiority by being submissive. They'll tip us off to their location by calling in. Then, of course, we'll be waiting when Art arrives."

"You're sure this will work?"

"As sure as I can be, but we *are* dealing with Art."

"Okay. Keep me informed."

"Yes, sir."

Vice President Art Klemp—Romney, West Virginia, 29 September

"Soldiers on foot!" Dayron called excitedly, pointing out the windshield.

Art had just driven into the town of Romney, West Virginia, on Highway 50, about fifteen miles from Prime. He stopped the truck and considered their approach. The soldiers wore hazmat suits, with their rifles slung over their shoulders. The lead soldier must have noticed the truck because he waved, obviously thinking Art's truck was one of theirs.

Art smiled. This might work, just like the sergeant had said. He knocked on the little window between the cab and truck bed, which was opened by one of his men.

"Get ready," he said. "We have soldiers directly in front of us, and they think we're friendlies." Art chuckled. "We'll give them a surprise. Follow the plan we discussed. I'll turn to the left, so go left. Here we go."

Art pulled the truck forward, cutting the distance in half and turning slightly to the side before stopping. His team piled out the back and came around the left side of the truck.

In her headset, Captain Marston addressed her team. "They turned to our right, so the attack should come from the right. No surprises, folks. When they point guns, raise your hands in the air. We follow their instructions explicitly. Here we go."

Art's team came around the side of the truck, eighteen in all, with weapons drawn and pointed at the soldiers.

"Hands in the air, people," Captain Marston said into her headset.

One of Art's team members yelled, "All weapons on the ground, carefully. No surprises and no one gets hurt."

Captain Marston and her team were outnumbered three-to-one; so, even though she was certain her trained soldiers could take control of the situation with few casualties, she complied, as she'd been instructed in the bunker. She carefully lifted her rifle off her shoulder and lowered it to the ground. Then she unbuckled her supply belt and lowered it to the ground. Her team members followed her lead.

Art and Dayron waited in the cab of the truck until the soldiers were disarmed, then walked over. Art reached out and undid the lead soldier's hazmat suit helmet, removed it, and stared in surprise. They'd sent a woman to stop him. No wonder they were so easy to capture.

"What's your name," Art asked.

"Captain Alyssa Marston,"

"A captain, eh?" he said, as he shook his head. They'd taken equal rights too far. "Why are you here?"

Captain Marston could see the wisdom in sending a woman. Vice President Klemp already underestimated her. In her pre-brief she was told that he had no respect for women. She had to fight to keep the smile from her face.

"Sorry, that's classified," she said, straight-faced.

"Nothing about you," Art sneered, looking her over, "or your team, is classified any longer. I own you. You will tell me what I want to know. You will do what I want you to do."

Captain Marston acted surprised by this comment, then feigned intimidation.

"We . . . we're here to find and stop you from getting to Prime, Mr. Vice President," she stammered.

Oh, I like that, Art thought. She was already cowed. She was going to tell him everything he wanted to know.

"Alright," Art called to his people, "gather up their weapons and hazmat suits and put them in the truck."

"Please, sir, not the hazmat suits," the Captain pled.

"Oh, you know about the virus still being contagious, do you?" Art smirked. "Well, that's too bad for you." Art grabbed Captain Marston around the neck with one arm, pulled her to him and kissed her, parting her lips with his tongue. She was no match for his strength. When he pulled away, he was grinning.

"That should do it. Now, take off the suit or I'll do it for you."

Art followed her gaze as she looked around at her team, all receiving the same treatment. When she didn't respond to his instructions quickly enough, he grabbed the front of her suit and started removing it for her. She immediately started helping and Art backed off to let her finish, but not before running his hands across her breasts. He grinned when she lowered her eyes, then finished removing her suit.

"They have wrist ties," one of Art's team members called out in surprise, as he inventoried one of the supply belts.

Why would they have wrist ties, when their assignment was to kill him? Maybe he'd misjudged Greg. Maybe Greg wanted to look him in the eye and gloat before having him killed. Well, that was going to backfire.

"Tie their hands behind their backs," he instructed his team.

"Where's your transport?" Art asked. Captain Marston hesitated as her hands were twisted painfully behind her back and tied. He slapped her face, hard. She lowered her eyes.

"Around that corner," she said, nodding her head to the left without looking up or turning.

"That's good. And the keys?"

"In the truck."

"Dayron, go get the truck. It's around that corner." Minutes later a truck started up and came around the corner, stopping next to Art's truck.

"Divide up. Put those five in the Captain's truck. The Captain will ride with me."

☢

As Captain Marston was lifted into the back of the truck, she was surprised to find three soldiers, two of them injured and anemic—possible loss of blood—with splotches on their exposed skin, a sure sign of smallpox. One of them was the sergeant who had reported his capture days ago—she hadn't known if he was still alive until now—and who she knew well. She tried to talk to him, but one of Art's women put a gun to her head.

"No talking," the woman said

"It's alright," Art said cheerily, from behind the captain. "Let her talk to them. Maybe that will help her cooperate when we need it."

Marston held a short conversation with the sergeant, discovering how they had been captured, contaminated, and injured. She could tell the sergeant was anxious to ask a question, likely wanting to know if the captain had a plan to get them out of their current incarceration, but he didn't ask. He knew her well enough to know that, if she had a plan, she couldn't say anything about it with the enemy this close. He would also know that her submissiveness was out of character, so it must be part of her instructions.

They didn't leave right away, which surprised Marston. After a few minutes the vice president came to the back of the truck and told her to get out. She stood awkwardly from her squatting position, without the help of her hands. He helped her down from the truck bed, led her to a bench on the side of the road, and settled in for a talk.

"Here's what we're going to do, Captain. I'm going to ask questions and you're going to answer them, truthfully. You can see what happens to those who don't cooperate."

She suspected he was referring to the gunshot wounds, so she took a quick look at the truck, to appear concerned, then looked down again.

"I understand," she said.

"How practical. I like that." He smiled, his face a grotesque mask. "Here's what I want to know. How many entrances are there to Prime?"

It was a simple question and answering it, she would begin to show a pattern of cooperation, which she needed to do to gain his confidence.

"Two," she said without hesitation.

"What's the approach like to each of them."

Again, she answered without hesitation. "The front approach is at the end of a narrow canyon. The rear entrance is down the back side of the knoll, along a fire break, behind a rock outcropping." She wasn't going to tell him about the emergency exit tunnel. She had only been told about it as part of her pre-brief. She wouldn't have known about it otherwise.

"Is there cover for our approach?"

"The entire area is heavily wooded."

"I have the GPS coordinates and a map of the area. You're going to show me where the security cameras are at both approaches and help me figure out the best strategy for getting in without being seen."

He held up a map in front of her. She answered all of his questions, without offering any suggestions. The psychologist in the bunker had told her that Art would become suspicious if she made suggestions. "Let him ask," the psychologist had said.

When Art asked for the locations of the security cameras, she tried to explain without pointing at the map, since her hands were still tied behind her back. Art called to one of his team to cut her wrist tie and retie her hands in front of her.

The captain showed him where some of the cameras were. When asked, she told him how to disable them, then warned him that if he disabled more than one or two, security would know they were there, just not be able to see or hear them.

"Can we sneak past the monitors?" he asked in frustration.

This is what she had been waiting for. She could now make a suggestion that he was likely to listen to.

"You can, but there's one trail that leads to each of the entrances without passing the monitors." It was a lie, but she needed to lull him into a sense of security.

"Why is that?" he asked, surprised.

"The security team uses them for training—for a surprise attack." She chuckled sarcastically. "It's also how we get out and back in without the brass knowing we're gone. All the soldiers know about it, but no one will tell."

"But you're going to show me."

She shrugged.

"Okay," he said, appearing pleased with her cooperation, "we're going to continue our conversation, but a little farther away from the bunker, in case Greg sends out a team to look for you." His smile distorted his face, making him look evil.

He loaded up the trucks and backtracked a few miles, to put more distance between his team and Prime. Then he quizzed the Captain again and again, to see if she would contradict herself or change her story, which she never did.

She noticed how Art's team wandered around, frustrated and bored, looking over at them periodically. They wanted to get going but he was oblivious to them. The lack of discipline made her smile inwardly: they would be easy to defeat.

Late in the afternoon, when the vice president seemed to be in a good mood and running out of questions, Captain Marston suggested that she would appreciate the opportunity to have her medic look at the other soldiers' injuries.

He smiled, then agreed, sending one of his men to get the medic.

Having succeeded in getting his cooperation once, she decided to risk making another request.

"We need to report in," she said apologetically.

Art frowned at her, then smiled wickedly. His mood shifts were scary.

"What are the security keywords for today?" he asked.

"White and truck," she said without hesitation and without changing expression. She was told to expect this. The keywords were actually red and table, but security had told her how to respond in a way that would fit naturally into the conversation they would have when she gave her report.

Art stared at her without speaking. The captain squirmed nervously, still looking down. She looked up for just a moment, to see Art staring at her. "I told you, I have no reason to withhold information," she said. "What do I have to gain? I probably already have smallpox. I have no desire to be tortured, too. It's not worth it."

☢

That convinced Art. She was too weak to hold out on him.

"Dayron, bring me the captain's radio." Art called on the frequency she gave him, then held the radio so he could hear both sides of the conversation.

She gave a generic report that everything was normal.

"No, we haven't seen the vice president," she said in answer to a direct question from the bunker.

"Where are you now?" the radio operator asked when she finished her report.

"Romney."

"Are you coming in now?"

"No, we'll probably stay out overnight again. I'm taking my team farther east, toward that table-like plateau," she said, so naturally and rehearsed that Art, listening as he was for the security keywords, had no idea she had just reported her capture.

"Okay. Take care, there are crazies out there."

"We will, thanks. We'll report again tomorrow if we don't get back."

"Roger that. Out."

Art smiled. This was perfect. They could approach Prime, right now, and surprise Greg.

President Gregory McCormick—Prime bunker, West Virginia, 29 September

Within minutes of Captain Marston's report, the president knew that she had infiltrated Art's team. That also meant that she and her team had been contaminated.

"What have I done, Jim?" The president asked his SecDef.

"Greg, those soldiers knew the risks when they volunteered," Jim replied. "There's a good chance they'll get smallpox. We may never have a cure. They did it for the love of country and I'm proud of them."

"I still feel guilty. How many people have died because I couldn't stop Al-Qaeda, Russia, North Korea and China? Because I couldn't foresee the actions of a handful of scientists? Because I couldn't stop Art at the shelter?" Greg was inconsolable, beating himself up. He wanted the madness to end, but it looked like it never would. He was living in a nightmare.

"Greg," Jim said, "berating yourself is not helpful. We have a good plan for stopping Art. We know where he is. We've infiltrated his ranks. He may have outmaneuvered us a couple of times, but we have him now."

"Of course, you're right, Jim. It's a good plan." Greg took a deep breath and let it out. Would Art outmaneuver them again? He wondered, as he smiled at his advisers half-heartedly. "Ok.

What's Art going to do?"

"The unexpected," Jim replied. "Captain Marston reported that they were heading away from Prime, so Art will attack immediately. They're about twenty miles away, so they'll hit today or tonight. If I were in his position, which I'm happy I'm not, I'd send half my team to each entrance and use the radios to coordinate an approach. We'll be watching and listening to them all the way in."

19

What could go wrong?

Vice President Art Klemp—Romney, West Virginia, 29 September

Captain Marston had given Art the exact location of the Prime bunker, in the hill country off the New Creek Highway, west of Romney and south of Keyser, on a heavily wooded knoll. Art called his team together, to review the conditions at each entrance, the safe approach at each location, and where to expect security monitors. They loaded up the trucks and headed west, Art already thinking of ways to humiliate Greg the way Greg had humiliated him, and chuckling with each new idea. The more he thought about it, the more excited he became.

Art and Dayron drove, with their other team members, captive soldiers, weapons and plenty of ammunition, divided between the trucks. When they reached the point on the New Creek Highway where the trucks needed to separate, the two men climbed down from the trucks and went over the details one more time.

"I'll take my truck up this farm road," Art said, and showed Dayron again on his map, which was identical to the one Art had. "I'll hide the truck in the trees and wait for you to be in position. You take your truck up this other road, over the ridge to the fire break and hide the truck in the trees, here. We stay in contact by radio to coordinate our approach, but use the radios as little as possible, just in case." With confirmation from Captain Marston, Art had changed the radio frequency to avoid being overheard—

or so he thought.

"Mr. Vice President," Dayron said when Art had finished.

"What?" Art asked.

"Jean asked me, 'What if that captain is just pretending to co-operate?' What if she's trying to trick us, sir?"

"No way," Art said with confidence. "She's scared to death that I'm going to torture her. She shivers when I talk to her."

"But Jean said—"

"Can it, Dayron! I've got her under control. Now, let's get going. We're almost home free."

Art reached the waiting point and had his team check their weapons. He took Captain Marston with him and left the other captives immobilized in the truck.

"In position," Art heard over his radio.

"Proceed," he replied and followed his team through the trees toward the entrance, along the secret trail, hand-drawn on the map by Captain Marston. He didn't see one monitor on the way.

☢

"Don't do anything stupid, Captain," Art said, standing behind Marston, with his gun in her back and his radio up to his ear, listening for anything from Dayron. "I'd hate to damage your nice body before we have a chance to get to know each other better," he sneered. "But rest assured, I'll shoot you if you try to give away our presence."

She shivered involuntarily at his remark, turned away, and started up the trail. He followed closely, his eyes on her hips, undressing her in his head.

Prime bunker, West Virginia, 29 September

The security team monitored the pre-planned frequencies and heard the vice president's team members checking their radios.

They also spotted both teams as soon as they left their trucks and entered the trees. Before the approaching men and women were within visual range, security personnel left the bunker and hid in the woods; their camouflaged military hazmat suits would help them blend in with their surroundings.

The monitors attached to the trees picked up portions of Art's conversation with Marston, as they walked along the trail, letting the security team know exactly where they were. They stopped near one of the monitors, and the security team clearly heard the captain's comment.

"What could go wrong?" she asked, meekly. "You're on a trail that isn't monitored, both teams have the access codes and should be able to enter the airlocks before encountering resistance, all the soldiers are tied up in the trucks, and I can barely navigate this trail thanks to the wrist tie." Despite her feigned awkwardness, walking with her hands tied, security could see that Marston was staying close enough that she could attack Art under the right conditions—with the right distraction.

Vice President Art Klemp—The canyon outside the Prime bunker, 29 September

Gunshots rang out, and two of Art's team members fell to the ground in agony, a few yards in front of Captain Marston. Angry shouting came from the radios, and Art looked around, startled by the suddenness of the attack. Realizing it must be a trap, he quickly recovered and turned toward the captain, prepared to shoot her, if necessary. Captain Marston, however, had already reacted. She removed the gun from his hand with one quick twist of his wrist, trapped his arm behind his back, and had his gun at the back of his head faster than he imagined possible.

Shocked by the sudden turn of events, he let the radio drop

in order to wrestle with her. He knew he was stronger, but was surprised to find he was no match for her, even with her wrists tied. Unable to move, Art registered the voice on the radio asking what they should do.

"Half of my team's been shot, Mr. Vice President. We're trapped. Whadawe do?"

"Pick up the radio," Marston said in a steely voice that Art didn't recognize.

Who is this woman? He'd had her under his control and couldn't understand what had just happened.

Despite his superior strength, with pressure applied to the trapped arm, she forced him to his knees next to the radio. When he resisted, she pushed him hard, almost pushing his face into the dirt. He picked up the radio, thinking he could still salvage this mess, by telling his team to come back and rescue him. He wasn't thinking about the fact that they would, undoubtedly, be shot if they moved from their hiding places.

"Talk to your people," she demanded. "They're asking you what they should do."

As soon as he depressed the talk button, she called in a loud voice, "I have the vice president. Come and get us."

Art released the talk button, but she had surprised him once again. He started to struggle, twisting his body in an attempt to reverse their positions, and almost escaped her grip. He didn't think she would shoot the vice president of the United States.

Suddenly, three soldiers appeared, surrounding them. One of the soldiers put an automatic rifle in Art's face and spoke, his voice distorted by the suit's hood. "I won't hesitate to shoot you, creep. Go ahead and resist."

Art stopped struggling and stayed on his knees. Captain Marston released his arm and grabbed the phone from him. "This is

Captain Marston. It's over. Throw your weapons out in the open. Raise your hands and walk out where you can be seen."

"How do we know they won't shoot us?" Dayron asked over the radio.

"You don't," Marston said, "but it will go much better for you if you surrender voluntarily. Don't make them come after you."

☢

Captain Marston hadn't been positive the security team could see and hear their approach but the shooting answered that question. Now that the tables had turned on the vice president, she wasn't surprised when a commanding voice echoed through the trees, "This is Colonel Ames in the bunker. Captain Marston is correct. No one will be shot if they cooperate."

Art's team members threw out their weapons, one by one, and began stepping out of hiding, arms raised.

"I count twenty, including the vice president," a voice said over the radio. "Is that all of them."

"Yes, that's it," Captain Marston said. "There are nine soldiers tied up in the trucks. All of us have been contaminated, two are seriously injured."

Armed soldiers materialized out of the trees and bushes, their automatic rifles aimed at the vice president's team members.

"We'll take care of those in the trucks, captain," one of the soldiers said as he cut the captain's wrist tie. "One of our security personnel will accompany you to quarantine."

She rubbed her wrists as she looked around, seeing soldiers picking up weapons and herding Art's team members, their hands tied, back toward the trucks. Two soldiers picked up one fallen man, obviously dead, and dragged him by the armpits down the trail.

Captain Marston watched a soldier cuff Art's hands and lift him from the ground while two others trained their weapons on him.

"It was a trap all along, wasn't it?" Art spit out the words, dripping acid, as the soldiers dragged him past Captain Marston. His face was twisted in rage and he was staring at her.

"You're an arrogant fool, Mr. Vice President," she replied, shaking her head. "Save your breath. I ought to shoot you right here."

"You can't. I'm guaranteed due process by the Constitution."

"Ahh, due process," she said, staring him down. "Did you forget already? We're under martial law and you threatened the life of the president of the United States? I could shoot you right now and no one would raise an eyebrow."

Art looked surprised, then awed, by Marston's bold remarks.

"You were just acting. You allowed yourself to be contaminated, just to trick me."

That the vice president's personality could change so quickly scared her. *Yes,* she could finally admit to herself, she had been frightened most of the time she had been his prisoner.

"You were easy to manipulate," she said. "I hope the president is as hard on you as you were to all those people you hurt along the way."

The soldiers prodded, pushed, then dragged the vice president away, kicking and cursing. She hoped it would be the last time she would have to see the disgusting man.

Captain Marston and the one remaining soldier stepped off the trail to let the other soldiers and their captives pass.

"That was brave, captain," the soldier—another female—said. "Even with a gun on him and his hands cuffed, he scares me. He's a devil."

The captain chuckled and shook her head. "That, he is. Shall we go?" They walked toward the trucks.

Quarantine Shelter, West Virginia, 30 September

"Captain Marston, this is Gregory McCormick." The familiar voice of the president emanated from a speaker in her quarantine room, which was in a shelter a few miles from the Prime bunker. It had been taken over by the military, the occupants having been relocated to another shelter, to make room. Captain Marston had been given her own room, where she sat at a desk, writing a report of everything that had happened during her time with the vice president. She'd been told what to expect, had been vaccinated again, then cautioned not to scratch the sores that now covered her body.

The other quarantined soldiers had been separated, male from female. The contaminated citizens, including Art, had been quarantined as well, but under arrest. Video and audio capability had been installed in each quarantine room.

The captain looked up to see the familiar face of President McCormick and jumped to attention.

"Mr. President," the captain said, saluting, "I'm honored."

"Relax, captain." She relaxed only slightly, reflecting her military training, and the respect she had for the man. "I want to thank you—"

"That's not necessary," she interrupted, embarrassed that the president of the United States would single her out for an apology.

"Don't interrupt me when I'm trying to apologize," the president scolded in mock anger.

"Sorry, sir," the captain said, meekly.

The president started to laugh. "No, I'm sorry." Then he continued, seriously. "I'm sorry you had to face Art. I'm sorry you had to take the physical, emotional and health risks you did. I'm proud of you. Your country is proud of you. I'll do anything within my power for you."

His words embarrassed her. She had just done her duty. She wasn't enjoying having smallpox and was sorry so many good people had gotten hurt, but she'd do it again, even knowing what she knew now. But she couldn't think of anything to say to the president that wouldn't sound melodramatic.

"Thank you, Mr. President."

"You think about it and let me know what I can do for you. Anything. I mean it. I also wanted to give you an update on the rest of your team. Everyone has been vaccinated and is going through the same transition you are. Unfortunately, Private Petersen developed a case of hemorrhagic smallpox."

She visualized the photos she'd been shown of the various stages of smallpox. She thought of Private Petersen with blackened flesh. "They always die," she remembered the doctor saying.

"He died?" she asked.

"He did. I'm sorry."

To think that Private Petersen had died that way frustrated and angered her. Art Klemp should have gotten hemorrhagic smallpox

The president was still talking. "All of the people who were in the bunker when you and Art entered have been vaccinated as well and all of the bodies have been cremated."

She was saddened by the needless death. She didn't know what to say. Finally, a thought came to her.

"What about the cure?"

The president was quiet for a few moments, which told her what she wanted to know.

"We've got everyone with any skill in that area working on it," he said sadly.

There was nothing else to say, and she couldn't remember either of them saying good-bye.

Art Klemp—Confinement, West Virginia, 3 October

After waiting in confinement for two days, soldiers in hazmat suits dragged Art, kicking and screaming, to another nearly empty room. They didn't strap him down to an electric chair, or put a hood over his head, or give him a lethal injection, as he was expecting. Instead, one of the soldiers told him where to sit so he could see and be seen, before leaving the room and locking the door behind him.

There were no wall hangings or other decorations, just like in the isolation room. Greg must have been afraid he would figure out a way to escape, if they gave him anything more than a chair bolted to the floor. Maybe he would, he thought, and chuckled.

After a few minutes, President Gregory McCormick's face appeared on the monitor in front of him.

"Hello Art," Greg said.

Art turned toward the monitor slowly, careful to keep his face blank, so Greg wouldn't know what he was thinking.

"A fine world crisis you've created, Greg," he said, trying to taunt the president into becoming angry and making a scene. He was sure this conversation was being recorded.

⊛

Greg wanted to respond to Art's accusation, but he knew that would play in Art's favor. He needed to be unpredictable.

"We need your help," Greg said with a smile.

"You're trying to trick me," Art said, his surprise showing on his face, "like that woman. What was her name? Captain Mar—something?" Art snarled, swearing and getting red in the face. He jumped up and stormed around the room, hitting the walls with his fists.

Greg let him vent for a couple of minutes, until it appeared that he would continue forever if Greg didn't interrupt. How could Art do that without taking a breath?

"You're right about one thing, Art," Greg said, staying silent until Art acknowledged his comment and settled down to hear what he had to say. "We do have a global crisis. Petty, selfish terrorists started it. When we couldn't prevent it, we tried to end it."

Art laughed maniacally. "You're admitting you failed."

"Oh, don't get me wrong, Art. We didn't fail to stop the terrorists. I'd be surprised if there are more than a handful of their leaders left, scattered around the world."

"Just like there are only a handful of uncontaminated Americans left," Art said—goading.

Greg smiled. "Thanks to you, Art, you may be right. The contamination has spread, although we believe it's still restricted to the Eastern States. That's why we need your help—to stop it. We want to find a cure."

Art stopped moving and looked at Greg curiously.

"How can I help?" He asked, seriously, suddenly sounding reasonable. "I'm not a viral scientist. You're trying to trick me again, aren't you?"

Greg thought it was scary the way Art's personality could change, so suddenly and dramatically, like Jekyll and Hyde.

"I'm serious Art. You can make up for all the deaths you've caused, by helping us find a cure.

"*You* are responsible for the deaths of millions of Americans," Art snarled, transforming into Hyde again, "maybe hundreds of millions"

"Sorry if your accusations don't upset me, Art. You can't make me feel any worse about the suffering of the American people than I already do. But I didn't start the war, I didn't release the smallpox virus, and I didn't intentionally spread it." Greg stared at Art, accusingly, and Art appeared to shrink back into himself. "In fact, you, Art, have personally killed more people than can be blamed on me."

"If you'd let me help run the government," Art whined like a child caught in a lie, "I wouldn't have tried to get back at you."

"That's really good, Art," Greg laughed, ruefully. "You couldn't have the glory and power you wanted, so you turned to sabotage, spreading the virus and attacking not one, but two, government bunkers. What the government needed, what it still needs, is people who put the country before themselves, like Captain Marston. That has never been in your makeup, not since I've known you."

Art bowed his head, perhaps in shame or contrition. "Marston," he said quietly. "Marston," he said again, as if trying to commit it to memory

Greg marveled at Art's behavior, wondering if it was an act, or if Art had finally lost his mind.

"If you want to help, Art, you will voluntarily assist with the search for a cure. For your information, the Russian scientists have now contacted the CDC director for help with their own outbreak of smallpox."

Art looked up, startled. "You're saying it was a global conspiracy to release the virus?"

"A conspiracy, yes, but we don't believe they were trying to release the virus,"—at least he hoped not— "just to prevent its destruction. The release of the samples from all three Level 4 facilities was the act of misguided scientists. They thought they knew better than their leaders what was good for the world. They paid with their lives."—he hoped they were dead— "Now the rest of us are paying a high price for their selfishness and greed."

Greg had never shared this much information with him—ever. Was it possible he could help resolve this global problem? Was Greg sincere? There was probably a catch. The thought made Art angry again.

"Are you sharing this with me because you're going to have me killed next?" Art asked.

"Sorry Art," Greg said, shaking his head, "I don't have time for this. I have a world to save." Greg stood, backing away from the camera. "You have a chance to make up for your stupidity. Help the scientists, voluntarily, and I'll grant you a pardon."

"A pardon?" Art asked, caught off guard.

"Oh, didn't I tell you? You've been charged with conspiracy to overthrow the government. That's treason, still punishable by death, with or without martial law in effect." Greg paused for a moment, then added. "You're going to volunteer to be one of the test subjects, to help the scientists develop a cure for the mutated virus. Your level of cooperation will have a huge influence on the outcome of your trial. Think about it."

Art stared at Greg, speechless, as the video monitor went blank.

20

Our latest test patient didn't die

President Gregory McCormick—Prime bunker, West Virginia, 3 October

"The team near St. Louis found an entire encampment of smallpox survivors," DNI Tom Mitchell said. "They claim a group of about eight people showed up last fall, and knifed one of their members, before being chased away. Two days later, people started getting sick and within a week, all of them—seventy-three people—had smallpox, and twenty-five of them died. That's got to be our Johns Creek people."

"Have you followed their trail beyond St. Louis?" Greg asked.

"The virus has spread out from that encampment," Tom said, "and I have teams searching, primarily north and west. We haven't found any other outbreaks."

"Keep looking. What do you have Jim?"

"Our estimate of the number of people the military has confined or eliminated as a result of the uncontrolled spread of the disease," SecDef Jim Seymour said, "is in the neighborhood of five thousand."

The president started ranting and swearing about the mess Art Klemp had caused. "Most of those deaths can be laid at the feet of Art Klemp," he said angrily. "He should have stayed put in the Johns Creek shelter and been eliminated like a good citizen."

His advisors wisely refrained from commenting.

⚛

"Mr. President?" his chief of staff, Eric Epstein said, opening the situation room door a crack and sticking his head in. He'd heard the end of the president's rant, but pretended that he hadn't.

"What is it Eric?" Greg said, appearing to calm himself with an effort.

"Director Lister is waiting, whenever you're ready for her."

"Let's have her join us now," Greg said, totally under control now, or so it seemed to Eric.

The VEEP bunker situation room monitor lit up, showing Ambassador Porter, with CDC Director Anne Lister sitting next to him.

⚛

Anne had traveled back and forth, weekly, between her research facility in a public shelter and the VEEP bunker, primarily to report on her team's progress—or lack thereof—to the president and his advisors, but she also took the opportunity to shower and change clothes before meeting with them. He'd given her two months to find a cure and her time was up.

The CDC and Ft. Detrick scientists had gone through a lot of patients in that time. With pressure from the president to find a cure, they hadn't had the luxury of running lab tests before using their test cures on live patients. Their attempts at a cure had, so far, killed almost a hundred patients, instead of curing them.

Fortunately—or unfortunately, depending on one's perspective—SecDef Jim Seymour had had no difficulty finding more guinea pigs for the scientists. They just gathered more smallpox survivors.

When she arrived to give her latest report, after her usual shower and clothing change, Anne was shown into the VEEP bunker situation room and seated at the conference table next to Ambassador Porter, where she fidgeted nervously while waiting for the president to finished up other business with his advisors. The Ambassador tried to make her feel comfortable by offering her coffee and tea cakes, which she accepted, then let them sit untouched.

She knew this week was no different from previous weeks—they still didn't have a cure—so she was reluctant to start out with her usual progress report.

"The scientists working on a cure want to name the mutated virus," she said instead, "to differentiate it from the original virus." She didn't get a chance to tell the President what the scientists wanted to call it.

"It should be named after that reprobate Art Klemp," The president said angrily, interrupting her. "Call it Smallpox K in his honor. How is our favorite son, anyway?" he asked sarcastically.

Director Lister didn't want to talk about the vice president—she thought the president would be unhappy with his condition—and she didn't want to think about how upset the scientists would be when she told them what the president had decided to call the virus.

When the president continued to stare at her, tapping his fingers on the tabletop impatiently, she realized she would not get away without an explanation.

"We vaccinated him yesterday after we received your instructions." She paused, trying to decide how to proceed.

"Yes?" the president said, motioning for her to continue.

"As I told Director Dickson at the time, we thought that version of the cure was promising," she continued tentatively, "but Vice President Klemp reacted to his vaccination and developed symptoms that lead us to believe he will die soon," she said meekly. She didn't know exactly what to expect—she knew the president had forced the vice president into the program because he was unhappy with him, but he was, after all, the vice president of the United States.

Greg surprised her, calming noticeably, his expression neutral, for several moments. "What kind of symptoms?" he asked.

"The spots on his skin," she began, wondering how to explain the vice president's condition, "the ones from the original contamination, appear to have become infected, and are oozing. We've attempted to control those symptoms," she hurried to report, thinking the president would accuse her of not doing everything she could for the vice president, but he listened without reacting.

"And?"

"He . . . his face has swollen, and his body and limbs have become bloated," she continued. The president's face contorted at her description, but he made no comment, simply motioning for her to continue.

"You said he was already suffering from mood swings?" she asked and the president nodded. "Well, they've become worse—extreme."

"How long do you think he'll live?"

"No way to tell. Others have suffered similar physical and psychological changes; some have died and some are still alive."

"I guess I should see him before he dies."

"It's not pretty."

"Doesn't matter. Nobody deserves to die more than Art, but I need to let him have one last rant against me, face-to-face. His name will forever be associated with the mutated virus that killed millions of people around the world, including himself. But I told him I would pardon him if he cooperated. The pardon is already printed and signed. I'm not going to have it remembered that I refused to pardon him personally."

Anne nodded without speaking.

"Are we any closer to a vaccine that works?"

She just shook her head.

Greg sat at his desk looking at the monitor that showed former Vice President Art Klemp in his detention cell. He chose to be alone for this meeting because he didn't want anyone interrupting or questioning anything that was said or done. Besides, he knew the interview was being recorded.

He studied Art's bloated face, covered with weeping sores, and noticed the jump suit they had dressed him in because his regular clothes would be inadequate to cover his swollen limbs. Although Art could have seen him if he'd looked up at the monitor on the wall, he hadn't. Instead, he twisted and turned uncomfortably, sitting on his cot, scratching his weeping sores and wiping his hands on his jump suit. His lips were moving, so Greg turned up the volume to hear what he was saying, discovering that Art was talking to himself and cursing, at times sounding rational, at others, completely insane. He heard his own name and that of Captain Marston mentioned several times, associated with the curses.

Convinced that Art had lost his mind, but believing he still needed to have this conversation, rational or otherwise, he spoke.

"Hello, Art," he said.

Art looked around suspiciously, not registering that the voice came from the monitor above him on the opposite wall, and continued to talk to himself.

"Look at the monitor on the wall, Art."

Art finally looked up and, seeing Greg, sneered, cursed and looked away again. "What do you want from me? Haven't I done what you asked? And what did it get me?"

"Art, look at me for a minute."

"Hah, you'd like that, wouldn't you? What did you bring me? Is that Captain Marston dead yet? I contaminated her, you know, and it was a pleasure. She was so surprised. Hah."

"Art, I wanted to tell you that because you cooperated with the search for a cure to the smallpox virus—"

"I have smallpox, you know. I let them inject me with something that was supposed to cure me, but it didn't. Greg told me to cooperate and I did but did he thank me? Oh no? Not him. He sits in his protected bunker and lets me do all the work."

"Art," Greg tried again, quickly losing patience, "this is Greg and I'm here to thank you for cooperating with the scientists, and to tell you I've pardoned you. I signed the pardon and recorded it."

"Is that captain dead yet? I contaminated her you know. She thought she was so smart. She tried to trick me, but I saw right through her. I hope she's dead. Is she dead yet?"

"Art, the scientists have found a cure for smallpox," he lied, not knowing why. "Do you know that I named the mutated virus after you?"

"Greg told me to cooperate and I did. Is he dead? Why hasn't he come to see me? Is that captain dead? I contaminated her, you know. I licked her face, hehe. I licked her lips and teeth and face. She should be dead. Is she dead?"

The recording of this conversation would show that Greg had done what he said he would do, whether Art was coherent enough to understand or not. As Greg shut off the connection, he thought about how out of control everything seemed. Convinced that he and his advisors had responded to each crisis the best they could, his wife's question came to mind again. Was he killing innocent people? Maybe Liz was right; maybe he would go to hell.

The Outcasts—Nebraska, 9 October

They stopped at the Platte River to bathe and replenish their water supply, then continued on to the city of North Platte where the river divided. They followed the South Platte river to what the pioneers called the Upper Crossing.

"The Oregon Trail follows the North Platte river," Beth explained, with her nose in a brochure. "But in pioneer days, it was easier to cross from the South Platte River to the North Platte, here at the Upper Crossing. This was the first major grade faced by the emigrants, climbing two hundred and forty feet in just over one and a half miles to the plateau between the two rivers. The brochure says that you can still see the trail ruts from the wagons in places. That would be interesting to see, don't you think?" No one had an opinion, so Beth led the way.

As they hiked, Beth pointed out orange stains on some of the rocks, which the brochure said were caused by the rusted iron rims that held the wooden wagon wheels together.

The hike wasn't difficult, because of their increased stamina, but Bryce kept his arm around Candy, and helped her in the steeper places. Candy periodically whispered in Bryce's ear, which kept them both smiling. Lisa and Kerri mimicked them behind their backs, by alternately pretending to struggle, then helping each other. The air, which had been cooler than normal in the south, was becoming chill here in the north.

☢

When they reached the Platte River at Kearney, Beth located Fort Kearney and led the others on a self-guided tour, breaking into the visitor center to look around.

"This says Fort Kearny was a military post established in 1848 to protect pioneers from the threat of Indian attacks," Beth read as the others looked around at the artifacts in glass cabinets. "The location of the fort was strategic, being located at a junction of several west-bound trails." After wandering the site and looking at the reconstructed fort, they rested at a picnic table and ate.

"You said this was a junction of several trails," Lisa said. "Does that mean that there's more than one Oregon Trail?"

"It looks like there were several trails from the east that joined here," Beth replied.

"They had Indians. We have the U.S. military," Bryce said.

"Hopefully the military isn't hanging around here looking for us," Candy said. Lisa and Kerri looked around reflexively, as if they expected to see soldiers appear suddenly.

"Would the military have protected us from the creeps in the tent city?" Candy wondered aloud.

"Or would they have protected the tent city from us?" Bryce asked, sitting thigh-to-thigh with Candy.

There wasn't a good answer for that, so Beth just shook her head.

VEEP Bunker, 10 October

Anne was exhausted. She patted her hair self-consciously. She hadn't had time to clean up—her last shower had been three days earlier—and she'd barely had time to get to the VEEP bunker and remove the hazmat suit before reporting to the situation room for a meeting with the president. Earlier, she'd indicated to Ambassador Porter that she thought her team had finally found a cure for Smallpox K. Minutes later the Ambassador had called back to say that the president wanted a progress report in thirty minutes.

The president entered the Prime situation room, sat at his conference table, and looked up at Anne. She noticed the surprised look that registered momentarily on his face, probably because of her disheveled appearance.

"Hello, Director Lister," he said. "I understand you have a report for us."

"Yes sir. Our latest test patient didn't die," she said tiredly. It came out sounding sarcastic.

The president blinked and sat up straight.

"I'm sorry, sir. That didn't come out right."

"It came out exactly right," he said, chuckling. "You met my deadline. I'm sorry I've been pushing you so hard. You look like you could use a break."

She thought he was just being polite. There was no way she could take a break until they confirmed they had a cure.

"Thank you, sir. I'll keep that in mind."

"So, you're ready to begin production of the vaccine?"

It was Anne's turn to be startled.

"No!" she said. "We're ready to begin the clinical testing phase."

"You've been testing for the last two months," the president said, looking confused.

"Well, no. All of our previous trials have been failures. Now that we have a possible cure, we need to perform clinical studies. We need to test the vaccine on multiple subjects, observe their response over time—"

"How much time do you need for these clinical studies?" He asked, interrupting. He was becoming agitated.

"In this case, I think we could limit it to four months," Anne said, feeling defensive.

"Unacceptable!" the president said, banging his fist on the table. "We've been waiting for this cure for two months already.

We can't wait another four months."

Anne continued quickly, in an effort to explain her position before the president cut her off again, as she suspected he would. She would have preferred a lot more time, but understood the urgency of the current situation.

"Sir, we have a highly unusual situation—"

The president cut her off again.

"I'll give you thirty days for your clinical studies, then I want you to begin production of the vaccine. The military will begin mass collections and vaccination, town by town, city by city, state by state, spreading out from the two testing stations." He was on a roll now.

Anne sputtered, trying to think of a way to slow him down. He was moving too fast for her, as usual.

"If you want to hold some of the vaccinated people longer than that, for observation, with an idea on improving the vaccine over time, you are free to do so. Chuck?"

"Yes, sir?" HomeSec Chuck Dickson asked. Anne thought he looked like he was trying to keep from laughing.

"Work with the director to make it happen." With that, the president stood and left the room, not giving Anne a chance to argue further.

Anne looked at Chuck, who raised his eyebrows and shrugged, then shook her head in defeat.

"It's too bad Vice President Klemp was vaccinated a week ago with an earlier version," she said, wondering if they could have saved him if they'd waited a week and given him this latest vaccine.

"The president told you to proceed, didn't he?" Chuck asked and she nodded. "Not your fault. What do you and your team need?"

Was it advisable to revaccinate him? She'd have to discuss that with her colleagues.

The Preserve, 11 October

"Mike's awake," Amos said, to sighs of relief. "His mother is with him."

Emily had invited everyone to attend this meeting, but Amos noticed that Jason and Nathan had chosen to stay away, which had helped him relax—he wouldn't have to defend everything he said.

"What's he saying?" Chris asked.

"Not much, Chris. He's, understandably, a little confused."

"Can we see him?" Rachel asked, sitting by Chris and squeezing his hand with both of hers.

"Not yet, Rachel. His body is healing, as it needs to, but we still need to evaluate his mental state. We'll do that and let you know. Any other questions?"

"What do you mean, 'his mental state'?" Chris asked.

Amos wondered how to explain in terms that Chris would understand. Chris was intelligent, but would he understand the medical terminology?

"Some types of injuries," Amos said, "are accompanied by memory loss."

"Like a concussion?" Chris asked, interrupting.

"Exactly," Amos said. "In these cases, we need to allow the patient—Mike—time to remember what happened gradually. Some memories can be so traumatic that it takes a long time, if ever, to recover them correctly or completely."

"You mean he may never remember what happened to him?" Rachel asked.

"That's a possibility. But we hope that's not the case with Mike."

"Can't you tell him what happened?" Matt asked.

"We don't know, Matt. We weren't with him."

☢

"Amos," Lillie said, "are these things Mike told me true?"

"That depends on what he told you," he said, smiling. "I didn't hear everything he said."

"Wipe that silly grin off your face and give me a straight answer."

"Okay," Amos said seriously. "I only know what Katie told me—what she heard before the gate closed, and which she's already told you—and what I saw when we re-opened it." He told her what he'd seen, heard and done, leaving out only the part about choking and threatening the three men. "How does that compare with what Mike told you?"

"He's pretty foggy about the whole incident, and doesn't remember anything about going through the gate," she said with obvious concern.

"What does Katie know?"

"I sent her out of the room as soon as he started talking. She was already uptight, and his incoherent speech just upset her more."

"Then we'll have to wait for him to become more lucid."

"Maybe he'll never remember it all," Terry said, sitting off to one side. "Concussions and head trauma can do that."

"Of course, you're right, Terry," Amos said. "What we need to decide is what to do about Mike's research. Do we continue investigating travel through the gate, or do we put a stop to it altogether?"

"And what do we tell Katie?" Lillie said.

"Are these decisions for the board?" Terry asked.

"Another good question," Amos said. "What do you think?"

"I think we need to hear what Mike has to say," Terry said. "If he doesn't remember anything, maybe we stop the research and don't tell him."

The Preserve, 12 October

"Mom, why won't anyone let me see Mike?" Katie asked her mother, Becca, who was in the kitchen preparing dinner. She hadn't left his side since the accident, until the previous day, when Lillie had made her leave. She'd wandered the Preserve—worried and trying to understand—looking for someplace where she didn't have to face the others or her memories. She was falling apart emotionally, so she went to the one person she thought would understand and help her.

"I don't know dear," Becca said sympathetically. "Have you spoken to your father?"

"I can't find him. Is he hiding in the lab?"

Just then, Lillie walked in.

"Becca, do you need some help?" Lillie asked. "Oh, hi Katie, how are you holding up?"

"Katie was just asking me why she can't see Mike," Becca said.

Lillie looked at Katie with concern.

"Let me talk to Amos, Katie. I'll see if he'll meet with you after dinner, okay?"

"That would be appreciated, Lillie. Thanks."

✺

It was Lillie who escorted Katie to the office, where Amos and Terry were waiting. Terry met her halfway across the room and gave her a hug.

277

"Hi baby. Sorry we haven't explained things to you. We're still trying to figure them out, ourselves," he said.

"Have a seat, Katie, Lillie," Amos said, pointing to two vacant chairs. "Katie, you told us you saw Mike go through the gate. Do you know what he was trying to do?"

"He said it was a parallel world and he was going to prove we all existed in this other world. I didn't understand, and told him I'd rather he not try it, because it looked like he was doing it behind your back."

"Did he say *why* he thought this was a parallel world?"

"He said he saw your name in a newspaper, and that you were an advisor to President McCormick, which he already told you. He was going to get a copy to prove it."

"Did he say anything else?"

"Not that I can remember, but he was pretty worked up over the whole situation."

"Worked up?"

"Well, more like, so excited that he couldn't stand still."

"Thank you, Katie. Now, you want to know why Lillie asked you to leave the hospital yesterday, just when Mike was waking up, right?" When Katie nodded, he could see light reflected off the tear in the corner of her eye. "You were worried because of Mike's physical condition. That's normal, when someone we love suffers. As a trained nurse—and an excellent one, I might add—Lillie noticed your anxiety level. When Mike started to wake, and not knowing what Mike went through, or his mental state, Lillie was concerned that what Mike might say, would make it harder on you—increase your stress."

"I don't . . . " Katie started to say, but Amos held up his hand to stop her.

"Katie, please accept Lillie's professional opinion, that it could be hard on you to hear what he might say when he's coming out from under medication. Her actions were not to punish you, but to protect you."

"But he's been awake for hours. Why can't I see him now?"

"I'm sorry it's taken us this long to get back to you, Katie. But, as I said, we're trying to understand what happened as well. Mike's had a very traumatic experience, and we want him to heal properly."

"So do I," Katie said, as tears started to roll down both cheeks. "I want to help."

Amos understood Katie's frustration; he'd dealt with it many times. Lillie, who was sitting next to her, took Katie's hand in both of hers and set them in her lap. Katie looked at Lillie pleadingly.

"Katie," Amos continued, "part of the healing process is to get Mike to remember what happened, without anyone suggesting things that he'll later think were his own memories. Until we know Mike's mental state, we don't want to say anything that will trigger a traumatic memory or plant a thought that's not his own. Do you understand that?"

Katie nodded, likely not trusting herself to speak.

"Sometimes, even seeing someone who was present during the traumatic experience can alter their memory of the event."

"Does that mean I can't be in the room with him?"

"If we let you sit with him, we'll be taking a risk; but we'll allow it on the condition that one of us will be with you, and you'll have to promise not to say anything to him."

Katie looked startled, as if this was asking too much, but nodded thoughtfully.

"It won't be easy, Katie. Think about sitting by him, with him asking you questions. You'll think it won't hurt to answer his questions. But that's exactly what we don't want."

Katie started to cry quietly, a sign to Amos that she understood and knew she had to accept their conditions.

"Terry, can we put a film on the observation window that will make it a two-way mirror, so Katie can watch Mike without being in the room with him."

Katie looked up at her dad expectantly.

"I'll do that as soon as Mike's asleep," he said.

"Thanks. Katie, you can sit with him, as long as you follow our instructions. If it becomes too difficult, you can leave, without explanation, and watch him through the window. Is that acceptable?"

Katie nodded.

"Okay. Now, the next thing I want to tell you, Katie, is confidential. You can discuss this with *no one,* not even your mother. Will you agree to that condition?"

"Why not Mom?"

"Right now, we are the only four who have any idea what actually happened to Mike. If you say anything about what you know, or what I'm about to tell you, to someone else, and it gets out, we'll have a heck of a time controlling life in the Preserve." Amos knew he was telling her a half-truth, since the board knew about the twin world, but he needed Katie's cooperation.

Katie's expression changed, like she was suddenly doubting Amos for the first time.

"Katie," Terry said, drawing her attention, "this is serious. Amos may be understating the difficulty it could cause. You need to promise us that you'll tell no one what you saw or did in the lab. In fact, no one can know that you've been to the lab, where no one else has been allowed to go. Do you understand?"

"I think so," she said. "Is that because what Mike told me is true?"

"That's exactly right, Katie," Amos said with a smile. "Who said you weren't brilliant?"

"Amos!" Lillie scolded, but they all laughed, while Katie wiped tears from her eyes.

"Okay," Katie said, "I promise not to share anything you tell me in confidence. Are you going to make Mike promise, too?"

"First, we need to get him healthy enough to leave the hospital, then we'll worry about what he might say to someone else. Is Matt staying away from the hospital?" Amos asked, looking at Lillie.

"He's so busy trying to manage the gardens," Lillie said, laughing, "that he barely has time for his wife."

"Okay. Katie," Amos said with a sigh, "what Mike told you about the gate is true, as far as we know. It appears that the world through the gate is a parallel world. None of the damage we've seen in our world has occurred in the twin world. I haven't seen the newspaper Mike told you about, but he swears he saw my name associated with the president's."

"You called it a twin world."

"Yes, we call the opening he went through, the Gemini Gate, or, the door between twin worlds. The reason I made Mike promise not to go through the gate is because we don't know what kind of harm we could cause to the other world or to us."

"He promised?"

"He did, and I'm a little upset that he let his curiosity cloud his judgment. However, what we've learned as a result of his little escapade is that there *is* an impact—to the gate, itself—by passing through it."

"You mean I didn't do anything to make the gate shut down?"

"No, Katie, you didn't do anything wrong. Let me try to explain. All of your body functions are controlled by your nervous system, which is the pathway for sending electrical signals from one part of your body to another.

"When your brain tells your foot to take a step, an electrical impulse jumps from one cell to the next in rapid succession, and makes your foot respond, almost instantaneously. When you're in danger, your heart needs to speed up. I'm sure you've felt that recently."

"Yeah," Katie said. "When the gate shut down."

"Alright." Amos continued. "Just as there are nerves running to every part of your body, there is a mass of nerve cells in your heart, called the sinoatrial node, or SA node, that tells your heart to speed up. The flow of electricity through a single nerve is very small. But the flow through the SA node, although still small, is much larger than through a single nerve.

"Mike and I have both put a hand through the gate, with no adverse reaction, as far as we can tell. We're going to study that some more. I should have guessed at the answer when we felt a tingling in our hands, like static electricity, but I didn't. What we suspect happened is that when Mike's heart passed through the gate, the SA node caused enough of a power surge that it changed the control settings on the gate, shutting it down."

21

Whatcha watchin'?

The Preserve, 13 October

"Physics lab at three thirty," a young female voice, with a rural Utah accent, said. Terry moved the gate to one side and rotated it, to focus on two students, walking on the sidewalk next to the science lab. Their long winter coats hid all but their faces. Terry looked at Amos, smiling, but didn't say anything that would give away their presence.

They'd been jumping between markers that Mike had set in the program, as places he might be interested in revisiting. So far, they'd been to twenty-two of the eighty-seven markers.

"Shut it down," Amos mouthed, so Terry closed the gate and turned off the Observer.

"What do you think?" Terry asked.

"I think Mike was right," Amos replied thoughtfully. "There's no other explanation. It's a parallel world."

"We thought we'd figured it out a couple of times before," Terry said with a barked laugh, "and we were wrong each time."

"The only thing we haven't seen is a newspaper report mentioning my role in Greg's government."

"Do you want to go through and start an internet search, like Mike suggested?"

Amos thought about it for a few moments, then sat forward and studied Terry.

"Have you figured out how to compensate for the electrical charge from the SA node?"

"An estimate only. We don't know if your SA node has the same voltage as Mike's or mine, and we don't have the equipment to measure it, except the Observer. If you go through the gate, we'll have an accurate reading. Now that we know the cause of *that* problem, we can respond faster."

"What about other problems?" Amos asked, trying to visualize himself going through the gate—into the unknown.

"No idea. Are you thinking that Mike might have been incapacitated by a shock to his nervous system, or some other problem, and not by the run-in with the three men?"

"How can we know? We've run every test that our medical equipment can perform. Are there other risks that we can't imagine and can't test for? Then, assuming I didn't run into problems immediately, how would I get around and where would I begin looking for information about our families?"

"If you can go back and forth through the gate without problems, I can program the Observer to drop you off anywhere you want."

"My own private bus, eh?" Amos asked with a smile.

"With faster service," Terry laughed.

"Mike thought he would get on the internet; but I can't imagine it. I could access the web in a public location, like an internet café; but I don't want to risk setting up an account."

"Maybe there are other ways to get information," Terry said, "like a public library. Do they keep back copies of newspapers?"

"One way to find out. I'll go look."

The Preserve, 15 October

"Whatcha watchin'?" Rylee asked innocently as she walked in on

Nathan, who sat on a couch facing the TV monitor, with the light from the screen dancing on his face.

Rylee's strength, stamina and confidence had been gradually building over the last few weeks, as she and Nathan had continued working out together. During their workout earlier that day, Nathan had inadvertently mentioned staying up late at night in the community center, so Rylee had slipped quietly out of her room—after Rachel had fallen asleep—to be with him.

As she entered, Nathan turned off the television—putting the room in darkness—before Rylee could see what he was watching. She sat on the couch, near him, and smiled tentatively, not knowing how he would respond.

Nathan didn't speak for several moments, making her nervous. She realized she still didn't know him well despite the time they'd spent together; and she couldn't judge his mood because the dim night-lights cast deep shadows across his face

"What are you doing here?" he finally asked.

From the coarseness of his voice, she couldn't tell if he was upset with her, or just tired, but his question hurt her feelings. She'd thought he would welcome the company.

"I just wanted to be with you," she replied meekly, wondering if it was a mistake to come. "Don't you want me to be here?"

Nathan sat up straighter and lifted his arm in invitation. She still couldn't see his face, to see if he was smiling, but decided it didn't matter, now that she was here with him. She scooted over next to him, under his outstretched arm, which he placed over her shoulder. She snuggled against him, inhaling his fresh soap smell, and decided she liked this even better than his musky smell.

He put his free hand under her chin and turned her head toward him. When she was looking into his shadowed eyes, he leaned in and kissed her. She had never kissed a boy, so she didn't know if she did it right, but it felt and tasted good. His stubbled face against her cheek surprised her; she hadn't noticed that he had facial hair, but she liked that, too.

He was awesome.

He kissed her again, then turned her toward him, reached his hands around her back, and rubbed her shoulders.

"Any pain from the exercises?" he asked.

"Not much," she lied. Actually, she'd been miserable the first couple of weeks, but was getting used to the soreness in her limbs. That must be normal, she'd thought more than once.

After a while, she started to doze off.

"That's enough," Nathan said, as he pushed her to a standing position. He didn't get up with her. "Go to bed," he added and waved her away.

She was disappointed, but knew she needed some sleep. As she left the room, she heard the TV turn back on. He was staying, she realized, watching videos. She was tempted to return, if only to see what he was watching, but decided it didn't matter; he had accepted her.

The Preserve, 16 October

"Amos," Terry said as Amos entered the lab to find Terry looking at the open gate. "I've looked at four public libraries and the Utah State and Weber State University libraries and can't find any newspapers. If they have them, they must be in electronic format, so we'd have to log into their website to look at them."

"Okay," Amos said. "Thanks for looking. What else can we try?"

"Well, I'm at the Logan public library right now. Do you want me to try to create an account?"

"Yes, and if it doesn't work for you, I'll try it."

It didn't work for either of them. The system must have known they didn't live in the city, or their addresses didn't match any city address, or something.

"Now what?" Terry asked, frustrated.

"Maybe Mike's right," Amos sighed. "Maybe one of us has to go through the gate and look around."

"While you think about that," Terry said, "I'll keep watching the newspapers."

"No," Amos said, becoming more animated, "Go to Smiths. We're going to start a newspaper subscription."

It took a moment for Terry to realize what Amos meant; he was going to start stealing the daily newspaper.

The Preserve, 19 October

"I haven't seen anything that's suitable to share," Terry said.

Amos wanted to share information with the others, particularly because so many had been asking questions. Chris had been hounding his parents for information ever since he'd learned that Amos was a friend of President McCormick. So, Amos had called a Board meeting to discuss what information to share. He indicated that they might want to comb through satellite footage of the war. He'd invited Matt, but had excluded Mike and Katie from the meeting. They were tending the gardens after what had been a near-miraculous recovery in Mike's health.

It had been weeks since anyone had looked at video footage, and what they saw now, which was precious little, Amos thought was not suitable for the younger family members. But they sat determinedly, watching a few videos that showed violence, death and destruction taking place around the country and the world.

"Well, we have to show them something," Becca said distastefully. "Chris won't be satisfied until we do."

"I've seen enough to last me a lifetime," Matt said, looking pale.

"This is the first time I've seen anything like this and I don't know why I wanted to." Emily had her face buried in Matt's shoulder so she didn't have to watch any more.

"Maybe you should tell Chris what you think," Becca said. "Maybe that will satisfy him."

"Chris won't care what Matt saw," Terry said, shaking his head. "He won't be satisfied until he sees if for himself."

"Terry," Amos said, "feel free to show Chris anything you'd like. I think the rest of us have seen enough."

"Will do," Terry said, grim-faced. "Chaos," he added, apparently speaking to himself.

☢

"How are you feeling, Mike?" Amos asked, clearly watching Mike's reaction.

Mike had just come from the gardens, where he'd left Katie working by herself. Mike knew that his dad had worried about him being around others who would undoubtedly ask questions, but as long as Katie didn't say anything, his dad thought it would be okay for them to work together; Mike and Amos both thought the physical movement would help him heal faster.

Mike had a smile on his face and a spring in his step. He'd recovered from most of the physical injuries, but had blank periods in his memory, including most of his experience in the twin world. He remembered going through the gate, but he couldn't remember Katie's involvement, and Terry and his dad refused to tell him. Amos had told him the blanks would fill in eventually and Mike had agreed to be satisfied with that, for now. He'd confided in his dad that he and Katie had become very close. It seemed like every time he turned around, she was there, and he was ecstatic about it.

"Fantastic, Dad."

"Any new memories?"

"No, but I can't help feeling like one of my missing memories has something to do with my relationship with Katie. I don't remember her being so affectionate before the accident."

"It'll come to you. Don't push it."

"I'm glad you changed our schedules so she could be with me in the gardens. She's very helpful."

"I heard that the two of you are working in the gardens alone—no helpers."

Mike was suddenly embarrassed, and struggled for something to say.

"We talk a lot," he finally said.

"Talk is good," Amos replied. "How's your back?"

Mike's back hurt—agonizingly at at times. He had suffered a herniated disk, and it seemed to be his final physical hurdle.

"I'm doing the exercises that Terry gave me, every morning. So, what's going on with the gate?"

"What do you remember?"

Amos listened as Mike recalled his memory of creating the jumps, and looking at a lot of sites in the twin world. He wasn't altogether surprised by Mike's failure to say anything about putting his hand through the gate, or anything about planning to go through the gate. It was as if anything to do with physically passing through the gate had been lost from Mike's memory.

Katie spent as much time as possible with Mike. She kept her promise to Amos that she wouldn't talk about the lab or Mike's accident. In fact, she spoke very little when she was with him, but she worried; about him, about the accident, about what Amos had told her, and about the future.

Lillie had permanently reassigned some of her other responsibilities, so she could spend more time helping Mike in the gardens, and everyone had realized quickly that Mike and Katie wanted to be alone. They could usually manage what needed to be done between the two of them, but if they got too distracted, paying more attention to each other than the task at hand, Mike would work longer hours for the next couple of days.

At the end of each day, if they were together, they would walk hand-in-hand to the bedroom cluster. If they were apart, they would meet in the community center or in the common area by their bedrooms, which were next to each other, and sit together holding hands, talking, and sometimes falling asleep on the couch together.

Chris realized how much time Mike had been spending with Katie, and knew that their parents had encouraged it, ever since Mike's accident—which still hadn't been explained. Chris couldn't tell how Katie had captured Mike's attention, but when he put all the puzzle pieces together, he suspected that Mike and Katie were doing more than just talking, late into the night. Maybe Rachel and Katie talked about things that they didn't share with him or Mike, and maybe she would tell him what she knew.

When he walked Rachel to her room that night, instead of kissing her good night and going to his own room, as he usually did, he stood looking at her, even after they'd run out of things to say.

"Do you want to come in?" she asked, after an awkward silence.

Realizing he'd placed her in a compromising position, he was suddenly embarrassed.

"No," he said, "Rylee's probably trying to sleep."

"Rylee's sleeping in Sydney's room tonight. They often do that."

Caught off-guard, Chris didn't know how to respond. But when Rachel opened the door wider, Chris entered. She didn't invite him to sit, so they stood looking at each other, Chris trying to read Rachel's thoughts from her expression.

"What do you think Mike and Katie do when they stay together late at night?" he asked.

"I think all they do is talk," Rachel said, "or fall asleep; they're so tired all the time."

"You don't think they're doing anything else?"

"No, Chris. Why?"

"They're spending a lot of time together. And Katie looks happier than I've ever seen her. You don't think they're—"

She cut him off. "No Chris, and you shouldn't be thinking that way either. I think you should go."

☢

Lillie looked at Amos and nodded toward Katie and Mike, who sat on a couch in the community center and appeared to be asleep, with Katie leaning against Mike. Even with the adjusted schedules, they stayed up late, just so they could be together. Several family members had commented on how tired they looked, and some of the mistakes they'd made in the gardens. Rachel had even told her mother what Chris had asked her, which Lillie hadn't shared with Amos or Chris's parents.

"What do you suggest?" Amos asked.

"I suggest they get married so they can get some sleep," Lillie said.

Mike might have sensed that they were talking about him because he opened his eyes just then.

"What?" he asked, looking at his parents, who were both looking at him. When he spoke, Katie also woke.

"I just suggested that you two get married so you can get some sleep," Lillie said.

Mike and Katie looked at each other and smiled.

"That would be okay with me," Katie said. "What do you think, Mike?"

Mike returned the smile and nodded, but looked embarrassed.

"Maybe another wedding will keep everyone's minds off what's going on outside," Amos said.

22

You screwed up!

The Preserve, 20 October

"Dad!" Mike called as he charged into the lab, followed by Lillie. "Dad, I remember."

Amos looked past Mike at Lillie, who nodded her head.

"Okay, Mike, sit down and tell us about it," Amos said.

Mike was so excited that when he sat down, he almost missed the chair. He got a worried look on his face and sat straighter, but still on the edge of the chair.

"Dad, I remember going through the gate and encountering three bad guys, who chased me, caught me, and beat on me until I fell down, then started kicking me. That's all I remember until I woke in the hospital. Did it really happen?"

"It fits with everything we know, but we didn't see any of that because the gate closed behind you."

"Why didn't you tell me?"

"You needed to remember it on your own, Mike. If we had suggested anything, you might have remembered what we said instead of the truth."

Mike was so excited, he fidgeted, tapping his shoes on the floor and slapping his legs with his hands.

"I did it, then, didn't I?"

"What you did," Lillie said, "was scare about ten years off my life."

"Sorry, Mom," he said, but he looked anything but apologetic. "So, you figured out what happened and brought me back. Did Katie accidently turn the Observer off and not get it back on? Is that what happened?"

"No, Mike," Terry said, speaking seriously. "You screwed up!"

Mike became still, glanced at his dad, then looked back at Terry, possibly trying to understand why he made such a serious accusation.

"Mike," Amos said, taking over for Terry, "what you did, was ignore my instructions and concerns about the gate and the twin world. You were lucky. We guessed what had happened and were able to get you out of a critical situation before it got any worse."

All of Mike's excitement and enthusiasm evaporated. He sat quietly and studied his dad.

"That's why I was in the hospital for so long?"

"We induced a coma to let your body heal. When I think you're ready, I'll tell you about the damage they did to your body." He didn't know if he would ever be able to tell Mike how close he came to being murdered. He hadn't and probably wouldn't tell Lillie either. "We're still evaluating the emotional and mental damage."

"Mental—?"

"You're *still* remembering things. We don't know how much more there is to your experience, and we don't want to suggest anything that may influence your recovery."

"What *can* you tell me?"

"I guess it wouldn't hurt to tell you about the SA node." Amos explained their theory and the effect of the SA node on the gate. Without waiting for Mike to ask, he explained that Terry had been attempting to estimate the impact on the gate if any of them went through it again, and how to compensate for it, but made sure Mike understood that anything they came up with was only a guess. And, they didn't know if there were other, unknown impacts.

"So, in a way, you advanced our research, but at a great cost to you, your mother, me, Terry, and especially Katie. She spent almost every minute with you while you were in the hospital. She was a nervous wreck."

"That would explain the difference I've seen in her since I woke up," Mike said, contritely. "I need to apologize to her."

The Preserve, 22 October

The wedding required very little preparation because they'd already been through one with Emily and Matt. Katie agreed that they should reuse the decorations from Emily's wedding, as much as possible, so that they didn't "waste any time".

After a busy day of celebrating, with Amos performing the wedding ceremony, Mike and Katie retired to their honeymoon suite, which had previously been Katie's bedroom.

Amos sat with Lillie on their favorite couch in the community center, after everyone had gone to their rooms.

"Did you see the way Chris and Rachel looked at each other all evening?" Lillie asked, interrupting his musings.

"What did I miss this time?" he asked. They both knew that he sometimes focused on one thing to the exclusion of others, even when those other things were going on around him. She had pointed it out to him often enough.

"Well, you *were* busy performing a wedding," she said. "I guess you could be excused for not noticing what everyone else was doing."

"And—"

"I'm concerned about the affect this second wedding will have on them. I don't think Rachel is mature enough for marriage yet. I trust her, but Chris is a little head-strong. I'd hate for him to pressure her into anything. And we have two young girls that don't pair up with anyone, except maybe Nathan, heaven forbid."

"You want me to talk to them?" Amos asked, surprised.

"I know it's my job to manage the children. I just think, maybe if you spent a little more time with Chris, your perspective on life would rub off on him."

"Terry's his father," Amos said.

"And I'm sure Terry's a good father," Lillie said, "but you're the religious leader in our home. He might respect that, and it wouldn't hurt for him to have a second adult male example."

"From an old man, who doesn't understand the younger generation, right?"

Lillie smiled and Amos sighed. He and Lillie already read scriptures and prayed together, as they had for years; but he had always left organized religion to, well, organized religion.

"And"—Lillie added, her expression serious, as though this was extremely important to her— "whenever Nathan and Chris are in the same room, the tension is palpable, especially if Chris goes into the weight room when Nathan's there. I think Nathan sees that as his exclusive domain and Chris as his nemesis. If either of them speaks, or if they come within feet of each other, they almost come to blows. It isn't comfortable for anyone in the same room with them."

"In the weight room?"

"Anywhere in the house. Becca asked Chris to figure out Nathan's schedule and work around it, so he could avoid a confrontation, because she didn't want to see either of them get hurt."

"What did Chris say?"

"He said he'd do it for her, but said it grudgingly. He's trying to protect Rachel from Nathan. He said he wasn't afraid of Nathan, and wouldn't put up with any of his crap—his word—and that she could tell Nathan he'd said so."

"What did Becca say to that?"

"She told Chris that Nathan was Brittany's responsibility, and that he should just try to avoid him. Becca said Chris got all huffy, and when she gave him a stern look, he said, 'Okay, okay. I'll avoid Nathan.' Anyway, Nathan's been seen less and less. He's always missed work assignments, not bothering to explain himself, but now he avoids everyone, all the time."

"Here's something you may not know," Amos said. "You remember our decision to start recording what's going on in the common areas of the Preserve, right?" Lillie nodded, so Amos continued. "Terry showed me a recording of Nathan sitting in the community center watching videos in the dark after we go to bed."

"No surprise there. Becca said that every morning now, there's evidence that Nathan's been in the kitchen. I spoke to Brittany about it. She said she'd asked Jason to talk to Nathan, but he refused to be responsible for his *adult* son. More and more, the only places we know Nathan goes are the weight room, to work out, the community center, to watch videos, or his bedroom, to sleep, usually during the day."

"That's what Terry said. How's it going with Rylee?" He had seen Rylee in the most recent videos of Nathan in the community center, but didn't want to tell Lillie that.

"She's started missing assignments, usually during the time Nathan would be in the weight room, so I suspect she's going there to work out with him; at least I hope that's all they're doing."

"I'll ask Terry to check on Rylee, too. What else do you want me to do?"

"I don't know. I'll think about it. What's going on with Jason?"

Amos ran his hand through his hair in frustration. "I don't

know what he's up to. He used to spend a lot of time in the library, reading, or in the weight room; but now he's acting restless, wandering the Preserve, when he isn't complaining about helping with housekeeping, the gardens, or the kitchen. Mike told me he caught Jason trying doors randomly, probably to see what access he has. When he was caught in the act, he made some lame excuse about being lost in the maze of the Preserve, and then challenged Mike about what we were hiding behind locked doors. He's been here for three months, for cryin' out loud. Why is he asking that now?"

"What should we do about our delinquent family members?"

"Well, with some of them, loving them might work; with others, maybe we should try shooting them."

"Amos!"

"Alright. What if we just tie them to an ant hill and see if the ants like them more than we do?"

Lillie reached over with her free hand and slapped Amos, open palmed on the chest. He pretended to be hurt.

The Outcasts—Nebraska, 29 October

In the North Platte River valley, the terrain changed from the vast farmland they'd passed through farther east to smaller farms along the river; and the ground rose slowly toward the mountains in the west.

"I think we should find someplace to spend the winter," Beth said as she studied the sky. What had been dust and smoke in the air, a few weeks ago, had now become real clouds, the air was colder, and rain fell frequently. She didn't know how much farther they could travel before they'd have to stop, but they agreed to continue until they found something suitable.

Beth pointed out prominent rock formations that they passed

along the way—Courthouse Rock, Jailhouse Rock, and Chimney Rock—which the pioneers had used to gage their progress. By the time they reached the Scottsbluff area, they were in heavy rain, with snow threatening. Ash covered the ground, the buildings, the plants—everything—and the rain turned everything a muddy gray. Beth hadn't figured it out yet, but they were in the fallout area from the destruction of the missile silos near Cheyenne, Wyoming.

"I recognize the corn," Lisa said, motioning to a field on the left side of the road, then pointed at low-lying plants on the right. "Are those weeds?"

"They're potatoes," Bryce said. "Obviously the farmers couldn't get their crops out of the fields before the weather changed."

"Look, there are people in the cornfield," Candy said, "and they're coming this way."

"We should leave," Lisa said, anxiously.

"Let's see what they have to say," Beth said, as one man looked up and waved to them, "but be prepared to run."

There were five of them; the two men that Beth had noticed first, plus a woman and two young girls. As they exited the cornfield, about twenty feet away, Beth could see that each wore a dripping wet waterproof poncho and had a large pack on their back. The older of the two men was smiling.

"They look like they're happy to see us," Candy said, surprised.

"That'll be a first," Beth replied cautiously.

"Hallooo," the man called, and waved again.

"Hello," Beth replied. "Kinda wet to be harvesting corn, isn't it?"

The man chuckled. "Gotta' get it while we can. Looks like this rain is gonna' turn to snow. Where're you folks comin' from and where ya' goin'?"

Beth wasn't sure if she could trust these people, but they seemed so friendly that she let her guard down a little.

"We're coming from Georgia and headed west," she said.

The man stopped suddenly and got a surprised look on his face. The others stopped behind him.

"You have sores all over your face," he said. "Are you sick?"

"We were," Beth said. "Very sick. I think we're better, but I don't know if we're still contagious. Best if you keep your distance."

"Well, we sure don't want to catch anythin'. How can we help you? I'm Harvey, by the way, an' this is my family."

"Hi Harvey. I'm Beth and these are my friends," Beth said, spreading her arms to both sides to encompass the rest of the Outcasts. "We were just admiring your cornfield. Any chance you can share a little?"

"Sure, Beth. We have plenty. There's just the five of us."

"Where's everyone else?"

"They left. Headed south. Before the explosions, everyone was in cars, truck and campers. A steady stream of 'em. After the bombs and power outage, most were on foot, bikes or horses." He snorted a laugh. "Even saw a few horse-drawn buggies. A whole row of 'em came through, with colorful streamers and frill hangin' from the top. It was real pretty."

Beth was surprised by Harvey's talkativeness. It gave her the courage to be bolder.

"So, you don't mind if we pick some corn?" she asked.

"No need. We'll give you some we already picked. And if you'll wait a few minutes, I'll have my boy go fetch a bag of potatoes we dug up earlier. Eddie, get one of the bags in the basement." Eddie, the young man who was with him, trotted across the road and through the potato field, giving the Outcasts a wide berth.

"Oh," Beth said, not sure how to deal with someone who wanted to give instead of take. "You don't need to do that. We—"

"No problem," Harvey said, interrupting and waving away Beth's argument. "We been pickin' corn and diggin' potatoes every day—except Sundays; we don't work on Sundays cause that's the Lord's day—since the president first mentioned the possibility of a terrorist attack.

The cellar's full and now we're fillin' the basement."

"Why did you stay?" Bryce asked. "Why didn't you leave with the others?"

"All the neighbors and everyone that came through here, acted real scared. They reminded me of my chickens, runnin' 'round and cluckin', but not knowing if where they were goin' was any better than where they were comin' from. We talked about it and decided we were better off stayin' here, where we had plenty to eat and drink, and a roof over our heads."

"That sounds real good right now," Lisa said.

Harvey went still and looked around at the Outcasts, as if considering options. Beth thought it best to explain Lisa's comment.

"We've been on the road for weeks," Beth said. "We're looking for a place to stop, farther west; maybe in the Rocky Mountains." Beth's comment seemed to reassure Harvey and he visibly relaxed.

"I felt real sorry for the folks passin' through here who'd left their homes," Harvey said. "Don't know why you left Georgia, and it's none of my business. Just hope you find what you're lookin' for. Ahh, here comes Eddie now." Beth turned and saw Eddie returning at a trot with a gunnysack over his shoulder.

Harvey took the pack off the back of one of the young girls and set it on the edge of the road. When Eddie arrived, Harvey set the gunnysack next to it.

"You're headed into bad weather," Harvey said, as he started to remove his poncho. "I hope you have warmer clothes than what you're wearing. The girls' ponchos won't do you any good, but you can have the three adult sized ones if you want 'em."

Beth started to object, but Harvey brushed her comment away again.

"Beth," he said, "when I said my prayers this morning, I told the good Lord that I missed a bunch of opportunities to help people that came through here. We gave out a lot of corn and potatoes, but that was it. I told God that if anyone else came by, I'd give 'em the shirt off my back if they needed it, and here you are."

Beth choked up and couldn't speak. She wasn't sure if the water on her cheek was rain or tears.

"Thank you," she finally said.

When Eddie and the woman had added their ponchos to the pile, the family of five crossed the road and walked into the potato field.

"By the way, Beth," Harvey called, "you need to wash the soot off the corn as soon as you can. We think it might be covered with fallout from explosions southwest of here." Then he turned and, with his family, hurried away through the rain. The Outcasts watched them go, returning the waves from the two young girls.

"He was right about the weather," Beth said. "Lisa, you're shivering. Take this poncho. It has a liner, so it should be a little warmer."

"Okay," Lisa said. It came out sounding funny.

Beth gave the other two to Callie and Kerri, who also looked extra cold. The rain had slowed to a light drizzle, so they all took the opportunity to find drier and warmer clothes in their packs.

23

Come back to me

The Outcasts—Wyoming, 4 November

They arrived in the town of Fort Laramie in a blizzard, the snow blowing horizontally. They were cold, even wrapped in the extra clothing from their packs, which wasn't much. They hadn't anticipated this weather.

"Bess," Ben said through chattering teeth, "yur libs're turnig blue."

Beth realized she couldn't feel her lips, or her fingers or toes. She looked around at the others, seeing their obvious discomfort. Lisa shivered so hard she looked like she could barely walk.

"I guezz tisss fars we go til Sprig," Beth replied, barely able to move her lips.

"Haf you notiss ta sno wis gray, like ta fils we walk trou earler?" Ben asked, as they trudged through snowdrifts that were already forming. "I tink tis area haseen nucleer fallou."

"I tink yu right," Beth agreed.

"Is too bad we haf to spen da wintr here. Cann be gud forr healt."

"Haf ta be carefo."

They stopped at the first house they saw. When no one answered the door, Bryce kicked the door repeatedly, eventually breaking it open. They carefully entered the dark interior. Their one remaining flashlight gave off a dim light, so Beth used it to locate the wood pile next to the fireplace and matches on the hearth. Bryce pushed the couch toward the door to block it shut, to keep out the snow.

"Ben," Bryce said, "les chek ta houss." They brought out their knives, took the flashlight, and left the room.

Beth and Candy started building a fire while Kerri and Callie huddled with Lisa to get warm.

When the men returned, to a family room that was feeling warmer by the minute, Bryce had both arms full of blankets, towels and dry clothes. He dropped the bundle on the couch and moved toward the fire to warm his hands.

"Nobody home," he announced, flexing his lips to get them functioning properly. "Also foun' candles," he added.

Ben, with one arm still in a sling, had tucked a couple of blankets under his arm, holding them against his body as well as he could, and carried more clothes in his good arm. He added them to the pile on the couch.

"And there're coatss, hatss and mittenss in the closetss," Ben added, with a crooked smile.

Ben and Bryce set up the candles around the room while the others sorted through the clothes, mumbling their gratitude through cold lips.

After finding some clothes that she thought would fit, Beth stripped off her wet clothes on the spot and put on the dry ones. She didn't care that the clothes didn't quite fit or weren't the latest fashion. After the first layer, she began pulling on larger clothes, layering as she went.

The others changed too, but Beth watched in admiration as Kerri changed, then helped Lisa, who clearly didn't have the strength to undress and dress herself.

"My fingers and toes tingle," Kerri said, zipping up a parka that was a bit too snug on Lisa's small frame. Then she pulled Lisa toward the fire, where they huddled together, in what Beth thought might be a futile effort to get warm.

A few minutes later, Callie spoke up. "I can't feel my toes."

Beth sighed. "Yeah. I should probably check everyone for frostbite."

"I can help," Ben said, starting to rise, awkwardly, when Beth did.

"No Ben," Beth said as she rose tiredly. "You stay there and get warm. I can handle this."

As Beth went from person to person, her initial worry began to ease. Everyone's hands and feet were bright pink from the cold, but looking no worse than her own. Until she got to Lisa. Several of her fingertips were frostbitten.

"Okay everyone," Beth began, after her initial evaluation. "If your hands and feet hurt, that's a good sign. Let's warm up some water. Soaking your hands and feet in the warm water will help. We'll need to try something else for Lisa though."

"There was no running water when I checked the kitchen sink," Bryce said.

"Bryce, find something to carry water in, okay?" Beth asked. "Callie, go look for a deep pan or a pot that we can set on the fire. We'll get the water from the toilet tanks and put it in a tub."

"That's not much water. Why not the water tank?" Kerri asked.

"We will if we have to, but we should save the water tank for drinking water, if we can," Beth replied. "The reservoir water should be clean enough to soak in and we only need enough lukewarm water to cover our hands and feet."

After locating the items they needed, they took turns with their hands and feet in the warm water. It didn't take long before most of them were feeling better. But while they sat, Beth went to work on Lisa. Her fingers didn't look that bad, really. She was certain that a little time and blood circulation would heal her completely. As Lisa sat with her hands in the bucket, Beth watched her carefully, rubbing her fingers gently in the warm water. Within moments, Lisa fell over, hitting her head on the floor with a loud thud.

The group sprang into action, but Beth had her up and cradled before the others even seemed to know what had happened. "I think Lisa has hypothermia," Beth said quietly, not wanting to cause a panic. "Kerri and Callie, we need to get her into the warm water. Help me get her undressed. Bryce and Candy, will you heat more water?"

"All that's left is the water heater, Bryce said.

"I know," Beth replied, "but we better do it."

Several minutes later, Bryce poured one final pot of water into the tub. "That's it. That's all the water I could coax out of the heater."

"Thanks. It will have to do," Beth said. Lisa was lying in about eight inches of warm water, with Kerri, Callie, and Beth sitting on the edge of the tub, gently massaging her limbs and pouring cups full of warm water on her, in an attempt to raise her body temperature. At Beth's request, Bryce took water from the tub and reheated it a couple of times, to extend the bath.

"Bryce," Beth said a few minutes later, "why don't you go see about getting some food going. I'd like to get some warm soup in Lisa, if there is any. Try to warm her from the inside as well, if we can."

"You got it," Bryce replied.

☢

Bryce and Candy found a fully stocked pantry and went to work getting food ready. Their first priority was to get something warm for Lisa. Thankfully, whoever owned the home before liked canned soup. There were dozens of cans, and Bryce picked a can of condensed chicken noodle soup. It took only a few minutes for the soup to be warm, but not too hot. Finding a spoon and small bowl, Bryce poured some soup, then took it to the bathroom where Beth and the others continued to work with Lisa. She looked so pathetic, and small. Of course, Bryce hadn't ever seen Lisa in her underwear before, and certainly not wet like this; but he wondered whether there was something worse than just being underfed as they had all been over the past several weeks. Lisa was conscious, and talking; and that, at least to Bryce, was a good sign.

"I think we're stuck here for the winter," Beth said, conversationally, as she spooned soup into Lisa's mouth. "Maybe we should relocate to get more centrally located. That way we can rummage around town for supplies."

"I don't want to go out in the cold again," Kerri said. "I'm just getting warm."

"Everyone's exhausted," Beth said, "so we'll stay here tonight, and talk about it in the morning, after we've rested."

Bryce listened for a few more minutes as Beth spoke with the other women about possible plans; But he was bored. He couldn't do any more for Lisa. There was plenty of food for everyone, when they got around to eating. So, he looked for another project, and soon decided on gathering wood for the fire.

Bryce bundled up, and then walked out the front door. He found a wood pile beside the garage and took several trips back and forth, carrying what he hoped would be enough to keep the fire going all night.

After bringing in his last load of firewood, he sat down on the couch to rest. Beth led Lisa out from the bathroom and into the living room and asked Kerri and Callie to help her find layers of dry clothes to wear. Bryce thought she looked better; he hoped she was. They had lost so many already.

⊗

"How are you feeling?" Candy asked, sitting down next to Lisa near the fire.

"Still a little cold," Lisa replied, "and very tired; but I'm feeling better. Thank you everyone for worrying about me."

Beth was relieved. She was worn out from worrying about Lisa and the others, and she needed sleep. They laid out piles of blankets on the floor, next to the fire, and began crawling under the blankets fully dressed.

"Beth," Kerri said, leading Lisa over to her. "Lisa's skin is still cold, even after the warm bath and the soup."

Lisa was still shivering, although not as much as when they'd arrived, and her face, neck and hands were still cold to the touch.

"I think her core temperature is still too low," Beth said. "We have to raise it some more."

"How do we do that?"

"We've tried warming her from the outside with a bath and the inside with warm soup—as much as she would eat. The other thing we can try is share body heat."

"You mean skin to skin, right?"

"Yeah. We can wrap you both in a blanket and your body heat will help raise her core temperature. You want to try that?"

"I'm not real warm myself," Kerri said.

"I'll help," Callie said from behind Beth.

"I'll help, too," Bryce said helpfully from his blankets a few feet away.

"No, you won't!" Candy said, slugging Bryce in the shoulder. "You need to keep me warm."

"Skin-to-skin?" Bryce whispered, hopefully.

"If you behave yourself," Candy whispered back, then they both ducked under the covers.

"Or, we could bathe her again and try to get more soup in her," Beth added.

"Let's go to bed," Lisa said, her voice so weak that Beth nearly missed it.

"Are you sure?" Beth asked and Lisa nodded once.

Beth was relieved. She was so worn out from worrying about Lisa and the others that she needed sleep. Maybe Lisa would be fine sleeping with Kerri and Callie.

She helped the two young women undress Lisa again and slide her inside the bed of blankets. Then Kerri and Callie slid in next to her and undressed under the covers, each piece of clothing eliciting an "ooh" or "aah" from Bryce and Ben as it came out of the blankets and joined the growing pile at their heads.

"Oh, grow up," Candy finally said, which stopped Bryce from commenting, but not from watching.

"Awk," Kerri said in surprise as she snuggled up to Lisa. "You really are cold."

"Wow," Callie said, involuntarily shivering. "Let's wrap ourselves around her like a cocoon."

Lisa moaned in reply.

☢

"Lisa?" Kerri whispered.

"Lisa?" She said more loudly.

"Lisa, don't leave me!"

Callie opened her eyes and could see Kerri in the dim light of the coals from the fire, leaning on one elbow over Lisa, shaking her and slapping her face lightly. Kerri's face was a mask of tension and fear. Callie had rolled away from Lisa sometime in the night. Now she looked at Lisa's sallow face and placed a hand on her arm. If anything, her skin was colder than when they had gone to bed.

"Lisa!" Kerri bawled, the anguish in her voice sending shivers through Callie's body. *"Come back to me, Lisa!"* Kerri cried in earnest. Callie placed a hand on Kerri's shoulder to comfort her, but Kerri shook it off.

Callie heard a rustling of blankets and an involuntary gasp, then Beth, in only her underwear, knelt next to them and felt Lisa's face and neck.

"No pulse," Beth said, throwing the blankets off of Lisa, so that she had access to Lisa's chest. "I'm going to start CPR." She started cardiac massage, then rescue breathing.

Kerri and Callie, both naked, squealed and grabbed at their piles of clothing.

"What can I do to help," Ben asked as he crawled out of his blankets. "Ouch," he added as he stumbled into something in the semi-darkness and started hopping on one foot.

Everyone wanted to help, but there was little they could do— build up the fire, light more candles, throw blankets over their shoulders. Bryce took over for Beth when she wore out; but, in the end, all any of them could do was sit and wait and watch Beth, then Bryce, try to revive Lisa.

"Kerri," Callie said quietly, as they sat side-by-side, near the fire, under blankets they had wrapped around their shoulders, "what did you mean, when you told Lisa to come back and not leave you?"

"She . . . she told me she was leaving me," Kerri said, choking on her words, "and not to worry about her. That's what woke me."

"I didn't hear anything," Callie said apologetically.

"You wouldn't. Her voice was in my head. She said she was happy." Kerri started crying again.

At some point, Beth had taken over again from Bryce, and after a few minutes, Lisa seemed to respond to her ministrations. When she started breathing on her own, between coughing and choking, Beth sat back to observe.

"Where am I," Lisa asked.

"You're in Wyoming with us," Beth said.

"Oh," Lisa said. "I thought I'd died."

"We thought you had, too. We worked very hard to bring you back."

"Maybe you shouldn't have. I think I was happy where I was."

"Where were you," Kerri asked.

"I don't remember, but it was peaceful and lovely and I was happy."

"Do you remember anything else about it?"

"Just that when I came back here, I was cold and miserable, then I saw all of your faces and knew everything would be okay."

Callie looked into Kerri's eyes, seeing the pain and the love there, then turned to Beth.

"Will she be alright?" Callie asked.

"I'm sure she will," Beth said. "Lisa, are you hungry? Would you like some soup?"

"That sounds wonderful, thanks."

The Outcasts—Wyoming, 5 November

By morning, the storm had passed and the wind had died. It was still overcast, but the world didn't look so dreary.

"With a good jacket on, it actually feels warm out there," Bryce said as he and Candy entered, wearing heavy coats, hats, and mittens, and stomping snow off their boots. They were smiling, their faces flushed from the cold.

"Did you see anyone on your walk?" Beth asked somberly. They'd made themselves at home in someone else's house—squatters—and she worried that if there were people still in town, they wouldn't be happy about it. They might even become difficult—violent.

"I don't think there's another soul in this town," Candy said smiling. "No footprints in the snow—"

"Except ours," Bryce interjected with a grin.

Candy looked at him and laughed at some private joke. "—and no chimney smoke—"

"Except ours," Bryce and Candy said together, still smiling.

"My goodness," Beth said. "What's gotten into you two?"

"It felt really good to go for a walk," Candy said. "Oh, by the way, we found a house that we think is perfect for us, near the center of town."

"That sounds like a vote to move," Ben said.

"I agree," Beth said seriously. "Let's take everything from this house that we want. We'll check out the neighborhood on our way."

"How's Lisa?" Candy asked, becoming serious.

"She's tired, but she's warming up, thanks to Kerri and Callie," Beth said. "They're fussing over her, feeding her and bathing her in warm water. I can't believe who close we came to losing her."

"You're acting like it was your fault," Bryce said.

"I should have done more last night."

"What more could you have done?" he asked.

"Maybe I should have taken it more seriously," she mumbled, "bathed her again, forced more soup into her—I don't know."

"She didn't want you to," Bryce said.

"Maybe she just gave up," Candy added. "It's been a difficult adjustment for all of us the last few months."

"I'm just grateful she's recovering. She was so full of life," Beth said.

"And we've been so inconsiderate, out having fun on our walk," Candy said.

"I'm glad you found something to laugh about," Beth said. "Lisa's sleeping in the bedroom and Kerri and Callie are keeping an eye on her."

☢

Ft. Laramie was a small town, with homes widely spaced. Beth and Ben checked the homes on one side of the street, while Bryce and Candy checked the other, as they walked into town. It looked like the people had left in a hurry, leaving most of their belongings behind.

"I see lots of footprints, made by two people who cavorted around the town," Beth said, when Bryce and Candy were within hearing range.

"Yeah," Candy said, smiling at Bryce, "we had a lot of fun this morning."

"Are those snow angels?" Ben asked teasingly.

"Yeah," Bryce replied self-consciously. "I haven't made one of those since I was five years old."

"No wonder you were in such a good mood," Beth said.

When they reached Laramie Avenue, Bryce and Candy stopped and looked at Beth and Ben, huge grins giving away the fact that they were pleased with themselves.

Beth and Ben looked around, trying to see what it was that Bryce and Candy wanted them to see. Beth's eyes settled on what looked like a two-story house, with an attached photography studio and motel, on one corner of the intersection. As she stared at it, Bryce and Candy came over and stood beside her.

"What do you think," Candy asked.

"It's the biggest place we could find," Bryce added.

"But will it keep us warm?" Beth asked.

"Yeah," Bryce said. "Fireplaces on both floors. Lots of wood behind the triple garage. I think it's perfect."

☢

When they returned to the house, Callie and Kerri had Lisa dressed warmly, bundled up for going outdoors. It was time to leave.

"Let's go," Beth said, as she turned and headed for the front door. They left, walking arm-in-arm, down the center of the snow-covered street, toward the center of town and their new winter home.

24

Are we all going to die?

The Preserve, 6 November

Rylee had quickly realized she couldn't join Nathan in the community center every night, but went to him as often as she could get away with it. They would kiss and hug—sometimes she would sit on his lap, but wouldn't do more than that—until he told her it was time for her to go to bed.

Rylee yawned continually at breakfast, despite her effort to hide her fatigue.

"What's wrong, Rylee?" Lillie asked.

"Nothing," she replied defensively. The late-night hours with Nathan were fun, but she was only getting a few hours' sleep each night, and she could tell it wasn't enough.

"Aren't you getting enough sleep?" When Rylee ignored the question, Lillie stopped eating and turned her full attention on her. "Rylee, if you're not sleeping well, maybe you need a physical to see if something's wrong. I'm going to the hospital after breakfast. Come with me and I'll give you a physical."

"I'm fine. Really. Let it go."

"I hate to interfere," Rachel said, apologetically, from across the table, "but Rylee has been sneaking out at night. I didn't know if I should say anything."

"Rylee! What are you doing at night instead of sleeping?"

"Nothing. I'm fine." Then she yawned again.

"Rylee!" Lillie scolded, drawing stares from farther down the breakfast table.

Rylee looked up. Several family members had stopped eating to listen as the conversation became louder and more confrontational. She'd already decided she was going to tell Lillie what she was doing, but she wouldn't have picked a time with so many witnesses. Nathan had assured her that she was grown up enough to make her own decisions about what to do with her life.

"I'm in love with Nathan. We're—"

Lillie didn't let her finish. *"No way, young lady.* You're too young for a serious relationship—"

"No, I'm not!" Rylee yelled, but Lillie talked over her.

"And Nathan will be a bad influence on you."

Rylee wasn't going to sit and listen to Lillie badmouth Nathan. Lillie wasn't her mother, even if she *thought* she was.

"Ohhh," she said, pushing herself back from the table so suddenly that her chair tipped over. She glanced at it, then stormed quickly out of the room without picking it up or finishing her breakfast.

☢

"Rylee!" Lillie called, but she was out of the room by then. Lillie looked around to see that everyone was watching her with surprise on their faces—whether because of Rylee's behavior, or Lillie's inability to handle the situation, she wasn't sure. What she *was* sure about was that she'd handled it poorly.

She felt like she should go after Rylee, but then what? As was her habit, she looked around for Amos—he usually had good instincts about how to handle people—but he'd already left. Then she realized that they'd never had unruly children that needed *handling*; their children had been into mischief, but never anything like this. So, she decided to talk to Nathan's mother, Brittany. She was also determined to give Rylee that physical.

Rylee went right to the weight room, where she found Nathan working out.

"Nathan!" she cried as she ran to him. He caught her in his arms and, while he ran his hand across her back affectionately, she told him about her confrontation with Lillie and how she'd handled it.

"Good for you," he said, chuckling. "I'm proud of you for not giving in." He wiped away her tears with the palm of his hand, gave her a kiss, and showed her a new exercise to try. She stayed with Nathan as long as she could, taking strength from his confidence and encouragement.

That evening, Brittany confronted Nathan. She'd wanted Jason to handle it, but he'd refused. When she'd told him what Nathan and Rylee were doing, he'd just laughed.

"Don't you care that your son is seducing a fifteen-year-old girl?"

"How much trouble can they get into in this beehive?"

She was so frustrated with him that she turned and left the room without answering. She crossed the common area to Nathan's room and knocked.

"What?" Nathan called.

"Nathan, can we talk?" Brittany said through the door.

"It's unlocked."

She opened the door and stood in the doorway, leaning against the frame with her arms folded, trying not to appear shocked at the appearance of his room. It looked just like his room at home had, with posters of heavy-metal bands plastered on the walls and dirty clothes cluttering the furniture and floor. She wanted to say something about it, but that would have to wait for another time. "What are you doing with Rylee Parker?" she asked bluntly.

A harsh laugh escaped his throat. "What do you *think* I'm doing?" he asked.

"I don't know. But if you hurt her, I'll make your life miserable."

He laughed out loud then. "Like it isn't miserable now? All we're doing is exercising together."

"Late at night?"

Nathan didn't answer for a moment. He just stared at his mother, as if he could intimidate her. "We watch movies," he finally said.

"I mean it, Nathan."

"Okay, okay. I get it. No more Rylee."

⊛

Nathan had known that his fun with Rylee couldn't last, but was surprised that his mother was cutting it off. He thought he'd have to do it. She was saving him the trouble.

Rylee was just a trial run, anyway. Now he could go after the real prize, Rachel Blund. She was his age, more mature than Rylee, better looking, and probably a better kisser.

He'd always watched Rachel, whenever the group was together, but had never approached her. Now that Rylee was off limits, he would correct that situation.

That night, he checked the next day's work schedule and saw that he and Rachel were both on the lunch crew. He would shift his morning workout to the afternoon, so he could help with lunch, and see how things developed. The only problem would be her jerk boyfriend, Chris Stephens.

The Preserve, 7 November

"Nathan," Becca Stephens said, when he showed up to help with lunch, "what a . . . pleasant surprise. Thank you for coming to help."

"Yeah," Nathan replied. Looking briefly in Rachel's direction. "I didn't have anything else to do right now."

Chris turned and glared at Nathan, then moved over and placed an arm around Rachel's waist, pulling her to his other side and staring at Nathan. Nathan grinned and looked away.

Becca noticed the interplay between the three and wondered what it meant. She decided she better mention it to Lillie, then promptly forgot about it, as she got busy with lunch.

☢

Rylee had been surprised when Nathan wasn't in the weight room for his usual morning workout, startled when she discovered that he'd been in the kitchen helping with lunch. She waited to see where he would sit, so she could sit by him, despite the looks she got from Lillie; but he didn't stay. He walked past everyone, including her, pausing for only a moment when he passed Chris and Rachel.

Did he smile at Rachel? Rylee wondered. What was that about?

After lunch, she tried the weight room again. She missed him already. She liked his seriousness, his sarcasm, and his strong, buff body. He was there, but he didn't greet her like he usually did.

She worried that Lillie, or Nathan's mother, had said something to him. They could ruin everything. She decided she would say hi and start working out next to him as though nothing had happened. They would talk and everything would be okay. She had to keep this relationship alive.

"Hi!" she said with cautious optimism. Instead of talking to her, he continued his reps. He seemed aloof and disinterested, which frustrated her. She stood watching him for a few minutes, thinking he would stop and talk to her; but when he finished his current set, he went to another machine and started another.

Why wouldn't he talk to her? She left a few minutes later, with tears in her eyes, when he failed to acknowledge her; but she would try again later.

The Outcasts—Wyoming, 8 November

Candy woke, with nausea bad enough to throw up, for the third day in a row. When she asked Beth if it was radiation sickness, Beth told her it sounded more like morning sickness.

"*Pregnant?*" Candy screamed, looking at Bryce accusingly. "I can't be pregnant. I don't want to be pregnant. It must be something else." They all looked at Bryce, who tried to look innocent.

"It was that night in the barn, wasn't it? One stinkin' time! How could you?" She swung at Bryce, who backed up and deflected her swing with an arm. She started to cry. "Why did I let you talk me into it?"

"Weren't you on the pill?" he asked. "Being an actress, I assumed you would be."

"Oooh," Candy fumed, making fists and stamping her feet. "Where would I get birth control pills?" She started pounding Bryce on the chest with her fists while he patiently submitted to her rebuke.

Finally, he grabbed her wrists to stop her ineffectual attack and started laughing. Then he turned to Beth. "She's really pregnant?" he asked. "I'm going to be a daddy?" He beamed with pride, realizing that his wife's inability to get pregnant before the war must have been her fault; he was obviously capable of having children.

"We'll be able to confirm it with time, but that's what I'd guess," Beth said, trying unsuccessfully to hide a grin.

When it had looked like the snowstorms would return, Beth had suggested that they gather what they could from nearby homes in town—things they might need for the winter—to their new home. They'd quickly discovered that the people had left most of their belongings behind—food, water, blankets, clothes, medical supplies, tools and other valuables. To their surprise, many of the homes had been left unlocked.

At first, they'd carried their treasures in their arms, but soon found sleds and piled them high with supplies, then pushed and pulled them across the snow.

As the wind picked up and blew the snow around, they retreated to their new house.

"They took their cars," Candy said, sitting next to Bryce on the couch as he counted the cash he'd found, "but they left so much behind. Why?"

"I've been thinking about that," Beth said as she sorted through canned goods she'd piled on the table. "They may not have had much warning before they had to leave."

"Why do you say that?" Candy asked.

"I think this area was in the path of the fallout from a nuclear explosion," Beth said hesitantly, worried how Candy, who'd seemed obsessed with dark thoughts since her near-death experience, would take that information.

"That would explain the gray snow when we arrived, wouldn't it?" Bryce asked, but didn't sound overly concerned about it.

"Are we going to regret staying here?" Kerri asked. "Are we all going to die?"

"I hope not," Beth said grimly, realizing that maybe she should be more worried about Kerri's feelings, since Lisa's near-death experience, than Candy's. "Perhaps the snow will keep us from getting too contaminated."

"We can really have all of these clothes?" Callie asked Kerri as she looked through the colorful tops and pants that she'd brought to the house. They sat side by side on a bed, with piles of clothes on either side of them.

"You like colors, don't you?" Kerri asked. "I remember from the shelter."

"Don't remind me." Callie's face fell and her eyes became moist. "Those were the worst days of my life."

"Yeah, that's probably true for all of us," Kerri replied. She remembered how hard those days in the shelter had been on her and Lisa.

Seeing Callie's distress, Kerri set down the dress she was holding and wrapped her arms around Callie's shoulders. It felt good to hug someone. She realized that that was what Lisa had always done to her when she was the one suffering. Was she becoming Lisa in Lisa's absence, borrowing Lisa's strength to help Callie?

After a few moments, Callie rested her head on Kerri's shoulder and cried, while Kerri rubbed her back.

"Thank you," Callie said, pulling away after a few minutes, and smiling through her tears.

"Any time," Kerri said, returning the smile, realizing she meant it.

The Preserve, 8 November

Nathan watched out of the corner of his eye as Rylee walked up to him in the weight room and started outlining the tattoo on his shoulder, the way he liked it. It felt good, but he couldn't encourage her or she'd never go away. Finally, he stopped, gave her his patented dirty look, and continued his reps, without talking to her. She looked like she wanted to scream.

He realized that she wasn't going to go away easily when she started rubbing the back of his neck, just the way he liked. He stopped and turned toward her.

"Go away, little girl," he said unkindly. "I don't have time for you."

"You had time before," she replied tearfully, "when you were kissing me and holding me." She started to cry quietly, her face scrunching up.

"I was just keeping myself entertained. I was bored, and you relieved my boredom for a while. Now I've lost interest."

She started crying in earnest and ran from the room.

"Good riddance," he thought out loud after she'd gone. He had other plans now. He started thinking about pretty little Rachel and what he wanted to do with her.

☢

"What's our purpose for meeting this time?" Terry asked Amos, knowing the board only met now when a board member wanted to discuss something.

"Nathan seems to have lost interest in Rylee," Lillie said.

"That's good, isn't it?" Terry asked.

"It would be," Lillie said, "except that he seems to be showing up for chores whenever he's on the same team with Rachel, and she's becoming nervous."

"But he's still not showing up for his other assignments, is that it?" Terry guessed.

"Correct," she replied. "I think we should have a party."

"Is a party the answer to every problem?" Amos asked with a chuckle, knowing that was exactly the way Lillie thought. "Maybe you should be Chairman of the Board," he said.

"Maybe I should," she said, with a twinkle in her eye.

Amos studied her for a moment. She might actually be serious. He decided to move on.

"What would our reason be this time?" he asked.

"Hmm . . . I'll have to think about it," she said. "I'll let you know."

President Gregory McCormick—Prime bunker, 8 November

Greg sat at the desk in his office and stared at the monitor showing a bloated Art Klemp in his detention cell, in a straitjacket, with his ankles tied to the bedposts. The scratches on his face and neck, where he had injured himself, oozed gore. His head swung back and forth violently, his lips moved, and his body thrashed as much as the restraints would allow. Director Lister had said that Art probably wouldn't last the night, so Greg had decided to see him one last time.

He increased the volume so he could hear what Art was saying and determine if Art was coherent enough for a conversation.

"dead yet? . . . contaminated . . . smallpox . . . cure me . . . dead yet? . . . contaminated . . . smallpox . . . dead yet? . . . contaminated . . . smallpox . . . contaminated . . . "

Suddenly, Art convulsed, grotesquely, his body arching as far as was physically possible without breaking, and screamed like he was being tortured, like his insides were being ripped apart. It was so loud that Greg had to turn the volume down. Art stayed that way for several seconds, then an alarm sounded in the room, and Art collapsed onto the bed, his head turning to the side, so Greg could see the blood ooze from the corners of his eyes and out of his nostrils.

Within moments, two people in white hazmat suits entered the room, pushing a gurney. There was no hurry. They checked a monitor on the wall that Greg hadn't noticed before. It showed that Art's heart had flatlined. They pushed a button that silenced the alarm, untied the straps attached to his ankles, disconnected the body sensors from the wall monitor, and transferred him to the gurney. As they turned to leave, they noticed Greg on the overhead monitor and saluted him, then wheeled the gurney out.

Despite Greg's negative feelings toward the former Vice President, he stood and saluted the retreating body of his former second-in-command. Art was dead; and his death was a similitude of the life they now lived: harsh, painful, dangerous and ugly. Life might go on, at least for some; but Greg thought it was a life barely worth living.

Whatever the cost, as he watched Art's body being wheeled away, Greg became resolute in his determination to change the final outcome of the war for which he felt responsible. The time was now.

Preview:

Battle for Aspen Valley

(Book 4 of the Gemini Gate series)

Rachel had just asked Chris to walk her to her room when his mother called out to him.

"Go ahead," Chris said.

Rachel cast a concerned glance at Nathan, who was sitting a few feet away reading a magazine, not paying attention to them.

Chris followed her gaze and whispered, "I'll see what Mom wants and be right behind you."

☢

Rachel left the community center and walked down the bedroom tunnel while Chris hurried over to his mother on the other side of the room.

Moments later, as Rachel unlocked her bedroom door, she heard footfalls behind her. Certain that it was Chris, she turned toward him with a teasing comment on her lips about entering a girl's bedroom.

"Don't you know it's not—"

It was Nathan. He grabbed her by both shoulders and pushed her into her room, kicking the door shut behind him so hard that it bounced off the frame and reopened a few inches.

Nathan continued pushing until Rachel banged into the dresser against the opposite wall, causing her to wince at the pain in her back. In the fraction of a second that her eyes were closed, Nathan had his hands under her untucked top, his hands warm against the bare skin of her stomach. As he pressed his face toward hers, likely for the kiss he'd tried to get earlier, she turned her head, so that his lips pressed against her ear.

"Now we're going to have some fun," he whispered into her ear, his husky voice making her shiver, "while your idiot boyfriend is occupied with mommy." As he moved his hands up her stomach, she folded her arms across her chest to stop his progress. She knew he outweighed her by at least sixty pounds and had been working out all winter. He was strong and she knew she couldn't stop him. She looked over his shoulder at the door, willing Chris to show up and rescue her. She later wondered why she hadn't cried out for help, but it didn't cross her mind at the time. She had never been treated like this before, and it happened so fast, the reality of the situation had yet to sink in.

Nathan breathed heavily into her ear and chuckled deep in his throat as he slid his hands upward across her stomach, obviously in no hurry. Leaving her left arm across her chest, she struck his face and shoulder with her right hand. He winced when she accidentally poked him in the eye, then growled and intensified his effort to get what he wanted.

Suddenly he was pulled backward—away from her—by strong hands that spun him around, off balance. Chris grabbed Nathan by the throat with one hand and punched him in the stomach with the other. Unaffected by the punch, as a result of his weight training, Nathan pushed Chris away and pulled a steak knife from his belt with his right hand, whipping it from left to right in front of him, cutting Chris's shirt and drawing blood on his chest. Chris winced and backed away a step.

Instead of pressing his advantage on Chris, Nathan took that brief reprieve to turn and grab Rachel with his left hand. He pulled her off balance and partially in front of him, then pressed the knife against her neck.

Rachel couldn't believe that Nathan intended to hurt her with the knife, but she didn't know what he was capable of and it scared her, both for herself and for Chris.

"You want to see your girl get hurt, huh?" Nathan asked. "You just back out the door and leave us to our fun."

About the Story

The Gemini Gate series combines real-world geopolitics, including a detailed, behind-the-scenes look at the White House and the possibility of a global thermonuclear Armageddon, with a fictional technological discovery that just might hold the secret to saving the human race. It takes a component of science fiction—a hypothetical, fictional technology—and embeds it in a realistic, present-day world.

This story is a work of fiction. All of the characters in the book are from the author's imagination and any resemblance to known persons is purely coincidental. Location names, government organizations and functions and the effects of man-caused and natural disasters mentioned in the story are accurate to the best of my ability to determine.

Background

The Three Mile Island Nuclear Generating Station, reactor number 2 (TMI-2) in Pennsylvania, suffered a radiation leak and partial meltdown on March 28, 1979. It was said to be 'the most significant accident in U.S. commercial nuclear power plant history'.

At that time, I worked as a project engineer at a nuclear power plant construction site in Washington State. Eventually, four of the five power plants that were under construction in Washington, were cancelled due to spiraling construction costs, that resulted from safety concerns and a labor dispute, at the same time that energy consumption declined in the northwest. The Washington Public Power Supply System (WPPSS, or Whoops, as it became known in the media and on TV in the eighties) was forced to default on $2.25 billion worth of municipal bonds—a humiliation for the financial industry. You can read about it on my website, www.StevenEWilde.com.

The failure of the nuclear industry to provide reliably safe, low-cost energy to the public made me wonder what would happen if an accidental or—heaven forbid—intentional nuclear accident occurred in the western United States, and my story about the Gemini Gate was born; but it took a few years for it to mature into a five-book series. It led me to speculate on the ability—or inability—of government leaders to work together to prevent thermonuclear war, and what it would take to survive the resulting chaos.

The premise of the Gemini Gate series is that: faced with the prospect of nuclear weapons in the hands of madmen—what we see in today's headlines would have us believe that there are radical ideologies in the world that would welcome another world war—the U.S. government feels compelled to confront the perpetrators and defend itself; while the people of the world suffer as a result of global political decisions, with the exception of a few, like the Blunds and Stephens's, who anticipate and prepare in advance, to survive the chaos.

When the idea for the story came to me, Aspen Valley existed, but only in my mind. Having travelled extensively throughout Utah over the years, visiting the beautiful and unique natural treasures of Utah's State and National Parks and forests, I tried for years to match up what was in my head with a specific location. Driving up Logan Canyon to a family vacation at Bear Lake a few years ago, I realized that we were in the right canyon. I just needed to find Aspen Valley. It's there, a little different than I've described it in the story, but close enough to recognize it. If you're ever in Logan Canyon and spot it, send me an email to let me know.

I've been to and loved many of the places I've written about in the series. Many of my characters are reflections of people I know and care about; I hope you see yourself in one of them.

One of my goals in writing this story was to give each character a unique and believable personality. So, many of the characters in the series are patterned after people that I know or have known. Just to be sure that I don't offend anyone, let's just say that if you identify with one of the characters, he or she was meant to resemble you—except for Jason, who is a composite of all the bad character traits I could think of.

Acknowledgments

I need to thank the people who've helped me develop, edit and publish the first three books in the Gemini Gate series. Steve Brown, Kevin Cook, Dan Duvall, David Noble, Felicia Osborn, Chris Palmer and Dan Wilde reviewed one or more of the volumes and provided valuable feedback on content and grammar. The people at IndieBookLauncher.com: Nas Hedron for editing the first two books and educating me on writing styles; and Saul Bottcher, for painting the first three book covers, setting up the books for publication, and putting up with all my questions. I couldn't have gotten this far without all of you pitching in to make me look good.

Most of all, I need to thank Marilyn for putting up with my obsession to tell this story. She's been my best critic and greatest supporter through the long hours at the computer. For your patience at all my interruptions, to run my latest idea past you, and each time I jump out of bed to finish a scene that has suddenly come to me, I love you.

About the Author

I grew up in Salt Lake City and graduated from the University of Utah in Civil Engineering. My wife, Marilyn, and I have five children and fifteen grandchildren. My life revolves around my family and most of my spare time is spent with them. Together we enjoy camping, hiking, travel and get-togethers with friends and extended family. In my quiet time, I enjoy gardening, family history, emergency preparedness, home remodeling, reading and now, writing.

I've traveled to six continents, either for pleasure or business. I survived two floods in Rio de Janeiro and a drenching rain forest in Costa Rica. I've been stung by a Ray on a California beach, I managed the construction of a graphite composite America's Cup race boat and watched it compete and win off the coast of San Diego. I managed the construction of a graphite composite prototype of the V-22 Tiltrotor aircraft. I managed the construction of five large steel wind turbines, which were installed in Washington, Wyoming and California. I managed and coached project managers in the U.S. and Canada and helped several of them earn their Project Management Professional certification.

Like many people, I had a story in me that wanted to be told, but life got in the way of actually writing the story until recently. My career as an engineer and project manager has led me through multiple industries and specialties, including electric utilities, nuclear power plant construction, water management, global mining and aerospace. Each of those experiences contributed to the broad perspective needed and the interest to research and write about the potential effects of global thermonuclear war on the infrastructure, on people and on the world, itself.

The premise of this story is that, faced with the prospect of nuclear weapons in the hands of madmen, the U.S. government chooses to confront the perpetrators and fight back, rather than sit idly and be abused. Like you, I hope we never see nuclear war. However, what we see in today's headlines led me to speculate on the ability—or inability—of government leaders to control the radical ideologies that threaten to engulf us in world war.

This story about a world in chaos is meant to entertain. I hope you enjoyed it. Don't miss the sequel *Battle for Aspen Valley* (Book 4 in the Gemini Gate series), available now. Be sure to check out my website, www.StevenEWilde.com for background information about the story, characters, locations, facts behind the fiction, and other relevant information.

Feel free to contact me with questions and suggestions.
Thank you.

Steven E. Wilde

Facebook: StevenEWilde_GG
Email: StevenEWilde@gmail.com
Website: www.StevenEWilde.com